# Before I Wake

R. J. WIERSEMA is a bookseller and reviewer,
who contributes regularly to Canadian newspapers.
He lives in Victoria BC with his wife and their son.
*Before I Wake* is his first novel.

*Praise for* Before I Wake

'A stunning debut. Robert Wiersema's novel is original,
thought-provoking and downright wonderful'
MICHAEL CONNELLY

'I wept over this book as I read it, and I'm still haunted by it.
Wiersema's compassion for us all shines through in writing
that is vivid and very often disturbingly powerful. He is a
beautiful writer, and this is a beautiful book'
GAIL ANDERSON-DARGATZ

'Inventively told using cinematic jump cuts and fantastical
interventions, *Before I Wake* provocatively dances along the
lines between faith and science, life and death. Robert Wiersema's
first novel shows a writer possessed with the kind of storytelling
instincts that make you care about the answer to the one question
that really counts: what happens next?'
ANDREW PYPER

"Riveting . . . Grips the reader in a chokehold on page one
and doesn't let go until the very last line'
*GLOBE AND MAIL*

'It's Dan Brown's *The Da Vinci Code* meets Philip Pullman's
*Dark Materials* trilogy – an age-old battle between good and
evil set against contemporary life'
CBC.ca

R. J. Wiersema

# Before I Wake

PAN BOOKS

First published 2007 by St Martin's Press, New York

First published in Great Britain 2007 by Macmillan

This edition published 2008 by Pan Books
an imprint of Pan Macmillan Ltd
Pan Macmillan, 20 New Wharf Road, London N1 9RR
Basingstoke and Oxford
Associated companies throughout the world
www.panmacmillan.com

ISBN 978-0-330-45222-9

A CIP catalogue record for this book is available from
the British Library.

Printed and bound in Great Britain by
Mackays of Chatham plc, Chatham, Kent

Visit **www.panmacmillan.com** to read more about all our books
and to buy them. You will also find features, author interviews
and news of any author events, and you can sign up for e-newsletters
so that you're always first to hear about our new releases.

*For Cori*
*Such is the principle of magic,*
*drinking from the same cup*

*Miracles are not contrary to nature,*
*but only contrary to what we know about nature.*

—St. Augustine

*I only looked away for a moment.*

That one phrase haunts a parent when something tragic happens to their child. It echoes in the mind like an accusation. Or a curse.

"I only turned my back for a second, but somehow he managed to reach the handle of the frying pan. . . ."

"I just went inside to answer the phone. I thought the gate to the pool was locked. . . ."

It's a cry for understanding, a challenge to the universe. I hear the guilt, the recrimination, and I understand: *If only I had been paying attention . . .*

*He wouldn't be burned.*

*She wouldn't have drowned.*

I didn't look away.

We believe that vigilance can prevent tragedy, that if we pay attention, we will be strong enough, wise enough, fortunate enough to counter fate.

"If I had been watching . . ."

It's a lie.

It's a trick that the universe plays, a way of increasing the guilt and despair while seeming to explain it away.

I *didn't* look away. I wish I had.

Sometimes we can only watch, mute witnesses as our lives change in a moment, in a heartbeat, in the time it takes a three-year-old girl to take a single step from our side.

I let go of her hand.

I *didn't* look away.

And my baby is gone.

# Part 1

*April 1996*

*"Jubilee, this is A32. We have two, repeat two, en route. Hit and run. ETA four minutes. Clear."*

*"Copy A32. Please advise condition. Clear."*

*"Copy Jubilee. Advise one adult female. Some bleeding. Shock. Holding stable. Clear."*

*"Copy A32. Advise."*

*"Copy Jubilee. Advise one female child, three years. Severe head trauma with decreased level of consciousness and spontaneous respirations. Severe bleeding from cranium. Clear."*

*"Copy A32. Trauma One will meet you at the gate. Clear."*

## Karen Barrett

Sherry and I were walking to the mall, holding hands.

Hillside Shopping Centre is only a few blocks from the house, and every Wednesday morning in the food court they have clowns and jugglers and musicians for the kids. I had dressed her in her little blue dress, the one with Winnie the Pooh on the front. She had chosen it herself: "My sky blue dress, because it matches the sky." I zipped up the back carefully, so as not to catch any of her wispy hair between the metal teeth. I tickled her gently under the arms as I finished.

Was that the last time I heard her laugh?

Sherry loved the clowns, and the noise of all the other children packed into the food court was like a wall of pure joy. We usually had a snack—a muffin or some french fries—before we walked home, and by the time we got back, it would be nap time for both of us.

It was a beautiful spring day. The sky was a clear, cold blue, but there was no chill to the air. In fact, the air was heavy with warmth and growth and green and flowers as we walked through our neighborhood. We stopped to pet familiar cats, to smell the lilacs just in flower, to pick up stones that weighed down my pockets.

I checked both ways before we stepped into the crosswalk on Hillside. I always do. The street is too wide to take any risks: three lanes in each direction with a concrete median, and the cars and buses just roar through. There's no light at the crosswalk, so I'm always careful to check. Better that we wait a few seconds than take any chances.

We waited for a station wagon to pass from the left, and I saw a truck a good distance away on the right, but it was perfectly safe. I took her small hand in mine.

Perfectly safe.

We walked quickly. Six lanes is pretty far for a three-and-a-half-year-old, but we'd done it plenty of times.

We should have waited at the median.

The next time I looked up, the truck was right there, maybe a hundred meters away. It was old and beat up, red with white fenders. And it was roaring toward us.

I felt her fingers slip from mine. Felt her moving.

"Sherry," I called as she skipped away.

We were in the same lane as the truck, so all we had to do was get to the next lane. It wasn't far. A meter. A meter and a half at most.

I should have picked her up. I don't know why I didn't pick her up.

She turned to look at me.

"Sherry!"

I watched her pudgy white legs scamper across the pavement, her little white shoes, her little blue dress.

Her sky blue dress.

When I looked up, I could almost see the face of the driver in the truck. He had shifted lanes to go wide around us, weaving into the next lane, the lane in front of us, the lane that Sherry had just quick-stepped into. The roar of his engine blocked out all other noise.

I reached for her, my fingers just brushing her blond hair before the truck pulled her away from me.

I could hear, over the roar of the engine, the sound of her body hitting the bumper, as the truck took her beyond my reach.

I could feel the wake of the truck as it sped past me, as I threw myself toward her. Tried to reach her.

There was a squealing of tires. A scream.

And the next thing I saw was the ceiling of a hospital emergency room.

*"Nine-one-one Operator. How should I direct your call?"*

*"I just killed a little girl. . . ."*

*"Sir—"*

*"I swerved . . . I swerved around her—"*

*"Sir, where are you?"*

*"I'm at the Hillside Mall. . . ."*

*"Where are you at Hillside Mall, sir?"*

*"I only looked away for a minute. I checked my mirror. I changed lanes. I swerved, but she—"*

*"Sir, where are you calling from?"*

*"I just killed a little girl. . . ."*

*"Sir . . .*

*"Sir?*

*"Sir?"*

### Simon Barrett

10:53.

I checked the clock on my desk as the two City of Victoria police officers opened the door to my office. Sheila followed them closely, her face tight.

"Mr. Barrett?" asked one of the officers.

A lawyer doesn't usually get unannounced visits from uniformed police, but it does happen, especially when you're handling accidents and personal-injury cases. I would have been more concerned had I been a stockbroker.

I rose from my chair. "How can I help you gentlemen?"

"I wanted to buzz you," Sheila started.

"That's fine, Sheila. Mary . . ."

She was sitting at my work table with the Anderson file.

"We'll finish this up later."

Mary rose to her feet, her eyes darting between the officers and myself. I shook my head slightly. She followed Sheila out the door.

10:54.

I came around from behind my desk and offered my hand to the officer nearest me. I have learned, from observation and experience, that one person's body position in relation to another is the key to determining seniority. The senior or more significant partner will usually stand just slightly forward from the other or the group. Perhaps just a half step, but enough to be noticeable. Enough to be significant.

The officer whose badge read CLEMENT took my hand and shook it. Not much of a grip. His hand was cool and soft in mine.

"What can I help you with?" I asked again.

The officer glanced at his partner, whose badge I couldn't read. That glance unsettled me.

"Mr. Simon Barrett? Of 2718 Shakespeare?" the second officer asked.

"Yes. What is it?"

"I'm sorry to tell you—"

"Yes?"

"Sir, there's been an accident. . . ."

"Sherry? Is it Sherry?" I felt for the desk behind me, and leaned my weight against it.

"Your wife and daughter were involved in an accident this morning near the Hillside Shopping Centre," Officer Clement continued. "If you'd like to gather your things, we'll take you down to the hospital. We can explain in the car."

"Is there—?" I fumbled for the words, but I pulled myself together. "I'll have Sheila cancel my appointments."

As I pressed the intercom button and instructed Sheila, the clock read 10:56. Grabbing only my jacket, I followed the officers through the reception area.

Mary was waiting just outside my office door. I didn't make eye contact with her as we passed.

*In the shadow of a fast food sign, the man in the black coat watched as the truck struck the child, as the mother fell away from the wheels. He watched, without moving, as cars squealed to a halt, as people rushed from buildings to crowd around the two fallen bodies. He didn't move when the mother screamed, as the sirens built in intensity, as the crowd parted to allow the white-suited medics through to the victims. When they stood up from their kneeling beside the girl, their knees were wet with her blood.*

*He clenched his Bible in one hand and worried a silver coin with the other. As the ambulance screamed away, lights flashing, the stranger turned and began walking toward the hospital.*

## Karen

At first, I had no idea where I was.

Everything was white, too bright and out of focus. All I could hear was confusion, a blur of voices and echoes. When I tried to rub my eyes clear, my hand tugged and flashed with a sharp pain. An IV line disappeared into my wrist, held with clear tape that pinched my skin.

The emergency room. Sherry.

I was covered with a green sheet but still dressed. There was a tightness around my head that, when I touched it, felt like bandages. My eyes were slow coming into focus.

Green curtains matching the sheet enclosed the bed. Simon was standing just across the steel rail.

"Simon?"

"The police came for me. At work."

"Sherry?"

I tried to struggle to a sitting position, but found myself swooning, tangled in the IV tubing, in the green sheet.

"Don't sit up yet. Lie back." His voice was calm and deliberate, the way it gets when he's upset and trying not to show it.

"Where's Sherry?"

"The doctors just want to be sure . . . Are you okay? They said you struck your head when you fell."

His use of the word *struck*—so clinical, so precise. Distancing himself, trying not to worry me with whatever is worrying him.

"No. Not me. Sherry. There was a truck. . . ."

He shook his head, and I realized distantly that no part of him was touching me. I wanted him to reach out, to touch my hand, my face.

"There was a second car. . . . The driver saw everything. . . . She called the ambulance from her cell phone."

"Where's Sherry?"

He took a deep breath, and in the pause between my question and his answer I could feel tears forming in my eyes, burning.


Simon

*Our miracle . . .*

That's what Karen has always called Sherry.

Our miracle.

Karen and I spent the first years of our life together struggling not to have children. It was a game for me to remind her to take her pill every evening as we went to bed, as if our continued happiness depended upon us remaining childless. I suppose it did.

We lived through some close calls. Missed pills, missed periods. Midnight talks about what we do if . . . The month in Thailand when we forgot the pills altogether.

Only after I was established with Bradford & Howe did we begin trying to have a child.

I guess we'd always wanted a family—children. It was just a matter of when. We both wanted to be ready, for everything to be perfect. Not when we were both students. Not when her job with the paper was barely putting me through law school and keeping us in tiny apartments.

It was almost a checklist: house bought, car paid for, trips to Europe and Southeast Asia and the Caribbean behind us.

Perfect conditions.

When we started trying, we thought it would just happen, that there would be no complications. Instead, we tried without success for three years.

Thirty-nine periods we didn't want.

Thirty-nine cycles of rising hopes and sudden disappointments, her blood haunting us, black in the blue toilet water.

We both went to the doctor. We were worried that we were getting too old, that our years of putting it off had cost us our only chance to be parents. He examined us, performed a battery of tests.

Nothing seemed to be physically wrong with either of us.

Karen took up yoga. We changed our diets. I gave up coffee and saturated fat. I started running again. We both took up swimming.

And after three years of trying, it worked.

Karen collapsed midway through the seventh month, while covering a story for the paper. Ironically, the story was about a nursery school. The doctor ordered her to bed: high blood pressure and anemia. Continued activity posed a substantial risk to the growing fetus. Child.

Sherilyn was born thirty-three days premature, tiny enough to cup in my hands.

She spent the first seventy-two hours of her life in an incubator. Our only contact was feedings, or momentary caresses of her tiny, soft belly, her silky legs, through the access holes of the Plexiglas box.

*Our miracle.*

I pushed the memories away.

"She's in surgery. The doctor said that there was severe trauma to her head. There was internal bleeding—" I stopped talking.

Karen seemed smaller than I had ever seen her, face blanched white, almost the same color as the gauze wound around her head. Her blond curls were matted with blood.

"Is she going to be okay?"

I leaned forward, wanting to touch and reassure her, but unsure of where it would be safe to do so.

"They don't know. They'll tell us as soon as they know anything. As soon as she's out of surgery."

Twin tears fell from her eyes, trickled into the green pillow on either side of her face. Her pupils were wide and black, leaving only a sliver of green around the rim.

My cell phone vibrated gently against my ribs. I knew that I wasn't supposed to use the phone in the hospital, but I couldn't turn it off. I couldn't be cut off. I stepped away from Karen's bed to answer it, checking my watch. 11:42.

"Barrett."

"Simon, it's me."

I held my hand up to Karen, turned through the green curtains and into the chaos and noise of the emergency room itself.

"Mary, why are you—?"

"Is everything okay?"

I tucked myself into a pay phone cubicle on the wall, my back to the noise and the bustle, my voice dropping. "There's been an accident. Sherry got hit by a car."

"Oh, God, Simon. Is she all right?"

"They don't know yet. She's still in surgery. Karen—Karen's hurt, too. She's okay. She fell. Hit her head. She's okay."

"How are you holding up?"

I shrugged, then realized she couldn't see me. "I'm fine."

"I was worried."

For some reason, the idea surprised me. "Why?"

"It's not every day you get taken away by the police before lunch." She laughed a little, awkwardly. "When will you know more?"

I could feel my shoulders tighten as I realized that I had no idea, that things were completely out of my control. "I don't know. Sherry's still in surgery. We won't hear anything until after that. Even then it will probably be too early to tell."

"But she'll be all right, right?"

"I don't know."

"Are you okay?" Her voice was nearly a whisper.

"I'm okay."

"Let me know if I can do anything? I'll be here, or on my cell."

"I know. Listen, work up Berkman and . . . check the records on Radinger, then call it a day. I'll call you later."

"You can—"

A hand fell onto my shoulder, gripping it tightly. I jumped and turned in a single motion.

Karen had climbed out of bed, wheeled her IV stand into the emergency lobby, and found me. She was still pale, but her cheeks were red from the exertion. Her pale lips mouthed, "Who?"

"The office," I mouthed back. Then, into the phone, "No, nothing that won't keep."

"Is Karen there?" Mary asked.

"I'll be in later to check on things. I left my briefcase—"

"Will I see you? Will you call me?"

"Right. Later, then. Thanks."

Karen was shaking her head. "Not a moment's peace. Not even now."

"They're all just worried. They saw me leaving with the police. Should you be up?"

"I'm fine," she said. "Who was it?"

"Sheila," I lied, taking her shoulder and guiding her to one of the orange plastic chairs.

Mary Edwards

Simon had been distant with me, but that wasn't anything new. He was always like that when we weren't alone.

In court when he cross-examines a witness or makes a summation, sometimes I don't even recognize him. The speech might be everything that we had talked about, everything that we had planned, but he'd make it fresh, like he was making it up as he went along. He was like a chameleon, completely adaptable no matter where he found himself, no matter who he was with.

Sometimes I feel like I am the only one who really knows him. And sometimes he's a complete stranger.

Like at this past year's Christmas party, when Sheila brought me over to where they were standing and introduced me to his wife. It didn't even seem to faze him. "Oh, yes, this is Mary. She's been a big help to me."

I just about dropped my punch cup when he said that, as if we hadn't spent the afternoon in my apartment.

I moved stuff around on my desk. I opened up the Berkman and Radinger files. I told Sheila that Mr. Barrett had phoned to explain what was going on. She must have known that I was lying—all incoming phone calls go through her desk—but she didn't let on. I'm sure she knew about Simon and me—what had been going on for months.

I had noticed the way she started to look at me.

I'm not a home-wrecker or anything. I don't want to be one of those little twenty-somethings that come to the Christmas party and are introduced as "My wife, Trixie," all dressed up in Armani or Versace, when it's perfectly obvious that not so very long ago Trixie was going to school with her current husband's daughter.

I wasn't interested in marrying him. Not really. I just liked what we had, those times when we were together, at work and alone.

I'm a lawyer. His junior, but from the beginning he really listened to my opinions. Respected my thoughts. I liked the way he looked at me, the way he nodded and kind of smiled when I said something that he was not expecting. We respected one another. That was the main thing.

But just once I wanted to be able to watch him sleep. Our afternoons were too short, so cramped by the time and excuses for being out of the office that we'd never had time to just relax, to really let go.

Instead, I would watch him as he dressed, his tight butt and legs, his narrow chest with its light dusting of dark hair. And after he disappeared into the bathroom, I would dress hurriedly, ensuring that my clothes were just right, that my makeup was just right by the time he returned.

I wanted to watch him sleep, watch his face as he drifted away, as the mask loosened and disappeared. To watch his face soften, just to see what it was really like, if I really knew him as well as I thought I did.

## Simon

I think time passes so slowly in hospital waiting rooms because there are so many ways to keep track of it. The rhythmic beeping of machinery, the patterns of security guards and orderlies with carts, the Muzak, the grating laugh tracks from the television mounted on the wall, the ongoing misery of the other people waiting. Time is an almost physical presence.

Nevertheless, I kept checking my watch until Karen put her hand over mine to stop me.

"Sorry."

Every time a doctor or nurse emerged from behind the desk we both half rose, and every time we were disappointed.

Karen paced. She sat. She called her mother in Winnipeg. She paced some more. She waved away the offers of more painkillers. She finally allowed a nurse to guide her back to the curtained bed she had vacated so that the IV could be removed from her arm.

I bought us each a cup of coffee from the vending machine near the nurse's station. The paper cups sat on the table in front of me—mine black, hers with a little cream. Piled alongside them were several packets of sugar.

"I thought that we should try to keep your blood sugar up," I explained. "Not being on the IV anymore . . ."

She laid her hand on my thigh and squeezed it gently.

"Mr. and Mrs. Barrett?"

The doctor, a vague shadow in green scrubs, was reading from a metal clipboard. We both stood before he finished saying our names.

"How is she? Is she going to be all right?" Karen asked. "Will she be okay?"

I watched his face—his mouth and his eyes—as he spoke.

"Mr. and Mrs. Barrett, let's sit down." Karen grasped my hand as we sat back down, and he took the chair opposite us.

"I'm Dr. McKinley, the on-call surgeon today." He didn't extend his hand. "I performed the surgery on your daughter."

"How is she?" I asked, still watching.

"I wish I had better news for you. . . ."

I took a deep breath. "Is she—?"

The doctor shook his head. "We had to open her skull," he said. "There was a lot of bleeding. A lot of pressure that we had to let off. We managed to stop the bleeding, and we removed some debris that could have caused some problems. . . . The surgery went very well."

"Oh my God," Karen cried, tears streaming down her cheeks. "Oh my God."

"Then she's going to recover?" I asked.

"In situations like this, there's often a lot of damage that we can't see, at least in these early stages." He took a deep breath. "I'm sorry. Your daughter is in a coma. It's too early to tell. . . ."

We waited for anything that might sound like reassurance.

"It's important to remember that the coma is a resting state, a chance for the body to heal itself in the places that we can't get to. In cases like this, quite often the patient will spontaneously pull themselves out. That's the way we're treating this. Your daughter is having some problems breathing, so we have her on a respirator, and right now it's just a matter of waiting."

Karen leaned toward me, whispering. I draped my arm around her.

"I'm sorry," the doctor said, leaning forward to hear better. "I didn't hear what you said."

"Sherry," I said. "She was telling you that our daughter's name is Sherry."

The doctor flinched. "I know."

"Our miracle," she whispered. I don't think the doctor heard.

Henry Denton

I didn't kill that little girl. She just floated away.

I turned away for a second, that's all. I saw her and her mother in the crosswalk, and I changed lanes to go around them. I checked my mirrors as I changed lanes, and when I looked back . . .

She rose up into the air.

She floated away.

I didn't stop. I couldn't stop. I just watched her as she floated away.

I watched her mother scream, but I couldn't hear it over the Tragically Hip tape and the sound of the engine. She was reaching out for her child.

I cut back around the block and parked the truck in my usual slot by the air and water and I called 911 from the pay phone at the gas station. My hands shook as I punched in the numbers. I wanted to try to explain, but I couldn't find the words. As I hung up the phone, I couldn't help myself—I threw up all over the wall of the phone booth, the concrete floor. I managed to miss my pant legs and shoes. I kept heaving until nothing else came out, until I could see these patches of light and dark with my eyes closed. My head felt like it was going to split open. I wanted to scream.

I kept seeing her, floating up, hanging in the sky just above me, watching me.

I stumbled out of the phone booth, dropping my keys on the ground beside it. I felt like I was going to be sick again.

One of the day-shift guys called after me, but I heard him the way you sometimes imagine hearing your name in a crowd. I don't think I could have answered even if I had tried. Instead, I turned toward Hillside, stumbling across the intersection. I followed the walk lights wherever they guided me, and everything behind me fell away.

Floated away . . .

Karen

I was expecting some sort of miracle, some technology or technique, a glassed-in room where doctors would fight for Sherry's life as we stood outside the window looking on. Instead, we were able to stand by her bed in the critical ward, no barrier between us and her profound silence.

Her head was bandaged tightly, a tracery of pink along the edge of the dressing. Her blood. Tubes entered her nostrils and her mouth, taped down to the soft skin of her cheeks. They ran to the respirator at the side of the bed, its accordion bag rhythmically inhaling and exhaling, filling and shrinking, Sherry's chest rising, falling, rising, falling. An

IV line ran into her arm, and under the covers she was catheterized, cloudy urine collecting in a bag at the edge of the bed.

But she was still my daughter. Still my Sherry, so tiny in the full-size bed. So fragile, she needed all these tubes, these adhesives, these machines to keep her together. I gently rubbed the inside of her left arm, the only place I could, telling her that she would be okay, that Mommy and Daddy were here, that everything was going to be all right.

Simon stood perfectly straight, fingers tight around the cold steel rail. The set of his jaw, the tightness of his shoulders, frightened me.

I lightly touched the back of his hand. "It's gonna be okay," I whispered, willing him to turn toward me. "She's gonna be all right."

He slowly faced me. "I know," he said, after too long a pause.

"She is," I urged him. I could feel the heat of tears on my cheeks. "She really is."

He rubbed away the tears on my face with his thumb, nodding in agreement.

"She seems so small, lying there." My words were too loud in the small room.

Simon took a deep breath, and checked his watch. "I have to go into the office for a couple of hours. I need to clear some stuff from my calendar, move some stuff around so that I can be here without them constantly calling."

"Really? Can't you—?"

"It shouldn't take too long. If you need me, call me on my cell. I won't be long."

I wanted to argue with him, to tell him how much we needed him here, how much *I* needed him here, but I just stared at him.

"I'll clear my schedule for tomorrow. That way I don't have to worry about it."

I pulled him close. "Don't be too long," I whispered into the wool of his jacket.

His hand came up to cradle the back of my head. "I won't be. A few hours." He kissed me fleetingly on the forehead. "I'll be back soon."

He looked back from the doorway, and I could see the worry stretching his face, but he was already reaching for his cell phone.

Already gone.

## Mary

I went to him the instant he came through the door. I'd been sitting on the couch with a Diet Coke, pretending to read A. S. Byatt. He had called me from the hospital to let me know that he was on his way, that his daughter was in a coma.

He looked terrible. His skin was gray, his hair unkempt, his tie askew.

"Are you okay?" I asked.

His eyes met mine before he could answer, and his expression seemed to break open. "Oh God, Mary," he said. "Oh God."

I gathered him into my arms. I could feel his back start to shake as I stroked it.

"She's so small. Oh God, Mary, she's so small. And all the tubes, there are all these tubes—"

"Shh," I soothed. "Shh." He buried his face in my shoulder and I could feel the heat of his tears through my shirt.

I let him cry. I held him until he went silent, his life, his pain, filling my arms almost to bursting. Then I asked, "Have you been outside today?"

"What?" He raised his red eyes to mine. "No."

"I thought—it's a beautiful day. Maybe a walk would help clear your head." I knew it wasn't going to happen, but I wanted to offer. We never take walks. It's one of the rules of being the other woman—the wife has custody of public spaces—but I felt like he might need the fresh air and shouldn't be on his own.

"No . . ." His voice trailed off. "I have to go back to the hospital soon. I think I'd like to just stay here."

I nodded. "Of course."

Our eyes met. Without warning, he pressed his mouth to mine. His lips were cold, hard, his breath a hot rush.

"I'm sorry," he muttered as he was kissing me, his voice cracking again. "I need . . ." His arms tightened around me, drawing me into him. "I need . . ."

"It's okay," I said. "It's okay."

I wanted to blanket the cold pain he had brought with him from the hospital.

He pulled my clothes off as we stood in my living room. He popped a button from my shirt, and looked down at it for a long moment, as if shocked that such a thing could happen. That something so small could be broken so easily.

After I was naked, he undressed himself quickly, his eyes never leaving me. He pushed the coffee table to one side and pulled me down onto the couch. He made love to me desperately, as if trying to hide within me. He controlled everything, his hands on my hips setting the rhythm, his mouth at my breasts, my lips.

After he came, he didn't release me like he usually did. Instead, he pulled me closer, laying his head against my breasts.

I could feel the rough tug of his whiskery face, and the heat of his tears, as he softened within me.

Simon

I hated myself for being there, for being so weak I had to run to her. Hated myself for lying there, watching Mary as she stood up, her high, small breasts, her pale skin.

I tried to rise, but she touched me gently on the chest with the palm of her hand, pressing me backward with an even pressure. "No, you stay here."

"I have to . . ."

"You can sit for a minute. There's time." The tone of her voice brooked no argument, but it wasn't her court voice. It was smoother, warmer, like honey in tea.

I glanced at my watch. 6:42. There was still time to stay, to sit. I had left the hospital at 5:32, caught a cab from the emergency room door, arrived here at . . .

## Mary

What was that expression? That little lift in his lips as he slept?

Was it satisfaction? Relief? Comfort?

Comfort . . .

Could I really settle for comfort? Probably not. But for now, I'd settle for the thought that I could help take his pain away for a little while.

I curled myself into the sofa between him and the picture of my parents on the end table. He slept with one arm at his side, palm up, the other hand draped across his belly, rising and falling gently as he breathed.

His hair was sandy, just beginning to hint at gray. I knew that he would comb it fastidiously before he left—he always did, no matter the weather, no matter if he'd have to comb it again once he got to wherever he was going. He never went out in public unless he was absolutely perfect.

If he were younger, it would have annoyed the shit out of me. "The great tragedy of middle age," my best friend Brian had once said about the carefully coiffed men who were always trying to pick him up, "is watching these guys trying so desperately to hold on to a youthful beauty they only imagine they had."

But Simon was beautiful. He hadn't let himself go. His belly was flat, his chest tight, his face barely touched by wrinkles at the corners of his mouth and eyes.

I liked that he wasn't young. He was old enough to be sure of himself, to be confident, to be powerful. He could change the mood of a room with a single glance, a curled lip, or a doubting lift of his eyebrow. His stare could make you feel like you were on trial, or that you were the most adored person in the world.

I should wake him up and send him back to his daughter. He shouldn't be gone too long.

I pulled the quilt up over my shoulders. Leaning my head back against the cushions, I watched him sleep, the flickering of his eyelashes, the tiny tremors within. I'd let him sleep just a little bit longer.

*Locking the door behind himself, the stranger turned the hot water faucet as far as it would go. Steam began to fill the small bathroom, and the rushing water drowned out the sounds of the emergency room next door. The stranger slipped out of his coat, hanging it on the hook on the back of the door with his satchel.*

*Plunging his hands into the scalding water, he began to scrub the dirt of the road from his nails, from the creases of his knuckles. He couldn't remember the last time he had been properly clean. The dirt of a continent stained the water brown.*

*With red and swollen hands, he set his wire-framed glasses on the back of the toilet tank before plunging his head into the steam. He splashed handfuls of water over his face and his closely shorn head. It burned, but he scrubbed at his cheeks, rubbed at his skin until it squeaked.*

*Shaking his hands, he tore off a strip of paper towel and dried his face and head.*

*From the hanging satchel, the stranger withdrew the cool, stiff white circle of a collar, which he laid on the back of the toilet, next to his glasses.*

*It took him a moment to button the top of his black shirt, closing the fabric over the scarred loop of russet twisted flesh around his throat.*

*The careful placement of the collar hid the evidence of his shame.*

*If they could see him as he truly was, he thought, all those who had come to him so willingly—who would come again, he knew—would turn away, repulsed by the sudden realization of his transgressions. But when they saw his collar, they saw their own chance at redemption, the promise of the glory, the rightness of the path. Who better to show them the way than a man of God?*

## Karen

The steady rhythm of the respirator was lulling, its cool, measured pace encouraging sleep. But it was impossible to ignore the reason for that rhythm, the ebb and flow of my daughter's breath. It was impossible to close my eyes knowing that.

The doctor had come in on his rounds about half an hour after Simon left. If he was surprised that my husband was gone, he didn't show it.

"How are you holding up, Mrs. Barrett?" he asked. I was relieved to see he didn't have to check the file for my name.

"You can call me Karen," I said, as if this were the most normal situation in the world, just a couple of people getting to know one another while a machine breathed for my daughter.

"Karen, then. Are you doing all right?"

"I'm fine."

"Have you had something to eat? You're recuperating, too."

My fingers strayed to the bandage on my head.

"I'll ask someone to bring you a dinner," he said, making a note in the file. "And later on I'll see if an orderly can wheel in a cot. These chairs are a pretty uncomfortable way to spend the night."

"Thank you." I was on the verge of tears again.

He waved it away. "It's too bad this room isn't a little bigger. There's only enough room for one cot, so someone's going to have to spend the night in the chair." He winked at me. "You'll have to draw straws."

I tried to smile.

"So how's our other patient?" He leaned over the rail, taking Sherry's narrow wrist between his thumb and forefinger, timing her pulse with his wristwatch. Untucking the stethoscope from his pocket, he gently folded back the bedclothes and raised the gown she was wearing.

I stepped back a little, feeling bile surge to the back of my mouth. Her body seemed to be a mess of bruises, mottled black and purple, bandaged in places.

He noticed me staring. "It's not as bad as it looks. Just bruises, from the impact of the truck and from the fall."

I nodded.

"We've bandaged up the worst of the contusions. They'll clear up pretty quickly. Nothing to worry about there . . ." He snapped the stethoscope in his ears and leaned over her, placing the cold metal disc just under Sherry's left nipple. He stared out into the middle distance as he listened, moved the stethoscope and stared into the distance again.

He nodded slowly as he straightened up, gently lowering Sherry's gown and tucking her back in.

Then he carefully lifted her eyelid with his thumb, moving the fore-finger of his other hand slowly across her line of vision before taking a small light from his pocket and following the path of his finger with it.

He slid the light back into his pocket and made his notations in her file before he spoke. "Well, all of her vital signs are stable. Her heart-beat is a little slow and her temperature is a bit high, but that's to be ex-pected."

"Will she—?" The words were out of my mouth before I realized it, and I wished immediately that I could take them back.

"Will she be all right?" he asked.

I nodded.

He took the briefest of moments before he spoke. "It's still too early to say, one way or another. We just don't know." He shrugged. "But we are going to do everything in our power to ensure Sherilyn's full recov-ery. Everything we can do."

I forced a smile.

"Okay?"

I nodded. "Okay."

"Good. Now I'm going to get you some dinner and we'll see to it that you get a cot in here." He turned toward the door, but then stopped. "I want you to take care of yourself, okay?"

I nodded again.

*File of Barrett, Sherilyn Amber*
4/24, 18:25
NOTES: bp 90/60, P 54. Pupils sluggishly reactive. Glasgow Coma Scale 6. Low-grade fever. Bibasilar rales and increasing oxygen requirements. Possible early ventilator-associated pneumonia. Start ceftriaxone and gatifloxacin now.

S. McKinley

### Karen

I pulled the chair to the foot of Sherry's bed and angled it so that I would be able to see when Simon returned. I looked up every time someone passed the open doorway. Nurses would stop and glance in, ask me if I wanted anything. An orderly brought dinner, covered with a brown lid, and left it on the table without a word.

I waited for my husband, listening to the machine breathe for my daughter.

"Mrs. Barrett?" The man in the doorway was a dark shadow against the bright lights from the corridor.

"Yes?"

He took several steps into the room, a tall stranger in a black coat, clutching a battered brown book to his chest. The light from above Sherry's bed reflected off the smoothness of his head, from the wire rims of his glasses and from the white of his clerical collar.

"Mrs. Barrett, I'm—"

"No." I shook my head. "No. We don't need you here."

He let the hand holding his Bible fall to his side.

"I'm no longer in the Church," I said.

He nodded. "I understand. But the Church can be a comfort and a source of guidance in these times."

I shook my head. "Did my mother call you? Did she?" Calling a priest to come to the hospital was exactly the sort of thing my mother would do.

"No, I was making my rounds."

"Please . . . I don't need you. We don't need you."

He nodded as if he had heard that response before. "There's a chapel here, if you change your mind."

He stood there for a long moment, staring at me as if waiting for me to speak.

I turned my attention wholly to Sherry. Eventually I heard his footsteps receding down the corridor.

The Church. That was the last thing I needed.

"Karen?"

I glanced up again, barely recognizing the woman who stood there.

"Jamie?"

I tried to remember how long it had been since I had last seen her. When she threw her arms around me and hugged me, hard, I was surprised by how familiar it felt.

"How is she?" she whispered.

"I don't . . . The doctors don't know. They say she could wake up at any time. . . ."

"Oh, Karen . . ." She kept an arm around me as I turned back to the bed.

We both looked down at Sherry as her chest rose and fell, rose and fell.

"It's been a long time, Jamie," I said.

"Couple of years."

"I sort of dropped off the map."

"You had a new baby. It was natural to want to stay at home."

"Is that how long it's been?"

She nodded. "I think the last time we really spent any time together was at the baby shower."

Jamie had been my best friend at the paper, the only confidante I'd had there. "I'm sorry."

"It was as much my fault as anything," she said, gently squeezing my shoulder. "Water under the bridge."

"How did you hear about Sherry?"

"Someone at City picked up the nine-one-one call on their scanner this morning. Did all the usual follow-up, and when it came back that Karen Barrett had been involved . . . Everybody's hearts are with you, Kar."

"Thanks."

"Are you okay?"

My hand went to the bandage. "Bumps and bruises. Nothing that won't heal."

"And Simon?"

"What?"

"Is Simon around?"

"Oh, he'll be back. He had to go into the office, clear his calendar."

"How's he taking it?"

"Well, you know Simon."

She didn't. Not really.

"Can I get you anything?"

I tried to smile. "No, I'm okay. But thanks."

"No big deal."

"No, I mean, thanks for coming. You didn't have to."

"Hon, I got here as soon as I could."

## Simon

The cabbie cut the corner sharply onto the Johnson Street Bridge, changing lanes and cutting off an Audi next to us.

Mary had awakened me with a kiss to my temple. So beautiful, the sight of her face as I opened my eyes. I was naked under an old comforter that had probably been on her bed when she was a teenager, that had accompanied her to university, to law school, and now into her apartment overlooking the Inner Harbor. Her apartment.

I jerked up. "I have to . . . How long have I been asleep?"

She glanced over at the clock on the VCR. "An hour or so."

"Shit." I dumped the comforter onto the floor as I stood. "Why did you—?"

"I thought you could use the sleep," she said. "I'm sorry."

I shook my head. "No, it's my fault. I should have known better. I shouldn't have—" The look on her face stopped me from finishing the sentence.

The cabbie leaned on the horn, cursing under his breath at a cyclist who dared to ride in the same lane, shooting past him with no room to spare.

"Hey," I said. "You want to ease off a bit, maybe get me to the hospital alive?"

He responded with a grumble, turning up the radio.

The taxi slammed to a stop at a light on lower Johnson Street, throwing me forward. Glancing up, I made eye contact with the cabbie in the rearview mirror.

Mary had wanted to drive me to the hospital, but I had shaken my head.

"You're right, that'd be stupid," she said.

"No, it's not that. I think I just need a little time to myself."

"Okay. Just call me when you can, all right?"

I nodded. "Oh, and listen—"

I guess she heard the work tone in my voice, because she interrupted me, smiling, to say "I've cleared your calendar for the next couple of days. Tom's going to argue for a postponement on Kitteridge. Bob Arnold was a little pissed, but everyone understands." She shrugged. "Won't be a problem."

As soon as the light changed, the cab squealed into motion, slamming into the right-hand turn lane, passing the sedan we had been behind, arcing back in front of it. I lurched from side to side. "Jesus Christ," I muttered, my voice rising as I found my balance. "What the hell are you doing?"

"You wanna shut up, pal, or should I drop you off right here?" He half turned in his seat to face me.

"Just watch your driving," I muttered.

He swerved the car to the curb and hit the brakes, jarring to a halt in a cloud of natural gas exhaust.

"You wanna get the fuck—," he started as he turned to face me again. I pulled back and punched him in the nose. There was a popping noise as the cartilage shattered and blood poured onto his shirtfront in a gush.

"What the fuck?" he sputtered, frantically holding his nose, spraying blood with every breath. "I'm gonna call a cop."

"Go ahead, Mr.—" I glanced at the license for his name. "—Fredericks. Go ahead. You can explain your driving, your recklessness. They'll probably take your license. Go ahead." I opened the door and extended one leg to step out.

"I'm gonna call my lawyer," he called after me.

Leaning in, I dropped a five-dollar bill on his seat along with one of my business cards. "Please do."

I slammed the door behind me.

So I was walking to the hospital, where my daughter lay dying.

Make no mistake—I knew what was going on. I knew how much the doctor was leaving out. "She could wake up anytime. . . . It's too early to tell. . . ."

Downtown was deserted except for the prostitutes, the street kids with their dogs and drums, the drug dealers and the junkies. The prostitutes stood brazenly at the curbsides in miniskirts and tank tops, or trench coats that flashed the nakedness underneath. I was subject to close study as I walked past, avoiding eye contact.

The doctor hadn't come out and said that Sherry was dying, that she would never wake up, that the damage was too great and that there was nothing that anyone could do. But I knew. For Karen's sake I was grateful for the dissembling. It gave her the time she needed, a chance to adjust, to accept, to say good-bye in her own way.

Good-bye . . .

Oh Christ, what sort of a world . . . What sort of a person . . .

No.

I choked back the rage I felt building, and the tears. I'd had my time for weakness. I still couldn't believe that I had run to Mary, leaving Sherry in that bed, leaving Karen hurt, and hurting. That was enough self-pity and weakness for one night.

The walk to the hospital passed in a blur. I steeled myself before walking through the emergency room doors, checking my watch. 10:04. I prayed that Karen wouldn't be too angry. That she wouldn't ask too many questions.

She was where I had left her all those hours before, leaning over the bed in a pool of harsh yellow light. She looked up as she heard me come into the room.

"Jamie was here," she said.

"Jamie?"

"From the paper? You remember."

Only vaguely.

"Where have you been?"

I set my briefcase on the floor beside the bed. "At the office." I leaned over the bed rail. "How is she?"

"I tried calling."

"You know how hard it is to get a call through once the switchboard closes. Did you try my cell?"

"I just . . . I needed you." She was biting her lip, and I could see that she had been crying.

"I know. I'm here now."

"Did you get everything done that you needed to?"

"I think so. I might have to go in for a bit tomorrow, but it should be all right." Such a bastard.

She nodded. I slipped my arm around her back, shifting as she snuggled into me. "How is she?"

"The doctor came in just after you left, checked her, said that everything was stable. They'll do some more tests in the morning. Have you had anything to eat?" She gestured at an untouched hospital tray.

Mary had made me a couple of slices of toast and a poached egg. The smell of the hospital room was making the food congeal in my belly. "I'm fine."

"They'll be bringing a cot up soon, so one of us can sleep there. I don't want to go home tonight. I don't want to leave."

"Of course not."

"One of us has to sleep in the chair, though. . . ." She gestured at the molded plastic furniture with a grimace.

"I'll take the chair."

"No, you take the cot. I probably won't sleep anyway."

In the end, neither of us slept. The cot stayed folded up where the orderly left it. We stayed at Sherry's bedside all night, not speaking, watching our daughter dying before our eyes, though only one of us knew it.

Henry

I walked downtown from Hillside Centre, through James Bay, then along the water and back into downtown. I needed to keep moving. I kept checking behind me, half-expecting the police or the mother of that little girl to be following me, but no one seemed to notice me. There was no eye contact with anyone, no strange looks.

But everywhere I went I could feel her with me. I could feel the little girl I had hit in the crosswalk hovering over me. I could almost see her.

It felt like I was just wandering, but I wasn't surprised when I found myself outside the hospital. It was where I had been heading all along, without even realizing it.

The little girl's mother was sitting in the waiting room, a bandage around her head. A man sat on the vinyl bench next to her. They each held a coffee cup, and they both looked up when I came into the waiting room. I took a step back, but she had no way of recognizing me.

They both turned away. I was completely alone, a ghost, a spirit haunting their lives.

A doctor brushed past me, and the two of them stood up as he came over to them.

I didn't hear too much of what he said. Coma. Accident. Their names.

Simon. Karen. Sherry.

Sherry was the little girl's name.

It was late in the afternoon before I even thought of Arlene and the kids. Would the police have come to the apartment looking for me? Arlene must be worried sick. For a moment I thought about going home, or at least calling to let them know I was all right.

But I didn't.

I wasn't.

*VICTORIA NEW SENTINEL,* THURSDAY, APRIL 25

## Hit and Run
### Girl, 3, comatose following accident
### Police Seek Driver

The family of 3-year-old Sherilyn Barrett waited anxiously last night for a change in their daughter's condition following a hit-and-run accident on Hillside Avenue yesterday morning. The girl has been in a coma since being struck by a vehicle while crossing at a marked crosswalk near Hillside Centre with her mother, Karen Barrett.

"It's really too early to tell," said a hospital spokesman yesterday afternoon. "We're optimistic."

Police are requesting that anyone who may have seen the accident please contact their local detachment to assist in their investigation. Police are also seeking Henry Denton, 24, for questioning.

## Karen

"Can I take a look at that file?" Simon asked, gesturing to the folder that Dr. McKinley was holding loosely at his side. The doctor was looking freshly pressed in clean greens. It seemed we were his first stop of the morning.

He hesitated just a beat before handing it over. "Let me know if there's anything in there you can't read, or would like me to explain."

"Simon does a lot of personal-injury work," I said. I don't know why. "He's good with charts."

The doctor glanced at me, then busied himself checking Sherry's breathing.

Simon rustled through the pages, taking it all in, nodding fractionally as he moved from point to point.

"What do you think?" I asked, lowering my voice as if the doctor couldn't or shouldn't hear us.

"Just what he said. Too early to tell." He closed the file.

The doctor looked up from where he leaned over the bed, listening through his stethoscope. He held up one finger, holding our attention and our silence for the few seconds it took him to finish. Then he folded the stethoscope and tucked it into a pocket. "I'm a little concerned with Sherilyn's lungs," he said.

A new sense of dread took hold.

"Her breathing seems a little . . . moist. I'm worried that she might be at risk for pneumonia."

Simon and the doctor exchanged a look.

"What's going on?" I asked. "What aren't you telling us?"

"It's the pneumonia that we're most concerned with right now. If she gets it . . . there's really nothing that we can do."

I started to speak, but he held out his hand to stop me. "I'm increasing her antibiotics. We'll do everything we can to stave it off, but while she's on the respirator she's at risk for opportunistic infection."

"Then take her off the respirator."

I could feel Simon's hand at the small of my back. That frightened me more than the doctor.

"We can't," Dr. McKinley replied.

"What? Why not?"

"They can't," Simon said. "They think—"

I turned my head away. I didn't want to hear.

"We don't think that Sherilyn is capable of breathing on her own," the doctor said.

Simon spoke to me in his courtroom voice, but I could hardly hear him over the roaring in my ears. "The trouble with the respirator is that with all the bacteria and viruses in the environment, what happens is that the patient . . . If she catches pneumonia . . ." He shook his head.

I took a step backward. I wanted to run. "Why are you saying this?"

"But we can't take her off the respirator because she can't breathe on her own," Simon finished, so logically.

"Is that true?" I asked the doctor, ignoring Simon altogether.

He hesitated a moment, then nodded.

"So what do we do?" I asked the room, Simon, the doctor, Sherry. "What do we do?" My voice almost broke against the words.

"We just have to wait and see," the doctor answered.

## Simon

After the doctor left, Karen turned on me.

"How can you be so calm? How can you be so cold? Sherry is dying. Don't you care?" She was shaking with anger.

"Of course I care," I said. But somebody needed to be strong, to be able to think things through. I didn't say that. I couldn't.

"You don't. You don't care at all!"

"Karen—"

"Get out," she said. "Get the hell out of here."

She didn't mean it. I was sure she didn't mean it.

"Get out!" she shouted.

I picked up my briefcase and turned toward the door. "I'm going to go home and get us both a change of clothes, okay? I'll be back in a little while. Is there anything else I can bring you?"

"You're going?" She called after me. "How can you just leave? How can you just leave us again?"

I could hear her sobbing as the elevator doors closed.


### Karen

"Are you okay?"

I jumped. I hadn't seen the doctor come in.

"What?"

"I saw your husband leaving, and I just wanted to check. . . ."

I nodded. "I'm okay."

"Listen, why don't we sit down," he said.

Using just the slightest pressure on my upper arm, he guided me to a plastic chair and sat next to me. "I'm sorry your husband's not here," he said.

I found myself shaking my head defensively, not entirely sure why. "That's just . . . Simon's got a different way . . ."

"No, it's not that. . . . You should both be here."

"He'll be back."

"Karen." He stumbled a little on my name. "I wish we had more time." He sighed heavily.

"What do you mean?"

"There have been some developments."

"Developments?"

"I've got some test results. Your daughter's already started to exhibit the symptoms of pneumonia. We upped the antibiotics already last night, so . . ."

"Then?"

*I will not cry I will not cry I will not cry I will not cry. . . .*

"Listen, Karen, we're going to take her for some tests this morning. CAT scans, MRI, neurological responsiveness, that sort of thing. We're gonna be gone for a few hours. Why don't you go home, get something to eat, try to get a little sleep. I know that you . . . that neither of you got any sleep last night."

More than anything the doctor recommended, I needed to talk to Simon.

## Simon

It was strange: coming home didn't feel like coming home. Something was wrong. Different. The house itself was unchanged, almost everything the way it was when I left for work the day before. There was a small pile of laundry in the middle of the living room, a basket of unmatched socks and underwear in front of the couch, a half-empty cup of coffee on the side table. A pair of Sherry's shoes sat next to the laundry basket.

Karen had done the breakfast dishes. The cloth hung sloppily over the neck of the faucet. A pool of water edged a chicken she had left to thaw on the counter. I picked it up and threw it into the garbage under the sink, washing my hands in hot water after, straightening the cloth over the faucet.

The bathroom light was still on upstairs, a towel in a wet ball in the corner. I turned off the light.

Sherry's door was open, her floor littered with stuffed animals and brightly colored toys, a little undershirt on the unmade bed, another pair of shoes on the blue carpet nearby.

It was only as I set my briefcase down on the floor of our bedroom that I realized what I had been feeling since coming through the front door. This wasn't home anymore.

This house was where I lived, where my family lived. This was where we had brought Sherry from the hospital, where we had planned and laughed and fought and cried and made love, struggling to conceive. This bed, these clothes, the office just off the bedroom, all of this was mine, ours. Or had been.

My life had changed in a moment, a dividing line between before and after. The house was before: unfamiliar to me now in its strange silence, like a garment belonging to someone else. Fundamentally alien despite its near perfect fit.

Leaning over the bed, I pressed the PLAY button on the answering machine to stop the red light flashing.

> *"Karen, honey, it's Mom. I just got your message.... Oh my... It's one thirty, Wednesday afternoon. I'm calling the airline right now. I'll call you right back.... I love you both.... I'm praying for you."*

> *"Karen, it's Jamie ... from the paper. Todd just pulled something in on the scanner.... Is everything ... Listen, I'll try later ... I hope ... I'll see you soon."*

> *"Mr. or Mrs. Barrett, it's Kent Lutz calling from CFAX radio, Victoria's News Authority. I was wondering if I could speak to either of you, or both of you, about what happened this morning. You can reach me at ..."*

> *"Karen, it's Todd Herbert from the* Sentinel. *I really hate to be calling at a time like this...."*

> *"Karen, it's Mom. I hope everything is okay.... The earliest flight I can get is Friday morning.... I'll be flying Air Canada.... I'll take a cab from the airport into town. Call me, honey. I'm praying for you...."*

> *"It's Tonya Hopper calling from CHEK TV. I was hoping I could have a word...."*

> *"Simon, Karen, it's Sheila from the office. I just wanted to let you know how terrible everyone is feeling. We're all praying for you...."*

> *"Oh my God, Karen, I just saw the paper. Is Sherry gonna be okay? Are you okay? Should I ... I'll ... I'll call you back...."*

I sat on the edge of the bed, listening to voices I didn't know, or couldn't remember. I couldn't move. Literally could not even shift my weight. Paralyzed.

The telephone rang, but the sudden noise didn't startle me. I could easily have picked it up; I didn't.

Looking at myself in the mirror on the closet door, I noticed the awkwardness of the position I was sitting in, weight shifted to one side, one leg balancing the body, a teetering support that could, at any moment, fall away.

The telephone rang.

I felt suspended, outside of time, separated from everything I loved, everything I had worked so hard for, as if within a plastic bubble.

Untouchable.

On the fourth ring my voice clicked in, distorted by the answering machine tape. "You've reached Simon, Karen, and Sherry. Please leave a message. . . ." My voice was cut off with a beep, and suddenly Karen was in the room with me.

"Simon? Simon? Are you there?" In the lengthy pause that followed, I watched the red recording light on the face of the machine. "I thought you were going home. . . ."

The connection broke with a click, followed by a shrill beep as the machine reset itself.

The room was now vibrant with Karen's presence—I could see her dressing, curled in sleep around a pillow, nursing Sherry in the chair by the window. Everywhere I looked I saw my wife, and everywhere I saw her, she was smiling.

My cell phone vibrated against me. I answered it before the second ring. "Simon Barrett."

"It's me."

"Hey."

"I tried you at home."

"I'm almost there. Just turning onto Shakespeare now."

"I spoke to the doctor. We need to talk. . . ."

I found myself nodding. "Okay, I'll come—"

"No. I think we should . . . Could we meet somewhere? They're taking Sherry for some tests, and I should probably eat something."

"How about John's Place in fifteen minutes?"

"I'll see you there."

The silence that followed was a pale shadow of our early days together, when neither of us could figure out how we wanted any given telephone conversation to go, or how it should end.

"I love you," she finally said.

"I love you, too. I'll see you soon."

Karen clicked off.

After I locked the front door behind me, I lingered on the front step for a moment before walking to our minivan. It seemed bewildering that the air was heavy with spring blossoms.

Karen was seated at a table in the window by the time I got to John's Place. I nodded to her as I opened the door, but she stared down into the dark depths of her coffee cup. She looked broken. I'm used to that look on people. I see it all the time in clients: the red eyes, the shaking hands, the pale skin. People weak from fighting battles they were unable to win on their own. It was shocking to see it on Karen. Her blond hair so dull, the pallor eating away her usual vividness.

"I'm here with someone," I said to the waiter as I moved around the few people lined up for tables to slip into the chair across from Karen.

She looked up.

"It took a little longer than I thought," I found myself explaining to her, unable to just sit in the silence. "I checked the answering machine." I pulled the folded piece of paper from my pocket. "Mostly newspapers, TV, radio. Jamie called. Your mom called a couple of times."

Her face brightened a little.

"She can't get a flight out until tomorrow."

"Damn."

"My mother called us back, too."

"You still need to call your dad, though."

I didn't say anything.

"Before he reads about it in the newspaper."

"He doesn't read the paper."

"Still, he's her grandfather. Even if they've never met."

I reached across the table and laid my hand over hers, trying to change the subject. "How are you holding up?"

"I talked to Dr. McKinley after you left. That's what we need to talk about."

I gently squeezed her hand. "Karen . . ." I waited until she met my eyes. "How are *you* doing?"

She pulled her hand away. "Fine, fine," she said. "I need a shower, and some food, and some sleep—"

The waiter materialized next to us. "Have you had a chance to look at the menu?"

I hadn't even noticed it lying on the place mat in front of me. I gestured toward Karen.

"Just toast, I think. Brown." She seemed drained, weakened.

"I'll have the same. And a coffee."

He scooped up the menus and disappeared back into the kitchen.

Karen sighed heavily, took a sip of her coffee. "I talked to Dr. McKinley after you . . . after."

I nodded.

"He said . . ."

Both her hands were wrapped tightly around her coffee cup where I couldn't reach them.

"He . . . uh, they . . ." She sniffed and ran the back of one hand over her nose. "They're taking her in for some tests. Scans. They . . ."

"MRI?" I asked.

"I think so."

"Another one."

"What?" she asked, confused.

"They took her for one yesterday. Before the surgery. If they're taking her in for another one . . ."

We both stopped as the waiter arrived with my coffee, setting the cup heavily on the scarred tabletop, dropping a handful of creamers next to it. "There you go," and to Karen, "I'll come around in a second to warm yours up."

Her face was tightly drawn in, straining, as if it might burst, as she nodded to him. "He said . . . He said she has pneumonia. That she . . ." Tears ran down her cheeks.

## Karen

He reached over and lifted my hand away from the coffee cup and held it between both of his. He was shaking his head, his eyes soft. "Let's not talk about this right now," he said.

"Simon . . ." I couldn't form a coherent thought, and I was embarrassed to be crying here in a restaurant.

"No, listen," he said, squeezing my hand. "We don't have to talk about this right now. . . ."

"I don't want her to die, Simon."

He shushed me and squeezed my hand again. "Don't even think about that right now. Just let it be."

"Simon . . ."

"Just let it be. We'll eat breakfast, get you home, get you showered. It's going to be okay."

I nodded, trying to smile a little.

"I love you," he said in a near whisper. "I'm here for you."

I could only nod again.

"I'm sorry I was such a jerk at the hospital."

## Simon

I checked the time as I answered my cell phone. 12:48. Karen was in the shower, and had been for over seventeen minutes. She had called her mother when we got home from the restaurant, hung up crying, and retreated into the bathroom with her robe over her shoulder.

"Barrett," I answered.

"Mr. Barrett? It's Dr. McKinley calling from the hospital. I tried a couple of times to get through on your home line and it was busy."

We had left the phone off the hook after Karen had spoken with her mother. While we had been out for breakfast, another half dozen messages, all from journalists, had been left on the machine. "It's probably easiest to get through to us on my cell. How is she?"

"Well, I know I told Karen that she should try to get some sleep, but

I think you two should probably come back as soon as you can. Sherry's running quite a high fever, and there is a lot of fluid present in her lungs. As well, we've run some tests. . . ."

"And . . ."

"And I'd like to talk to both of you about the results."

I closed my eyes before answering. "We'll be right back. Where will we find you?"

"Have them page me."

He hung up without saying good-bye. I sat for a moment in the silence, the only sound my breath, a quaver noticeable with every inhalation.

Karen had turned off the shower, and a moment later the bathroom door opened with a burst of light and steamy warmth redolent of raspberry shower foam. She was wrapped in her green robe, and gently drying her hair with a towel. She stopped when she saw me on the bed, telephone in hand. "Is it—?"

I nodded. "We need to go back to the hospital."

She retreated into the bathroom, closing the door behind her.

## Karen

We were holding hands when we got back to Sherry's room. I don't think I would have been able to get through the door without Simon holding on to me.

Dr. McKinley was staring at her chart. "I just took Sherry's temperature—"

"How bad is it?" Simon asked.

"A hundred and three degrees," he said, double-checking his note.

"Oh, Jesus," I whispered, my knuckles white around Simon's hand as we stood by Sherry's bed.

"Is that—?"

"Is that why I called? No. The tests we ran this morning—CT, neurological scans, I jumped the line for the MRI again. . . ."

We waited.

"Since the surgery, there's been considerable swelling, and some bleeding." He paused, suddenly unable to meet our eyes. "Unfortunately—"

I fumbled for the bed rail with my free hand.

"We failed to detect any trace of brain activity." He turned his gaze on Sherry, lying as if suspended within the institutional sheets. "I'm sorry," he said.

"Brain dead?" I whispered.

"We don't . . . ," he stammered as he caught Simon's look. "That's not what we call it anymore."

"Are you saying she's never going to wake up?"

I wanted him to argue, or to reassure me, but the doctor didn't say anything.

"So what do we do now?" Simon asked.

"I want to say that we should wait. That there might be some change . . . But I can't." The doctor lifted his eyes to ours.

"She's never going to wake up," I repeated, watching her chest rise and fall.

This time he shook his head. "No. No, she won't. There's just too much damage. . . . I'm sorry."

"Is she in pain?"

He seemed surprised by the question, and it took him a moment to answer. "No. No, she's not feeling anything."

*Not feeling anything.*

"I know that this sounds terribly sudden, but we should probably discuss the possibility of organ donation."

"Yes."

"There are a number of children—"

*Not feeling anything.*

"Sherry could help a lot of—"

"No," I said, the firmness of my voice hiding the confusion I was feeling. I wanted to scream. I wanted to tear things into pieces. I wanted to push these men away from my daughter and take her in my arms and not let her go. Instead, I repeated myself. "No."

"I'm sorry?" The doctor turned toward me.

"Karen, it's for—"

"I can't. I just can't, Simon." I shook my head. "It's all moving too fast. It's all just . . . Yesterday I was holding my daughter's hand as we walked down the street, and today—today you're asking me to decide, to decide if she should live or die. And I can't. It's all too fast. It's all too—"

"I'm not—"

Simon glanced at the doctor.

"There's still some time—"

"She's not in any pain?" I asked again.

The doctor shook his head.

"Then I'd like to wait. I'd like to wait, and I'd like to get a second opinion. Maybe the tests were wrong. Maybe he's wrong, Simon."

"Of course," Dr. McKinley said. "Of course. I'll leave you alone."

Simon shuffled out of my way as I sat down in the chair at Sherry's bedside. I took her hand and held it in mine, its warmth burning into me.

*Not feeling anything.*

## Simon

It began to rain shortly after three that afternoon. At first, I noticed only because I was standing at the window, but the wind quickly picked up and started to drive the drops against the glass.

Karen had not looked away from our daughter since the doctor left, rubbing her thumb in a slow circle on the back of Sherry's hand as she held it.

I had tried talking with her, but she hadn't responded. I couldn't tell if she hadn't heard me or if she was ignoring me.

So I stood at the window, watching the water run in dirty rivulets down the glass, across my reflection.

In the gray light, the room could have been a painting. Everything was still, shadowy, except where the bedside lamp cast a pool of golden light on Sherry's face, a warm circle over my daughter and her mother in a world of cold gray.

I walked over to the bed.

"I'm going for a walk," I said in a whisper, not wanting to startle her. She didn't move. "Do you want me to bring you anything?"

I waited a moment for a response—a word, a gesture, anything—
but there was nothing. It was like I wasn't even there.

Karen

Will I ever have this moment, this time, again? Will I ever be able to sit
with my daughter, just sit with her and watch her sleep? Watch the rise
and fall of her breath, trace the curve of her cheeks?

No. Never.

The machine breathes for her, and when it stops . . . No amount of
wishing will make her whole. No amount of watching will bring her
back.

How do you hold a moment, knowing that it is the last? How do
you take in enough to last you through a lifetime of absence? How do
you remember enough to see you through?

How do you know what will last?

Will I be surprised someday to realize I've forgotten the color of her
lips, barely pinker than her face? Or the way the corners of her mouth
lift naturally to hint at a smile? Will I need photographs to remind me of
the way her hair falls? The way her smile bursts open in pure happiness?

What of my daughter will I take with me from this room? Nothing.
Nothing if I can help it. I don't want to remember her like this—broken
and bleeding, the sound of the machine that presses air into her tiny
lungs.

I don't want to remember this room, the sound of the rain and the
sight of her here. I want to remember yesterday, the way she laughed
and ran, the way she looked at the flowers and rocks, the way she was so
alive, so filled with joy. I want to hold the stones in my pocket—the
three stones she picked up on the way to the mall—as a reminder of
Sherry growing and learning, smiling and running.

But I know that I can't choose. I know that I'll remember this room
as much as those mornings with the three of us in the big bed, snuggling
and tickling and refusing to face the day. I know that I'll remember
these bloodstained bandages as much as I'll remember last Christmas,
her look of wonder as Simon read her the note that Santa Claus left her,

thanking her for the cookies and the carrots for the reindeer. I know that I'll remember the moment I choose to let her go, the moment I feel her last breath, as vividly as I remember that gush of blood and love I felt as I heard her first cry, as I first saw her, tiny and twisting and perfect, wailing to raise the moon.

Ashes to ashes. Blood to blood. Cries to silence.

## Simon

It was cold outside the emergency room doors, but sheltered from the wind and the rain. A small crowd had gathered around the garbage can, and the air was thick with smoke.

"Can I buy a cigarette from someone?" I asked the group in general. "A cigarette and a light?"

A kid near me, no more than sixteen or seventeen, fumbled for his pack. "Here," he said, handing me the pack of du Mauriers. "Take a couple." He waved away the money I offered.

"Thanks," I said, inhaling the first lungful of smoke, handing him back the cigarettes.

My cell phone rang as I was taking another drag. I didn't need to check the number to know who it was.

## Karen

Simon came back just before nightfall. No sunset tonight, no warm orange glow, just a slow darkening of the rain, the sky, the room.

"How are you?" he asked when he saw me looking at him.

I shrugged.

"I brought food." He set the bags on the swing table next to the bed. "And coffee."

I tried to smile. "Thank you."

He leaned over the bed and smoothed back Sherry's hair, careful to avoid the bandages.

"You missed the doctor," I said.

"What did he have to say?" he asked without looking up.

"Not Dr. McKinley. Dr. Tompkins. A specialist."

He straightened up. "And?"

I couldn't do any more than shake my head before bursting into tears. Simon came around the bed and held me until I stopped crying.

"So nothing has changed," he said as he stepped away from me.

I nodded.

He busied himself with the food on the table. "It's not much."

"What?"

"The food. It's not much. Just doughnuts." He shrugged, and I tried to think of where he might have found a doughnut shop nearby. "I thought we could get something from the cafeteria a little later."

Eating was the last thing on my mind. I couldn't bear to watch as he picked up a jelly doughnut and bit into it, the sugar sticking to his lips. He washed it down with a mouthful of coffee.

"I talked to your mother," he said, his voice thick as he chewed. "She called my cell. She'll be here around one."

"That's fine."

"She sounded like she really wanted to be here."

I nodded. "I know. She'll have a priest in here, she'll be praying—"

"It's a comfort to her."

"I know. But it's not a comfort to me. It makes everything so much harder."

I could imagine trying to tell my mother that there was nothing that we could do, that there was no hope for Sherry to recover.

"Of course there's hope," she would say. "There's always hope." Staring up at her god.

I wouldn't want to fight with her; I never do. But that's how we relate, I guess. She puts all her faith in a god who either doesn't exist or who takes a particular delight in testing her very limits. The Lord will provide? The Lord will save my daughter? Where was your Lord when Dad was dying? What good was your faith when he was wasting away before our eyes? Where was your god yesterday morning when a truck hit my little girl?

"One o'clock?"

Simon nodded. "She'll take a cab in from the airport so we don't have to worry about picking her up."

One o'clock. It would all be over before then.

## Henry

I couldn't do it anymore.

The day of the accident, I walked until I couldn't walk anymore, and then I collapsed in a small park, on the grass next to a cedar tree. I could barely feel my legs, and I thought I'd fall asleep right away. But I didn't. Every time I closed my eyes, I could see her, Sherry, hanging in the air in front of me, her eyes locked to mine, the sound of the engine drowning out her scream.

I wanted her to go away, but she didn't, and I lay there all night, not sleeping. By morning I was wet with dew.

I had nowhere to go, nowhere to turn. I had tried to go home, had stood in the hallway, listening to the sound of my family, but I couldn't bring myself to open the door. What would I tell Arlene? That I had hit a little girl with my truck, and then run away? How could I face my boys, knowing that?

I kept replaying the accident in my mind, seeing her appear in front of the truck, spinning skyward. I couldn't shake the image. I couldn't turn it off.

I walked back to the hospital, in the pouring rain, trying to reassure myself: *She's still alive. She has to be.*

*If she made it through the first night, she'll make it.* Isn't that how it's supposed to work? She would make it. I knew she would.

I saw Mr. Barrett just outside the emergency room. He was leaning against a wall with his eyes closed, a cigarette burned to a column of ash between his fingers.

It took me a few minutes to find her room, just around the corner from the nurse's station on the fifth floor. I was standing outside the door when the specialist examined Sherry. I couldn't hear what he said, but the way Mrs. Barrett looked after he left—the way she fell against

the bed, sobbing with her face buried in the blankets—told me all I
needed to know.

She had made it through the first night, but she wasn't going to
make it.

I had killed her. I killed that little girl.

The little girl who I could see, hanging in the air in front of me, as I
fled the hospital.

I couldn't do it anymore. I couldn't keep seeing her, seeing the accident, over and over in my head.

I needed to make it stop. I needed to escape.


## Simon

I fell asleep in the chair. I wouldn't have thought it possible; I don't
think I've ever been less comfortable. But I guess it all catches up with
you.

The dark window reflected the room, the half-drawn curtain, the
bed. I checked my watch: midnight.

My back seized a little as I straightened up.

Karen was still at the side of the bed, her hands tight around the
steel rail.

"Hey," I said quietly.

"You fell asleep," she said, not looking at me. Her voice was flat.

"Yeah." I stood up and stretched. "Sorry."

"You probably needed it."

When I reached over to rub her back she flinched, and I drew my
hand away. She finally turned to look at me. Her eyes were deep-set in
gray pockets, her face lined and tight and pale. She looked like she had
been beaten up, like she was barely able to stand of her own volition.

"How is she?" I asked, resting my hand on Sherry's knee.

"The same," she whispered.

I looked away from Karen, down at my daughter under the sheet.
"Right."

"Dr. McKinley said we could call him. Anytime."

I lifted my eyes to meet hers.

"I think we should call him," she said.

## Karen

I don't think I breathed as Dr. McKinley laid the stethoscope on the pale skin of Sherry's chest.

You can talk and talk and talk. You can make it all make sense in your head. You can lay it out and cry and plan and think and accept. . . .

He lifted her eyelids and shone a light into her wide pupils.

Accept the inevitable.

He laid his fingertips against the warm inside of her wrist.

But when it comes down to it, it doesn't make sense. You haven't really accepted anything. I mean, how can you let your child die? How can you make that make sense?

He added his notes to her file, all without saying a word.

"Well?" Simon finally asked.

Dr. McKinley took a deep breath. His face was ashen, and there were dark circles around his eyes, too. "It's not looking good. Her temperature is dangerously high. She's nonresponsive. Her heart rate is weak, and I'm hearing a lot of fluid in her lungs. I've ordered an increase in her IV antibiotics, but we haven't seen much of an effect—"

"And there's no brain activity," I said, not lifting my eyes from my daughter.

"No," he said. "And with the pneumonia—"

"I think that we should disconnect the life support," I said.

"Are you—?"

I looked up at Dr. McKinley. "I want you to disconnect my daughter from the life support."

"Well, usually we—"

"You what?" I asked. "You treat her? You bring her temperature down, clear up all the symptoms, keep feeding her antibiotics, knowing that she's not going to wake up?"

"Can we discuss—?"

I shook my head. "I can't. I'm sorry, but the idea of organ donation, right now, it's more than I can bear."

The doctor nodded. "I understand," he said. "It's just that you'd be helping so many people."

"I know. I know we would. I know that this is selfish, but I just can't."

"We both have organ donor cards in our wallets," Simon said, as if that might make up for this selfishness.

The doctor was silent for a moment. "Do you need more time?"

"We know that this isn't a decision that you can make, or that you can counsel us to make," Simon said, looking down at our daughter. "You'll want us to sign a waiver," he added.

I don't know how I spoke the words, how I was able to keep from screaming, let alone crying, as we stood around her bed, knowing that Sherry was going to die. Was really dead already.

Our miracle.

Henry

Off Dallas Road, the wind whipped from the ocean, and the trees leaned away from the cold. The air was thick and damp with spray, and the moon and stars were bright and full over my head. It smelled of salt and rotting seaweed.

I walked the concrete path toward the cliff's edge with my hands in my pockets, shivering but focused on the lights of Port Angeles across the strait. There were a few other people out, bundled against the cold, but I brushed past them and nobody seemed to notice me.

We used to bring the kids here for the afternoon to play catch on the lawn. Arlene always warned them away from the drop down to the rocks and the beach below. The boys and I would tease her—see how close we could get to the edge before she'd yell at us. Then we'd take one of the narrow paths down to the beach and walk along the water. Connor would shriek when his legs got drenched by a wave, and we would all laugh.

I would never be able to tell Connor what I had done. How do you tell your son that his father is a murderer, that he had killed a little girl the very same age as him?

How could I ever look Dylan in the eye?

And Arlene . . .

When I reached the end of the sidewalk, I stood facing the black water at the edge of the grass. The beacon at Clover Point turned and flashed, but the light was cold and far away. The surf boomed against the rocks and sand.

I didn't deserve to have a family—not when I had stolen one away.

I didn't deserve a normal life.

The lights of Port Angeles across the strait shimmered orange on the dark water. I stood on the edge of the world, in the black and the cold, and even the stars seemed to have gone out.

I had been trying to get home as fast as I could after my shift.

I had looked away for only a moment, but that was enough. When I turned back, I saw her fly into the air. I didn't even have time to touch the brakes.

I killed that little girl. Sherry. She would never wake up. She would always be with me.

*I'm sorry,* I said to her. *It was a mistake. I didn't mean to . . .*

A gust of wind buffeted me, and I nearly lost my footing on the edge of the cliff. My heart raced with the fear of falling.

It was so ridiculous, I almost laughed.

I couldn't think of anything else to do, anywhere else to turn. And if I was going to do it, it was important to do it right, to hit the rocks headfirst, to end it quickly. Not to struggle as the waters dragged me away from the shore. What a coward, worrying about my own suffering while that little girl was dying.

Drawing a breath, I raised my arms above my head. Leaning over, I bent my knees—

*I'm sorry, Arlene.*

—and pushed off into the night sky.

*I love you, Dylan.*

My feet left the ground.

*I love you, Connor.*

I angled down, headfirst, toward the surf and rocks below me.

*I'm sorry, Sherry.*

The black water looked like asphalt after the rain.

*I'm sorry. . . .*

Without warning, I felt myself wrenched backwards, and started to twist in the air. The wind caught in my shirt, my hair. It felt as if a hand had grasped my shoulder and pulled me back toward the cliff. I landed heavily on my side on the wet grass. The force of the impact left me breathless, and I struggled to sit up.

"What the hell . . ."

The beacon light flashed, and the shadows of the trees danced in the wind, but there was no one else there. No one else who could have pulled me to safety.

I was completely alone.

But I could feel the pressure of the hand, of the fingers, on my shoulder. By morning I'd be bruised, the handprint clearly visible on the pale skin.

Simon

Dr. McKinley summoned a night nurse from the station down the corridor to witness Sherry's death. Once she was in the room, he closed the door. The sound of the medical equipment was overwhelming.

"Mr. Barrett, could you please make your request one more time?"

I cleared my throat. "Knowing that the damage to her . . . Knowing that there is no chance that my daughter will ever wake up, I would like you to remove her from the life support equipment."

The doctor glanced at the nurse to make sure that she had heard. When she nodded, he turned to Karen. "Mrs. Barrett?"

She had moved to the head of the bed and was smoothing Sherry's few loose curls back from her forehead. Tears were running steadily down her cheeks, and she was biting her lower lip.

"Mrs. Barrett?" he asked again.

She nodded, unable to speak.

"I'm very sorry," he said, stepping forward and reaching for the control panel.

His fingers had just touched it when Karen choked out, "Wait."

Everyone in the room turned to her.

"I can't do this. I can't just watch this. . . ." There was no longer any pretense of control: her face was flushed bright red, eyes swollen almost shut with tears.

"Do you mean you don't want to . . ."

"Help me," she said to me. "Help me turn her over."

I hurried to help her clear away the tubes and wires so she could reach under them to roll Sherry onto her right side. "She always sleeps on her side," she explained tearfully.

"I know," I answered, shaking as I held the wires and tubes away from my daughter's body like a veil.

Karen slipped her hands under Sherry's neck and hips, and turned her to her side. Out of the corner of my eye I could see the doctor lay a restraining hand on the nurse's arm as she started forward.

Karen carefully arranged Sherry's legs, drawing them upward slightly, curling her like a comma, smoothing back her hair again and whispering, "I love you, baby," into her ear.

I hoped she could hear.

I hoped she couldn't.

I was about to lower the weight of tubes and wires, the weight of my daughter's life, when Karen touched my arm. She had kicked off her shoes. Instead I raised them a little higher so she could lower the rail and slip into the narrow bed with our daughter.

I draped my burden over both of them. Karen nestled herself around Sherry's tiny, still body, cradling her, and buried her face in the soft bed-pressed hair on the back of Sherry's head. Her body was racked with silent sobs.

I rested my hand on Karen's shoulder more for my own good than hers, and looked across the bed at the doctor.

Our eyes met, and I nodded just once.

He stepped to the machine and, with the touch of one finger, turned it off.

### Karen

She was so small, so light, it was like she wasn't even there. Like I was holding, trying to hold, a handful of rain.

I could feel her breath, the steady rise and fall of it under my hand, the steady warmth of her . . .

*. . . thou shalt not grow cold . . .*

The smell of her, her shampoo . . .

*. . . may God bless and keep you always . . .*

Her breath . . .

I whispered in her ear, where only she could hear me. . . .

*Now I lay me down to sleep . . .*

. . . A breath

. . . . . . And then nothing . . .

*I pray the Lord my soul to keep . . .*

I heard her saying it along with me, felt her arms around my neck as I kissed her good night, pulling the covers up to her chin. . . .

Felt her chest stop rising in midbreath.

*And if I die before I wake*

Felt the soft rain of her heartbeat under my hand stop, like a passing summer storm.

*I pray the Lord my soul to take*

Nothing.

It was as if I could actually feel the life pass out of her, a motion of breath, of wings, an actual physical presence I wanted to catch.

If only . . .

Was she cold? Already?

It seemed so soon . . .

Too soon . . .

I tightened my arms around her, pulling her to me, trying to pull her back inside me, where I could protect her, where I could keep her warm and safe.

I would not let her go.

I would not let her go.

I would like to start again.

I wanted that moment back, the moment that the truck pulled her away from me, the moment that I let her go . . .

In my arms, her chest fell, and I could hear the breath, her last breath, escaping from her.

Could I catch it?

No.

Just let it go.

*May angels guide you. . . .*

And then her chest rose. There was a wheeze as she breathed against the pressure of the machine, against the tubes in her mouth and nose.

I could feel her heart.

Beating.

Another breath.

And then choking . . .

Choking . . .

## Simon

The silence of the room was broken as Karen arched upright on the bed, screaming, "She's choking! She's choking!"

I leaned in, whispering, "It's all right. Just let her go—"

"She's choking!"

And from the corner of my eye I could see motion on the heart-rate monitor. "Holy . . ."

The doctor had seen it, too. "She's got a pulse. Janet, we have a pulse. Let's get those tubes out."

I pulled Karen off the bed as the nurse and the doctor stepped in, turning Sherry back onto her back, swiftly removing the tubes from her mouth and nose.

As her airway cleared, she coughed and sputtered. "Let's turn her back onto her side," the doctor said. "In case she vomits."

As they turned her, she coughed again, a small pool forming on the pillow under her mouth and nose. The nurse cleared it away.

The heart-rate monitor was still beeping out its rhythm. The doctor hastily pulled on his stethoscope and pressed it between her shoulder blades where her back was exposed. He listened for several seconds, as if he couldn't believe what he was hearing. He changed position and listened again.

As he straightened up, the nurse asked, "Doctor, what—?" She couldn't even form the question.

He waved her silent, glancing at us across the bed, huddled together, shocked and confused, unable to take our eyes from our daughter.

Using the digital thermometer, he took Sherry's temperature from her inner ear. He shook his head as he stared at the readout. "Son of a bitch," he muttered, but everyone in the room could hear him.

"What is it?" I asked. "What's going on?"

"I don't know." He was too shaken to be anything but completely honest. "Spontaneous respiration has resumed. And when I listen to her breathing, I don't hear any fluid in her lungs. It's like the pneumonia is . . . gone. I'll schedule some tests."

For a moment, we looked at one another. Then all our eyes turned to rest on the small form on the bed, curled into the fetal position, looking for all the world as if she were only sleeping.

*Halfway down the corridor, the stranger watched as nurses rushed into the little girl's room. Seconds later, the elevator doors slid open, disgorging more doctors and nurses, all rushing to the same room. Then in twos and threes they came out into the hall. Most of them were half-smiling, half-confused, not sure about what they had just witnessed in that room.*

*The stranger knew.*

*One nurse, young, pious, the chain of her crucifix visible at the neck of her uniform, was in tears.*

*As he drew on his coat, he heard her say, "It's a miracle."*

*A miracle. Yes.*

*The stranger turned away.*

*It had begun.*

# Part 2

---

*November*

# Karen

Some mornings everything seemed normal.

I would lie in bed, letting myself wake slowly from dreams I could not remember, the house silent around me, the bed warm. I would dress in comfortable clothes—jogging pants or Simon's flannel pajama bottoms. I'd splash cool water on my face. In the hallway, I would pause outside the closed door to Sherry's room, straining to hear any sign of waking within.

It was only as I walked past the doorway to the living room that reality would reassert itself. Where once Simon and I had sat with friends, laughing and drinking wine, now the furniture was pushed against the walls, the couch and coffee table crammed into the corner, Simon's chair tucked almost into the closet. The room where we used to sit around the Christmas tree was dominated by a hospital bed, and the mixed smells of antiseptic cleanliness and the thick, cloying cut flowers that failed to conceal it.

Sherry lay motionless on the bed, the covers tight around her.

Seeing her lying there, on those mornings when I had been fortunate enough to forget, would almost kill me. I had to force myself to breathe as I watched for the rise and fall of her chest under the covers.

I wanted to mess up the bed, to make it seem as if she had stirred during the night, to hold on to the hope that she was only sleeping, that at any moment she might open her eyes, sit up, and wonder why I was crying.

But she hadn't moved the night before, or the night before that. She hadn't moved since Simon and I brought her home from the hospital.

And she didn't stir as I touched her forehead with the cool back of my hand, checking her temperature.

"Hello, Princess," I said. "It looks like it's going to be a beautiful day outside. A little cold though. Mr. Squirrel will be putting on his winter coat. . . ."

On the windowsill I had placed the three stones she had asked me to carry on our walk to the shopping center that morning.

"No more than three," I'd said.

"Four?" she asked, smiling at me, testing her limits.

"How about none?"

She stuck her tongue out, then spent several minutes carefully choosing three stones from a gravel driveway.

For a moment, as I pulled back the curtains, spilling sunlight into the room, I almost expected to turn around to see her looking up at me, shifting groggily and burrowing more deeply into her blankets.

I knew she wouldn't, but that moment, as the light fell across her, that second of possibility, was the only vestige of a normal life that remained.

## Henry

At first I tried to take care of myself. I looked for somewhere to sleep and to eat, somewhere warm where I could rest. I tried the Mustard Seed, the Salvation Army, the Upper Room, anywhere a crowd of men gathered on the sidewalk outside—the sort of men who are used to looking up at people as they walked past without making eye contact.

Everywhere I went it was the same: I would line up for a bed and no one would see me. The man behind me would get a bunk as the volunteer passed me by. When I lined up for food, the servers in their hairnets didn't offer me anything.

I tried to speak, but nobody heard me. Even screaming got no reaction.

The first few days, I screamed a lot.

So I stopped going to the shelters. But even when I found a place to lie down, in an alley or a park, I didn't sleep. I would close my eyes, feeling the tiredness in my muscles and the coldness in my bones, but I couldn't drift off. I ached with hunger, but I couldn't eat. Any food I scavenged from the Dumpsters behind restaurants or corner grocery stores sat like cardboard on my tongue. Eventually the hunger disappeared, and I stopped noticing that I was tired.

And I discovered soon enough that I wasn't being ignored: I really wasn't seen. I could stand directly in someone's path, and they would only veer around me, no recognition in their eyes.

I had disappeared.

Not eating, not sleeping, not seen, I had nothing to do but walk. Along the shoreline, on the cliffs high above the surf, the cold wind in my hair, blowing through my thin clothes. I barely felt it. Along crowded downtown sidewalks, through shopping malls, bars, churches. I could feel people as they brushed against me, hear their voices, smell their perfume, their breath, their hair, their skin. They shuddered sometimes when I passed, like a chill had come over them, but they never saw me.

For the first few weeks, I kept going back to the hospital. I would wait for Mrs. Barrett to step out, for the doctor to disappear—and I would sneak in to stand beside Sherilyn's bed. I knew I had watched another child sleeping, but I couldn't remember. . . . A brother, maybe? Did I have a brother? I didn't know anymore. Everything from my life before the accident had disappeared. Nothing seemed to exist for me before I watched Sherilyn float away, before that night on the cliff.

I kept walking. It was like I was looking for something, but I wasn't sure what it was, or how I would know when I found it.

Simon

The shower turned off on the other side of the bedroom wall. Even with my eyes closed, I knew that the curtains were open, the room bright with morning. I nestled farther under the covers.

Half-asleep, I was only vaguely aware of the bathroom door opening. Then there was a new weight on the bed, the shifting of covers, a radiating warmth alongside me.

I groaned a little and rolled onto my back.

"Are you awake?" She slid her leg over mine, damp and hot.

I moaned this time as she ran her fingers over my bare chest, across my stomach, gently wrapping them around my penis, which thickened at her touch.

"*You're* awake," she whispered.

"You're awake, too."

"Here," she said breathily, sliding atop me. "Here." Using her hand, she guided me inside herself, hot and wet. Raised herself up . . .

Any last remnants of sleep were burned away. "Oh, God, Mary. You're gonna kill me." And I opened my eyes to this vision in the sunlight, her head thrown back as her body moved on top of me, the Inner Harbor behind her through the tall glass.

## Ruth Page

Mrs. Barrett always had a pot of tea waiting for me when I arrived at the house in the morning.

I would let myself in with my key, hang up my coat in the hall closet, and then check on Sherry. I noted her temperature, pulse, and blood pressure—anything significant—on her chart before joining Mrs. Barrett in the kitchen.

The first few days she had offered me coffee, and seemed quite puzzled when I said no, thank you. Then I explained about my ulcer. The next day she had a cup of tea ready for me, the bag dropped directly into a coffee mug. The tea was almost as black as the coffee she was drinking herself.

I thanked her, keeping a smile on my face.

The next day when I got there, she had set a proper teacup and teapot on the kitchen table, with the tea bag on the edge of the saucer and the kettle on the boil.

She wasn't sleeping very much after they brought Sherry home from the hospital, and it was worse after her husband left. When she had coffee with me each morning, I couldn't help but notice the dark circles, bruiselike around her eyes. Already slim, she'd lost weight, and her hair had turned brittle and dry. Her hands shook as she cradled the mug.

"Are you all right?" I asked her one morning, as both a nurse and a friend. "Are you sleeping enough?"

She shrugged ungracefully and took a sip from her coffee. "It's hard. I know she's fine through the night, but I still wake up every two hours. I have to check on her."

"Would it be better if we arranged for a night nurse? It's not helping Sherry at all for you not to sleep."

She set her mug on the table, then sat for quite a long time, just staring at it. "No. No, it's not that. It's . . . I keep seeing the accident," she said quietly. "I lie awake and it just . . . plays. Like a song you can't get out of your head."

I nodded.

"Simon was like that with cases. Even when he'd win a big one, he'd spend weeks afterward focusing on what he *should* have said, the things he missed . . ." She took a sip. "It doesn't help that all of a sudden I'm alone with all this."

The friend in me wanted to reach out to take her hand, while the nurse in me knew I should sit back and let her work through what she needed to work through.

Leaning forward, I curled my fingers around her hand, meeting her eyes and holding them with my own.


Henry

I got to know the city in a way that most people never get a chance to. Some mornings I would hang out at the Inner Harbor, watching tourists as they stepped off the ferries or floatplanes. I'd see some of them again over the next day or two, shopping downtown or walking through Beacon Hill Park or along the waterfront, taking the whale-watching tours out to the San Juan Islands.

I got to know people without ever meeting them. The businessmen and the people who worked in the stores all had their own routines.

They went to the bank at this time, had lunch at that time, at this table. The students up at the university, the bankers on Douglas, the homeless people under the Johnson Street Bridge . . . I saw all of them, and none of them saw me.

I started going to the library every morning to check the paper, to see if there was any news about Sherry. I would sit at the same table every day, reading that morning's *Sentinel.*

A few days after the accident, there had been an update. Sherry's condition was "stable," but they said she was in a coma. There was a picture of Sherry and her parents in front of a Christmas tree, dressed up, smiling and happy. For a while, there were updates on the search for the driver of the truck that had hit Sherry, who seemed to have just disappeared.

The first time I read that, I sank a little lower in my chair, peering carefully around to see if anyone was watching me. Nobody even knew I was there.

The newspaper had interviewed a woman named Arlene and showed a picture of her in her apartment, not quite looking at the camera. I recognized her, but it was like I had once dreamt about her. The newspaper said that she lived with me, that we had two children. Sons. The same article mentioned that the police had contacted my parents, and asked for people to please keep their eyes open for me.

Parents, children, a wife. Why couldn't I remember them?

There wasn't very much news for a while, just little things that I really had to look for. My insurance had agreed to pay out for the accident. Sherry went home with her parents. A picture of them at home, a nurse standing next to the family. Occasional updates on Sherry's condition. A brief mention of marriage difficulties, then the news that Mr. Barrett had moved out in a "trial separation." A short article about her fourth birthday, with no change in her condition.

After that, news about Sherry just faded away, replaced by the latest drug bust, the most recent pit bull attack, a crackdown on panhandlers downtown.

But I still went to the library and read the paper.

Waiting.

---

### Simon

I took the bus across the bridge to the house every morning.

The first few times, Mary drove me, letting me off down the block, kissing me good-bye, and taking my briefcase with her to the office. But when she saw that my visits were going to be routine, she shook her head. "I can't keep driving you there," she said. "I know you need to see your daughter, but I can't."

I made a point of arriving on the 7:56 bus, which dropped me across the street from the mall, near the crosswalk where the accident had happened. I used the few minutes' walk to steel myself before walking up our steps and ringing the doorbell. I had learned not to just let myself in; this was no longer my home.

"Good morning, Ruth," I said as the nurse opened the door.

"Hello, Mr. Barrett." She always smiled. I knew that I was likely not her favorite person in the world, but she never let it show. Always professional.

"Your payments coming through on time? No problems there?" I asked about the insurance every so often, letting her know that I wasn't the complete bastard that Karen and her friends believed I was.

"Oh, yes. No problem. No problem at all." She always made a point of leading me to the living room, as if I didn't know my way or couldn't be trusted on my own in the house.

"How's Sherry this morning?"

"She's doing well. We're listening to some Mozart."

The curtains were open, the blinds up. *Eine kleine Nachtmusik* played at a dominating volume.

I leaned over the bed and kissed Sherry on the forehead, surprised to feel how warm she was under my lips. "Good morning, sweetheart," I whispered. "Listening to Mozart this morning? Good for the brain." I glanced up at Ruth as I settled myself into the chair next to the bed.

"I'll leave you be for a little while," she said with something approaching a smile.

Some mornings I would talk to Sherry about the weather or something from TV, or I'd tell her a story she used to like. If there wasn't any music playing, I would sing to her, from my limited selection of lullabies and kids' songs or the folk songs I used to play in university. Eventually, I would find myself just sitting, not saying a word, listening to the gentle in-and-out of her breath, unconsciously counting, only later noticing that I was doing so. I would listen to the familiar noises of the house around me, the sound of water in the pipes, the furnace, footsteps, and distant voices.

I would stroke her soft hair.

## Karen

After he had had a little private time with Sherry, I brought Simon coffee.

I would probably have been better off to ignore him, to stay in the kitchen or my bedroom until the cab pulled up to take him off to work. But I wanted to be the bigger person.

So I put on a happy face, stood ramrod straight in the kitchen, and prepared myself for the meaningless pleasantries that should never come between a husband and wife.

When I came in, he was sitting in the chair alongside the bed, his hand resting on Sherry's arm, just staring into the distance.

"Coffee?" I asked, walking around the end of the bed so I wasn't reaching across Sherry as I extended the mug toward him.

He smiled a little. "Thanks." He took the mug and held it on his lap. In the light from the window I would see that his hair was thinning. I wondered if that had started recently, or if I had just never noticed before.

"How's work?" I asked, sitting down on the couch, maintaining my distance.

"It's fine. Busy."

I nodded, wondering if he was still working as late as often as he used to, or if having Mary at home had solved that particular problem.

"How's Mary?" In my mind, the question was dripping with venom, but he only shook his head, as if he couldn't believe I was asking.

"She's fine."

"Good. That's good."

He touched the side of the mug with the back of his hand to check its temperature, and blew across the surface to keep from burning his mouth. He took a sip. "Do you need anything?" he asked, somehow managing to be flat and earnest in the same breath.

*My daughter.*

*My husband.*

*My family back.*

*My life the way it was.*

I shook my head. "Nothing I can think of."

"You'll—"

"I'll let you know."

He smiled. "Good. And Sherry's . . ."

*In a coma.*

*Gone.*

"No change."

"She seems a little warm to me. . . ."

"She always seems a little warm to you. The chart should be here if you want to check it." I handed him the folder.

He looked at the top sheet. "She seemed warmer," he muttered. Setting the file down on the table, he glanced at his watch, took another swallow of coffee, and stood up. "I should go," he said, sweeping the front of his suit for imaginary crumbs.

"Okay. Do you want me to call you a cab?"

*Wouldn't you rather stay?*

He shook his head as he crossed the floor. "That's all right. I'll walk. I didn't get a chance for a run this morning."

I tried unsuccessfully to stifle the picture that rose in my mind. "Say hello to Mary for me." Bitchy, bitchy, bitchy.

He looked at me for a long moment, then shook his head. "I'll be by after work." He closed the door behind him.

At the clicking of the lock, my strength left me in a great rush. If he knew how difficult his visits were, I could accuse him of being incredibly cruel. As it stood, all I could accuse him of being was incredibly dense.

———————

## Simon

Leaving the house—closing the door behind me, walking down the path and through the gate to the street—was the hardest thing I had ever done, and I did it twice every day, once before work and once after. I never looked back, worried I would see Karen watching me through one of the front windows, or maybe worried I wouldn't.

On the days I walked to work, I cut through Fernwood, taking the crow's path downtown. The twenty-minute walk gave me time to consider things without interruption. And invariably, I found myself thinking about the same things.

I had become a cliché—the older man who left his wife for a younger woman—but I certainly wasn't going to use a midlife crisis as an excuse. I didn't feel old, and Mary was certainly no ditzy trophy.

I was keenly aware of how other people viewed the situation. My secretary, Sheila, no longer spoke to me—to either of us—with anything other than deliberately exaggerated professionalism. The associates never mentioned it, but I'm sure they spoke of it.

Mary and I.

Strange how a single phrase could signal so many changes. A few months before I had been part of "Simon and Karen," almost a single proper name. Husband, wife, father, mother, family.

Mary brought me more joy than I had felt in a very long time. I felt young again, open to possibility, in a way I'd lost. No. In a way I hadn't even noticed I had lost.

It's not like I just walked away from my family. I wanted to be there for Sherry. I needed to be there with her, and twice a day wasn't really enough.

I called Karen the first Sunday night after I left, asking if I could visit Sherry on my way to work the next morning. I was careful to keep my voice as detached as I could manage. For a long time Karen didn't say anything; then she answered. "I suppose I can't stop you."

I hadn't missed a day since.

## Henry

I spent whole days in the library. After I finished reading the morning paper, I would check out another part of the building. I was amazed by how many books and magazines and files there were, the dusty, dry smell, the billions and billions of words. I couldn't remember ever reading a book. I had no idea there were so many.

The library was two full floors. Large windows at one side looked out over a glass-covered courtyard. Inside, the carpet was a dark orange brown, worn thin in places by foot traffic. The ceiling was low, with all the ventilation and heat pipes exposed and painted brown.

What really amazed me, though, was all the people who came in, finding books and leaving, or finding a place to sit at one of the tables and lingering, reading for hours if they wanted. Kids did their homework, people looked things up, or planned trips, notebooks open, stacks of reference books on the tables in front of them.

And then there were the others.

At first I only noticed them because they seemed so out of place. Their clothes were ratty, their beards grown in, with dirty, untrimmed hair and skin the color of concrete on a sunny day. They would take a newspaper or magazine and sit at one of the tables, slowly reading their way through from front to back. They didn't miss a single word. Their eyes were haunted.

It got so I recognized some of them from day to day. They always sat in the same places, and slipped away when they were finished. They never disturbed anyone, and no one ever disturbed them. No one even seemed to notice them.

Just like me.

One day I was standing beside someone at one of the paperback racks, watching him choose things to read. One of the covers caught my eye. The book was dark red and seemed familiar somehow. I pulled it from the rack to look at it. The front and back cover both said *The Catcher in the Rye* in bright yellow letters.

I held on to the book and wandered back to the chairs near the magazine section, settling myself in and starting to read. From the first line, it was like the writer was speaking directly to me. I followed the words with my finger as I read, laughing out loud in some places.

The next time I looked up, the lights were dim. I set the book on the chair and walked toward the main desk. There was no one there.

The library was closed. I had read the day away, and I was locked inside.

## Ruth

It is always a delicate balance to work with families in crisis. I knew I had to be ever so careful not to become personally involved with the Barretts.

Oh, who was I kidding?

I had been personally involved from the moment I saw Sherry in that hospital bed. She looked just like she was sleeping, dressed in her pink nightshirt, head turned slightly to one side. I kept expecting her to give a little sigh and turn onto her side, suck her thumb, or kick off the covers. But in the four months I had been coming, she had moved only when I moved her, for her exercises and her baths.

Her world had changed around her, and she didn't even realize it. Her father had left, moved in with his young girlfriend. Her mother cried in the kitchen when she was washing the dishes.

Karen was a good woman. I really admired her. The way she cared for her daughter, read to her, changed her. Even something as small as my cup of tea every morning was a remarkable achievement under the circumstances. If Sherry had been my daughter, I don't know what I would have done. Probably curled into a tiny ball and died.

But Karen carried on. She didn't have many friends, but she talked to her mother on the telephone regularly, and Jamie Keller from the newspaper came to the house to visit. Karen dealt with the newspaper and the television reporters well—she was never terse, but never too open when answering their questions, either. Her life revolved around her daughter.

There were times, though, when I would speak to her and she wouldn't hear. I knew exactly where she had gone. She was reliving the accident, or the night in the hospital when Sherry should have died, but didn't.

I had heard that story from several people. A number of nurses I knew claimed to have been in the room when it happened. And Dr. McKinley himself told me he still didn't honestly know how to explain how Sherry had survived.

"I could show you the file," he said. "I could show you the records from the machines. She was gone. There was no heartbeat, no respiration . . ." He shook his head.

When he spoke about Sherry's mother, his tone changed. "I couldn't believe her, crawling into the bed like that. It . . . it broke my heart, her holding her daughter as she died. I've never seen anything like that in my life."

We have to be so careful to keep our distance.

I have never hated anyone, but I imagine it would be easy to hate Mr. Barrett if you didn't know him.

But who among us can really understand why anyone else does the things they do? If we can't understand, then how on earth can we judge them? "Walk a mile in their shoes," as my mother used to say.

I was working at the house the day Karen found out about Mary. There was no screaming, no hysterics. Instead, she seemed to shut down, to shut Simon out.

He was apologizing, stuttering, trying to explain. She didn't seem to hear a word he was saying. Finally, she asked him to leave. She was calm and cold. He packed some clothes into a suitcase and a garment bag, and he carried his computer under his arm out the door to wait for his girlfriend to pick him up in her little white Volkswagen convertible.

He said good-bye to Sherry before he left. And he said good-bye to me.

I didn't expect to see him any too soon, but the following Monday, he made the first of his morning visits to the house.

I worked with Sherry Monday through Friday, but there wasn't really that much for me to do. When she first came home from the hospital, she had full-time care. I worked the day shift, and other nurses came in at night and on the weekends. There was a physiotherapist every afternoon, and Dr. McKinley visited every couple of days.

I think the idea was that the insurance on the driver of the truck would pay us, and then Karen would be able to go back to work at the paper when she was ready. But Karen wasn't ready, and with Mr. Barrett and the insurance money taking care of the expenses, she didn't have to work.

And then we noticed that Sherry didn't require full-time care. No one could explain why, but her condition didn't deteriorate. Her vital signs were absolutely normal, her temperature and blood pressure never varying. The physiotherapist cut back his hours, to three times a week, then one, then not at all. None of the things we would normally be on the lookout for, from bedsores to muscle atrophy to infections, ever manifested. When Karen expressed an interest in taking a greater role in her daughter's care, the night and weekend nurses were let go.

I still performed my job scrupulously. I made sure that Sherry was turned regularly to prevent bedsores. I took her through her physiotherapy every day, bending her arms and legs, flexing her knees and elbows, rotating her wrists and shoulders to prevent her large muscle groups from atrophying. Every second day I gave her a full bath, carrying her into the tub and using the specially designed rack to immerse her. It was probably more often than was necessary, but the water all around her likely acted as a stimulant to her. It couldn't hurt.

On the other days, I gave her a sponge bath, carefully washing between all ten toes and all ten fingers. Every day she got a clean nightie, and every second day I changed her bedding.

I checked her carefully, monitoring the color of her urine and smell of her breath. I checked the feeding tube that snaked under the blankets and into her abdomen throughout the day. Karen had become very good at changing the bags, but I still checked.

She was such a sweet little thing. You could tell, just by looking at her, that Sherry had been a happy one, the sort of child that lit up a room just by toddling into it. Even her motionless face spoke volumes about her—the way her lips naturally fell into a half smile, as if she had a secret she was refusing to share.

If I claimed to be uninvolved, I wouldn't be fooling anyone.

I had retired from hospital work because it was too easy for me to get swept up into people's stories, caught up by the raw force of life and death struggling all around me. I had worked in pediatrics, and it was always so difficult for me when it came time for the children to go home. Some of the parents wrote or called, usually only once, to say thank you and to give me a bit of an update.

I had forced myself to take early retirement. I did have legitimate medical grounds, and all my benefits came through without any problem. The arthritis that had messed up my hips had settled into my fingers so badly that it was becoming difficult for me to keep up with the demands of the ward.

My fingers . . .

*"Barrett."*

*"Simon. John Richards."*

*"How are you, Sergeant?"*

*"Same as I ever was. Just older. You?"*

*"Weathering the storm."*

*"Like an old sailor or an old building?"*

*"Depends on who you ask. Do you have anything?"*

*"I'm sorry, Simon. . . ."*

*"Come on, John. People don't just disappear."*

*"You know better than that. People disappear all the time. The last we've got on Henry Denton is that phone call right after the accident. Nobody's seen him since. He hasn't made contact with his wife or his family. He's gone."*

*"So?"*

*"So we're keeping it open. The case'll stay open until we find him. I think we're looking for a body at this point. But Simon, we can't . . ."*

*"Uh-huh."*

*"I mean, it's an open case, but the most we can do with this guy, if we ever find him, is talk to him. We likely couldn't even get a charge of driving with undue care. Maybe leaving the scene . . ."*

*"You don't understand. . . ."*

*"No, I do understand. But seeing this guy, even talking to him—it's not going to explain anything to you. It's not like it's all gonna make sense all of a sudden."*

*"Thanks, John."*

*"I wish there was more that I could tell you. I still owe you one."*

*"We'll see."*

## Henry

It was kind of exciting being locked in the library when I wasn't supposed to be there.

It wasn't too dark. There were orange security lights, and the computer screens glowed orange or green. The shelves loomed in the shadows like entrances to a maze. I went down a few aisles, my heart beating faster, but they were the same aisles they were in the daytime.

— I don't know why I had expected them to be different.

As I wandered I whistled, not a tune or anything, just whistling. I wasn't even really aware that I was doing it.

Until someone whistled back.

## Ruth

I waited until I got home to make the telephone call. I let myself into the apartment, scratching both cats under their chins as I took off my shoes. I set my purse on the kitchen table before dialing. I didn't sit down; I couldn't sit down.

Sarah answered after the third ring. "Hello?" Her voice was rough and weak.

"Sarah, it's Ruth." I had to stay my impulse to speak too loudly to her, as if she were deaf as well as dying.

"Ruth." I could hear the surprise in her voice. We didn't have the sort of relationship where one of us would just call out of the blue. My sister lived less than two miles from me, but for the past few years we'd really seen each other only on birthdays and Christmas. "How *are* you?"

"I'm well. How are *you?*"

"I'm not dead yet." She chuckled at her own joke, which started her into a fit of coughing I could feel in my own lungs. My hand clutched at my thick winter coat over my chest.

"Not yet," she sputtered out of the cough. "It's been a while. Are you working?"

"I am. I'm still with that family. The little girl in the coma?"

"I heard her parents were having troubles." My sister had a memory like a leg-hold trap. It had served her well when we were working together on the ward. I had retired first. She filed for disability a few months after I did, but by the time the tumors were removed, they had already metastasized, cancer clinging to her lungs "like Christmas lights," she said. The doctors had predicted six months for her, at the outside. That was three years ago. I got the impression that she stayed alive mainly to prove them wrong.

"They separated a couple of months ago."

"Poor little thing."

"She's a sweetheart. Listen, would you like to meet her?" I tried to make it sound as if the idea had just then occurred to me.

"Well, I don't . . ."

"No, it would be good for you to get out. Karen—Mrs. Barrett— goes out sometimes in the afternoon, and you could come over then."

"That would hardly be appropriate, would it?" Her voice was a hoarse wheeze. She was two years younger than I, and dying.

"Mrs. Barrett won't mind. She's told me that if I ever wanted to have anyone over for a visit . . . You could meet her if you'd like. I just thought it might be nicer just the two of us. And Sherry."

"What have you got up your sleeve?"

Sarah was still able to see right though me.

"Nothing. I just thought it might be nice for us to have a visit. We're the only family we've got left." Our parents had died during Sarah's last year of high school. I was away at nursing school, and our older brother, John, had taken care of her until she graduated. Then she came to Victoria and stayed with me while she took her own nurse's training. John had died four years ago of lung cancer, just before Sarah had been diagnosed.

The cancer was a family legacy that I had been lucky enough to dodge. Maybe because I didn't smoke two packs of cigarettes a day.

"Have you been reading those self-help books again?"

I knew she was joking with me now, and that she would come over to the Barretts'. "Well, there is this one you might be interested in. . . ." I played along.

"Okay, okay, stop. I surrender. For Christ's sake, no more self-help books!" I could hear her restraining her laughter and the choking cough it would bring. "So how do I get to this place?"

I gave her directions, and hung up after telling her she was welcome to come anytime in the afternoon. The next day was Tuesday, and Karen went to a movie most Tuesday afternoons with Jamie.

After hanging up, I raised one hand level with my eyes and held it flat, fingers extended.

There were no tremors, no shaking. Not even the slightest vibration. My hand was as steady as a rock.

Then I slowly curled it into a fist, which I clenched tightly, not releasing it for several seconds.

When I did release it, there was no pain, none of the tearing in my knuckles that I had lived with for so long, none of the dull, continuous ache that had been my companion, even at rest. There was no pain as I reached into my pocket, gripping the Barretts' house key between my thumb and forefinger, turning it from side to side, fully rotating my wrist.

There was no pain, no hesitation, no restriction of movement.

My arthritis was gone.


Henry

I stopped short at the bottom of the stairwell, suddenly chilled. Somewhere above me, the whistle echoed through the empty building.

It might be the janitor. I had seen him in the distance, and done my best to avoid him.

My mouth was dry as I pursed my lips and tried to whistle again. I tried a little bit of "Dueling Banjos" this time.

In the distance, I heard the next part of the song.

It wasn't different enough, though. It could have just been an echo, distorted by the books and shelves.

I whistled a bit more and listened as the whistle came back, followed a moment later by the next line.

The silence waited for my response.

It took a moment for it to hit me: someone knew I was in the library. Someone could hear me.

I took the stairs two at a time, my footfalls echoing off the bare walls. The landing on the second floor was a narrow space, clogged with paperback racks and bins of records.

I slowed just as I was about to round the corner. I peered into the reference area, the rows of tables that during the day were filled with students writing essays.

I couldn't believe my eyes.

The chairs were full and the tables piled high with books. People wandered between the shelves, taking armloads of books back to their seats. Dozens of them, all like me, shabbily dressed, dirty, unshaved. I recognized some of them from the newspaper tables.

"Had we but world enough and time," a voice boomed out. My heart jumped in my chest. "Your coyness, boy, would be no crime . . ." There was a skittering sound, like dry leaves, as the people all started whispering at once.

"You," came the voice again. "You out on the landing . . ." My stomach dropped into a deep hole between my feet. "What are you waiting for? What are you afraid of?"

I stepped around the corner and into the reference area.

Everyone stopped their work and turned toward me, silent again, not surprised by my presence.

"Well it's about time," the large man at the back table said, in the same resounding voice. "Of course, time is the one thing we have no shortage of."

## Karen

It was hard to say just what was the hardest part. I found myself wanting to preface every conversation with Jamie or Ruth or my mother on the telephone, by saying, "But the hardest part is . . ." But I couldn't make such a distinction—*everything* I prefaced with that statement would be true.

Getting out of bed, knowing what lay ahead of me in the day. Showering, washing—for who? No one cared. Eating . . .

I invited Ruth for dinner most nights, hoping to have someone to eat with, but she always declined. I could see her point.

So I ate alone. In the first few weeks after Simon left, I ate whatever was at hand: tins of soup, boxes of macaroni and cheese, ravioli, all that crap stuff we'd give Sherry once in a while as a treat. I'd heat it up on the stove, dump it onto a plate, toss the pot into the sink.

I couldn't bear to sit at the table. The table was for family dinners, and Sherry was all the family I had left. I'd eat alongside her bed, mindlessly shoveling forkfuls into my mouth, staring out the front window, at the overgrown yard, the sidewalk, the cars going by on the street.

I made sure I did the dishes each night, but that was only because I knew Ruth would be in the kitchen the next morning.

I don't know how long I would have continued eating that garbage if it hadn't been for Ruth. One morning in early September she arrived carrying a large brown paper bag.

"I hope you don't think I'm trying to mother you," she said. Setting the grocery bag on the table, she began pulling items from it. A head of lettuce. A small cauliflower. "I know that with everything that's going on you haven't had a chance to get out to the supermarket." Several stalks of broccoli. Pale green celery. A bundle of carrots with the tops on. "So I thought I'd pick up some veggies for you while I was out doing my shopping last night." Four apples, each a different variety. Several oranges, a grapefruit that almost rolled onto the floor. "If you want me to, I can pick up whatever you need when I go." Setting a bunch of bananas with the rest, she artfully folded the bag.

I don't think I had ever seen anything so beautiful. The table looked like a child's treasure chest. I felt a craving so deep, it was primal, a desperate need for the sweetness, the fibers, the textures.

When I turned to Ruth, I realized she knew exactly what I was feeling. "Of course, if you wanted to," Ruth said, "I could stay here with Sherry and you could go for a walk, buy yourself what you needed. I know that in a lot of places, people shop every day, just for what they need. Everything so fresh." She inhaled heartily, as if swept away by the thought herself. "There's a little market not far from here, isn't there?"

I smiled at her. "What do I owe you for—?" I gestured at the table-top.

She shook her head. "We'll call it insurance money."

I bit into an apple, the skin exploding under my teeth, the sweetness flooding my mouth.

Ruth smiled at me and went to check on Sherry. I finished my apple in private.

So most days, early in the afternoon, I walked to the market. And I loaded up the basket with what called to me as I passed: a glossy red pepper, a purple onion, snow peas, a cauliflower, grapes, a chicken breast. And I took my time walking home, canvas shopping bag slung over one shoulder, the warm sunlight on my face, the breeze cool against my skin.

The meals always seemed to come together as naturally as the shopping did. I lived on stir fries over rice or noodles, maybe a piece of fruit afterwards, and I ate at the table.

Every so often, though, I looked at the empty place across from me, the empty chair. These chairs were the first pieces of furniture we ever bought new, for the kitchen of our first house. This house. The house where I live alone with my silent daughter, where the man who used to be my husband visits twice each day, knocking on the door like a sales-man.

We had lived here together for five years; I had been alone here for five months. Lifetimes.

*When he went to services around the city, the stranger kept the collar and his Bible in the pocket of his coat. He usually sat near the back, in a pew of his own. He paid little attention to the sermons and homilies—what interest had he in the purported wisdoms of some provincial priest?*

*He was there to watch the congregations.*

*He knew the sort of person he was seeking. There would be something in their eyes. They would be devout, building their lives around their faith rather than paying lip service with once-weekly observances. They would sit close to the front, close to the altar, close to the aisle. They would carry their own Bibles with them.*

*Soldiers. He was looking for soldiers of the Lord. There were many candidates, as he knew there would be. As there always were. They would come to him when he called. They would serve.*

*But there had to be a first, and he soon knew who it would be.*

*He was a huge man, nearly six and a half feet tall, and solid through the body. He carried his Bible like a shield. His face, though, was soft, open. Malleable.*

*The man brought his mother to Sunday Mass. They walked slowly, her arm looped in his, his Bible in his other hand. He bowed his head as he walked with her, listening to the old woman, nodding. For several weeks, the stranger walked behind them. His mother called her son Leopold, but the priests at the cathedral called him Leo.*

*Leo came to the early morning weekday services alone. He always smiled, and as he walked up the aisle he raised his eyes to the stained glass. A little simple, perhaps, but the stranger knew there was an inner steel in the big, soft man that the stranger could shape to his purpose.*

*Leo was always the first to his knees, dropping with a purity of faith and a fervor no one else matched. His belief burned in him like a torch, and the stranger could feel himself warmed by the flames.*

Mary

Most days, we had dinner after our run. It helped us work up an appetite, and by the time we got to the restaurant, there usually wasn't much of a lineup.

We had started running together not long after Simon moved in. I used to do aerobics in the afternoons, and Simon would run every morning with his male colleagues and play racquetball or squash a couple of times a week. After we moved in together, though, his friendships started to fall apart. At first people came up with excuses—the kids were sick; sorry, slept in—but then they didn't even bother. And Simon gave up, both on them and on exercise.

After a couple of weeks of Simon being surly, I suggested that we should start running together.

"You don't run," he said, lying in bed and staring at the ceiling.

"No, but I've always wanted to try it."

"Really?" He turned to look at my face.

"Really."

"That'd be great, Mary. It's always better if you've got someone to run with. When do you want to start?"

"How about tomorrow?" He was reaching for the alarm clock as I interrupted him. "No way. I'm not getting up at some insane hour to run. Let's go after work. You know, when I usually go to aerobics."

He withdrew his hand from the alarm clock, sliding it instead over my hip. "Thank you," he said after a moment, his voice a mere whisper.

The tone of relief, and of appreciation, warmed me.

It took a little while before I was able to keep pace with him over his usual distance, but I think I surprised him with what good shape I was in.

"That's what aerobics four times a week will do for you," I panted after our first run, hunched over, barely able to feel my legs but refusing to let on.

Most nights, after showering, we'd retrace our route, hand in hand, the golden lights of the legislature reflecting off windows and waves.

At first we'd both felt awkward being together in public, but as summer turned to fall and beyond, we became comfortable. It was such a pleasure to be able to walk outside and not be afraid of who might see us.

We usually went to Pagliacci's at least once a week, avoiding the weekends when you had to line up for an hour for a table. Even on a Thursday night the place was packed.

The walk over had been frosty, the sidewalks surprisingly busy for a chill November evening.

Simon carefully poured more wine into our glasses, sliding mine toward me past the candle.

I took a sip of my wine. "I was thinking that maybe we should go away for a bit—"

The idea obviously took him by surprise. "What?"

"Well, it's been so busy. I mean, today was what—eleven hours? And last weekend?"

"I'm not arguing the need; I'm just wondering what you had in mind."

"I thought maybe pack up the car, go up to Tofino, get a room right on the beach. Maybe the Wickaninnish."

He sat back, cradling his wineglass in his right hand. "Right on the beach," he repeated. "Maybe a fireplace, whirlpool tub? That sounds really nice. When were you thinking of going? The next couple of weeks are pretty tight. What about over Christmas?"

"I told my folks I'd be up at their place from the twentieth or so. You could come, too, if you like."

"What about the weekend of the seventh? We could even head up that Wednesday afternoon, make a four-day weekend of it. I figure the firm owes us a little time." He slipped past the invitation to spend Christmas with my family.

I didn't want to bring it up, but I had to ask. "Will you be okay leaving Sherry for a few days?"

"She's . . ." He paused, and I could almost hear him sifting through everything before he spoke. "It's only for a few days. . . . I'll let her know what's going on. Tell her when I'll be back."

"And Karen . . ."

"Well." He took another sip of his wine. "I don't think Karen's going to be too pleased about it. She always wanted to go to Wickanninish. . . ."

That thought made me strangely happy.

"So. December fourth?" he asked.

I nodded. "I'll make the reservations tomorrow."

## Henry

"Well, come on," the big man called. "Time and tide wait for no man."

I hesitated in the doorway. The people were all staring at me.

"Okay, the rest of you, back to what you were doing," the big man said.

As if he had flicked a switch, everyone went back to work, back to the shelves, to their tables, their heads down in their books.

"Well." He waved me toward him. "Come on."

I crossed the crowded room to where he sat.

"Good, good," he said as he looked me over. "I was worried there for a minute that maybe you were a bit tetched."

"What are . . . What are all of you . . . What are you doing here?" I stammered. My mouth was not quite under my control.

"Well, reading, of course." He laughed heartily, and I felt less afraid. He was a great bear of a man, with graying hair and beard still touched with red, his face full and rosy. His clothes were rumpled and plain, and he seemed to blend into the background, the sort of person you wouldn't notice asking you for change.

Static suddenly whirred over the PA system; then horns kicked in with a blast.

"And listening to music, apparently. Would you turn that down," he bellowed. "There's people trying to hear here."

The volume fell as quickly as if he had turned the knob himself.

"Better," he muttered. "Hot Fives. Louis Armstrong. Nineteen . . . twenty-seven, I believe." He shook his head. "Great set, great set. Great man, that Satchmo . . ."

"Who *are* you?" I asked, completely baffled. I felt like I had just stepped into a movie or a fairy tale.

"Good question," he answered, not answering. "I'm pleased that it wasn't the first thing you asked. Just don't ask me how I make a living, and we'll get along fine."

"But . . ."

"The real question is, who are you?"

"I . . ." For a moment, I considered lying. "I'm Henry. Henry Denton."

"*Ah.*" He settled himself into his chair, gesturing for me to sit down across from him. A look of understanding filled his face. "So you're *that* new, then."

I sat down. "I guess, but . . . who *are* you? No. Why . . . How can you see me? I thought—"

"You could also ask why you can see us, Henry, when no one else can."

My chest tightened. "You mean you're . . . People can't see you? But—"

"But why?" The big man sighed. "Not an easy question to answer. Not easy at all . . ." He pushed back from the table, stood up, and began to pace. Behind him, there was a wall of windows, and through them I could see streetlights and the lights in the buildings across the street, along with a reflection of the room. I wondered what people would see if they happened to look up. Probably nothing. An empty room in a deserted building.

"There are no easy answers," he said. "Especially not as far as who I am." He gestured around the room. "Who we are"—turning his gaze back to me—"who you are."

I pulled back. "I know who *I* am. I told you already—"

"No," he interrupted gently. "You told me your name. That's got absolutely nothing to do with who you are."

I guess I looked confused. I was confused.

"Let me ask you this: Why are you here?" He ran one hand over and through his beard. "Why are you here, in a closed library, in the middle of the night?"

I couldn't answer. It would have meant telling him about Sherry, about what I had done.

He watched me for a moment. "Well, what about everyone else? Why do you think everyone else is here?" He set both hands on the tabletop and leaned toward me. "Why do you think *I'm* here?"

I responded without thinking. "You already told me—you're reading."

"Clever boy." He nodded his head, grinned a little, and started pacing again. "Yes, we're here because we're reading. But why are we *here?*" This time, when he looked at me, his eyes asked a deeper question. "*That's* what we're trying to figure out."

"You mean you don't know?"

He smiled. "You sound so disappointed. Do you know how few people know why they're anywhere? How few people ever find out? When they do, we turn them into saints. Or martyrs. Or gurus." He paused. "Or gods."

"I don't . . . understand."

He shrugged. "Of course you don't. Most people go through their entire lives without understanding, without ever stepping out of the day-to-day to really look around. . . . But you see, we're luckier than them. We know what we are."

"What are you?" I asked, because he wanted me to.

"We, Henry? We're the damned," he answered, his eyes locking on mine. "We're doing penance for our crimes. We just don't know when that penance will end."

Damned? Penance? The words echoed in my head as I looked around at the men and the stacks of books and papers, echoed what I had been feeling for weeks. "The answer's in here?"

"The answer's in here," he said, pointing at the books on the table in front of him. "Maybe." His eyes twinkled, but I didn't think he was joking. "Who's your favorite author?"

The question took me by surprise. I struggled for a moment to remember the name of the person who wrote the book I had spent the day reading. "Saminger," I said, feeling pleased with myself.

His smile was patient, and suddenly very warm. I realized that I had gotten something wrong. "Salinger. That's a good place to start. See where he takes you."

He sat back down in his chair and opened the top book of the stack in front of him. I realized he was finished talking, that I had been given a task to do and now I was expected to do it.

"But what's . . . What do I call you?" I asked, before his attention disappeared into his book completely.

He looked up as if surprised to see me still standing there. He straightened, and when he spoke, his voice was commanding, thick with a different accent. "You may call me . . . Tim." Nearby, one of the others snickered, and Tim waited expectantly.

I was missing something.

When I didn't respond, he sagged a little. "Oh great and powerful Tim," he said, waiting for recognition, his eyes bright. When it still didn't come, he sagged and slumped against his chair. "Oh, for Christ's sake," he muttered. "Monty Python? *Holy Grail*? John Cleese?"

"I don't think I've . . ."

He shook his head. "That's the trouble with youth today. No knowledge of the classics." He picked up his book, opened it again to his page. "Just call me Tim," he said as he started to read.

As I turned away, he was muttering to himself. "Great man, John Cleese. Great bit. Great bit . . ."

I made my way back downstairs to where Salinger was waiting for me.

# Ruth

Sarah arrived just before Karen left to go to the movies the next after-noon. Her friend Jamie was sitting at the kitchen table with her. When the doorbell rang, I called out from Sherry's room, "I'll get it!"

I hadn't seen Sarah in weeks, and I was shocked at her deterioration. Her flesh sagged away from her cheekbones, and her skin was crepey. She was dressed in a loose blue-and-purple floral print blouse and navy slacks. She had obviously bought the clothes after she had started to lose weight, but she still seemed to swim in them.

With her right hand she held the handle of a small rolling oxygen tank, its plastic tubing snaking up, then splitting into each nostril. Her shaking left hand held a cigarette, which she pressed unsteadily to her lips.

I must have given her a look.

"Oh, give up, Ruth," she rasped, exhaling a blue plume of smoke. "Keep your judgments to yourself."

"I didn't say a word." I leaned forward to give her an awkward hug. She smelled terrible, a mix of stale cigarette smoke and acrid sweat, as if she hadn't bathed in weeks. "It's good to see you, Sarah," I said as I pulled away. My words hung in white clouds in the chill air.

"You, too, Ruthie," she answered. "You're looking well." She took a heavy drag off her cigarette. "And don't even try; I know I look like hell." She blew out the smoke.

"You don't look . . ." I trailed off. She did look terrible, and she knew it. "Did you drive?"

She turned partway around and gestured at the sedan parked across the street. "Am I okay where I'm parked?"

"Yes, that should be fine. Come on, let's go inside. I'm freezing." I added, "You'll have to leave that out here."

She gave me a withering look as she dropped her cigarette to the con-crete stoop and ground it out with her foot. "Do I look like an idiot to you? Of course I'm not going to smoke in someone else's house. And around a patient . . ." She shook her head and hefted the oxygen tank up over the doorsill in a practiced yet still uncomfortable-looking motion.

I led her toward the kitchen. "I'll just introduce you to Mrs. Barrett. . . ."

Karen and Jamie stood up as we entered the room.

"Mrs. Barrett," I started. "This is my sister, Sarah Page. Sarah, this is Mrs. Barrett."

"I'm pleased to meet you," Karen said a little stiffly, taking Sarah's hand and shaking it. I could tell she was surprised by the way Sarah looked. I should have prepared her.

"And this is my friend Jamie Keller," Karen said. Sarah reached for Jamie's hand, forcing Jamie to reach past Karen in order to shake.

Sarah gave a watery smile. "I'm pleased to meet you both." Her voice cracked as she spoke.

Karen's eyes flicked to mine, then away. "Ruth, I put some water on to boil when the doorbell rang."

"Thank you, Mrs. Barrett."

"We shouldn't be much later than four." They never were.

"I'll be here," I said, smiling.

Karen's eyes gleamed a little. Her spirits were always lifted by her Tuesday afternoons out of the house. "Sarah, it was very nice to meet you."

"Very nice," my sister repeated.

"I hope we'll be seeing you again."

"God willing," Sarah muttered with the same watery smile.

The kettle on the stove started to whistle, and I lifted it away from the element. "Shall I make us a pot of tea?" I asked.

I heard the front door close.

"God no," Sarah said to my surprise. "I'll be up all night; the bladder's not what it used to be." I didn't like to imagine.

"Let's go into the living room, then. I'll introduce you to Sherry."

She followed me, the wheels of her oxygen tank squeaking along the hardwood floors. Vivaldi was playing, and I turned it down a little as we came into the living room.

"Music therapy?" she asked, teasing me the way she always did.

I shrugged. "Well, she might be able to hear."

She pulled her cart to the edge of the bed. "Oh, she is a pretty little thing, isn't she?" she cooed softly. She actually cooed.

"Yes, she is." I stepped over to the bedside, gently stroking Sherry's cheek with the back of my hand.

Sarah clung to her oxygen rig like she needed the support. "They never found the fellow who did this? The driver?"

I shook my head.

"He must have been drunk."

I shook my head again. "The police don't think so. He had just worked a night shift, and they figure he was in a hurry to get home. He had two boys of his own."

"So sad."

"Apparently he tried to go around her."

She pursed her lips. "Is there any—?"

I shook my head. "No. The doctors don't think she'll ever—"

She nodded, saving me from having to say it.

"You can touch her if you want to. Go ahead."

Sarah double-checked my face to be sure I was serious, then gingerly reached out her left hand. Her yellow fingertips trembled as she stroked Sherry's cheek. "I don't know how you do it," she said, barely above a whisper. "It must just break your heart."

"Sarah," I said seriously. "Listen, there's something I want to tell you. . . ."

She drew back from the bedside, all her attention on me. "What is it? What's wrong?"

"No, no." I shook my head. "Nothing's wrong with me. It's . . . I wanted you to come over here. . . ." I took a deep breath, trying to figure out the best way to broach the subject with her. "Watch this."

Holding my hand in the air in front of her face, I clenched my fist, flexed my fingers, rotated my wrist.

I didn't meet her eyes again until I had gone through the whole routine.

It took her a moment to realize what she was seeing. "Oh my God, Ruth," she gasped. "What happened to your arthritis?"

I hesitated before I answered. "Gone."

Her face shifted in confusion, her fingers tightening around the handle of her oxygen tank. "But how? A new medication? A new . . . Some experimental drug? Oh God, Ruth, I'm so happy for you!" Her eyes sparkled. "When did this happen?"

"I . . . I'm not really sure."

I had spent a long time trying to answer that question, but I still hadn't been able to figure it out. The trouble with chronic pain is that it is so easy to become accustomed to it, both mentally and physically. At first it's absolutely agonizing; it's the only thing you think about, like a rock in your shoe that rubs your foot raw with every step. Then the constant rubbing, the pain, and the limp all become part of the status quo, the occasional stabbing pain just a reminder.

You are set to endure, hunched against it—and when it starts to ease, you don't really notice, until the absence washes over you like a balm.

"Sometime in the past few months," was the best I could do.

"And you're only telling me now?"

"I . . . I didn't really notice right away. The pain is always better in the summer. But when the cold weather hit, it didn't come back."

"You must have known," my sister snapped. "It's not like someone was slipping the pills into your food like you were a pet cat."

"There weren't any pills."

"What?"

"There weren't any pills." I turned my eyes away, suddenly embarrassed.

"So what was it? Some sort of spontaneous remission?" She spat out the words with all the venom of a fallen true believer.

"I think . . ." I turned my gaze back to Sherry, motionless on the bed. "I think it was her."

Sarah just gaped at me.

"I know how ridiculous that sounds. . . . I know it sounds like I'm turning into one of those old women, the ones who send in all their money to the television evangelists, but it's the only thing that makes any sense to me. My arthritis was terrible last winter. Then I started working with Sherry every day. And now—" I clenched the fist again to demonstrate. "—I'm not taking any pills, I haven't changed my diet. It's the only thing I can think of."

"You think this little girl healed your arthritis?" she rasped, leaning a little farther over the bed, eying Sherry curiously.

I nodded, bracing myself for her derisive laughter.

Instead, she asked softly, "And me? Is that why you wanted me to come over here?" For just a moment her voice was that of a sixteen-year-old girl, and I had a sudden vision of a funeral in a country church-yard in the rain, two coffins, two daughters holding one another.

I hesitated, then nodded.

"I don't believe in God," she said, looking me straight in the eye.

The remark took me by surprise. "I hadn't—This isn't about God," I stammered.

"Well, what, then?"

"I don't know." I shook my head. "I just know that I'm healed." Again I clenched my fist, demonstrating, still transfixed by that simple motion, by the emotions that the movement raised in me.

"Well," she said. "I'm at the point where I'll try anything. How do we do this?"

"I don't know," I confessed.

She grinned at me with her yellowing teeth. "Well, that doesn't do me much good, does it?"

"Well, I'm in contact with her all day. I bathe her and turn her and—"

"I know the routine."

"So I don't know when exactly it happened."

"*If* it happened."

"Or how," I countered, glaring at her.

"Well," she said, changing her tone, studying Sherry. "What if we try this the old-fashioned way?" She gently took the covers down from Sherry's still form, freeing her arms.

"Here, let me," I said, coming around the bed to stand alongside her. "I'll take care of Sherry," I said, taking hold of her tiny arm. "You . . . maybe you should unbutton your blouse . . ."

Sarah leaned forward slowly, opening her blouse to expose her brassiere. It looked new, and loose on her diminishing frame. I gently raised Sherry's arm, supporting it under the elbow, turning her wrist to shift her hand.

For a moment, I felt guilty. I glanced at the doorway, feeling suddenly as if we were being watched. There was no one there. Guilty conscience.

As I turned back, I glanced at Sarah's face. Her eyes were closed, her lips parted, her features . . . hopeful.

It would be worth the guilt.

Gingerly, I touched Sherry's hand to the pale, oddly smooth skin of my sister's chest, just above the barely noticeable rise of her breasts. Carefully, I applied just enough pressure to smooth the tiny palm flat against the white skin, and then I held it there.

"Lower," Sarah said softly, not opening her eyes.

I slid Sherry's hand between her breasts, nestled over her heart. "Can you feel anything?" I asked.

She shook her head. "I don't know what to expect. . . ."

I had no idea either. I held Sherry's hand there for just a moment longer, then removed it, tucking her gently back under the covers as Sarah buttoned her blouse. "There you go, sweetie," I told her. "All bundled up again."

Straightening up from the bed, my eyes met Sarah's and we just looked at each other for a long moment.

She smiled a little, bit her lip, and shrugged. "Well," she said.

# Part 3

*November 27–December 5*

## Karen

Simon was singing when I brought him his cup of coffee.

"Hush little baby, don't say a word . . ."

The weather had turned cold almost overnight, the late gales of November blowing icy off the strait, the last of the leaves clinging to the wet pavement, the trees skeletal against the gray sky.

"Daddy's gonna buy you a mockingbird . . ."

Simon actually had a nice voice. Back when we were in school, he used to play a bit of guitar. We'd have people over to our place, a tiny apartment in one of the big converted heritage houses near downtown. Friday nights of songs, soup, and jugs of homemade wine.

"And if that mockingbird don't sing . . ."

But that was a long time ago. I didn't even know where his guitar was. Probably up in the attic somewhere.

He broke off in midline as I came into the living room, setting the two mugs down on the table.

"You didn't have to stop."

He smiled. "Well . . . Listen, Karen, there's something I wanted to talk to you about." His tone was careful. Too careful.

"What? Is it Sherry?"

"No, it's nothing like that. It's just that Mary and I are going away next weekend. Four days. Head up to Tofino."

"Why are you telling me this?"

"I thought you should know—"

I could feel a hot rush rising in me. "You thought I should know that you and your girlfriend are getting away for the weekend? That's nice. Have a great time." I stood up. I couldn't bear to be in the same room with him.

"Karen—"

"Oh, for Christ's sake, Simon," I snapped. "What made you think that this would be a good thing to share with me?" I was trying to keep my voice under control, but it was starting to rise.

"I just wanted to let you know that I wouldn't be coming by for a few days."

"Good for you. Thanks for the heads-up."

"I thought you'd want to know—"

"You thought I'd want to know?" I said, dripping sarcasm. "That's sweet. Now when I wake up in the middle of the night next weekend, I can think about you and your girlfriend fucking in Tofino. That's great. Thanks." I should have left then, but I couldn't stop myself. "I hope you get a room with a fireplace. Maybe a hot tub. I imagine doing it in a bed must be getting pretty boring for you."

"Karen—"

"Oh, right. I forgot. She's all of what? Twenty-four? Twenty-five? Shit, you probably won't get bored with her for another ten years."

"Jesus Christ, Karen. Sherry's right here! Keep your voice down."

"The next time you're looking at her ass, be sure to check the expiration date!"

He headed for the door and I followed him. I couldn't stop.

"Simon, what you fail to see is how little I care about what you do. You may not have noticed, but I have a little more on my mind than that. Come or don't come, I don't care. Sherry doesn't care. It's all the same to us."

He stopped at the front door. "Listen, this isn't . . . I'm just going to go."

"Fine. Go. That seems to be what you're best at."


"*Hello?*"

"*Ruth? It's me.*"

"*Sarah?*"

*"Listen . . . I just had a doctor's appointment. . . ."*

*"Are you okay?"*

*"Well, I had started to notice some strange things a week or so ago."*

*"Are you okay?"*

*"So I made a doctor's appointment."*

*"Sarah! Are you okay?"*

*"It's gone, Ruth. They did X-rays, tests . . . Spontaneous remission. That's what the doctor said."*

*"Spontaneous remission."*

*"Yes."*

*"Oh my God."*

*"Yes. That's what I was thinking. Exactly."*

*"Hello?"*

*"Hello. Is this Pam?"*

*"Yes. Who's this?"*

*"It's Sarah. Sarah Page."*

*"Sarah Page?"*

*"From the group. Sarah from the Tuesday-night group."*

*"Oh yes, yes. Sarah from the group."*

*"How are you feeling, Pam?"*

*"Oh, not so good, Sarah. It's not a good day. But how are you?"*

*"Well, that's why I'm calling."*

## Ruth

For the whole morning after the phone call with Sarah, I alternated between staring at Sherry and not being able to look at her. I tried to find some physical sign of what she could do, but I didn't know what I was looking for. An aura maybe. A halo. Stigmata. But there was nothing—just a little girl who will never wake up.

"Who are you?" I asked her at one point. She didn't answer.

Anything that I had read about healers and saints, all my Sunday

School lessons so long ago, led me to believe that I should have been able to see *something,* some trace of the divine. Her ordinariness—it scared me.

How would I tell Karen? For that matter, what would I tell Karen? That her daughter had cured my sister of cancer? My arthritis? That she could do miracles, but she would still never wake up? How could she heal us but not herself?

I bathed her carefully. Not that I was at all rough with her usually, but now I took an exaggerated care, cradling her as though she was an object of great value, not just a little girl. Sacred. I looked for some sign that I had missed, but no. It was still just the same pudgy, pale body I had washed so many times before.

This mortal vessel . . .

Karen was distracted. She had been upset yesterday morning. I had heard the raised voices from the front room as I sat in the kitchen with my second cup of tea, heard Mr. Barrett slam the door as he left. He hadn't come for his regular visit last night or this morning, and I had caught Karen checking the clock as it got later and later, until it finally became clear he wasn't coming.

She was gone three hours on her walk, and when she returned, it was obvious she had been crying. I wanted to do something to comfort her, but she retreated upstairs to the privacy of her bedroom.

She was a little better this morning, but her face was drawn with trying not to let anything show.

If I told her about my sister, maybe it would help to put her problems with Mr. Barrett into perspective. Or maybe not. Maybe it would all be just too overwhelming. Or maybe it would be just what she needed.

How could the miraculous and the painful exist so close together?

"I'm going out," Karen said from the doorway, startling me. I hadn't heard her footsteps.

I glanced up at the clock. 11:30. That was pretty early, even for a Tuesday.

"I'm meeting Jamie for lunch downtown before the movie," she explained, as if she'd read my thoughts. "I'll be back well before five, though."

I nodded. "All right."

She looked past me at Sherry. I had dressed her in her green nightie after her bath. "How is she today?" she asked. It wasn't like her to have to ask.

"Oh, she's doing just fine. We were just about to listen to some Bach."

She nodded. "I'm sorry, Ruth. I haven't been very . . . It's been a tough couple of days."

"That's fine," I said. "I know there's been some . . . drama."

She smiled. "I guess it's pretty hard to keep anything a secret around here, isn't it?"

I returned her smile, but her words struck very close to home. Secrets.

She glanced down at her watch. "Shoot. I have to go. I'm walking . . . Listen, thanks. I'll try to be more together tomorrow."

"Don't rush anything," I said as she was turning away.

She looked back, and I forced a smile. "These things work themselves out."

"Not this time." The front door clicked shut.

I sat down next to Sherry and brushed her hair away from her face. The light coming through the windows didn't seem to penetrate as deeply into the room as it had even a few weeks before.

"That's okay, Sherry. Your mom and dad are having a little argument, but it's going to be okay. It'll all turn out okay."

I spent the next while listening to the music, leaning back a little in the chair, my hand touching Sherry's hair where it spread out across the pillow. I wanted to ask her what I should do, how I should tell her parents what she was capable of. . . .

I was awakened from a light sleep and a vague dream by the sound of the doorbell. The music had finished, and for a moment I didn't recognize where I was.

Then the doorbell rang again.

Sarah was standing on the front step. Gone was the oxygen tank, the pallor, the lifelessness. Her cheeks were flushed, her eyes bright and full of life. She held her overcoat around herself against the cold, but she seemed stronger. Taller, even.

"Hello, Ruth," she said, a little too cheerfully. "I'm sorry for not calling first. . . . This is my friend Pam."

As bad as Sarah had looked when she arrived at the house two weeks ago, Pam looked even worse. A much younger woman, no older than thirty, she seemed withered, almost weightless. Her hair had fallen out in chunks, leaving bright spots on her scalp. She clung to my sister as if Sarah were all that was holding her to life.

"Sarah . . ." The thought of what Sarah was asking me to do chilled me.

"Can we come in, please?" She spoke with forced joviality. "It's really too cold out here for Pam."

I knew that by letting them into the house, I was condoning what would happen. I looked again at Pam and stepped aside. I couldn't leave this frail person standing on the doorstep in the cold.

Pam's steps were slow and tiny. Sarah carefully guided her along, over the doorsill, into the house, supporting her weight and rubbing the back of the hand that clutched her arm. I closed the door behind them.

"You have a seat, Pam," Sarah said, walking her into the living room and settling her on the couch.

"Can we talk?" I gestured for Sarah to come back into the hallway, out of Pam's sight.

"I'm sorry, Ruth," were the first words out of her mouth. "I would have called, but I knew you would have said—"

"No?" I finished her sentence. "Sarah, what do you think you're doing? Do you know what Kar . . . Mrs. Barrett would say?"

"Have you told her? About . . ." She gestured with her head toward the front room. "About Sherry?"

"Not yet. I'm not sure how to."

"She's dying, Ruth."

"What?"

"Pam. She's dying. She's in this support group that I was going to. For terminal patients."

"Sarah." I didn't want to hear Pam's story. But Sarah was not going to stop.

"It started off in her breasts. She had a double mastectomy, but . . . it's metastasized all through her now. They've taken out most of her stomach, pieces of her lungs. The doctors say she doesn't have more than a couple of weeks."

"Sarah, I can't."

"Ruth, she has two little kids. Both under five. I could show you pictures."

"Sarah . . ."

"Please?"

I was stunned: it was the first time Sarah had asked me for something in years.

I took a deep breath before speaking, knowing that I was going to regret my decision, whichever way I decided.

"All right," I whispered. "We'll give it a try."

"Thank you."

"But listen," I interrupted. "This is *it*. You can't tell anybody else. This can't get around, okay?"

"Okay."

"No," I said. "This is important."

"I said okay." She looked at me unflinchingly. "I *do* understand."

"Okay," I breathed. "Let's try to get you both out of here before Mrs. Barrett comes home."

I started back toward the living room, but Sarah reached out for my arm. "Thank you," she whispered.

I touched the back of her hand, and squeezed it softly.

### Simon

The last thing I wanted to do was to upset Mary by telling her about the fight with Karen, so I kept it to myself.

Mary worried so much. One night, when I was almost asleep, she started a conversation by saying, "Are you ever sorry you're here?"

I rolled over to face her. My eyes were dazzled by her skin, glowing in the darkness. "What?" As if I either hadn't heard or hadn't really understood.

"Are you ever sorry you're here?" she repeated, her voice small.

"Why would I be sorry to be here?" I curled my arm around her, surprised to find her cool despite the temperature of the apartment.

"Well, I feel . . . Sometimes I feel like I stole you from your wife." Her voice dropped even lower.

"There were problems between Karen and me before I met you."

"Yes, but if it weren't for me—"

"If it weren't for you, I'd be very unhappy right now."

"And with me?"

"With you I'm very happy."

Her eyes lit up, and after that she fell asleep quickly, but that wasn't the end of it. Occasionally she would look at me and almost speak, but then she'd change her mind.

The reactions at the office hadn't helped. Everyone was still very civil to my face, but it was different for Mary. People treated her like she wasn't even there. Sheila wouldn't acknowledge her presence. If she brought files or records to us while we were working, she would hand me everything I needed, but leave Mary's materials on the table or desk out of reach. She would bring me coffee without bringing anything for Mary. She would ask if I wanted her to order lunch for me, ignoring Mary entirely.

I spoke to Sheila about it a couple of times, and she assured me that I was mistaken, that it had been an oversight, that it wouldn't happen again. That was, of course, a lie, and we both knew it.

"How's Karen holding up?" Sheila would ask.

Karen.

I had picked up the phone half a dozen times in the forty-eight hours since the fight, punching in what used to be my home number, disconnecting each time before the phone had a chance to ring. What would I say?

I would apologize.

But I hadn't done anything wrong.

What was I thinking? Hadn't done anything wrong?

I might as well have rubbed salt in her eyes, kicked her while she was down.

Mary had been quite concerned when I told her that I wasn't going over to visit Sherry the morning after the fight.

"The doctor's going to be there."

"Well, shouldn't you be there, too?"

"Karen'll let me know what he has to say." I cleared my throat. "Sometimes the doctor and I don't see quite eye to eye. It's best if I just . . . give him the space to do his job."

She seemed to accept that as a valid reason, and didn't pursue it any further. That afternoon I deliberately let a meeting run well past five, the time I normally left to see Sherry.

"Are you still going to stop by the house?" Mary asked after the client left.

I pretended to think about it, then shook my head. "No, I don't think so. I don't want to disturb Karen at dinnertime. Besides, I really feel like a long run tonight."

She eyed me strangely. "Don't you want to hear what the doctor—?"

Caught in my own lie, I said, "I'll call her later."

Mary didn't say anything more, and we drove home together in silence.

The next day's excuses were even more lame.

And then it was 1:42 A.M., according to the red digits of the clock radio. Mary's breath was as regular as a metronome, and I had lain awake for almost three hours, watching the soundless changing of the numbers, listening to the distanced, muffled noises from the other tenants.

Mary shifted a little in her sleep and moaned softly.

Without disturbing her, I slid out from under the covers. By the light from the windows, I navigated out of the bedroom, shutting the door behind me before I turned on one of the table lamps in the living room.

I looked around in the low amber glow. I had been living with Mary for months, but I didn't seem to have made much of an impression. There were a few of my books stacked on the floor next to her bookshelves, but all the art in the room was hers—reproductions of a Lichtenstein comic panel, a blue Matisse "Jazz" figure, a Navajo-style blanket. There was a small stack of my CDs on top of the stereo cabinet, but the stereo itself, the television, the furniture, the apartment, were hers. Sometimes, it was as if I were not even here.

I crossed the room to the CD rack. There were almost no artists that I recognized among her CDs. Each time I looked, it brought home the fact that an entire generation separated us.

Sighing, I turned to the stack of CDs I had bought over the last couple of months, comforted by their spines. Van Morrison. Bob Dylan. Neil Young. The Grateful Dead.

I slipped a Sinead O'Connor CD into the player, plugging in the headphones before pressing PLAY. This was one of the first CDs I had ever bought, when I began to make the transition to digital after Karen bought me a player for my thirtieth birthday.

The sound was immediate and true, insinuating itself directly into the middle of my cranium: *"God grant me the serenity to accept the things I cannot change. . . ."*

I found myself thinking, for the first time in a very long time, about my guitar. It was a cheap little Yamaha acoustic, but I had spent hours playing it as an undergrad, building calluses on my fingers, irritating Karen to no end with countless renditions of "Tangled Up in Blue." I found my fingers unconsciously curling into chords, sliding along imagined strings with a beautiful, steely rasp as I listened. Why had I stopped playing? When was the last time I had even seen the guitar, which had once rested so proudly in the corner of our tiny book-lined living room in its battered black case?

I wished I had it now, and could cradle the comforting, familiar weight of its body in my arms. Strange how we let things slip away.

As I listened to the album, a hour of loss and sadness and understanding, I became inescapably, deeply aware of two truths, beyond words, beyond the capacity of rational thought, beyond any possibility of reconciliation.

I was in love with Mary. This wasn't the silly midlife infatuation that everyone seemed to think it was. She pulled me out of my accustomed form in ways that I hadn't thought possible. With her, I felt a sense of possibility, of potential, that I hadn't felt in years.

But that recognition was made almost unbearable by my second, simultaneous realization.

I loved Karen. Still. After everything I had done, the problems we had and everything I had subjected her to, I loved her.

I loved her, and I couldn't stand myself for hurting her. I knew I was too far gone to ever go back, but I couldn't bear to lose her.

*I couldn't bear to lose her. . . .*

The trouble was, these words were equally true of both Karen and Mary.

I sat, in the silence of the headphones after the music ended, until the barest light of dawn began to touch the world outside the window.

Henry

A cold hand fell on my shoulder. "Jesus Christ!" I yelped and jumped out of my chair, dropping my book, spinning to face . . .

Tim—who grinned at my distress.

"You scared the hell out of me," I mumbled, trying to recover a little dignity.

He pulled out the chair next to mine and sat down, gesturing for me to do the same. Leaning over, he picked up the book I had dropped and studied the cover. "*Tao Te Ching*," he muttered. "However did you end up at that?"

I had to think for a moment. "Well, I started off with Salinger, which sent me to . . ."

He waved my words away, as if he hadn't really meant for me to answer. "What do you think of it?"

"I don't know if I really get it. I mean, I understand the words and everything, but they just don't seem to pull together."

"That's the thing with the Oriental philosophies," he explained. "Zen, all the schools of Buddhism, Taoism . . . it all makes sense when someone else processes it for you, like Salinger. But when you go back to the sources"—he gestured at the book in my hand—"you realize how very foreign, how very different the cultural framework is. And that makes the ideas quite difficult for the Western mind to wrap itself around. We don't have a common vocabulary. . . ."

I nodded, mostly understanding him.

"It's good you're prepared to tackle it, but you might want to try something a little closer to home. Some Western philosophy. The Bible, perhaps."

I felt a surge of pride at his compliment. The Bible. That would be next.

"Is it just your reading that's keeping you away from us?" he asked, his voice dropping a little.

"What?" I asked, pretending not to understand.

"We haven't see too much of you on the second floor," he said. "You seem to spend most of your time down here. Some people think you're hiding."

"Well, I've been . . . ," I stammered, gesturing at the books piled on the table in front of me.

How could I explain?

*I killed a little girl. Well, I didn't kill her exactly: I put her into a coma that she'll never wake up from. I tried to kill myself, but I can't seem to die. I don't deserve to be with other people.*

I couldn't bring myself to say the words.

"I guess I'm just a slow learner," I said.

He nodded. "You'll find that a lot of us are. That's why we're here."

"Maybe . . . Maybe in a little while . . ."

"Whenever you're ready. No pressure. No rush." He rose to his feet, started to turn away, then changed his mind. "It's not so bad, you know," he said.

"What?"

"What you've done. Whatever you've done. Whatever you think is so bad that you shouldn't be allowed to associate with people. It's not as bad as you think." His smile seemed more sad than happy. "It's probably not nearly as bad as some . . ."

Without waiting for me to answer, he disappeared into the shadows of the library, leaving me to puzzle over his words.


Mary

Something was going on.

Simon had been distant, preoccupied and secretive, as if there was something on his mind that he didn't want to tell me about. And he was behaving strangely, changing plans at the last minute. Not visiting with Sherry the last few days. Not sleeping. One night, I woke up at about four and he wasn't in bed. The bedroom door was closed, but I could see a splinter of light under it.

I got up and opened the door, just a crack, to look out into the living room. He was sitting on the floor next to the stereo, leaning against the wall with his knees up to his chest. The headphones were over his ears, his eyes closed.

I wanted to go to him, but thought somehow that I shouldn't. I stood in the doorway for several minutes. Then I went back to bed, hugging his pillow against me.

Just after five I woke up again. He had come into the bedroom, grabbed a pair of shorts and a shirt off the dresser, and ducked back out. A few minutes later, the front door clicked shut.

What was going on?

I stared at the white textured ceiling. How had I ended up living with a man with a wife and a daughter across town? I got up, too, and showered, mindlessly soaping, shampooing, rinsing, then got dressed and made myself a cup of coffee.

If it had been something with Karen, or anything wrong with Sherry, he would have told me. Wouldn't he?

I almost called Brian. If anyone could cut through the BS and help me figure out what was going on, it was Brian. But I hadn't spoken to him, to any of my friends, since Simon had moved in. Pathetic. Was I really turning into one of *those* women, the sort whose lives revolve around their men, their fucked-up relationships?

A couple of mornings later, Sunday, I was sitting in the living room, coffee cup on the table in front of me, glancing through the *New Sentinel,* when the doorknob rattled and he came in. He was wet from another solitary run, his shirt plastered to his body, his face red, his breath harsh. I wondered how far he'd gone, how hard he'd pushed himself without me.

I wondered how much I held him back.

"Good run?" I asked.

"What are you doing up?" He glanced at his watch. "I was just coming to wake you."

I shrugged, as casually as I could fake. "I woke up when you left. Couldn't go back to sleep."

"I'm sorry. I tried to be quiet. I wanted to blow out the cobwebs. I'm having problems sleeping."

"I noticed. Are you going to tell me what's going on?"

He looked at a loss for words. It was a state I don't think I had ever seen him in before.

"Everything's fine," he finally said.

"Simon, you can talk to me."

"There's nothing—" Then he looked at me and sighed. "Yeah, I should have talked to you. I had a big fight with Karen the last time I visited Sherry. It got pretty loud—"

"And that's why you haven't been going over there?" I didn't dare allow myself to feel relief. It was Karen; it wasn't me.

He nodded, but didn't meet my eyes.

"Well, why didn't you say something?"

He was silent.

"It was about me, wasn't it? That's why you didn't say anything."

"I told her about our trip next weekend. . . ."

I waited silently for the other shoe to fall. When it didn't, I asked, "And?"

"And she just lost it. Screaming. Cursing me out. It was ugly." He paused, as if to shape the words before speaking them. "Right over Sherry's bed . . ." He shook his head, as if he were having difficulty understanding the situation.

I was stunned. "That's it?"

"What?" He seemed surprised by my response.

"You kept me in the dark, you made me worry, because you had a fight with your wife?"

"Well . . ."

"Because she's pissed off that we're going away for the weekend?"

He shrugged.

"Damn it, Simon. I thought you were mad at me for something. Of course Karen's pissed off we're going away for the weekend." I shook my head. "How dense are you? She's alone in that house, looking after Sherry every moment of every day, and you come in and tell her that we're going away for a nice weekend at Tofino? How did you think she was going to react?"

"Oh, Mary," he finally said. "I'm sorry." I got up to hug him. I rubbed his hair, sweaty and cool. "I didn't mean to . . ."

"I thought I had done something wrong."

He leaned back, looked up at me. "That's exactly what I didn't want you to think. That's why I didn't say anything. It's just . . . This is all so hard."

"Of course it is. Did you think it would be easy?" He started to answer, but I cut him off. "That was rhetorical."

He smiled.

"Go shower." I messed his hair. "We're going for brunch."

He leaned in and kissed me gently; then he lingered for a moment, his face almost touching my own. I could feel a crackling of energy in the air between us. "You're going to be a very wise woman when you grow up," he said, his eyes dancing.

I smiled. "Maybe. But by the time that happens, I'll be too busy caring for you in your old age to enjoy it."

---

*On the nights that he hunted, the stranger did not wear the collar. There were things best done in the shadows, and times when the objects of the light were best left behind.*

*Victoria, he discovered, was a small town masquerading as a city. Within weeks, he was familiar with everyone he would need. He recognized them going to work and coming home, he followed their routines, and sought out the secret habits they were convinced no one knew save themselves.*

*Secrets. He always knew where to find the people he needed, the people whose vulnerabilities he could turn into his strengths, his power. The power of secrets and lies.*

*Everyone had secrets that, if confronted, they tried to explain away as mistakes, momentary lapses of judgment.*

*If confronted.*

*But secrets, the stranger knew, had their own power. Those things people hide could be used to reveal the truth, in time. Untold stories could bring other stories to the light.*

*The weakness of others would become his strength.*

## Karen

I hoped Sherry hadn't heard. Couldn't hear. What had I been thinking, tearing into Simon with Sherry right there? The memory of it still pulled at me, days later.

I hated that we had fought in front of her.

We?

Let's be realistic: Simon had nothing to do with it. That was my own freak-out, all by myself. He was trying to be polite, to keep me aware of what was going on, where he was going to be, why he wasn't going to be around. And I totally lost it.

"You probably just needed to vent." That had been Jamie's insight when I told her.

"Maybe . . ."

"I mean, look at the facts: your daughter's in this horrible accident, she comes home from the hospital requiring *extraordinary* amounts of care, and within a couple of weeks Simon's up and gone, moving in with his secretary or whatever she is, who it turns out he's been sleeping with for months. I think you're entitled to vent."

"But it was so stupid."

I had wanted to call him ever since. I don't know how many times I had dialed his cell phone, hanging up before it could connect.

"I should apologize."

"Why? For calling him on his bullshit?"

"He was just trying to be polite."

"Oh, for Christ's sake, Karen. How much more of this are you going to take?"

Over lunch yesterday, she had handed me a business card. I had vaguely recognized the name. "She's one of the best," Jamie had volunteered, taking a bite of her linguine. "I talked to her for a feature I was doing on the state of marriage in the nineties. Very pro-woman. Very smart. I think you'll like her."

I stared at the name and realized that I had been introduced to her at a party with Simon at some point. For the opera, maybe? A fund-raiser? One of the firm functions, whatever it was. She hadn't seemed very cutthroat, drinking a champagne cocktail.

"You're starting to sound like my mother. I'm not looking for a lawyer."

"Well, you probably should be. I mean, if Simon's behavior should prove anything to you, it's that he's moved on. You're not his priority anymore. Don't think he hasn't been talking to someone already."

I had shaken my head. "It's not like that. He comes to visit Sherry every day—"

"Which is exactly the sort of thing a lawyer would tell him to do. It looks good in court if he seems to be a devoted father."

"God, you're hard, Jamie."

"Someone has to be realistic."

I had tucked the card into my purse, trying to forget that it was there, trying to ignore the sound of Jamie's voice in my head.

This wasn't supposed to happen to us. Not after all the lean years—the studying, the macaroni and cheese, the thin soup, the shitty basement suites and scrounging change for the bus. Everything was supposed to be smooth sailing now. We had our house, our daughter . . .

What had happened to my life?

What could I do? Simon wasn't coming back—I knew that. So what did that leave me? Fighting? Bitching? I couldn't just accept things the way they were: Stop thinking of Simon as my husband and reimagine him just as Sherry's father? Accept that he was gone, that his life was with someone else now? I couldn't. But what other choice did I have? How much could I give, could I fight, for something that wasn't going to change?

*"Hello?"*

*"Is this Sarah?"*

*"Yes . . ."*

*"What did that little girl do to me?"*

*"Pam?"*

*"I was just at the doctor. He wants me to come in for more tests. He says he's never seen such a remission—"*

*"Pam, slow down—"*

*"He says it's a miracle. He actually used the word. He says that after my appointment on Friday, he wasn't expecting to see me again. He thought that I would probably die over the weekend."*

*"Pam, what—?"*

*"He thought I was going to die. And now the cancer's gone. All gone."*

*"Pam, what did you tell the doctor?"*

*"About what?"*

*"About Sherry. The little girl. What did you tell him about Sherry Barrett?"*

*"Nothing."*

*"Thank God. Pam—"*

*"But we have to tell someone—"*

*"No. I promised Ruth—"*

*"Sarah, listen to what you're saying. This little girl cures cancer. Do you know what that means?"*

*"We can't—"*

*"People are suffering. How can we keep this a secret?"*

*"We have to."*

*"Why?"*

*"I promised Ruth. "*

*"People are dying, Sarah."*

*"Let me talk to Ruth."*

*"We have to tell people."*

*"Let me talk to Ruth first. She took a big risk letting us . . . helping us. I can't go back on my word. Just let me talk to her. Please?"*

*"Okay."*

*"Promise me you won't say anything before I call you back?"*

*"All right. I promise. But call me soon."*

*"I will."*

*"People are dying every minute."*


*"City desk. Todd Herbert."*

*"Is this the* Sentinel?"

*"Yes, ma'am. New Sentinel city desk."*

*"I need to speak to someone."*

*"Is this a delivery question? I can transfer you to circulation. Hold on."*

*"No. I have a story you might be interested in."*

*"What sort of story, ma'am?"*

*"It's about that little girl. The one who was in the accident . . ."*


FROM: therbert@ns.ca
TO: jkeller@ns.ca
Jamie—

   Bit of a situation here. Woman calls me up, says she's got a story for me about a little girl who was in an accident. I figure it has to be Karen's daughter, so I let her talk. Long story short, she claims Sherry has miraculous powers, that she cured her of terminal cancer. Normally, I'd just blow this off, but the lady seems to have some pretty solid information, so I figured I'd run it past you, get your read on it before we take it any further. Have you heard anything like that? Could be guesswork, but she gave what sounded to me like a pretty solid description of Casa Barrett—right down to white carnations on the table in the room the daughter's in.

Any thoughts,

th

FROM: jkeller@ns.ca
TO: therbert@ns.ca

Sorry, Todd—talked to Karen. I don't think there's any news here. Good human interest, maybe a short feature—follow up the accident, etc. As far as miracles go—Simon and Karen wish. Apparently the woman you spoke to is the nurse's sister. They're pretty close and she's been over to visit at the house a few times. Yes, there were carnations in the room with Sherry. Don't get excited, though: according to the nurse, her sister's never been sick a day in her life. Approaching senility, apparently. I've met her myself and she's no sicker than I am. Thanks for the reminder, though—I think maybe I'll do a follow-up for the "Life" pages next Thursday. What do you think?

Jamie

Oh—Karen says hello.

*"Simon, it's me. Listen, I just wanted to let you know that Jamie's working on an article for the paper, for next Thursday. Sort of a, you know, a human interest, "where are they now" kinda thing. . . . I know you'll be out of town, but I thought you might want to get a copy."*

## Simon

I woke to the sound of thunder, a throaty rumbling that rattled the bed. No, not thunder. The roar of waves, mere meters from my head. For a moment, I was completely disconcerted. Nothing about the room was familiar—the honey-colored timber ceiling, the chair, the beige carpet stretching to meet the sliding door onto the balcony. Then it came to me: Tofino. The Wickanninish.

We had driven up the night before, stopping in Nanaimo for dinner before addressing three hours of winding wilderness roads, the headlights illuminating only trees and undergrowth until we emerged on the west coast of the island. The clerk at the front desk was the only person in the firelit lobby when we checked in.

Arriving at the room, we had fallen into bed. The promised view was nothing more than a reflection of the inside of the room on the clean, slick glass.

I rose from the bed, careful not to disturb Mary. The room wasn't at all cold, but with a single flick I ignited the gas fireplace, which purred to life.

"Oh my God."

"What?" Mary asked groggily, rustling as she turned to face me. "Oh, wow."

The balcony seemed to dangle precariously over the waves crashing against the slate-black barnacle-encrusted rocks right before our eyes. The sky was cloud white, and there was nothing in the distance save a thin line of silver where the water met the sky. Every crashing wave spewed foam skyward, toward where we stood, always falling just short of the balcony.

The sensation as I looked out at the ocean reminded me of church, the tiny Anglican chapel my mother dragged us to when I was a boy, and the breathtaking cathedrals in Europe that Karen and I had visited during our backpacking trip in university. I felt awe, wonder, and fear in the face of the sublime, and a limitlessness akin to weightlessness, as if some sort of internal gravity had been lifted away. Even behind the glass, I felt tiny, nearly overwhelmed by the roar and the spray.

I could hear Mary's footsteps on the carpet as she came up behind me, sliding her arms around my waist, the softness of her bare breasts and warm belly against my back. "This is amazing," she said, looking out around me at the view.

"Yeah." I entwined my hands with hers.

She kissed me just inside my shoulder blade, resting her face there for a moment. "I'm happy we're here," she said, her voice muffled.

"I am, too."

After a moment, she asked, "Do you want to go for a walk on the beach?"

"Actually, I'd like to get some breakfast." As if prompted, my stomach growled. "Let's go out, find a little café."

"Do I have time for a quick shower?"

"No rush at all."

"Good. I'll see you in a sec."

She was just closing the bathroom door behind herself when I decided I needed a shower myself.

*"Jamie? Are you there? If you're there, pick up. Shit. It's Karen. Have you seen the paper? What the hell is this? Jesus Christ, the phone's ringing off the hook, I don't know what to say. What the hell happened? Where are you? Listen, give me a call. . . . No, never mind, you won't be able to get through—just get over here."*

Simon

It was cool outside; the moisture in the air chilled us as we hurried to the car. The air was heavy with the smell of the ocean. We drove the few minutes into Tofino and parked in front of the Cranberry Cafe, weathered wood with white curtains in the front windows.

Next to the door there was a busker—the typical West Coast Generation X type with his rough goatee, knit toque, shapeless jacket and pants—driving out an old Bob Dylan song on a battered guitar. He couldn't sing, and could barely manage the chords, but he swayed, eyes half-closed, as if in a trance. I dropped a few coins into the open guitar case at his feet as we went through the restaurant door. Mary looked a bit surprised.

"Good morning," called out the heavyset girl behind the counter as we came in. "Sit wherever you like. I'll be able to find you."

We sat in the window, overlooking the rough street, the cracked pavement, the row of small stores. She was there with the menus and the coffeepot, filling our mugs, almost before we sat down. The waitress smiled. "The specials are on the board." She gestured to a dusty chalkboard on the wall behind the counter. "I'll be back in a few minutes to take your order. If you get bored waiting for me, just wave."

She turned to walk away.

"Before you go, do you have a copy of today's *Sentinel* that I could take a look at?"

Mary smiled as the waitress answered, "I've got one at the counter. I'll bring it when I come to get your order."

Mary looked around the restaurant. It was a cute place—tablecloths on all the tables, lots of plants, plain walls with lots of natural wood trim, decorated with watercolors. "I like this place," she whispered.

"I like you," I said without even thinking about it.

I wasn't usually prone to emotional blurtings like that.

She reached across the table and laid her hand across my own. The gesture seemed utterly natural. "I like you, too." She grinned, and blushed a little. "I like *this*."

"Me, too."

We sat looking out the window, until the waitress returned, setting a folded copy of the *New Sentinel* on the table in front of me. "Are you guys all ready to order?"

"I think I'll just have some pancakes—butter on the side, please."

The waitress turned to me, jotting down Mary's order. "And for you?"

"Bacon and eggs, sunny side up, hash browns, multigrain toast, and a glass of tomato juice."

She scooped up the menus and headed back to the kitchen.

The folded copy of the *New Sentinel* lay on the table between us. Mary smiled and shook her head, watching me deliberately not looking at the paper.

I took a sip of my coffee. Neither of us said anything for a long moment.

Finally, Mary broke the silence. "You might as well read it."

I shrugged. "I'm not in any hurry."

She grinned at me. "Well, I'm in a hurry. I'd like you to read it so that we can get it out of the way and get on with our weekend, okay?"

"Well, if you insist . . ." I unfolded the paper. "It's not like there's going to be anything new."

I skipped the front section entirely, guessing that the story Karen had called about would be in the "Life" section. "I expect it'll be the typical six months later—"

My voice caught. Under the fold, C3. A small picture of Sherry, and a headline that I couldn't believe even as I reread it.

"Holy shit," I muttered.

"What is it?"

I couldn't stop reading to explain. "Oh my God."

*VICTORIA NEW SENTINEL,* THURSDAY, DECEMBER 5

# Miracles?
### Can Injured Girl Cure the Dying?
by Todd Herbert

According to one grateful woman, 4-year-old Sherilyn Barrett is much more than the victim of a tragic accident last spring. "She's an angel," says Pamela Harding, 28. "*She's* a miracle." The miracle is that Harding is alive to say anything at all: according to Harding, two months ago she was informed by her doctor that she had mere weeks to live. "It was cancer," says Harding. "I lost both breasts, but it was all through me. The doctor said that there was nothing he could do. He said that I was going to die." Today an expert confirms that no cancer remains in her system. "It's the most amazing thing I've ever seen," says Dr. Herbert Katz, on-cologist at Royal Jubilee Hospital. "There seems to have been a complete remission. I can't explain it."

But Pamela Harding thinks she can explain it. "It's a miracle, and it's all because of that little girl." According to Mrs. Harding, who is married with two young children, she was taken to the Barrett's Fernwood home by a friend who had also been healed by Sherilyn Barrett. "She told me that her lung cancer had completely disappeared. I didn't believe her, but I thought, 'Well, it can't hurt.' "

According to Harding, her contact with Barrett took place almost two weeks ago. By the following morning, her cancer had disappeared. "It's a miracle," Harding says, radiating her new-found good health. "I've got my life back, and it's all because of that little girl."

Karen Barrett could not be reached for comment. According to Harding, "They're trying to keep it all a secret. They don't want anyone else to know. But I had to tell you: it's a miracle, and everyone should know."

## Simon

"Simon? What is it?"

Unable to speak, I handed her the newspaper. "Here," I said, tapping the article. "This."

As Mary scanned the article, I punched in my home number as quickly as I could. Busy. Of course.

I dialed again.

"Simon, what is this?"

Still busy.

"I have no idea." I dialed again.

Still busy.

"Shit," I muttered. Several of the other patrons turned to look at us as I dialed again.

Still busy. I slammed the phone to the table. More people turned to look.

Mary stared at me as the waitress came rushing over.

"Is something wrong?" she asked, her face creased with concern.

"No." I shook my head, clearing my throat and trying to pull myself together. "Just a . . ."

Mary's eyes lowered to the table, and she shook her head. She touched the waitress's arm. "Actually, could we have our breakfast to go, please? It turns out we need to head back to Victoria."

"Sure, sure. Of course. No problem. Right away."

"What are you doing?" I asked.

"We'll stop at the hotel, just grab the stuff, and head out. If we drive straight through, we should be back in Victoria by—" She stopped, checking her watch. "—three thirty or so."

Without even thinking about it, I looked at my own watch. "Yes, but—"

"You need to be home for this. Your daughter needs you. Karen needs you. If nothing else, they probably need a lawyer."

"Mary . . ."

I could see how hard she was trying to hold on to her calm facade. "You need to be there, Simon. It's as simple as that. We'll get away some other time."

It was clear that neither of us completely believed what she was saying. We both knew that our lives had changed again in a single moment. The waitress returned with two Styrofoam trays, and neither of us said anything more.

### Ruth

It was even worse than I had feared. By the time I got to the house at 8:30 that morning, the front yard was surrounded by reporters, bunched together on the sidewalk, at the edge of the lawn, in the driveway. They all turned to watch me as I drove up, and rushed toward me when I got out of the car.

"Are you the nurse . . ."

"Can you comment on . . ."

"Have you seen any . . ."

"Mrs. Page . . ."

"Ma'am, what about . . ."

"Has Karen Barrett ever . . ."

I tried to be polite, but they pressed around me, a wall of voices, shoving and pushing. I walked as quickly as I could across the front yard, opening the door with the key Mrs. Barrett had given me, slamming it behind myself.

I wondered how long it would be before she asked for the key back.

All the lights were off, except one in the kitchen.

I hung my coat on the hook. "Hello?" I called quietly. "Hello?"

Karen was sitting in the dark in Sherry's room. She didn't flinch when I turned on the light. I was the one who jumped.

"Mrs. Barrett. I didn't . . ."

She stared at me without saying a word, a folded newspaper on the table next to her.

"I've been on the phone all morning—"

"Mrs. Barrett—"

"It just kept ringing and ringing. Finally I just left it off the hook."

"I can explain—"

"Can you?" she asked, turning to me. "Can you really?" Her face was pulled so tight, it looked like she might tear.

I sighed. "I can try."

She just stared at me, waiting.

"I didn't mean for any of this to happen." When the words started coming, I could do nothing to slow them. I told her everything, from my retirement to when I had first noticed that there was no longer any pain in my hands.

"I couldn't believe it," I said. "I had lived with that pain for so long. I'd tried all the treatments. Nothing worked. I couldn't figure out what had happened, until one day—" I stopped. I hadn't told anyone. I didn't want to sound ridiculous. "I was giving Sherry her bath, and I was holding her head to wash her hair, and I saw my hand on her forehead. I couldn't . . . I couldn't think of anything else that explained it."

Then I told her about Sarah, and inviting her to the house, about Sarah's remission, and about opening the door to find Sarah on the doorstep with her dying friend Pam.

She didn't say anything when I was done. Unable to bear the silence, I busied myself with Sherry's routine as if it were any other morning. The curtains were drawn, but with all the reporters outside, I didn't want to open them. My hands were shaking as I wrote the notes in her file.

"Did you have any problems with the reporters?" she finally asked.

"No. No. I just got into the house as fast as I could."

She stood up and peered through the crack in the curtains. "They're staying out on the sidewalk . . . ," she muttered. "I could call the police and complain about trespassing if they came into the yard."

"When did you know about the article?" she asked, her back still turned.

I hesitated a moment. "I thought that Jamie's article was going to be in the paper today, so I bought a copy this morning."

"You didn't know?"

"I didn't know that Pam had told."

I couldn't say anything more. I had betrayed Karen, betrayed Sherry. I stared down at the carpet.

"I'm sorry, Karen. If I wouldn't have invited Sarah, none of this would have happened. But I . . . she's my sister."

She sighed, and turned to face me. "Ruth, did you leave her—either of them—alone with Sherry?"

"I would never do that. They were never alone with Sherry—"

"I can't . . . I can't be lied to anymore," she said.

"I'm sorry."

"There has to be honesty here. *Here*." She stressed the word. "I have to know that there's someone, one person, I can count on."

She didn't seem angry; she seemed close to tears. "I'm so sick and tired of being surprised by things. Of always being the last to know. Do you know what I mean? I can't, I just can't . . ."

I nodded. "I won't. I won't lie to you again."

She nodded, and looked at me without saying anything for several seconds. "I made tea," she said then. "I'll bring it in here."

She turned to leave the room.

"Do you—?" I stopped her. "Do you want me to come to the kitchen with you?"

She turned back to face me. "You're asking if I still trust you alone with my daughter?"

I didn't say anything.

"I'll bring the tea in here," she said.

I sat down heavily, my eyes wet.

When she came back, she set the tray on the table and reached out to me. "Take my hand," she said.

"What?"

She wiggled her fingers a little. "Take my hand," she repeated.

Gingerly, I took hold of her extended fingers.

"Squeeze it."

"What?"

"Squeeze my hand. As hard as you can." Our eyes met, but I didn't quite understand what I saw there.

Without breaking our gaze, I squeezed her fingers as hard as I could. I saw her jaw clench, saw her flinch with the pressure, until finally she jerked her hand away. "Jesus," she muttered.

"I'm sorry," I started.

"And last winter . . ."

"You should see my cupboards at home. I had to go out and buy all those gadgets, like the can openers with the big rubber handles, so I could get a grip. But now . . ."

She stared at me for a moment, then turned her attention to her daughter. "And Sherry . . ." She drifted toward the bed, resting her hands on the rail.

Standing next to her, I just nodded.

She stared down at her daughter. "How?" she whispered.

"I don't know. For me, it just happened. I guess I was in such close contact with her all the time, washing her . . . But with Sarah, and with Pam, I thought that laying on hands might work."

"You mean they just touched her?"

I shook my head. "No, I lifted Sherry's hand."

Karen pulled the sheet back from Sherry's still body. With great care, she picked up her right hand, carefully cradling the wrist as she turned it slightly, gazing down at the pale palm, the tiny curled fingers, the pale skin almost entirely free of line or mark. Karen didn't speak, just ran her thumb gently over the smoothness.

She was crying, thin rivulets of tears trailing unchecked down her cheeks, collecting at the corners of her jaw, falling soundlessly away.

*"This is Kent Sellers for* News at Noon. *I'm outside the Barrett residence in Fernwood, where, sources tell us, miracles have started to happen in Victoria. I'll be joined by Pam Harding, who was apparently miraculously cured of cancer by Sherilyn Barrett last week, and Todd Herbert of the* New Sentinel *in a few moments, but first a little background . . ."*

## Karen

"You need to explain," I said, holding fast to the doorknob, my body between Jamie and the house. "You need to tell me what the hell is going on."

"Karen, I had no idea."

Jamie glanced over her shoulder at the other reporters watching us from the far side of the fence, and at the small crowd that had gathered behind them. "Can we do this inside?"

I didn't move for a long moment, then stepped back, allowing her enough space to slide past me. I closed the door behind her and shot the dead bolt. I could hear the shouts of indignation from the sidewalk.

She started to take off her jacket. "No," I said, turning to her. "You're not staying. Not until I find out what's going on."

"Karen, how can you even think—?"

"There's a story in *your* paper about how my daughter is some sort of healer. What am I supposed to think?"

"Damn it, Karen, I tried to protect you." Her voice came out in a squeak.

"What?"

"Can we please . . ." She started toward the kitchen, and I followed. Ruth was at the table, and neither of them said anything when Jamie sat down across from her. I sat down between them.

"So."

Jamie shook her head. "Karen, I tried to stop this."

"So what happened?"

She glanced at Ruth. "Have you asked—?"

"I'm asking you."

She sighed. "Todd—you remember Todd—sent me an e-mail. Said he had received a phone call from a woman who claimed that Sherry had healed her."

"Pam," Ruth said quietly.

Jamie nodded. "That's what he said. Anyway, he was asking a lot of questions, talking about how she could describe the inside of the house, right down to what flowers were on the table. White carnations."

She sniffed.

"So I told him I'd check it out. I told him that I didn't think that there was anything to it, but that I'd check it out."

I just sat and waited.

"So that day I came over, and I made a point of looking around Sherry's room."

"Oh, Jamie."

She shook her head. "No, I wanted to prove to him that this woman was making the whole thing up. I tell you, I've never been happier than when I saw that there weren't any carnations anywhere in the room."

"So what—?"

"Until I looked in the garbage can," she continued, as if I hadn't said anything. "And there they were. Broken stems, all crunched up, gone brown. A bunch of carnations."

I felt like I was going to be sick. "So you told him."

She shook her head firmly. "No. No, I didn't. I tried to misdirect him. I tried to protect you. You and Sherry. I made up something about your sister, Ruth. I didn't know anything about any Pam. . . ." She dropped her head.

"So if you didn't . . ."

She shrugged. "I guess he didn't believe me."

"So what happened to the story you were working on."

"They killed it. They weren't interested in anything from me. At least that's what Ron Kozak said."

"The managing editor?"

She nodded. "It's a hell of a way to start a day. Being told that you've lost your objectivity. That you've betrayed your employer. It was a nice little chat. And then I packed up my desk."

"You were fired?"

"Suspended, with no fixed date of return. I got the feeling they wouldn't be calling anytime soon."

"Oh, Jamie." I stood up and moved to her, intending to embrace her, but she pushed me away.

"No," she said, looking across the table at Ruth. "I need to know what's going on around here."

*"This is Troy Shepherd with the* CFAX *News Cruiser. I'm here at the home of Karen and Sherilyn Barrett. I'm talking to Todd Herbert of the* New Sentinel, *who wrote a story in this morning's paper. . . ."*

### Karen

The house was dark, silent. None of us were speaking, so focused were we on trying to ignore the murmur from outside the windows. We were playing a waiting game, but none among us knew what we were waiting for.

After Jamie had heard Ruth's side of the story, I borrowed her cell phone. I dialed Simon's cell, then pressed CANCEL before it could ring. Instead, I called Stephen McKinley at the hospital.

"I saw the paper. What's going on over there?" I could hear genuine concern in his voice.

"Well, my phone's ringing off the hook, and I've got reporters on the sidewalk." I pulled back the living room curtain to check on the journalists. I was surprised to see about a dozen people milling around on the front lawn, right under the window. They turned to look as I parted the curtain. Several of them rushed up to the window and pressed their hands and faces against the glass, trying to see in. Trying to see Sherry.

I dropped the curtain, but images of their faces lingered in my mind: blind eyes, scars, patches of hair, yellow skin . . .

"Karen? Are you still there?"

"I'm here. It's, it's a little bit crazy. . . . Could you . . . ," I stammered, not even really sure what I was asking.

"I'm done here at two. I'll come right over."

When Stephen arrived, I let Jamie and Ruth explain it to him, all of us sitting in the family room, away from Sherry, away from the crowds of reporters and onlookers who were separated from my daughter, it seemed, by only a curtain. When they finished, he looked between the two of them, first at Jamie, then at Ruth.

"Total remission?" he asked.

Ruth nodded her head. "That's what Sarah said."

Stephen nodded. "We should get her checked out by an independent physician."

"Why?" Jamie asked.

"In case this is all a big scam. So we can go to the paper with the test results, maybe get them to back off a little."

"But it's *not* a scam," Ruth said, quietly but forcefully. "It's not."

"The records can be checked. There must be tests we can do."

"On who?" Jamie asked.

"On you," the doctor said to Ruth, who looked at the floor. "On your sister." He turned toward me. "On Sherry."

"I don't want this," I whispered, afraid that if I met anyone's gaze I would start crying again. "I just want all of this to go away."

Jamie came over and, perching herself on the arm of the chair, rubbed my back. Her hand was cold through my thin sweater, but I was grateful for her touch. "Kar, I don't think that this is going to just go away." She gestured toward the front of the house. "I don't think those people out there are just going to go away."

"I know," I whispered. "I just, I just want my old life back."

At that moment, there was a knock at the front door.

Instinctively I rose to my feet, stepped toward it, stopping as Jamie took my arm.

"Leave it," she said.

Instinct and habit were at war with rationality. I couldn't let a telephone ring unanswered either.

Stephen rose to his feet. "Let me get it."

I shook my head and pulled free of Jamie's hand. "No, I'll get it. I can't just sit here anymore."

Bracing myself, I opened the door a crack, holding tightly to the knob in case I needed to slam it shut again.

"We got here as soon as we could," Simon said. Mary was standing just behind him.

Fanned out at the foot of the steps were more of the damaged people, their ranks swollen in the dimming light.

"Can we come in?" Simon asked.

## Simon

For several seconds it seemed as if Karen might not let us into the house. She looked at me as if she didn't even recognize me, then at Mary. Finally, biting her lip, she stepped to one side and allowed us in, closing the door behind us.

Out of habit I bent down to take my shoes off. Mary followed my lead.

"Just leave them on," Karen said, walking past us toward the family room.

I led Mary into the living room to see Sherry.

"Hello, baby." I leaned over her bed, touched her face. "Daddy's here. Daddy's here."

Mary stood stiffly next to me.

"This is Mary, honey," I reached out and found Mary's hand, took it into my own. "Do you remember her from Daddy's office?" I glanced up at her, smiled a little, feeling at a loss. I turned my attention back to Sherry. "So I hear you've been getting into trouble," I teased my silent daughter. "What did Daddy tell you about that, eh?"

Straightening up, I turned to Mary. "You can talk to her, if you want. I don't know if she can hear it or not, but I like talking to her."

"It's so sad," she said, her voice rough. "She's so small. . . ."

"I know. That's what everyone says."

"I should go," she said. "I should go home."

She hadn't wanted to come in at all. I'd spent most of the last hour of the drive down-island trying to persuade her. I asked, "Why?"

She shook her head. "It's not right. I shouldn't be here."

"No, it's fine," came Karen's voice from the doorway. We both jumped, turning to face her like children caught misbehaving. "You came all the way back down. You should both stay."

It was hardly the response that either of us was expecting, and I suppose our surprise was apparent in our faces. Karen took a deep breath. "I don't care. . . . Just stay."

She was pale and worn, as if she might disappear into the painted wall behind her. Her eyes were darkly outlined, her face stretched taut.

"Everyone else is in the family room," she said.

I knew that Mary still wanted to leave, despite what Karen had said. Or perhaps more so because of it, I couldn't be sure. I also knew that I wanted her to stay. We walked into the family room in silence.

Karen was standing with her back to the window. "Find a seat. I'll get you some coffee."

The room felt like a minefield. "Yes," I said. "Coffee would be nice. We've been driving for hours."

Her jaw tightened. "Mary, why don't you sit here." Karen gestured back to the chair as she crossed the room.

"Uh, no, that's okay. I'll just find a piece of floor."

I caught the sidelong glance between Jamie and Ruth as I sat down on the couch next to Dr. McKinley. Mary folded herself into a sitting position, leaning against the couch by my legs. I reached out and smoothed her hair.

There was an awkward pause. To cover as I pulled my hand away, I asked the doctor, "So where are we at right now?"

He shifted a little in his seat and shook his head. "I don't really understand it myself. Ruth?"

After Ruth finished speaking, there was a lengthy silence. It took me a long time to realize that everyone was waiting for me to say something. To have an idea. A plan.

I drained my coffee cup and rose to my feet, beginning to pace the room. I always think, and speak, more clearly if I'm in motion. "Well, leaving aside everything else," I started, then stopped short. I had no idea how to continue. "I . . ."

I looked at Mary, who smiled at me, clearly believing that I would know what to do. Looking at Karen, though, was like seeing a reflection of myself—trapped and frantic, with absolutely no idea of what to do.

"I . . ."

From the front yard, I could hear the sound of singing, voices raised in a hymn, people calling out my daughter's name.

## Henry

The library was closed for the night. Tim was in the children's section, his massive frame squeezed into one of the tiny little chairs, pulled up to one of the tiny little tables. He was chuckling over a picture book.

"Tim."

He glanced up. "Ah, Henry." He didn't seem surprised to see me, folding his book closed on the table and looking at me expectantly.

I sat down next to him. "Can I ask you a question?"

A smile touched his lips. "You just did."

"I wanted to ask you." I struggled to get my focus back. "I wanted to ask you about miracles."

He raised an eyebrow, his face spreading into a smile. "What about miracles?"

Everything. Ever since reading the newspaper articles that morning, I needed to learn as much about miracles as I could.

"Well, just . . . well . . . what are they, to start? I mean, I know what they are, but . . ."

He paused for a moment, looking at me. "Well, there's really no single answer." His voice trailed off. "If you're King Lear, well, then, your life, sir, is a miracle. If you're having a wedding at Cana, and you have no food, then you hope there's a messiah nearby with some loaves and fishes." He waited, I think expecting me to comment, but I had nothing to say.

"But if it's a little girl you're talking about, a little girl more dead than alive, who seems to be able to heal people without being able to heal herself, well, then, that's something completely different, isn't it?"

I felt the blood leaving my face, a sudden lightness as if I might pass out. "But, how—?"

"How did I know?" He laughed. "You make such a point of reading the local paper every morning. When I saw you reading this morning, I thought you might want to talk about that little girl that you almost killed in the spring."

I still couldn't speak.

He sighed deeply. "Let's talk about miracles, then."

I nodded.

"How did it feel when you couldn't kill yourself?"

I felt like he had punched me in the face. "What?" My body tensed, ready to bolt.

"You still don't understand it, do you?" he asked.

"Understand what? I don't understand anything."

"You think you're so different from everybody else, that you're not fit to associate with anyone, that you don't even deserve to be a member of the human race." I nodded slowly. "But you see, we're all like that. That's why we're all here. We all have our own stories, our own secret shames."

I couldn't meet his eyes.

"So how did it feel when you couldn't kill yourself?" Tim asked again.

"I . . . it scared me. I was angry. Sad. Frustrated."

"Trapped?"

I nodded. "Trapped."

"And yet you're immortal. Free to go anywhere, to do anything. You're virtually a god. That's a miracle, isn't it? Immortality?"

"It doesn't feel like it."

He shook his head. "No, it doesn't. But that's the flip side. That woman gets cured of cancer, gets to live a few more years with her children, and you and I and everyone in this building just want to die, but can't. When does a miracle become a curse?"

He chuckled. "I'm sorry. I'm not being very helpful, am I? I guess I don't really know the answer, any more than you really know the question." He smiled at me, but it seemed sad. "Go back to your reading. You'll find what you're looking for. Or at least some point on the way."

I nodded again, not knowing what to do.

"But, Henry, I do know this. Miracles don't come easy. They're not a gift. There's always a price in return. And it applies to everyone, not just us. The price of miracles is dear. You have to remember that."

## Mary

Simon was a different person when he was with his family. I had always known him to be caring and emotional, but these qualities seemed to be heightened, more sharply focused, being with Sherry. Being with Karen.

I hadn't been able to escape that realization since we arrived that afternoon.

I'd never been inside their house before. I had never met his daughter.

There was a whole side of Simon I didn't know. He was so very careful, when we were together, not to call this place *home,* even reflexively. He always called it *the house*: "I'm going to the house." "When I was at the house this morning . . ." I guess he thought that hearing this place referred to as home would upset me. Instead, I always noticed the slight hesitation as he consciously shifted from *home* to *house* before he spoke. But really, this was home.

And Karen. You could see how everything was wearing on her, but somehow she held herself together. I wouldn't have been able to cope with it. And having me here . . . insult to injury.

After sunset, people began lighting candles on the front lawn. The doctor and the nurse had left together, and the four of us sat mostly silent in the family room.

Karen rose to her feet. "I guess we need something to eat," she said, starting toward the kitchen.

"Why don't we order something in?" Jamie suggested.

Karen paused to consider the idea. "I don't know how keen I am on answering the door at this point," she concluded. "Besides, it's no big deal. I can whip something up."

As she slipped from the family room, Simon called after her. "I'll give you a hand." Jamie and I sat for a few moments, looking at each other awkwardly.

"Well, all the best parties usually end up in the kitchen," Jamie said, standing up to follow, leaving me alone.

Simon was chopping vegetables on a maple block on the kitchen table when I got there, carrots falling under a large chef's knife, a tea towel draped over one shoulder. The kitchen was bright and clean, large and well organized. Karen was at the stove with a wok. "I could open wine or something," she said.

"Yes," Simon said, glancing at me. "Let's have some wine."

As Simon finished chopping the carrots and swung toward the

stove, Karen stepped away, leaving a space between her body and the wok, allowing him to slide the cutting board through and to empty the carrots in, never breaking Karen's stirring. It was a dance between two people who had been partners for years.

I couldn't watch. The easy intimacy, the comfort and custom, it was all too much.

I left the kitchen, then lingered in the family room for a moment, running my eyes along the bookshelves, over the CDs and records beside the stereo. The light was still on in the living room, but it was even gloomier than it had been in the afternoon. For some reason I was surprised that Sherry was still in exactly the same position she had been earlier, that she hadn't turned in her sleep, or kicked off her blankets. Looking down at her, she seemed completely natural, as if she might at any moment open her eyes, sit up, and start speaking.

The sound of someone clearing her throat in the corridor made me turn around. Jamie entered the room tentatively, carrying a glass of red wine in each hand. "It's really sad, isn't it," she said, looking at Sherry, handing me a glass.

"Thanks," I replied, shy at being caught at the bedside. "I was—"

"You don't smoke, do you?"

"No."

"No, of course not. You probably do aerobics or something, too, right?"

"I run," I said.

"Nobody smokes anymore," she said. "It's a curse." Going to the corner she picked up her purse, fumbling for a moment before coming up with a package of cigarettes and a lighter. "Normally I'd go out onto the front step." She pondered for a moment. "I can't smoke here." She started out the living room door. "Coming?"

I followed her up the stairs and down a darkened corridor and into a room at the end. It took me a moment to realize that we were in the master bedroom. Karen's bedroom. Simon and Karen's bedroom.

It was immaculately clean. The bedframe, the dresser, and the nightstands all matched in glossy pine. The linen complemented, but didn't match, the curtains. Jamie slid open the window above the dressing table, sitting down and lighting a cigarette before she noticed that I was still standing in the doorway.

She gestured toward the bed. "Come on in. Pull up a seat." It took a moment for her to catch on. "Oh, shit," she muttered, standing up again. "That's awkward."

I shook my head. "No, it's okay." I perched on the foot of the bed.

She leaned back and crooked her neck to exhale a breath of smoke through the open window. "Yeah. Awkward."

I didn't say anything. From the open window came the faint sound of singing.

"I can't imagine how hard this must be for Karen." Another drag. "That sounded horrible. I didn't mean you. I meant those people outside, the reporters, the whole situation."

I waved it away. "No, you're right. This is all pretty awkward." Sitting on the bed that Simon had bought with his wife, the bed that Sherry had probably been conceived in. Sherry, who lay in another bed downstairs, in another kind of sleep.

"That was a pretty gutsy move, actually coming into the house. I think most people in your situation would have dropped him off at the curb."

"I wanted to," I started. "But he was so . . . He needed me." While I was saying it, I almost believed it.

She nodded, blowing out more smoke. "I know. It's pretty obvious."

I was taken aback. "It is?"

"The whole time you've been here, he's never been more than a few feet away from you. Always within arm's reach."

"Until now."

She shrugged. "He loves to cook."

"He does?"

"You didn't know that?"

"We go out a lot."

She nodded. "Oh yeah. He loves to cook. I mean, Karen's a good cook, but Simon, when he's got the time—"

"They work really well together."

"Oh, they used to have the best dinner parties."

All this information, all these things I didn't want to know. "I shouldn't be here," I said quietly.

"Neither of us should be here," she said. "But we're here for Karen. And for Simon, too, I guess."

For a long time we sat there in silence. I watched as the blue rivulets of smoke from her cigarette winnowed through the air, gradually drawn out the window.

"How long have you been seeing him?"

"What?"

"Simon. How long have you been seeing him?"

I paused to think. "Well, we've been working together for about a year and a half."

She raised an eyebrow. "That's not what I asked."

"A year or so," I answered, feeling my face warm.

She nodded slowly. "Simon and Karen were together, I don't know, fifteen years, I guess. Married more than half of that. I can't even imagine that kind of intimacy with another person." Standing up, she flicked her cigarette butt out the window, then reaching out shook the ashes from her palm.

"I know. It's . . . I think I'm in love with him." It was the first time I had ever said the words out loud.

"From where I'm sitting, it looks like Simon's pretty in love with you, too." I was amazed at how casually she could say it, how matter-of-fact it all seemed.

"The trouble is," she continued, "in love with you or not, Simon is still in love with Karen. You can see that, can't you?"

It wasn't really a question.

"I think that the only people who might not know that are Simon and Karen themselves."

I nodded, reluctantly. "I never thought that Simon would leave Karen. I didn't expect it. I didn't ask for it. And then the accident happened. It all got crazy. Simon needed me. He started taking stupid chances and one day . . ." I just shrugged. I assumed that she had already heard Karen's side of the story, that she knew all the details. "He wouldn't have left, but she wouldn't let him stay."

"I know."

"I still don't know how it happened. All of a sudden we're living together. I'm the other woman, the home-wrecker. Nobody at the office will have anything to do with me. With either of us." I couldn't continue.

She closed the window, cutting off the cold breeze. "I was involved with a married man at one point. It's an impossible situation you're in. I know."

We sat in silence a few moments. "I'm going to go," I said, more decisively than I actually felt.

Jamie seemed surprised. "Why?"

"This isn't about me. This is about Simon and Karen. If I stay here, it'll only confuse things. This is something they need to deal with on their own."

"You're not staying for dinner?"

I shook my head. "No. Would you mind, if Simon asks, can you tell him I've gone home?"

She nodded, reaching for another cigarette.

Descending the stairs, I noticed that the house was heady with the smells of meat and vegetables, rich with spices. From the kitchen came the sound of soft voices. Karen's voice. Simon's voice.

I stood in the doorway of the living room for a long moment, looking at Sherry.

Nobody inside the house noticed me leave, but the eyes of the people in the yard were upon me, following me as I walked up the sidewalk to my car.

# Part 4

---

*December 6*

# Miracle Vigil for Sherry

"Please go home," says distraught father.

A group of several dozen seekers and pilgrims, many suffering from life-threatening diseases, kept a cold candlelit vigil outside the Fernwood area home of Sherilyn Barrett last night. They had been attracted by news reports that the four-year-old girl, comatose following a hit-and-run accident last April, had healed two women of cancer in the last month. "We just want to see her," said Eliza Cox, 54, of Cobble Hill. "It seems to me that if she's been chosen by God, then she's been put on earth for a reason."

"My son is dying," said Donna Kelly, 24, of Seattle, accompanied by her six-year-old son Jeffrey, who suffers from leukemia. "There's nothing more the doctors can do. If there's any possibility that this little girl can do what the radio says she can do, then I don't mind waiting."

Cox, Kelly, and the other pilgrims may not get a chance to find the answers they are looking for. In a written statement delivered late last night, Simon Barrett, Sherilyn's father, pleaded, "I'm asking you as a father, please leave my daughter alone." His words went largely unheeded by the crowd, who clustered together in the Barretts' front yard, lighting candles and waiting.

### Simon

For the second morning in a row I awoke with no idea where I was. As I opened my eyes I saw bookshelves, distorted by the angle at which I was lying. The shelves sat against a dark-green papered wall, coving into a cream ceiling—the paper Karen and I had put up when we moved into the house, before we had Sherry. The family room, flooded with morning light from the east-facing windows.

I was home, on the couch in the family room.

The moment I thought of the word *home,* I thought of Mary.

I hadn't even noticed her leaving.

When I went looking for her last night, Jamie said, "She's gone home."

"Did she say why? Was something wrong?"

"Maybe she wanted to give you and Karen a little space."

Karen.

I jerked to a sitting position, the comforter falling off my shoulders. She was leaning against the doorframe. "Finally," she said. "There's coffee on. I brought the paper in." She slipped away before I could respond.

I pulled on my pants and yesterday's shirt, and put on my watch. 7:40. Running my fingers through my hair, I found Karen at the kitchen table, two coffee mugs and the morning paper spread out in front of her. "Morning," I said.

Her eyes flicked up to me from the newspaper, then returned.

"Did you have any problem getting the paper? With the . . ." I didn't know what to call the people outside.

She shook her head. "I think I took them by surprise. I checked to see if anyone was on the step, but they all seemed to be over by the living room window. I cracked open the door and grabbed it. By the time they realized I was there, I was already gone."

I gestured toward the paper. "So? What does it say?"

She wrinkled her nose. "You're not going to like it." She closed the paper and turned it toward me.

It took me a couple of seconds to register what I was seeing. Just below the banner headline were four photographs. The smallest was the picture of Sherry that we had taken at Sears on her third birthday—we had given a copy to the *New Sentinel* at the time of the accident. Somewhat larger was a picture taken at the scene of the accident, paramedics huddled around the tiny blanketed form of our daughter.

Dominating the page was a large night shot of a group of what the paper called "pilgrims" in front of the house, their faces lit from below by their candles, the orange glow of the living room visible behind them. Inset into this larger photo was a black-and-white shot of a young boy, smiling into the camera.

"Oh my God."

"That's what they're saying, too," Karen muttered. "Lots of human interest. Lots of sick people." I scanned the story as she continued speaking. "They'll be posting copies of it at Lourdes."

I took a swallow of my coffee. "I don't like to think of how many people this article will attract."

"It's already started. There were ten or fifteen people out there when I got the paper, and cars have been pulling up steadily."

I shook my head.

"So what should we do?" Karen asked.

I shrugged. "I have no idea. We could get an injunction."

She raised her eyebrows. "Do you want to be the one who has terminally ill kids dragged off by the police?"

"Well, it would keep them away," I joked.

Karen took a long sip of her coffee. "So." She looked at me. "What happened to Mary last night, anyway? She just sort of disappeared."

I shifted uneasily in my chair. "Jamie said she went home. I tried calling, but she wasn't there."

"I'm sorry," she said.

"For what?"

She waved her hand as if I should know. "For that, for that whole thing with your trip up-island. That whole freak-out." She seemed really uncomfortable. "I'm sorry, that's all."

"Yeah. Me, too."

The silence between us was thick. Neither of us knew what to say next.

I drained my coffee and set the mug on the table. "Uh, listen, would it be okay with you if I had a shower?"

Her eyes flashed up at me. "Oh, sure."

"I just . . . I won't feel really awake unless I—"

She cut me off. "No, I know. I remember." She gave a wry smile. "Your clothes are where you . . . where they usually are."

"Okay." I pushed away from the table. "I'll be back in a few."

### Karen

I don't think I breathed again until I heard the shower starting in the upstairs bathroom. I hadn't known it would be so easy. Or so hard.

The last time I saw Simon, I had all but thrown him out of the house. Then to have him show up when I needed him so badly—to show up with Mary.

My first impulse had been to slam the door. My next to fall into his arms. In the end, all I could do was let them in.

Them.

I couldn't even think about it.

I pulled the paper toward me and took another look at the front page. It was unsettling, seeing your life there—your own home, your daughter, your husband. All your problems, your tragedies—public knowledge.

Setting aside the paper, I went to the living room to check on Sherry. I wanted to open the curtains to let in the cold sunlight. Instead, for the second morning in a row, I flicked on the lamp.

"I'm back, baby," I said, judging her temperature with my hand. "Your dad's in the shower. Are those people bothering you?" The crowd on the front lawn was singing again, but I couldn't make out the words. "Are you hungry? It's almost snack time. Another hour or so."

It was Friday, but with Simon spending the night, I had given Ruth the day off. She offered to come in just in case, but I'd shaken my head. "I think we'll be all right."

As she left, she turned in the doorway to look at me, unsure whether I was angry or understanding.

I wasn't sure either.

I went to the window and peered out, pressing my eye to the crack between the frame and the blind, hoping not to be seen. Probably twenty-five people were now milling around on the front lawn.

No one even seemed to be looking at the house. No one except a little boy, at the front of the crowd, eyes locked on the living room windows, staring directly at me. He was tightly bundled in a winter coat, head covered by a red toque, and sitting on a sleeping bag. Our eyes met, and he smiled, then looked down at the ground in front of him.

I let the curtains fall back. I recognized the little boy from the front page of the paper—Jeffrey, six years old and suffering from leukemia.

At the kitchen table, I examined the group picture of the vigil outside the house, the faces in a luminous half circle. And there he was, barely visible in one corner, partially hidden by sets of legs. He was seated exactly as he was now, his back to the camera, his attention completely focused on Sherry's window.

It was as if he hadn't moved in—what, twelve hours? Fourteen? Fourteen hours on the cold ground? And for what?

For what?

Simon

It was strange to be naked in the bedroom after such a long time away. It felt familiar yet at the same time alien. Most of my clothes were still in the drawers and hanging in the closet. I pulled out a pair of jeans and a shirt, socks and underwear, folding the dirty clothes I had just taken off and leaving them outside the bathroom door.

I showered using the same soap, the same shampoo, as if the last few months had been only a dream. I found one of my razors in the cupboard.

When I got back downstairs, Karen was still staring at the front page of the newspaper.

"Much better," I said with a gusto I didn't entirely feel, picking up our mugs from the table. "Can I get you another cup?"

She didn't answer me for so long, I began to wonder if I had actually said the words out loud. Then she looked up at me. "What are we going to do, Simon? What are we going to do?" Her eyes were desperate.

"I don't know. I feel like it's out of our hands."

She pushed the paper toward me. "Look at this," she said, tapping the photograph with an extended finger. "Look. His name's Jeffrey. He's got leukemia—"

I nodded. "I know. I read the—"

"He's only six years old, Simon. He's six years old and he's dying and he's been sitting out in front of our house all night."

"What are you saying?"

"He's got no chance. Can you imagine being six years old and being told that you're not going to get any older? That you'll never grow up?"

I wanted to reach out to her, to make it all go away, but I couldn't.

"Can you imagine having no hope?"

"Karen—"

"No hope, except for a little girl—"

"Karen—"

"What if someone told us . . . What if someone said there was someone who could help Sherry?"

"Karen, what are you trying to say?"

"What if Sherry can help that little boy? How can we let all of those people suffer, when—"

"We don't know that Sherry can—"

"We *do* know, Simon."

"We *don't* know," I repeated. "I would have thought that you of all people—"

"I know, but—"

"Fairy tales. That's what you called them, all of those stories about saints and miracles, all that dogma your mother tried to ram down your throat. Fairy tales."

"I know. But Simon," she said, "look at the evidence. Look at what happened to Ruth. And to her sister. And to that woman who reported it to the paper—Those things *happened.*"

I walked over to the counter and poured myself another cup of coffee. "So what do you want to do?"

"You're angry."

I shook my head. "I'm not angry. I'm—scared. What happens if we bring him in here? What happens if . . . if Sherry *can't* heal him? And what if she *can?* What then? Do we let everyone in? And what does it do to Sherry, every time she . . ." I choked on the word. "Every time she heals someone?"

"But what—?" Karen was cut off by a loud knock at the front door. She rose automatically from her chair, but I waved her down.

"I'll get it. It's probably a reporter."

"Be careful."

I was surprised by the concern in her voice. "I will."

I opened the door just a crack at first.

"Mr. Barrett?" the stranger asked, meeting my furtive eye. "I'm Father Peter." He was dressed in crisply pressed black trousers, coat and vest over a black shirt, buttoned all the way to his neck, and topped with a stiff white collar. He was almost bald, save for a light trace of hair along the ridges of his scalp. He wore a pair of wire-rimmed glasses over cold gray eyes. Tall and painfully thin, his skin stretched tight over his chin and cheekbones. He wasn't an old man, but with the shaved head and the dour expression, he seemed skeletal.

"Yes?" I answered, not loosening my hold on the door.

"Mr. Barrett, I'd like to speak with you and your wife." He glanced back. The crowd was beginning to gather behind him.

"Why?"

"It would be better if we discussed that inside the house."

I opened the door, seeing little to fear in a priest. As he slipped in, there came shouts of protest from the people outside.

Karen was standing just beyond the foyer.

The priest stepped forward, his hand extended. "Mrs. Barrett, I'm Father Peter. I'm very pleased that you're giving me this opportunity to speak with you." There was a chill in the air, and the cold seemed to radiate from him. "I'd like to meet Sherry, if I could," he said, lowering his hand when Karen didn't take it.

"Why?" she asked flatly.

He sighed. "I was sent to see you by the archbishop—"

"We're not Catholic," Karen said.

The priest smiled, revealing yellow teeth. "That's why he sent me. I'm not directly affiliated with the diocese. I don't preach, I don't have a home church—"

"Yes, but why are you here?" I interrupted.

"The archbishop called me this morning, quite concerned about the story in the newspaper, the coverage on the television news. He asked me to stop by—informally—and try to find out what was going on." As he spoke, he toyed with a coin in his left hand, the way people might finger a rosary.

The coin caught the light, flashed through his fingers, tumbled.

Surprisingly, Karen stepped to one side. "Sherry's right through here." I followed them uneasily into the living room.

The priest went directly to Sherry's bed and turned back the covers. Karen stood to one side; I could see how tense she was. I felt the same way. He lifted Sherry's right arm, turning it to expose her palm.

"What are you doing?" I asked.

Karen answered before he could. "He's looking for stigmata."

"And there are none," he said as he checked Sherry's other hand. "That makes it considerably easier."

"That makes *what* considerably easier?" I asked.

He ignored me, tucked Sherry back in, then straightened up. "I've come to make you an offer," he said. "The archbishop has authorized me to tell you that the Church is willing to undertake an investigation into . . . these matters." He leaned forward, his tone confiding. "You do understand that an investigation must be done."

I shook my head. "Why?"

"To make her into a saint," Karen muttered.

"No." The priest turned to me. "The investigation will find that absolutely nothing miraculous has transpired here. The newspaper will print a correction. You and your family will be left in peace. The three people who claim to have been healed by your daughter will be revealed to be—" He waved his hand as if pulling the story from the air. "—fraud artists trying to take advantage of you, or religious fanatics, or perhaps to be suffering from dementia." He was completely casual, his voice utterly flat. "Upon examining their medical records, it will be revealed that they never suffered from the conditions your daughter supposedly healed them of. Cancer, whatever." He smiled again, and I was reminded of a dog showing its teeth.

"It will be quite a scandal for a while," he continued. "But the investigation will find that neither of you had any knowledge of what was going on, that you and Sherry had been victimized." He shrugged, as if this plan made such perfect sense there was no need to explain further.

"Why?" I asked. Karen's eyes moved between the priest and me.

His tone had the exaggerated care and condescension I imagined he used to speak to a child. "The Church finds that it is in its best interests if any claim of miracles is refuted as quickly as possible. Can you imagine what it will be like as the stories of Sherry start to spread? It must be very difficult for you now, with even those few people out there, holding you prisoner in your own home. Do you know how many people visit Lourdes each year? Don't you want this problem to disappear?" He paused, an effect I recognized from the courtroom.

"That doesn't explain what the Church—"

"It's about faith," Karen said, her thoughtful gaze on the priest. "Right? What's faith worth, what's heaven worth, if there are everyday miracles? What role does the Church have if people have direct access to God?"

The priest smiled his cold smile, neither confirming nor denying what she was saying. "Mr. and Mrs. Barrett, I came here to offer you a way out of the dilemma you currently face. I urge you to consider this carefully, and consider the repercussions of any decision you make. How your lives will be affected—"

"How our lives will be affected?" Karen repeated. "And what about them?" She gestured toward the window. "What about all of those people who Sherry could help? Is the Church comfortable denying them hope?"

"Mrs. Barrett," he said in measured tones. "There is no reason to believe that anything miraculous has occurred here. And frankly, the Church is not concerned with what happens to people who put their faith in snake handlers or faith healers." He started for the front door. "Those are choices people make. Your concern should be with the choices you make."

"Are you threatening us?" I asked.

The priest turned, and we both stepped back despite ourselves. "Mr. Barrett, I have considerable experience with matters like this. Things can become very difficult if these situations are not resolved quickly and quietly." The darkness of his eyes left no doubt—this *was* a threat, not a warning. "I'll check back with you in a couple of days."

He opened the front door and set off down the walk as if we had just had the most casual of visits. I hurried to close the door behind him, trying to ignore the press of faces staring in. I caught sight, out of the corner of my eye, of the boy with leukemia still sitting on the front lawn, still staring at Sherry's curtained window.

As I came back into the room, Karen was pacing, muttering to herself. "It's all the same old bullshit you think went out with the Dark Ages."

"A lot of people think that miracles went out with the Dark Ages."

"That's not what my mother would say. Christ, when she was here last month, she told me that she had asked her priest if they could do some fund-raising so we could take Sherry to Lourdes. And the priest agreed." She stopped her pacing, shook her head. "I thought I'd left all of that behind. How the hell did we get into this? And the worst part is, what he was saying made sense. In a way. Wouldn't it be easier if all this just went away?"

"I was thinking the same thing."

Of their own accord, my arms opened and I found Karen in them, her arms around my waist, her head against my chest. It felt like the most natural thing in the world to stroke her back, breathe in the scent of her hair.

"What are we going to do?" she asked.

## Leo Tanner

I parked the van behind the truck from the TV station. I turned off the engine and looped the springy key ring around my wrist, just like Mr. Perkins always told me. I sat there for a minute, looking at the newspaper on the other seat.

The little girl was so beautiful. Sherilyn Barrett. She looked just like an angel. Or like the Holy Mother in those paintings where she looks so peaceful, her eyes looking up to heaven.

The newspaper didn't give the whole address, but this had to be the place. Why else would there be TV trucks everywhere? Why else would all those people be in the front yard? I sat there, though, looking out the windshield. I wanted to be sure.

"Be careful, and you won't make any silly mistakes." That's what Mother always says. I didn't want to make a silly mistake.

So I read the article again, even though I knew it almost by heart already. I'd been waiting all morning for my lunch break so I could come, ever since Mr. Perkins had showed me the newspaper in the break room when I got to work.

"I guess you'll be interested in this," he said, pointing to the picture of the little girl who looked just like an angel.

I read the story while I had my coffee and a chocolate doughnut. Then we had to go out to fix a broken sewer main and a flooded basement. I did all the digging and lifting, but then I had to wait for the other guys to do their jobs. So I couldn't come to the house until lunchtime. I could hardly stand it. I just had to see her, to see if what the papers said was true.

Taking a deep breath, I opened the door and climbed out of the van. I made sure to lock it after I closed the door. Better safe than sorry. That's something else Mother always says. Mr. Perkins was really nice to let me use the van, and I didn't want anything to happen to it.

There was a crowd of people with cameras and Bibles and cups of coffee on the sidewalk in front of the house, and I had to walk on the street to go around them.

I walked up to the crowd in the front yard. I was trying to smile, but I had a funny feeling like butterflies in my belly.

I stood near the back. I smiled at the people around me, and some of them smiled back, but they all looked a little scared. It's because I'm so big—nobody ever wants to talk to me. So I just stood there, holding my newspaper, talking softly to the Holy Mother.

"Hail Mary, full of grace . . ."

Everybody jumped when the front door opened. A priest came out of the house, and the door slammed behind him. I could tell he was a priest. He looked like one even though he was only wearing a collar and no robe. His long black coat was sort of like robes, anyway.

Everyone on the lawn backed away from him. He started down the walk, but he stopped when he saw me standing in his way.

He looked me up and down from my head right down to my toes. He looked at the paper in my hand. He was playing with a nickel or a quarter. The sun caught the coin as he twisted it and flipped it between his thumb and finger.

Then he smiled at me. I wasn't expecting that, and I smiled back.

"Hello, Leo," he said, extending his hand.

"How . . ." I tucked the newspaper under my arm and took his hand and shook it, not too hard and not too soft, just like Mother taught me. I'm always careful not to hurt people. There's no reason to be a bully just because you're bigger. "How do you know my name?"

He smiled again. "It's on your overalls."

I looked down at the patch on my uniform. LEO TANNER.

He held on to my hand with both of his. "Why are you here, Leo Tanner?" he asked.

"I came to see the little girl. The one who can do miracles."

"You saw the story in the newspaper?" Without really noticing it, we had gone through the gate and I was walking with him along the sidewalk toward the van.

I nodded. "I've got a big book about miracles at home," I told him. "I never thought I'd actually get to see someone who could do miracles for real."

"I could tell you about miracles," he said. "Would you like that?" He had a funny look on his face. I couldn't tell if he was smiling or angry.

I nodded, and then stopped.

"I'd like to learn about miracles," I said.

This time I was sure that he was smiling.


*"Thanks, Diane. I'm Bill Stewart, live at the Barrett home here in Fernwood, where we've had, in the last few minutes, what may be a significant development in this story. Moments ago, Simon Barrett, father of Sherry Barrett—who you'll remember is the little girl who was in that tragic hit-and-run accident back in April, and may in fact be capable of healing—Mr. Barrett moments ago came out of the house, onto the front step for his first public appearance. Let's go to the tape."*

*SIMON BARRETT: Is Donna Kelly here? Donna Kelly? Donna, I'd like to have a word with you and Jeffrey if I could. Just for a moment . . . Come right through here. . . .*

*BILL STEWART: As I said, that was a few moments ago. No one here knows what is going on. There are some in the crowd who believe that they've called Jeffrey Kelly, who is a six-year-old with terminal leukemia, there are some who believe that he has been called in to be healed by Sherry Barrett, although we have no confirmation of this.*

DIANE OLIVER *(in studio): Bill, what's the mood like in the crowd?*

BILL STEWART: *Diane, that's an interesting question. There are a couple of dozen people here, a lot of them have been here all night. A number of them protested after Mr. Barrett closed the door, but overall the crowd is very calm. There are a number of very sick people here, wanting a chance to see Sherry Barrett. If Jeffrey Kelly has been called in to be healed, then maybe it bodes well for everyone else here.*

DIANE OLIVER: *Thank you, Bill. That was Bill Stewart live. . . .*

## Karen

As Donna Kelly and her son Jeffrey stepped into the foyer, they both bent to take off their shoes. "Don't worry about that," I said.

"We really should," Donna said, helping her son with his shoes. "It's pretty muddy on your lawn."

"You were really out there all night?" I asked.

She nodded sheepishly.

"Let's go into the family room."

She was a small woman, young and fit, and she looked like she might once have been happy. With her blond hair pulled into a ponytail, she had the look of someone who worked with kids, in a day care or a preschool. Jeffrey was everything a six-year-old boy should be—small and cute and shy, blushing and turning away as Simon and I introduced ourselves to him. But there was a brittle brightness about him from the taut translucency of his skin. Under the toque he was bald.

No one seemed to know what to say once we were all sitting down. I decided to lead with honesty. "We, Simon and I, we don't really know . . ." I smiled at Donna, and at Jeffrey sitting next to her, craning his head toward the living room. "We don't really know what we're doing with all of this. It sort of took us by surprise."

Donna nodded. "It must be terrible for you. I mean, I can't imagine being in the position you're in, but I know . . . I know what it's like to face losing a child. . . . And then all this. This circus—"

"That's a good word for it." I didn't point out that she was part of that circus.

"I'm sorry we were out there . . . ," Donna stammered. "We were at the hotel when we saw the thing on the news and we caught a bus up to the mall right away. It was pretty easy to find your house, with the reporters and all." She looked down at her hands, folded in her lap.

"Hotel?" I asked.

"We're not from here. We live in Seattle. We're just up for a few days."

"Holiday?" Simon asked.

Donna glanced at Jeffrey. "It's . . . You know those Make-A-Wish people? Jeffy's been seeing the ads for Victoria on the TV and he wanted—they're paying for us to have a few days up here in a nice hotel. See the museums and stuff. I never would have been able to afford it on my own."

Simon looked at me out of the corner of his eye. "It can't be easy for you."

She pursed her lips. "It's hard, yeah. The medical expenses have pretty much wiped us out. I had to quit my job to take care of Jeffrey, and we moved back in with my mom."

"And his father?"

She shook her head. "High school. I haven't seen him since graduation." Donna laid a hand on Jeffrey's thin leg and squeezed it. "But we do okay, don't we, bud?"

"When can we go see Sherry?" Jeffrey asked, as if discussing a visit to McDonald's. He looked around the room for someone to answer his question.

Donna patted his leg. "We'll see, baby, okay? You remember that this was a maybe, right?"

"Maybe right!" he repeated.

I looked across at Simon. He cleared his throat. "We don't really know how this works. We don't know why. Or how—"

"Mr. Barrett," she interrupted.

"Simon."

She blushed and looked down at her lap again. "Simon, I'm sorry, and please don't misunderstand me, but the why and the how of it aren't really that important to me. Is it true? Did the news get it right? Did your little girl cure that woman's cancer?"

I glanced across at Simon, then nodded. "We think so. Yes."

"Oh my God," she said. I watched her fingers tighten on Jeffrey's thigh. After a moment he pushed her hand away. "Ow, Mommy!"

"Sorry, honey," she said, but her attention was focused entirely on Simon and me. "Would you . . . Do you think it would work on Jeffrey?"

Before I could speak, Simon answered, "We really don't know, but let's give it a try."

"Oh God," she whispered, tears streaking her face. "Thank you—"

Jeffrey turned toward her, his face twisted with worry. "What's wrong, Mommy? What's wrong?"

"It's nothing, hon. Mommy's just—"

"Hey, Jeffrey," Simon called out playfully. "Would you like to go and meet Sherry now?"

He stood up. "Yeah."

"I'm sorry," Donna sobbed after they'd left the room. "This is so stupid."

"No, it's not," I said, crouching in front of her, gently touching her knees. "It's not stupid. I just hope it works."

She shook her head again. "No. No. Even if, even if it doesn't, just the thought that maybe . . ."

I could hear my own thoughts in her voice. "I know. If someone were to tell me that Sherry . . . that there might be a way—" I shook my head. "We should go in there."

She smiled through her tears and nodded. As I started to stand up, she grabbed my hand, pulled it to her, and kissed the back of it, then pressed it to her tear-damp cheek. "Thank you, Karen. Oh God, thank you so much."

I didn't know what to say, so I pulled her up and led the way to Sherry's bedside.

Simon was explaining the feeding tube to Jeffrey. "So the food—"

"The juice," Jeffrey interrupted.

"The juice," Simon played along. "Goes down through this tube and into Sherry's tummy. So even though she can't eat, she still gets to have all the good stuff that she needs."

Jeffrey nodded. "I have something like this when I'm in the hospital, but it goes in my arm."

Simon noticed us over Jeffrey's head. "Here's your mom," he said.

Jeffrey looked up. "Mom, look, this is Sherry. She was—" He glanced at Simon, who nodded. "—she got hit by a truck and now she's never gonna wake up." He touched the side of Sherry's face, his tiny hand in perfect scale with her features. "Isn't that sad? She'll never wake up."

Glancing at me apologetically, Donna gently touched the back of her son's head. "Yes. Yes, that's very sad."

"Is that what's going to happen when I die?" he asked his mother, as if it were of no greater consequence than taking an afternoon nap, or being forced to eat his vegetables.

Donna looked like she was close to breaking. "It's something like that, honey."

Simon cleared his throat and beckoned me with a surreptitious twitch of his head. "How do we . . . ," he asked in a whisper as I reached him. Donna was looking over at us.

"Ruth said that she used Sherry's hands."

He nodded and stepped forward. "Hey, Jeffrey," he called, and the little boy turned toward him. "Can I show you something else? Do you want to feel how soft her hand is?" Simon gently lifted her arm, turning her palm to face the boy. "Here, go ahead. Touch it.

Jeffrey slowly reached out and, with a single finger, touched the center of Sherry's palm, pulling back quickly with a giggle.

"Oh, you didn't feel it!" Simon mock-scolded him. Jeffrey responded with another giggle. "Try it again."

Jeffrey shook his head, giggling still, making strange.

"Here, I know what . . . ," Simon started, shifting his hold on Sherry's arm. "Close your eyes."

Jeffrey closed his eyes, then opened them again.

"No peeking," Simon warned.

When Jeffrey closed his eyes the next time, Simon covered the boy's eyes with one hand. "Hey," he protested.

"I have to make sure that you're not peeking," Simon explained.

With his other hand, he gently laid the palm of Sherry's hand against Jeffrey's forehead, pushing back his toque.

"What's that?" Jeffrey asked, smiling brightly.

Donna held her breath.

"Guess," Simon said, pressing on the back of Sherry's palm.

"I don't know."

Donna's hand was at her mouth, choking back a sob.

"Come on, guess."

"I don't know!"

"Does it feel soft?"

"Uh-huh."

"Does it feel warm?"

"Uh-huh."

"Does it feel like it's got fingers?"

"Uh-huh." Jeffrey slowly brought his hand up, touching the back of Sherry's hand. "Is that Sherry?" He traced her fingers, and I heard Donna gasp.

Blood roared in my ears.

"It is," Simon said, lifting his hand away from Jeffrey's eyes and Sherry's hand away from his forehead in the same motion. "Aren't you a smart guy!" he joked, gently tucking Sherry back in. "Aren't you smart." He playfully pulled the toque low over Jeffrey's eyes.

Jeffrey pulled his hat up. "Is that how she's going to make me all better?"

His mother bent to hug him and scooped him into her arms, crushing him to her. "I don't know, baby. We'll see. We'll see what happens." She whispered, "Thank you."

"You're welcome, Mommy," he said.

Simon and I looked at each other across the room, both of us aware of the bridge we had just burnt behind ourselves.

There was no turning back.

*"This is Bill Stewart, live at the Barrett residence in Victoria, where just moments ago Simon Barrett announced that he'll be holding a news conference in a half hour. We'll bring coverage of that to you on the news at five. Meanwhile, it's been a very strange day here. A few*

*hours ago, the front door you see behind me opened and Simon Bar-*
*rett asked for Donna Kelly. Ms. Kelly and her son Jeffrey, who suffers*
*from leukemia, entered the house. Ms. Kelly left almost an hour*
*later, carrying her son and refusing to answer any questions. It's un-*
*clear what happened inside the house. Perhaps that's the reason for*
*the news conference we'll have for you at five."*

## Simon

It was cold on the front step. The reporters were in position below me,
a phalanx of microphones, of necks craned to get the best view, cameras raised to get the best shot. Behind them, the pilgrims stood vigil.

"Thank you for being here," I began, as if they were doing us a favor. "I have a brief statement, then I'll take a couple of questions." The
door opened behind me, and Karen came to stand next to me.

"Ladies and gentlemen, we are the parents of a little girl who was involved in a horrible accident. Our instincts are to protect Sherry at all
costs. At all costs. No parent would argue that instinct." I paused, making eye contact where I could with the journalists, as if they were a jury.
"When the news broke about the miracles for which our daughter was
supposedly responsible, we were taken completely by surprise. Our
first instinct was to pull back, to lock the doors and do everything we
could to protect Sherry from all of this." I gestured at them, at the cameras and the crowds.

"This afternoon, as you know, we spoke to Donna Kelly, and her son
Jeffrey. Jeffrey has terminal leukemia. Six years old, and no hope of
growing up. We spoke to his mother, another parent whose instincts are
the same as our own—to do anything she could to save her child.

"We still don't have enough information to confirm the rumors you
have heard. I don't know if we ever will. But earlier this afternoon—" I
shifted from foot to foot. "—earlier this afternoon, we attempted to
replicate the conditions of those healings with Jeffrey Kelly."

I pulled myself up to my full height and directed my gaze over the
fish-eyes of the cameras, toward the pale faces bent toward me, eyes
rapt.

"We're parents," I continued, speaking directly to the pilgrims. "And one of the things that being a parent requires us to do is to be good role models for our daughter, to teach by example. One of the things—" I found myself choking up, paused for a second. "—one of the things we wanted to teach Sherry is that she has a responsibility, as a human being, as a member of a community, to reach out to people if they need help. Not to walk past the beaten man at the side of the road."

I took a deep breath. "We don't know if what people claim about Sherry is true or not, but we just can't just walk past." As I watched, the hope that had been building in the pilgrims' faces peaked. Stress and worry spontaneously gave way to expressions of relief. Hope. The reporters looked stunned, as if this were the last thing they were expecting.

"So on Monday morning, at ten A.M., we're going to open the doors of this house to allow people access to Sherry. We don't know how this is going to work out." I had to raise my voice to be heard above the murmurs and whispers, the snapping of camera shutters. "We don't know how this is going to work out, so I'd like to ask for your patience and consideration as we try to come up with some sort of system. I don't know how hard this is going to be on Sherry, so we'll have to see, but I think that just a few hours a day . . . maybe ten to two? We'll have to see. Are there any questions?"

"Mr. Barrett, Suzanne George, *New Sentinel.* Are you confirming reports that your daughter is able to heal people?"

I fought the urge to snap at her. "As I stated, we're not confirming anything. If there's any possibility, though, I think we need to be open to trying to help as many people as possible."

"Mr. or Mrs. Barrett, Brad Roberts, CBC. Have you spoken to anyone from any of the churches or religious institutions about your daughter, about what's going on here?"

I glanced up to see Father Peter at the back of the crowd, studying me intently. Our eyes met. "My wife and I are agnostic. Religion doesn't enter into this."

The reporter from the *New Sentinel* started to ask another question, but the reporter from the CBC cut her off. "How can you claim that religion has nothing to do with this? If there are miracles—"

"Perhaps you should be talking to someone from one of the churches. I don't have the background to discuss the theory or the theology behind all of this. Next?"

Father Peter turned and walked down the driveway, quickly merging with the shadows. I guessed he wouldn't need to check back with us.

"Mr. Barrett, don't you see this as exploiting your daughter?"

I started to answer, but Karen stepped forward, laying her hand on my arm. "I love my daughter so much, I can't even begin to describe it. If someone told me that there was some way . . . If someone told me that there was a way that my daughter might be able to wake up, might be able to smile at me again, I would do anything in my power to make that happen." She took a deep breath, calming herself. "If I was in that position, and someone might be able to help, I would hope that they'd be willing to do so. That's all we're doing." With that, she went back into the house, closing the door behind her.

"That's all for now," I said, ignoring the cries for "just one more question, just one more."

I continued: "I'd like to ask, please, everyone go home. We'll be here at ten o'clock Monday morning, so there's no need for you to put your health further at risk by sitting out here in the cold. Go home, please. Take care of yourselves."

I ducked back inside, ignoring the voices behind me, closing them off with the front door.

From behind the curtains in the living room, Karen and I watched as most of the crowd dispersed. The press left first, hopping into cars and speeding away. I wondered what sound bite the five o'clock news would choose to run, and how the paper the next day would deal with the whole thing.

The pilgrims who had been at the house all night were slower to slip away. Some stayed to clean up, picking up their garbage, rolling up their sleeping bags before leaving the yard. Someone even cleaned up the mess of coffee cups and take-out wrappers the press had left scattered in the driveway. Someone else rolled up Jeffrey's sleeping bag and left it on the front step as they were going.

By five o'clock the yard was empty. The last pilgrim to leave shut the gate. It was as if nothing had happened.

## Mary

All day I managed not to answer the phone when it rang. Instead I'd pause in the middle of whatever I was doing—a long overdue cleaning, another chapter in my book—to listen to the answering machine as he left his messages.

Four messages in the past twenty-four hours. The first an hour after I had left his house, while I was out walking along the water. "Mary? It's Simon. Are you there?"

I'd gotten into his habit of checking a clock every time something happened, making a mental note of the time, measuring my life out in increments. Just like him.

9:40 A.M. "Mary, it's Simon. What happened to you last night? You just disappeared. I was worried. Listen, give me a call on my cell."

His voice was low. Not a whisper, but pitched low enough that Karen wouldn't hear him. I could picture him, sitting in their family room speaking softly into his tiny black phone, keeping one eye on the door, ready to cut it off should his wife appear.

I'd been through all of this before.

12:10 P.M. "Mary, it's Simon again. Are you there? Are you okay? Please call."

His voice was touched by tenderness and care, by worry. I should have explained why I had to go.

But what would I have said? "I'm leaving you so that you can choose between me and your wife. I'm leaving because you want me to leave—you just don't know it yet."

I almost picked it up. Too late. He'd hung up.

3:40 P.M. "Mary, it's Simon. Listen, I know you're mad at me. I know we need to talk. Please, just call me, okay? I love you."

Mad at him? Not a chance. I was too furious at myself even to think about him: what was I thinking, destroying a family like that? Taking a father away from his daughter, a husband away from his wife. Mad at you? God, no, Simon. And that last, that *I love you,* as if just saying it could make everything all right.

But love was easy. I had loved Simon long before he ever moved in, long before it was even a possibility that we could have a life together. Loving him was easy.

*Had been* easy.

5:55 P.M. "It's me. . . . I've . . . It's been a really long afternoon. . . . I don't know if you saw the news or not, but . . . I really need to talk to you. If you get this, please call."

I hadn't watched the news; I hadn't been doing anything except sitting around, putting CDs into the player, changing them after a few songs, unable to find anything that seemed to speak to me.

I couldn't stand to hear him in pain. I was reaching for the phone to call him when it rang. I jumped a little, then answered it. "Hello?"

"Party girl!" came the loud, familiar voice, almost a shout over the music in the background. I don't know if I was saddened or relieved that it wasn't Simon.

"Brian?"

"Who else, party girl? Where have you been hiding?" I hadn't spoken to him, to any of my friends, since Simon had moved in. "We thought you'd died!"

"No, not dead. Just in love . . ."

"That doesn't sound as happy as it should."

"Is it ever?"

"It's always a man, isn't it?" he said, more sympathetically.

I didn't need to answer. Brian and I had known each other since we were undergraduates, both headed for law school.

"Married, gay, or stupid?"

I found myself smiling. Brian can always do that. "Married. And stupid, I guess."

"Is this a bad one?"

"The worst," I answered. "And you?"

"This is the lawyer, right?"

I was a little surprised, but I shouldn't have been. Just because I hadn't spoken to Brian in the past few months didn't mean that he was out of the loop. "Yeah, it's the lawyer."

"I just saw him on TV. On the news."

"Him and his wife, right?"

He ignored the question. "Listen, party girl, I've got just the thing for you. Big rave, up the Peninsula somewhere. Love bus leaves at ten—"

"Brian, I'm not—"

"Listen," he said, suddenly serious, oddly maternal, his voice dropping an octave. "You need to get out, right?"

"I don't think—"

"Let me guess: you've been puttering around the apartment all day, not answering the telephone, in a cleaning tizzy, not eating, trying to think of anything else but him, right? Changing the CDs every half hour?"

Ah, Brian. "Right."

"So you need to get out."

"Brian, I'm not—"

"Look, we'll dance. We'll drink some smart drinks, we'll talk, we'll just hang, okay?"

He was impossible to resist. "Well—"

"I'll be there at ten," he jumped in. "Wear your Day-Glo lipstick." He hung up.

As I cradled the receiver, I looked at the answering machine, the red light flashing four times, pausing, then flashing again. I thought for a moment about calling, just to let him know I was okay.

Instead, I pressed the button and erased the messages.

The light went out.

## Karen

I was afraid to admit to myself how good it felt to have Simon at home. It was like what Donna had said, about getting accustomed to the worst and accepting it, and how anything else, any slight hope, was almost too much to bear.

Sitting at the table, a glass of merlot in front of me, watching him cook, I was reminded of the early days of our relationship. That first basement apartment, so tiny, so dark. We had rented it furnished with a god-awful cream vinyl chair and couch, a bed that felt like it had no mattress on it at all, and a rickety table with two chairs. We had no money, but it never felt like suffering. He could whip up a good meal from a few vegetables, some noodles, and the tiniest pieces of meat—all that we could afford. It was so easy to romanticize the poverty of those days, both of us in school, no TV, always working or reading or going for walks or making love. There was no sense of a real world outside dictating our actions. Not yet.

When the telephone rang, Simon looked at it with suspicion. I couldn't blame him. I'd just hung up after a painful near-hour with my mother.

"Is it true?" she had started, without any warning or preamble.

"Mom—"

"Father Jean just called me and said he had heard from someone in Victoria—"

"Mom—"

"It *is* true, isn't it?"

I could picture her clutching her rosary beads to her heart.

"I was going to call. . . ."

"Oh, Karen, you must be so happy."

"Happy?"

"To be so blessed."

I sighed, and Simon shook his head, obviously piecing together the conversation.

"I wouldn't say happy, Mom. I'm . . . the house is under siege. There are reporters and people everywhere—"

"They just want to see the miracle," she answered. "They just want their questions put to rest. Just like you."

"Mom," I said warningly, gritting my teeth.

"It's true, Karen. It's what I've always said: God doesn't depend on your belief or disbelief, He just is. And now you see proof—"

"Mom, I really don't want to—"

"I've called Air Canada," she interrupted. "They can get me on a flight Monday—"

"No," I said, so firmly Simon looked startled.

"I beg your pardon?"

"I said no, Mom," I said, trying to stay calm.

"But, Karen—"

"Now is not a good time, Mom. Let us . . . give us a couple of weeks to get used to this. Maybe right after New Year's—"

"That's a month!"

"Mom, you were just here, not three weeks ago."

"But that was before—"

"Before what, Mom? Sherry's the same as she ever was."

I could hear her sigh over the phone. "I know how tough it must be for you," she said. "To have everything you believe—or don't believe, I guess—fall apart with this proof."

The conversation degenerated from there.

So when the telephone rang again, mere minutes after I had hung up, I hesitated.

"It's up to you," Simon said. "The machine will pick it up if you don't."

I decided to chance it.

"Karen, it's Jamie." I waved Simon's concern away. He turned back to his cooking. "I just saw you on the news. How are you holding up?"

"Fine, I suppose."

"Are you guys really sure about this, this whole thing with letting people in to see Sherry? It's going to turn into a zoo."

She was repeating my own fears back to me. "We don't really have a choice in the matter."

"Well, yes, you do."

"We can't just—" I couldn't finish the sentence.

"I suppose."

There was an uncomfortable silence.

"Do you need any help? I know you'll have Ruth there. But Simon?" She trailed off.

"Simon's still here." He glanced toward me at the sound of his name. "He's cooking dinner."

"Ah. Well, he's going to have to go to work, and, well, I seem to have the time." I hadn't often heard Jamie at a loss for words.

"I'd really appreciate that," I said. "We've got no idea what to expect, so . . ."

"I'd be happy to come over."

"Thanks, Jamie."

"Don't worry about it. I'll be there, what, eight o'clock? Just to be sure everything's all ready? Or should I come earlier? Or—"

I couldn't help but smile. "Whenever works for you. I'm just happy you're coming."

"Me, too. I'll see you Monday morning, then."

"Yeah."

"Jamie wants to help on Monday morning," I explained when I hung up.

He nodded. "Good. We'll need as much help as we can get."

"Are you going to be here?" I asked, not even realizing the magnitude of my question until he glanced at me. "I mean, don't you have to go to work?"

"Actually, I thought I'd call in, take some personal time."

"Really?"

"Really."

I was speechless for a moment. "Okay, then. Jamie will be here, and Ruth, and you and I. We should be okay."

He returned his attention to his cooking. I took a sip of my wine. "Have you spoken to Mary?" I asked before I lost my nerve.

He shook his head. "No, not yet. I've left a couple of messages."

"I'm sorry," I said.

"Sorry?"

"This must be very hard for her. And you."

He looked at me for a long moment, then nodded. "Grab a plate," he said. "Dinner's ready."

After we had been sitting in silence at the table for several minutes, I said, "Can I ask you something, Simon?"

"Of course." He was watching me warily.

I set my fork on the edge of my plate and picked up my wineglass. "You and Mary. How long had that been going on, you know, before . . ." I took a sip of my wine.

He sighed, and leaned back in his chair. "I . . . it was . . . I don't know, I guess a year or so before I moved out." He spoke without looking at me, without meeting my eye.

I shook my head. "I never even suspected."

He was still looking away.

"I was . . . stunned," I continued, filling up the empty spaces between us.

At this, he turned to me. "Do we have to talk about this now?" he asked quietly. "Haven't we got enough to worry about?"

"I'm sorry. I was just—"

"Don't be sorry. But let's not talk about it, okay? Not right now," he said.

I bit my lip. "Okay."

But I needed to ask him why. I needed to know why, after being together for more than fifteen years—

"No. Not okay," I said. "I'd like to know why."

He stood and picked up the bottle. Filling both our glasses, he said, "Why don't we go sit in the family room?"

Ruth

I pulled my car to the curb and turned off the engine. I left the keys in the ignition as I looked up the street at the front of the church, the doors flung wide, spilling light into the dark of the evening.

I still wasn't sure if I was going to go in, or if I was going to start the car and drive away. I had already driven past three times over the course of the day, but something kept drawing me back.

The rational, professional part of my mind tried to dismiss the feeling, to play it down the same way I had been doing in the weeks since I had noticed the absence of pain in my hands.

I had been around doctors, around patients, my entire adult life. I had seen people recover from the most dreadful of conditions, seen the look of relief on people's faces. Every recovery was a miracle, in a way.

Wasn't it?

But after seeing the people at the Barrett house, I couldn't fool myself anymore. What Sherry had done was something of a different order altogether. It was the hope in their faces that awakened me, that reminded me of what a gift I had received. I couldn't downplay what had happened.

But there were so many questions. Everything had changed. I had spent my life concerned with the how of things: how a treatment worked, how a patient recovered. And now that I was confronted with questions of why, I didn't know what to do. I didn't know what to think.

I pulled the keys from the ignition and locked the car, then walked slowly up the sidewalk toward the church. There were a few other people around, and they smiled when they saw me. We walked up the stairs together.

## Simon

"I just need to know why you threw everything we had away," Karen started as she settled on the couch. I sat down across from her, the wine bottle on the table between us. "Knowing the truth, even if it's unpleasant, has to be better than not knowing. Or imagining."

"I don't really understand it, myself," I said. I braced myself. "This will sound stupid. Clichéd. But I suppose there's nothing really original about any of this, is there?" I sipped before continuing. "We went out for a drink after work. There was a whole crew of us. Stevens had just—" I thought for a moment. "—Stevens had just won Dempster, and we all went out to celebrate." I could remember that night with perfect clarity. "Mary had been working for the firm for maybe a couple of months? No more than that. We sat next to each other. Had a few drinks."

"Did you sleep with her?"

I shook my head. "No. Not then. We just talked. She asked me, point blank, if I was jealous of Stevens. I mean, Jesus, Kyle Stevens? But for some reason, I told her the truth. I told her I was." I could picture the sweater she had been wearing, how her hair, still long at that point, was held back with a comb that came from India, the smooth skin at the base of her throat. I remembered wanting to feel the pulse beating there. More than that, though, I could remember the tremendous openness of her expression as she asked me about my jealousy—her forthrightness, her attention.

"I mean, Stevens, Christ, what a yutz. But she read it right. He was coming off the biggest case of his career, and I was jealous. And I admitted it."

"You never told me."

"No, I never did."

"But you told her."

I nodded. "Yes." I tried to figure out a way to put my thoughts into words. "She had no expectations of me. I could say, I could do anything. I felt—"

"Free," she finished.

It was the word that I had been going to use, but hearing it spoken aloud, especially in Karen's voice, I could see it wasn't right. "No. No, that's not it. I felt genuine. I felt like I could be myself."

She seemed shocked. "But we've always been honest with one another."

I didn't respond.

"I guess I should know better than to believe that, shouldn't I?" She shook her head. "So what else didn't you tell me the truth about?" she asked. "Beyond the obvious, of course."

"It's not about honesty, so much," I tried.

"Then what is it about?"

"It was about me. At least, me more than it was about us. I just . . . I felt like I hadn't been able to be myself for a long time." I waited.

The reaction I had been expecting didn't come. She blinked, trying to understand. "But I never—"

"It wasn't you," I interrupted. "This isn't, this was never about you."

She shook her head sharply. "No. You can't betray me, leave me for another woman, then try to tell me that it's not about me. You don't get let off that easily."

"I'm not trying to get let off. I'm just trying to explain—"

"Then what *is* it about, if it's not about me?" she asked.

"It's about us, I guess. In part . . . about the relationship. The roles we play—"

"What *roles*?" she asked, sliding sarcastically over my word.

I thought for a moment. "Do you remember how hard it was, back when we were trying to get pregnant?"

She nodded.

"How hard it was on you?"

"And you were there for me."

I nodded this time. "Yes. Yes, I was." I tried to smile. "But who was there for me?" She gaped at me. "That sounds stupid. Stupid and self-ish and weak, but it was like I didn't have anyone. *Anyone*."

"You had me," she said quietly, already knowing herself that this wasn't true.

I shook my head. "How could I talk to you? You were so scared, so upset. Could I have told you how scared I was? How would you have reacted?" I didn't allow her a chance to answer. She didn't need to. "It would have made everything worse." I tried to make the words, the terrible words, make sense.

She bit the inside of her lip as I spoke, staring into her glass.

"So I didn't. I couldn't. I just kept it all in. I was trying to be strong for you—"

"I'm sorry," she said without looking up.

"No, it's just . . . That was the right thing to do. I know that. It was the only thing I could do. But I ended up being stuck in that role. Always strong. You leaned on me—"

"I leaned on you," she whispered.

We sat for a long time without speaking, without looking at each other.

"Why didn't you ever say anything?" she said finally, setting her empty wineglass on the coffee table, next to the bottle. "To me—I mean."

"I didn't even know anything was wrong," I answered. "Until Mary asked me about Kyle Stevens, and then I knew that there were some things that I just couldn't talk to you about anymore. Things that, by the way we had defined our relationship, couldn't exist in it."

"And Mary was someone you could be honest with."

"She was someone I didn't have to play a role with," I corrected.

She smiled wryly at me. "It's the same thing."

I didn't know whether to agree or disagree.


Henry


Tim was on the roof of the library, leaning against one of the ventilation shafts, looking up at the sky. The smoke from his cigar seemed to shine as it curled away, the tip an orange glow.

I had to wait for him to look up at me.

"I've been doing some reading," I said.

"Ah, yes. Well, come and sit down. Tell me what you know." He gestured at the roof, his motions a shadow against a shadow, barely visible.

I was carrying several books, and holding my place in one with my index finger, but I managed to settle myself next to him.

"Isn't it a gorgeous night? A little cold, but look at those stars."

"I've been doing some reading," I started again.

"Would you like a cigar?" he asked. "I've got a couple of extra. I steal them from the shop around the corner."

I shook my head. "No, no. I don't smoke."

He shrugged. "You're missing out. There's really nothing quite like it." He held the cigar before him at arm's length, rolling it between his fingers. "More of a meditation than a vice, really."

"I've been reading . . . ," I tried again.

He sighed, took a gentle pull on his cigar. "Let me guess: you've discovered old Ahasuerus?"

"What?" I was surprised to hear him say the name. I carried on, trying to keep my thoughts organized now that I had his attention. "There's a story," I fumbled with my books for a moment before realizing that, even with the light of the city around us, it wasn't bright enough for me to read. I had to rely on my memory. "There's a story, in the Bible—"

"*Not* in the Bible," he interrupted. "Apocryphal. Scholars seem to think it was added in the Middle Ages, but accounts go all the way back to the time of the Gospels."

I shook my head, amazed. "So you know."

"You'll find, young Henry," he said, "that there's not a lot that surprises me anymore. Not for a very long time. But tell me, what did you find?"

"There's a story, about a man who was cursed—"

"Punished."

I glanced over at him, but I couldn't read his expression in the dark. "Doomed to wander the world until the end of time because he hit Jesus as he was on his way to be crucified."

"The avenue of sorrows . . ."

"So he was cursed—"

"He didn't hit him."

"What?"

The tip of his cigar glowed as he took a long pull. "The Jew. The Wandering Jew. He didn't hit Christ. Oh, I know what the books say. This man pushed or shoved or hit or spit on Christ as he walked the avenue of sorrows toward Calvary, dragging his cross.

"Truth is, Ahasuerus was a shopkeeper. A simple man. A wife, six kids. And that day was just like any other day. Another execution. A couple of thieves, another one of those cult figures. Jerusalem was full of them in those days.

"Crucifixions were like big festivals. There was always a parade. People would follow the Romans and the victims along the route by the hundreds. A good day for business if you were lucky enough to have a shop right on the route like Ahasuerus did."

I could almost picture it in my mind as he spoke.

"Christ was weak. He'd been beaten; he hadn't eaten in days. The cross was heavy, and he just couldn't continue. So he stopped in the doorway of this shop. Right in the doorway. And the shopkeeper came out, took a look at the crowd of people following along behind the Romans, took a look at this, this criminal who was blocking the way into his store, and he just told Christ to move along. Told him that he couldn't stay there." His voice dropped. "So Christ turned to him and said, 'I won't wait here. But you will. You'll wait until I return.' And he picked up his cross and carried on to Calvary."

Tim blew a big cloud of cigar smoke into the night. "The shopkeeper didn't think anything of it. Just another day. Another execution. He forgot all about it until his wife died, years later. And then his children died. Not young. They had lived their whole lives. It's a terrible thing when a child dies before his parents. It's unnatural. But the shopkeeper outlived his children. And his grandchildren. And on his hundredth birthday, this shopkeeper, who had meant no offense, was still thirty-eight years old, the same age he had been on the day of Christ's crucifixion. He hadn't changed. He hadn't aged, not even as everyone he loved grew old and died around him."

"And then?"

He continued speaking into the middle distance. "He ran. There was nothing else he could do. There were obviously powerful forces at work. He had stepped between—"

"Between?"

"Imagine a curtain on a stage. Out front, there are people, there's laughter, there's life. People making their entrances and exits. All of us merely players and all that. And backstage, backstage are the forces that make it all happen, the things that you don't see, the mechanics of the world. The Wandering Jew stepped between, between life and the mystery behind the curtain. He was no longer of the world onstage. He couldn't stay.

"No one knew him. No one knew that he was the same man. No one could know. So he took another name, and he ran. And he's been running ever since."

"So this," I gestured with the book. "The story's true?"

Finally he turned to me. "You'll find that many of the stories you'll read are true. Stories like the Flying Dutchman. Thomas the Rhymer. Dorian Gray. Prester John. The Emperor Barbarossa. The lore is full of stories of people who have stepped between. And there are hundreds—thousands—about whom nothing is written."

He took a long breath through his cigar.

"You."

He was telling me what I already knew, what I had put together without being able to put into words. What I knew, without believing.

"You've stepped between, Henry. Just like we all have. Whether it was when you hit that little girl with your truck, or when you tried to kill yourself, you stepped between."

"I don't understand."

He shrugged. "I've had much longer to think about this, young Henry, and I don't understand it either. I just know. You've stepped between, outside of the world you knew, but you're still connected to it."

"That's why no one can see me."

He nodded. "You're not a part of that world anymore. You have your own story now. The only people who can see you, who can hear you, are people inside your story. People who have a role to play . . ."

"People like you."

His smile disappeared. "And others. You must be careful, Henry, not to assume that you're invisible to everyone. There are people who have reason to see you. They won't always be jolly fat men with a love of books and good cigars."

I waited for him to continue. He didn't.

"Why can't I remember anything from before?"

"When you tried to die, you left your life behind, even your memories of it, but you couldn't pull away. Your story wasn't done. That's why we're here, waiting."

"Waiting? Is that it? Am I being punished for hitting that little girl? Am I waiting for the Second Coming?"

He chuckled. "It's strange to talk like that, isn't it? As if the Second Coming of Christ were Halloween, or New Year's Eve, a finite time . . . I don't know what you're waiting for, Henry. I don't know what forces are at play for you. I know that the Wandering Jew is waiting to make his amends. He's waiting to apologize, to beg for forgiveness, and he has to wait for Christ to return for that to happen." The cigar had burned down to a stub, and he dropped it to the roof between his feet, where it smoked for a long moment, then slowly went dark.

"How do you know so much about this?" I asked quietly.

He rose to his feet, stretching himself against the chill that the roof had brought to his muscles. "Time," he said. "I've had a lot of time to think about it."

Then he walked in silence back to the stairwell and disappeared inside, leaving me alone with the stars and the city.

*It was dark when the stranger arrived at the newspaper building. He had left this stop for last; the editor of a newspaper would always be near his newsroom until the next day's issue was safely put to bed.*

*He had taken off the collar after leaving Bradford & Howe. The senior partner had practically genuflected when the priest had asked for a moment of his time. In the end, he had come away with everything that he wanted in exchange for no more than a few moments of private confession and counsel.*

*For this meeting, however, the collar would be a liability.*

*He knew, before he opened the door to the newspaper, how the conversation would proceed, how the lies would break into heated denials, then dissolve into pleading and panic in the face of the proof. He had seen it many times.*

*And they always seemed so relieved when they learned his silence could be bought, so surprised that the cost of his silence was so low.*

*"Truthfully, I have no use for your money. What I need amounts to no more than a few column inches."*

*Within minutes, it would be accomplished. Months of planning, of waiting and watching, would have served their purpose. The stranger would walk into an office with nothing more than words—secrets—and walk out with promises.*

*The promises were more precious than silver, and the most powerful weapon he could wield.*

## Karen

Night sounds, both familiar and strange.

The dripping of the bathtub faucet a little slower than a heartbeat; the otherworldly click, then roar as the furnace burst into life; the slow, occasional pops and wheezes as the heat pipes cooled when the furnace went off, the motor and the fan of the fridge, the occasional voices of people walking past on the sidewalk.

After dinner, after the wine, Simon and I had worked together to get Sherry ready for bed. He had carried her into the bathroom, lowering her carefully into the tub, cradling her head as her hair floated in a nimbus around her face. He had held her as I dried her with a fluffy towel, as I powdered her and slipped a nightie over her head. While I warmed her nutritional supplement, Simon reconnected the feeding tube to the pump and diapered her. He told her a story while the machine fed her and I did the dishes. Without saying much, he made up his bed on the couch in the family room.

And then it was just Sherry and me, as it had been for so many nights. Her breath was slow and hypnotic, warm against my cheek as I bent to tuck her in, to kiss her face. Headlights falling across the curtains, laying shadows across the wall.

Door locked, porch light out, hall light on by force of habit—if Sherry woke and had to go to the bathroom, she would need to see her way.

I peered into the family room before I went upstairs. Simon's breath was rough and irregular. He slept with the sleeping bag pulled up to his throat, twisted onto his side on the narrow couch, face buried in one of the spare pillows.

What do you dream, Simon?

I dream of that first apartment, the funky smell from the unit down the hall that we used to joke meant that they must be "cooking dog for dinner again." I dream of the weight of your body in our first bed, the taste of you on my lips, the breadth of you inside me.

I dream of my father's funeral, the way you held me. I dream of Sherry's birth, the way you held her, your hands shaking, a look of awe, wonder, and terror in your eyes, and an openness I so rarely saw there.

I dream of Mary, of her long legs spread wide and you between them, the pale half moons of your buttocks thrusting into her, your fingers in her hair, her calling out your name in my voice.

I dream of killing you in your sleep, pressing my thumbs into your Adam's apple, the look in your eyes as you awake.

I dream of kissing you in your sleep, pressing my lips gently against your Adam's apple, the look in your eyes as you awake.

"Good night, Simon," I whispered.

As I walked away, my shadow followed, leaving the light from the hallway to fall on his closed eyes. He groaned a little, turned deeper into the pillow.

At the foot of the stairs I turned the light off and started up in darkness. I had gone three steps when I changed my mind and turned around.

Lifting the covers gently, I slid into Sherry's bed, nestling against her, losing myself in the smell of her, her hair, her skin, her warmth. I carefully curled one arm around her, sheltering her, protecting her. I drew her to me, lay waiting for her to press herself against me, the way she had when she was smaller. I waited. And waited.

## Leo

I did everything just like Father Peter said.

I waited until Mother had fallen asleep and then I picked him up downtown. I was real quiet when I got ready to go so I wouldn't wake her.

He was outside the cathedral like he said he would be. I didn't see him at first in the dark, so I stopped the van and waited. He opened the door without knocking. It scared me a little.

"Hello, Leo."

"Hello, Father."

He closed the door, but I didn't pull away. He looked at me.

"I can't go anywhere until you put on your safety belt," I told him. "That's what they taught us in Young Drivers. The car doesn't move until everybody puts on their safety belts. That's the rule."

He smiled and put on the safety belt. "There," he said. "It's important to follow the rules, isn't it?"

I nodded. "Very important." I started the van. "Where should we go?"

"Do you know how to get to the Dallas Road waterfront?" he asked.

"Where?"

"The waterfront at Dallas Road. Near the park, I think."

I thought for a minute. "Is that the place where people bring their dogs for walks?"

"Are there cliffs there? With benches?" he asked.

"I think so. Mother and I go there sometimes after church to watch the people with their dogs."

"Do you know how to get there?"

I nodded, and he smiled. "Good."

We parked under one of the trees that looks like it's always being pushed back by the wind. I had started to pull into a spot under the streetlight, but Father Peter said, "No, over there," pointing to the shadows. When we were walking away, I looked back and I could hardly see the van at all in the dark.

A few people were still playing with their dogs even though it was so late, but we went the other way. It was kind of scary. The bushes on either side of the walkway reached over my head like a tunnel. It was so dark, I couldn't barely see anything. It sounded like the ocean was right there, just past the bushes.

When we came out of the bush tunnel, we were right on top of the cliffs. I was scared to look down. Stay back and be careful. Better safe than sorry. It was cold and it was windy and I felt kind of like I had to pee.

Father Peter walked all the way to the bench at the very end of the sidewalk, turning a coin in his right hand. There was a big fat man sitting there smoking a stinky cigar. He stood up when he saw Father Peter.

"I see you've brought a bodyguard," he said, with a funny sound to his voice, like he came from somewhere else.

"Leo's a friend, Tim," Father Peter said. "That is what you're calling yourself these days, yes?" The fat man nodded. "I see you've come alone. Couldn't convince one of those thieves and liars from the library to come along?" He sat down on the bench, facing the cliffs and the ocean, and the fat man sat down next to him. He took a big puff on his cigar and blew out a big cloud of smoke.

"Don't I usually come alone? It's lonely work. I'd have thought you'd know that by now."

Father Peter smiled. "Aren't you afraid of me, even a little bit, after all these years?"

"Should I be? Should I be afraid of you wrestling me over these cliffs? We both know we'd just end up damp, and it's too cold a night for that."

I didn't really know what the fat man was talking about, but hearing him talk about the water and the cold made me have to pee even more.

"I can't say that it's good to see you," Father Peter said.

Tim shrugged. "It should hardly be a surprise."

"It's been quite some time, though."

"Since Lima. Those little girls. The twins."

Father Peter smiled. "I remember. Terrible what happened to them. And who was it before that? That whore in Oregon?" Father Peter shook his head. "It won't do you any good this time either."

"So you always say."

I really had to pee. I started to bounce up and down a little, but I stopped when I remembered what Mother would say about that.

"I don't know why you go on trying, Tim. I always win. That should be clear to you by now." Father Peter smiled, but I didn't think he looked very friendly. I thought that maybe he was angry with the man he called Tim. "Do you remember the French girl? The one who would be king?"

"Joan."

"Joan. Yes. You tried so hard to save her."

"Yes."

"And all you could do in the end was to watch as she burned."

"I remember you there. You were . . . a cardinal then, I think."

"The most powerful woman in the world. A beloved leader. And they burned her. They came out in the thousands to watch her die. She saved their country, and they spat on her ashes. Because I told them to."

"That was a long time ago."

Father Peter shrugged. "It's only become easier. With the little faith people have these days, all it takes is a few well-chosen words. A rumor here. A whisper there. And the problem takes care of itself."

"That doesn't mean I stop trying."

"No," Father Peter said. "No, it doesn't. How long have you been here?"

Tim looked like he was thinking. "Four years or so, I guess. It's a nice little city."

"From the very beginning."

The fat man nodded. "And you?"

"A few months. Just before the accident."

The accident? I couldn't understand what they were talking about. I had to pee really bad.

"That poor little girl."

Father Peter snorted. "I'm not here because she's a poor little girl."

The fat man looked sad. "No, you're here because you're the worst sort of zealot. You're the sort who destroys people's lives, who kills in the name of all you believe."

"All that I was taught, you mean. I'm just doing God's will in this world. Wasn't it He who rained down fire on Sodom? Who flooded the world?"

"I think you've forgotten all you were taught," Tim said. "I think you've spent so much time beweeping your outcast state, you've forgotten the very foundations of all you believe. The Flood? Sodom and Gomorrah? What about 'Thou shalt not kill'?"

"If it comes to that, I'll not stay my hand. I'll make my own reckoning when my time comes. I will be judged—"

"And found wanting. Again."

Father Peter shrugged.

"You would kill that child?"

"She wouldn't be the first I've put to the flames. Thou shalt not suffer a witch to live."

"She's not a witch. She's a little girl who has never done anyone wrong."

"She is an insult, an aberration. Whether she is evil, or a vessel for evil, makes no difference to me. There is only one savior, only one path to salvation. I will defend Him and the purity of His name from these pretenders, no matter the cost. This little girl cannot be suffered to spread her poison, and I will do whatever it takes to stop her, to stop her family. It's the Lord's work."

"So it has begun, then."

Father Peter nodded.

"And he's the first?" Tim gestured to me.

Father Peter nodded again. "The first of the true."

The fat man shook his head.

I couldn't stand it any longer. I turned around and ran back down the path, pulling open my pants as I went. I was peeing almost before I stopped at the edge of the bushes.

When I got back to the bench, Father Peter was alone. I couldn't see the fat man anywhere. "We're done here," he said quietly, not looking at me.

# Part 5

*December 8–9*

# Karen

Simon and I spent most of Saturday working around the house: planning, cleaning, moving furniture to clear paths for access. Access to our daughter.

It had been a long time since he and I had worked side by side on anything. It felt good to break a sweat with him, to laugh at our mutual ineptitude when it came to anything remotely handy. I was surprised, though. Simon actually built a credible ramp up one side of the front porch, out of a couple of sheets of plywood over some two by fours. When it was finished, we both jumped on it, and it held. Thankfully the reporters had left by that time.

I slept in on Sunday morning for the first time in months.

I had been dreaming of Simon. Nothing in particular, just the sense of being with him, of spending time with him, of being in the same bed. It had been so vivid, I was surprised when I woke up alone. I was even more surprised when, rolling onto my side and glancing at the alarm clock, I saw that it was after eleven.

"Shit," I muttered, sitting bolt upright. Adrenaline coursed through me, but I calmed as I realized that Simon was downstairs. I wasn't alone.

I pulled on a robe, cinching it tightly around my waist before stepping into my slippers and opening the bedroom door.

I heard voices from the kitchen. I was surprised to see Simon and Ruth both sitting at the table.

They looked up as I came in. "Good morning," I said, still groggy. "Did I sleep all the way through the weekend?"

Ruth smiled and shook her head. "No, but I thought . . ."

"Ruth thought that we might like a little time out today, to run some errands, or—"

"I saw the news last night," Ruth explained. "It's going to be pretty crazy around here tomorrow, so I thought I'd come over, see if you wanted me to watch Sherry today, so you could get anything done that needed doing."

"Thank you, Ruth, but I don't think so," I said, shaking my head.

Simon and Ruth exchanged a glance. "I already said yes," he said.

"Oh."

"I thought we'd get away for a couple of hours. Maybe walk downtown, have something to eat. Get out of the house while we can."

"Oh."

"We don't have to, though."

"No, no, that'll be good. I'm just . . . I'm not used to sleeping in anymore, I guess. I'll be better after I shower."

A little unsteadily, I turned back to the stairs.

Simon and I walked downtown. We kept to the residential streets as far as we could, savoring the quiet. We made small talk, stayed away from anything of any importance.

We had no destination, no place we had to be. We spent a while drifting around bookstores. Simon gravitated away from the sections in which he usually browsed. At Munro's, I found him in the poetry section, reading E. E. Cummings.

"What's this?" I asked.

He jumped, blushing a little. "It's, ah, it's . . ." He showed me the cover.

"This is kind of unusual for you, isn't it?" I joked, only realizing what I'd said after the words were already out there.

"I always used to read poetry," he said. "I used to write some, too. I thought you'd remember that."

"I do, I'm sorry," I answered in a whisper, ashamed of myself. I tried to meet his eye, but he didn't look at me.

It was like that for the rest of the afternoon. We meandered from shop to shop, stopping for coffee at one point, walking along the water through the Inner Harbor, through Market Square and finally into Chinatown. We avoided the furniture stores and kitchen boutiques where we used to spend so much of our time.

Despite being on the news so much in the past few days, thankfully no one recognized us.

"Are you hungry?" he asked as we were walking through Chinatown.

"Yeah. Yeah, I am."

"Do you want to get a bite to eat?"

My first thought was of Sherry. "What time is it?"

He glanced at his wrist reflexively, then pulled back his sleeve to reveal his naked arm. "I forgot to put my watch on this morning."

I checked my own wrist. "Sure. I guess we've got time."

"I can't stop thinking about her either."

I nodded.

"Ruth's there," he ventured. "And I've got my cell."

"Lunch would be good."

"What about right here?" He gestured at the restaurant where we had stopped. It was one of a dozen in that single block. Most of them were indistinguishable from one another, but this one stood out.

"It's been a long time," I said.

"Maybe they still do the special."

The lunch special was almost twice as expensive as it had been the last time we had eaten there, but the chairs and tables seemed to be the same. The waitress, tall, willowy, and young with a tattoo in the small of her back, was different, but familiar nonetheless.

"God, we must have come here every week for a year," Simon said, sipping his ice water.

"It *was* every week," I answered, smiling. "It was the only place we could afford."

In his last year as an undergrad, Simon had worked as the night clerk in a convenience store. Three ten-hour graveyard shifts each week. I hated being alone in the apartment, so I would bring a book or some homework with me and set up in one corner of the store for the night. He'd get off at eight in the morning and we'd go back to our basement apartment and fall into bed, too tired even to make love, sleeping through most of the day.

When we woke up, we'd walk downtown, stopping at this restaurant for the lunch special.

He cleared his throat. "I've been thinking about that time a lot recently. That first apartment. Working those stupid hours."

"Me, too," I said.

He smiled. "It's amazing, isn't it? That we even survived."

"We were young."

"Yeah. I guess." His gaze was far away. "Still. I think it was the last time I can remember feeling that there were more doors opening in front of me than there were closing behind me."

His hand was on the table, next to the bags from the bookstore and the record store.

I was startled by how close I came to taking it in my own. And then I noticed his wedding ring.

"When did you put that back on?" I asked.

He looked down at his hand. "This morning. I don't know. I just put it on."

I nodded, unable to look away.

"Is that all right?"

"That's really up to you," I said; then I stopped myself. "No," I started again. "No, it's not. I don't want to close any doors on you. . . ."

"But?" he said.

"I don't think . . . I like having you at the house. I like all this, being with you like this. But I don't think you can stay. Not now. Not yet. Not with everything we've been talking about the last couple of days."

I waited for him to argue. "Yeah," he said, instead.

"I know that it's not fair, but I'm worried that we'll slip into the same old patterns."

"No, it's fair. I've still got some things I need to figure out."

I looked down at his hand, the ring, on the black tabletop. I didn't want to ask. "Will you go back to Mary's?"

He shook his head. "No. That wouldn't be fair to her. To either of you."

He glanced at the space on his wrist where his watch should have been. "Could I stay at the house one more night? I'll find a place tomorrow."

He looked so open. I wanted to believe him. To believe in him. "Of course. It'll be good to have you there first thing. I think tomorrow's going to be a difficult day."

I looked once more at his ring, the ring he had put back on this morning, then glanced at the matching gold band I had never removed.

## Leo

Father Peter was already at the edge of the cliff when I got to Dallas Road. It had taken me a little longer to get Mother settled than I thought it would. She wouldn't let me leave until I had eaten some lunch.

The wind was blowing Father Peter's coat back like a cape when I came up behind him. I stayed by the bench, not wanting to get too close to the edge. It was even scarier than it was at night because I could see how high up we were.

The park was busy with people walking after church, dogs running around with no leashes, people flying kites. The wind off the water was cold, though.

"I'm sorry it took me so long to get here," I said to his back. "My mother—"

"That's all right," he said. "It gave me time to think."

He didn't say anything for a long time. Then he said, "Why don't you come over here, Leo?"

"I, I'm a little bit scared," I answered, holding on to the back of the bench.

"You're scared? Of falling?" He held out a hand to me, turning the coin he carried in the other. The silver flashed in the light, flashing, flashing.

"Come to me, Leo. I won't let you fall."

I took a deep breath and walked toward him. Baby steps. I tried not to look over the edge as it got closer and closer. I didn't feel safe until I took his hand.

"That's good," he said. "I won't let anything happen to you. You know that."

I nodded, too afraid to look away from his face.

"You know that you're safe with me."

I nodded again.

"You can look down," he said. "It's all right. I won't let anything happen to you."

I knew he wouldn't. I knew that if I did what I was told, Father Peter would keep me safe.

So I looked down.

There were bushes at my feet; then the cliff fell away and all I could see was the gray water and the rocks way down below. It looked so cold. I felt like I might throw up.

"You see?" His soft voice was close to me, almost inside my head. "I won't let anything happen to you."

"I know." I looked down at the rocks and the water.

"You were right to be scared, though," he said. "Your soul is in grave, grave peril. That little girl, all of this talk about miracles. Your soul is teetering on the edge of a vast abyss, hundreds of times higher than this cliff."

I felt a sudden gust of cold all the way to my heart, and I imagined myself falling.

When I looked at him, Father Peter was staring at me, looking worried and a little sad.

"I can save you," he said. "I can save you from those rocks, from that endless fall."

Save me.

"I can save your soul. I can keep you safe."

I nodded. "What do I do?"

"We need to talk, you and I," he said, turning us toward the bench and guiding me until I was sitting. "There is so much that you don't know. Are you ready to learn?"

I looked into his face, then toward the cliff—imagining myself falling into the water, into the flames—and nodded.

*"Barrett residence."*

*"Karen?"*

*"No, I'm sorry. Mrs. Barrett isn't available to come to the phone right now. This is Ruth Page speaking."*

"Oh. Is . . . is Simon there?"

"No, I'm sorry. Mr. Barrett isn't available either. Is there something I could help you with?"

"No, I . . . Will they be home soon? I need—"

"I'm afraid I don't know exactly when they'll be home. Is there something wrong?"

"No. No, I just . . . Can you take a message?"

"For Mrs. Barrett?"

"For either of them, I guess. It doesn't really—"

"Of course."

"Tell them . . . This is Donna Kelly. My son Jeffrey . . . Could you please tell them . . . tell them we're sorry."

"Sorry? Sorry for what? Mrs. Kelly? Are you still there? Mrs. Kelly? Hello? Hello?"

## Simon

Neither of us was particularly hungry after our late lunch in Chinatown, so we had a salad for dinner. A little lettuce, a little endive, some red cabbage and grated carrot, a honey vinaigrette—light and sweet with a little bitterness.

After dinner, Karen looked at me. "Would it be okay with you if I had a bath? I never feel comfortable having one when it's just Sherry and me in the house."

"Of course."

Once I was done with the dishes, I went upstairs.

Access to the attic was a pulldown ladder at the end of the corridor. The only light was a bare bulb hanging from the rafters, catching motes of dust in the air. Karen and I had talked about building an apartment up here for Sherry when she got to be a teenager. It had seemed so far in the future, then—now, it seemed to belong to a distant past.

The attic wasn't cluttered, but it still took me a while to find the guitar, the black case leaning in a corner. I dusted the case off with the dish towel I had brought up with me, then pulled the chain to turn off the light, closing the attic door behind me.

My new books were on the coffee table in the family room, alongside my watch and wallet. Sitting down on the couch, I lifted the guitar from the case and the fingers of my left hand curled around the neck. I carefully rubbed it down with a chamois, bringing the color back up to a rich honey-colored shine. I changed the strings, and then spent several minutes tightening the keys, plucking each string, bringing the whole into tune.

I'd heard stories of guitars that had been destroyed by being stored for a lot less time than this one. Sometimes an unloved, untouched guitar just faded away, incapable of holding a note, flat and lifeless. Casualty of neglect.

I strummed the strings lightly. The sound was far from clean, but that was probably more my technique than the guitar itself. I fumbled for the chords. My fingers were stiff, and my transitions were awkward, but the guitar sounded fine. Its vibrations pulsed through my belly and filled me with a remembered warmth. The strings cut small troughs into my fingertips as I moved through the chords, first slowly, gradually faster.

Karen had bought me the Yamaha for my twentieth birthday. I asked Chris, this pothead who had lived on my floor in residence, to show me some chords. After that, I practiced every night for an hour, a good break from studying. The first time I played in front of people, I was drunk. I played "Tangled Up in Blue" to the crowd at one of our house parties, stumbling a little on the changes at first, but quickly getting caught up in the flow. I even sang.

"Well, you're not as bad as Bob Dylan," Karen told me that night after everyone had left. I took it as a compliment and kept playing. Soon, a couple of the other guys started bringing their guitars with them and we'd play together.

I wondered where those guys were.

I fumbled in the pocket of the case for my bridge, fastening it to the neck of the guitar, bringing it up a bit to suit my voice. I tried to find the pitch, then took the bridge off, dropping it back into the case. Apparently my voice wasn't as high as it had been.

Clearing my throat, I began to sing.

## Karen

He was playing with his whole body, leaning into the notes, the chords, bending into the song, his eyes closed. His shirtsleeves were rolled up, and his voice strained a little to keep even close to the tune. He mumbled the words he didn't remember, or just hummed over them. I drew my robe closely around myself against the cooling of the house.

He played each song all the way through, never stopping, as if he needed to finish, needed to see each one through. They were all songs I had heard a hundred times, songs that seemed more fragments of dream than of memory.

I finally crept away without him seeing me, turning off the lights as I went. As I crawled into bed, I could still hear the guitar echoing through the heat pipes, the hallways, the otherwise silent rooms, his voice weaving in and out of the notes.

For some reason, the sound of it made me feel both warm and frightened.

*VICTORIA NEW SENTINEL*, MONDAY, DECEMBER 9

## Miracle Fraud?
### Investigation Reveals False Healings, Fraud

In a surprising development late Sunday, a source close to the Catholic church announced that an inquiry may take place into the healings attributed to four-year-old Sherilyn Barrett, comatose since a hit-and-run accident last spring. According to confidential reports, those healings may be part of an elaborate fraud devised by her parents, Karen Barrett, a former journalist, and her estranged husband, Simon Barrett,

a junior partner with Bradford & Howe.

The *New Sentinel* spoke to one pilgrim who says she no longer expects a miracle.

"It's all about money," says Donna Kelly of Seattle. Kelly's six-year-old son Jeffrey suffers from leukemia, and was invited into the Barrett home on Friday. "They sit you down and give you this story about medical bills, and how all of the money goes to caring for Sherry. It's pretty clear that if you don't cough it up, they won't let you see her." Although Miss Kelly wouldn't divulge the amount she contributed, she is very clear on the cost to her. "They catch you in this untenable position. You're ready to do anything if you think there's a chance that maybe it'll save your child's life."

A source who has investigated such claims in the past discussed the nature of miracles. "We usually find that these supposed miracles are psychosomatic. People experience temporary recovery because they *believe* in the possibility of having been healed. For the sufferers, it's all about faith. People who are less scrupulous can easily take advantage of these believers. That's what makes fraudulent situations so repre-

hensible. That people can prey on other people's desperation, taking advantage of tragedy for their own gain, is terrible."

According to a statement released by the Barretts Friday afternoon, they will be allowing people access to their daughter and her alleged powers beginning at ten o'clock today. "It looks like a textbook situation," says the source. "You hold people off, start the rumors going, then just let the demand build. The higher the demand, the higher the price."

The Barretts could not be reached for comment, nor would they allow investigators access to examine Sherilyn. Victoria Police would not confirm whether they would investigate the situation, or if criminal charges would be pending. According to a spokesman, "It would be premature to say anything at this point."

## Karen

I awoke to a familiar but unaccustomed weight at the foot of the bed. "Simon?"

"It's me," he whispered, squeezing my foot through the blankets. I could see the vaguest outline of him, sitting on the bed and looking toward the bedroom door.

"What are you doing? What time is it?" I struggled up to a sitting position.

"It's a little after seven."

"Okay."

"But I . . . can I turn on the light?" He stood up, and the mattress shifted.

"Yeah, sure," I said, fumbling for the bedside lamp.

He turned on the ceiling lamp before I had a chance to flick the switch. The light was painfully bright on my sleep-darkened eyes. "Sorry," he said as I winced.

"What's going on?"

He sat down on the bed next to me, wearing only his socks, underwear, and an undershirt. "You need to look at this," he said, laying today's newspaper on my lap.

"What is it? What's—?" The black headline, over the picture of our house stopped me cold. MIRACLE FRAUD? "Oh my God," I muttered, skimming through the article.

"I'm going to guess that the unnamed church source is likely—"

"Father Peter," I finished Simon's sentence for him.

I stared at the headline. "Why would Donna Kelly say we asked her for money?"

"Father Peter likely showed up at her hotel room with a bag full of money and some variation on the line he tried to sell us. She didn't really have a choice. She's not working—"

"I know, I know," I said, shaking my head, able to imagine myself in her position. "I guess that's what her phone call was about yesterday."

I wanted to curl up and go back to sleep, to wake up a few hours later and discover that this was all a dream.

Instead, I asked, "So what do we do now? Can we sue them, or—?"

"We can try," he said. "It's pretty difficult to pursue a libel action."

"So what are we going to do? Nobody's going to come if they think the whole thing is a fraud." A moment later, I realized what I'd just said.

"Wouldn't that be better?" Simon looked at me. "Not to have to worry about it . . . Just like Father Peter was saying the other day?"

"No," I said. "No. It might be easier, but if Sherry *can* help people, then it's not better. I want the people to come."

I waited for an argument, but he just nodded.

"That's good," he said. "Because there were four people waiting on the front step when I went out to get the paper."

"Had they seen it?" I couldn't keep track of all the things that I was feeling.

"One of them mentioned it to me," he said, shaking his head in disbelief.

"There were already people waiting?"

"As of seven o'clock."

*"Sheila, it's Simon."*

*"Simon, I was just . . . Is everything all right?"*

*"It's been a strange couple of days. That's why I'm calling. I think I need to take a couple of personal days to try to get through the worst of this. Can you please—?"*

*"Simon, I was about to call you."*

*"Why? What is it?"*

*"The senior partners want to meet with you at nine thirty."*

*"Did they say—?"*

*"In Mr. Fitzgerald's office."*

*"Oh. Well. Let them know I'll be there."*

Mary

I was sitting on the leather couch in Simon's office, pretending to make notes on a yellow pad, when he opened the door. I stood up slowly, my heart rushing in my chest.

"Good morning," he said, closing the door.

"Hello," I said. "I saw the paper."

He set his briefcase on the floor. "Yeah."

I had no idea what I wanted to say. The silence stretched for almost a minute, before I asked, "So what are you going to do?"

"About what?"

"About the newspaper?"

He shrugged. He seemed distracted, not really there. "There's not really a whole lot we can do. If we threaten to sue, they'll just print a correction on page H17, where no one will ever see it. And I'm not going to go after that poor kid's mother." As he was speaking, his eyes were darting around the office.

Leaning over his desk, he rifled through the pink message slips. "I tried calling you this weekend," he said without looking up. "After you left."

"I went home. Back to my apartment. I got together with some friends Friday night."

"Why?"

The question caught me off guard. "What do you mean *why?* You were at home with your wife and daughter. I didn't think there was a whole lot of room for me in that picture."

"I needed you."

"You don't know what you need."

"What?"

"Simon, I love you," I started, as coolly as I could. "But you—you just don't know. You don't know where you're going, you don't know what you want. Who you want to be with." He started to protest, but I held up my hand. "No. Don't. I don't want to be the girl who broke up your marriage. And I don't want to be some bit on the side. Not anymore. That's why I left. If there's any chance that you're going to go back to Karen, I don't want to stand in the way, but I sure don't want to participate in it."

He stared at me, speechless.

"You didn't come," I said.

"What?"

"To the apartment. *Home.* This weekend, after I left. You called. You left messages on the machine, but you didn't come."

"I didn't know if I should," he said. "I didn't know if you wanted me there."

"Of course I wanted you there. I just wanted you there for the right reasons. I wanted you there for me, and for you, and for us, not just as a reaction to your wife."

He looked as if he wanted to argue, but he didn't.

"*You* have to decide, Simon," I said. "It's got nothing to do with me now." The truth of what I was saying startled me.

"I know."

"I've got your stuff in the car. I'll—"

"I'm not sleeping with her," he blurted. He seemed almost like a little boy, so quick and earnest with the denial. It almost made me smile.

"Maybe you should," I said. "Maybe that's what you need. Maybe that's what you both need."

He glanced at his watch, and I looked reflexively to the clock on the wall. 9:25.

"I'm sorry," he said. "I have to go."

I looked at him as he straightened his tie and smoothed imaginary wrinkles from the sleeves of his jacket. "Go where?"

His face was pale. "The senior partners have requested my presence in Garrett's office."

"Mr. Fitzgerald?" I'd only met the firm's founder once.

He nodded, and faked a smile. "It'll be fine," he lied.

## Ruth

There was already a crowd in front of the Barretts' house when I arrived at 8:30. Both sides of the street were lined with cars and TV vans. I was forced to park several houses down and walk.

Rather than clustering on the front lawn again, the pilgrims had formed a loose line from the foot of the front steps and along the walk. No one said anything as I walked up to the front door, though several people smiled at me.

"Are there many out there?" Karen asked as I shut the door. I was surprised to see how well she looked. I had been expecting her to be more frantic.

"A dozen or so," I answered as I hung up my coat. "But there are more people coming. Looking for places to park."

"I thought maybe there wouldn't be that many."

"Because of the newspaper article this morning?"

She nodded, starting toward the kitchen. "Did they talk to you? The *New Sentinel*?"

I shook my head. "No. And no matter what they said in that article, no one called here yesterday afternoon from the paper."

"I didn't think they had. But I'm surprised to see so many people here, considering," she said.

"I think that most people, if they're going to try something like this, they've got enough faith—"

"Or desperation—"

"Or desperation. They won't be swayed by anything they read in the paper. Did Simon . . . Do you know if Simon . . ."

"Yes, he saw the paper." I explained, "He stayed here last night, but he had to go into the office."

"I wasn't prying."

"I know. I told him yesterday that I didn't know if I could handle having him in the house," Karen said. "I mean, I like it that he's here. It's comfortable. It's safe. It feels right."

"Well, it is right. He's your husband."

She shook her head. "No, no, it's not. Like this morning. He had to go into the office, and all I can do is worry about him seeing Mary, talking to her. I mean, I know he's in love with Mary, but having him here feels so natural, like maybe we can just go back to the way we were before, but we can't. We can't go back to that."

"Why not?"

She sighed and stood up, leaning on the counter with her back to me. "Because I don't want to go back. Because what we had wasn't good, and it wasn't until he left that I realized that." When she turned to face me, I was surprised to see that she wasn't even close to tears. "And now it's all about him. All about his feelings, his problems. I'm stifling him. I'm not letting him explore himself. Be himself. What about me? Aren't I allowed to have feelings?"

"Of course you are."

"Then why won't anyone listen to them?" It was just a question—there was no self-pity in her voice.

I waited.

For a moment, her gaze drifted away. "I liked being at home with Sherry. I liked watching her grow. Watching her change. But I didn't have a choice. That's it, right there. I never got to choose. I wouldn't have gone back to work at the paper—but I never got to choose. It was always just assumed that I would stay home." She drained her cup, then set it gently on the table in front of her. "This is stupid. I'm being selfish."

I deliberately didn't say anything.

She understood. "I'm sorry. You're not the one I need to be having this conversation with."

## Karen

Dr. McKinley was leaning over Sherry, his back to the door, as I came into the living room.

"How is she?" I asked.

Stephen didn't turn to face me. "The same," he answered, closing the file.

"I wasn't expecting to see you this morning." I approached Sherry's bed, and he shifted away, toward the couch.

"I thought I'd check in." His voice was cool. "I wasn't doing anything else."

"You're off at the hospital?"

"Indefinitely," he said, turning to face me. His face was ashen and tight, his eyes ringed with circles.

"What?"

"The hospital has suspended my privileges, 'pending a hearing,' " he explained.

"Because of the article in the paper this morning?"

He started to shake his head, then stopped. "Probably. I got called in yesterday afternoon, but it was about the same stuff as the article. The board had a few questions about my conduct 'regarding the Barrett matter.' " He smiled bitterly. "They told me that they 'knew what was going on,' but that they were willing to give me the benefit of the doubt and schedule a hearing." He shook his head slowly. "I had no idea what they were talking about. It was like a Kafka story. And then I saw the paper this morning."

"Oh God, Stephen, I'm so sorry. I'm so sorry."

"So, would you mind telling me what the hell is going on around here?" he said.

I led him toward the kitchen and we sat down at the table where Ruth had refilled the teapot. I recounted the events of the weekend: the visit from Father Peter, the decision to bring Jeffrey Kelly in to see Sherry, and then to open up the house.

"Has a doctor looked at this Jeffrey Kelly since?"

"I wouldn't think so. His doctor is in Seattle, and it only happened Friday afternoon, late—"

"Then how can they claim this is a fraud? I mean, if they haven't run any tests on him, how do they know he hasn't gone into remission?"

"Maybe they had someone check him."

"No. No, I don't think so. If there had been any tests, they would have mentioned them in the newspaper article." Another thought occurred to him. "Do you have any way of contacting Donna Kelly?"

"She gave me her number in Seattle." I was already in motion, going to a small basket on the counter. "Right here."

"Let's give her a call."

My hands shook as I punched in her telephone number. Stephen's face was still curiously blank.

The line rang once, then switched over with a sharp click and a change in the tone of the line to a recording. "We're sorry. The number you have dialed is no longer in service. Please check the number and dial again." As the message began to repeat itself, I hung up. "The number's not in service."

Stephen nodded, as if he had already guessed.

"Well, there's probably a good reason why she doesn't want to talk to you," he said.

I looked up at the clock. It was almost 9:30. "There's nothing we can do about that right now. Are you thinking of staying?"

He shrugged carelessly. "I've got no other plans."

"But what about—?"

"I can't say that I support this, Karen. But I'm Sherry's doctor. I should keep an eye on her. And if this is actually going to help people . . ." He didn't need to finish the sentence. The words had been going through my mind like a mantra for the past several days.

*If this is going to help people . . .*

I nodded at him, then said, "So. How are we going to do this?"

## Simon

Garrett Fitzgerald didn't rise as I entered his office. He didn't even acknowledge that I had arrived. He was sitting in his famous burgundy leather wing chair, leaning toward Martin Stoller and Steven Ross, our senior partners, who were seated on the matching leather sofa. They glanced up as I closed the door but then quickly looked away.

Garrett cleared his throat and leaned back into his chair.

I stood my ground, a few steps inside the door. There wasn't a place for me to sit that didn't require my asking permission, which I wouldn't do. I didn't say a word. The dead air in the room wasn't about to force me to start this conversation.

"You know why you're here," Garrett said.

"I can guess."

"We're very concerned. The three of us have spoken several times over the weekend, and we met first thing this morning." Garrett's voice was smooth, his phrasing delicate.

I did not take the bait.

"Simon, could you please explain to us the article on the front page of this morning's *New Sentinel*?"

"The track record of the *New Sentinel* in matters such as this—"

He sighed heavily to interrupt me, and Ross burst out like a bulldog. "Simon, cut the crap. What the hell is going on here? Why the hell is the name of this firm in a story about fraud?"

There it was, on the table.

"The paper got it wrong today," I said. "The previous articles were more accurate."

"You mean to tell us that your daughter is some sort of miracle worker?" Stoller stared at me as if I'd lost my mind.

"I didn't say that. There were some occurrences that aren't easily explained. The newspaper got hold of them. I didn't even know about it until I read the paper last Thursday morning."

"Yet you're opening your home to strangers." Ross this time, flat-voiced.

"It would seem that way."

"What about this Donna Kelly and her little boy?" Stoller leapt in again. "What about your attempt to extort money from her?"

"I can assure you—"

"Well, that's not good enough, is it? Is that how you win cases? By assuring the jury that your client is innocent, and that they should just ignore any statements to the contrary? Does that usually work for you?"

I suppressed the desire to snap back. "I believe that Karen and I are being harassed." Less than impressive.

"That's as may be, Simon." Garrett's soothing voice. "But we have to look out for the firm."

"I've done nothing to impugn the firm, Garrett." I struggled to keep my voice even.

He shook his head slowly, portentously. "You were named, Simon. We were named. And what would you have us say when the clients call? Because they have been calling. All morning. Should we say that despite an article that mentions a police investigation, we have complete confidence in both your abilities and your integrity?" Garrett paused. "Do you expect us to lie, Simon?"

He let the words hang in the air.

"Just how long are we supposed to turn a blind eye to your indiscretions?" Stoller asked after a long moment.

"Indiscretions?"

Ross sighed. "While you might think it's acceptable for one of our associates to have an affair with a junior member of this firm, you should be aware—"

"Gentlemen," I interrupted. "Are you asking me to leave?"

Garrett's face lifted in surprise. He seemed about to speak when Toller interrupted.

"There's no 'asking' involved, Simon," he said. "There's no option here."

"We can't have you making a laughingstock of this firm," Ross added.

Garrett watched me in silence.

I paused for a moment, and then I began to pace—the slow, deliberate steps of a final summation, but this time there was no script, no notes to follow, no jury. "I assume you're offering a severance package."

Garrett cut Ross off with a gesture, his eyes never leaving my face.

"You have absolutely no grounds to dismiss me." I didn't wait for confirmation or argument. "Given my length of service, my billings, the fact that there have been no prior complaints or reprimands and no investigation on your part into a defamatory newspaper report, I expect an amount equal to my last two years' gross salary and billings, including my bonus, to be paid out within seventy-two hours."

Stoller rose to his feet. "You've got to be—"

Garrett waved him down again.

"I also expect to maintain my medical benefits, and to have my pension plan transferred to a fund that I'll set up. And finally, Garrett, I'll need a letter of apology from you, deeply regretting the circumstances that have arisen that have forced you to take this action, as well as a letter of reference. Carla will know all the right things to say. And, in the future, if I hear that you've been expressing any reservations to potential employers, I'll have you in court."

Stoller and Ross seemed dumbstruck.

I kept my eyes locked on Garrett, knowing that, in the end, there were only the two of us playing the game.

"Pay him," he said, his eyes never leaving mine.

"What?"

"Pay him," he repeated. "Have human resources put the package together and have it ready for him by three this afternoon." He shook his head. "If you're in the building after three, we'll have you arrested for trespassing."

I didn't even go back to my office.

Karen

By the time Jamie arrived, the crowd had grown to two dozen.

"How are they?" I asked as she slipped out of her coat.

She shrugged. "Patient. I don't think they're going to be any sort of problem. I'd be more concerned with the group on the sidewalk."

"What group on the sidewalk?"

We peeked out the crack between the blind and the frame of the window. "*That* group."

Father Peter was on the sidewalk in front of the house with a group of protesters waving placards that read WORSHIP NOT FALSE IDOLS and JESUS DIED FOR YOUR SINS. They seemed to be singing as they marched in a looping line. Father Peter was at the epicenter, his black coat pulled tightly around himself. To one side of him, a wiry young man clad only in jeans and a T-shirt, feet bare against the cold December concrete, almost buckled under the weight of a rough-hewn wooden cross almost twice his height. On his other side was a huge man dressed in coveralls, his arms folded across his chest.

"They're singing hymns," Jamie added in a whisper, as if they might hear her and discover our hiding place.

And then, as if that was exactly what had happened, Father Peter's stare met mine. It was all I could do not to jump back.

"He's looking right at us," Jamie said in a tense whisper. "Who is that?"

I let the curtain fall back against the window frame. "Lock the door behind me," I said, not pausing to pull on a jacket or shoes.

"Karen, where are you going? What are you doing?"

"Just lock the door behind me," I repeated, striding down the concrete steps in my socks and past the pilgrims.

I don't know where the courage came from. Anger, more than anything else. If I had stopped to think about it, I would have stayed inside. Instead, I pushed through the even line of protesters, their song and their ranks falling to pieces around me.

Father Peter smiled coldly. "Mrs. Barrett."

"What are you doing here?"

His smile widened, revealing his yellowing teeth. "Demonstrating my right to free assembly."

"And what was that in the paper this morning?"

He stood easily a foot taller than me, and the man in the jumpsuit loomed over him.

"You were warned," he said, too quietly for the bystanders to hear. Then, a little louder, and for their benefit, "We won't allow you to make a mockery of our faith."

A few people in the crowd grunted their support.

"And that's how you do it? By spreading lies about us?" Letting my voice rise.

"What lies?" he demanded. "You're the one who claims that your daughter can heal people, but where are those people you claim she's healed? Where is the woman who first went to the newspaper? Where is this Jeffrey Kelly you claim was cured? Why isn't he here, standing up in your defense?" He held my gaze just a moment too long, enjoying himself.

"What about Ruth Page? Sherry—"

"The nurse?" he scoffed. "Do you think that someone in your employ is to be trusted? There are no miracles here. Just desperate people trying to make some money out of their daughter's tragedy."

"We haven't taken any money."

"Liar," he shouted. "Blasphemer. You make a mockery of our faith."

The crowd started to close around me.

"Get out of here. Get away from my house."

"We're on public property here. We'll stay."

"We'll stay," one of the protesters shouted.

"I'll call the police."

His eyes gleamed. "Oh, the police will come. They're eager to speak with you and your husband."

My anger condensed into a cold, hard ball of resolve. "You want miracles?" I asked as I started back to the house. "I'll give you miracles."

Jamie opened the front door as I reached it.

"Let's start allowing some of these people in," I said. "Do you mind looking after the door while I stay near Sherry? I want you to get full names, addresses, phone numbers, doctor's names, everything. We need thorough records."

She nodded. "How many should I let in? How fast?"

I hadn't even considered this. "Just a few at a time, I guess. I'll let you know."

I pulled open the front door, filling the foyer with cold, bright light. Stepping out into the chill, I leaned over the woman who was first in line, helping a young man in a wheelchair. His head lolled back and his mouth twisted into a spasming rictus, his eyes moving independently of each other as his hands jerked and jumped. She looked at me with a face touched with sadness and exhaustion.

"Would you like to come in?" I asked. My throat was thick with emotion.

As I helped her with the wheelchair, I glanced up the driveway at the long line of people waiting for a miracle. And, on the sidewalk, the dark shape of Father Peter watching it all.

## Henry

I don't know what I was expecting at the Barretts' house. I had read the article in the paper and I wondered if I would arrive in time to see the police arresting them, or people throwing things at the house.

Instead, it was pretty quiet. There were people with signs on the sidewalk singing hymns, but in the lineup to see Sherry everyone spoke as if they were in the library, or clutched their crosses, mouthing silent prayers.

Sherry's mother came to the door, speaking to the crowd in a voice most of them couldn't hear. The message passed quickly down the line: it was almost three o'clock. They'd start seeing people again at ten the next morning. The crowd trickled away with little fuss.

Inside, someone closed the blinds, and I found myself staring at a reflection of the yard in the suddenly mirrored surface.

"Show's over," came the voice from the driveway, directed at me.

The man was tall, wrapped in a long black coat. A chill ran through me.

"I've startled you," he said, walking toward me. "Henry Denton, I presume?" He stopped just close enough to make me uncomfortable. "You're wondering why I can see you."

I could barely nod. His eyes were a flat gray, his pupils barely noticeable. He radiated cold the way a road radiates heat in the summer.

"My name is Peter," he said, extending his hand. "I've been waiting for you."

I took his hand reluctantly.

His grip was machinelike in its steady force. His smile widened. "I knew you would come," he said, just before I pulled my hand away.

I backed away. "Who are you?" I asked, finally finding my voice.

He stepped forward, maintaining his uncomfortable closeness. "I told you. My name is Peter. I know your fat friend in the library. I know what you're doing here, watching this house." The wave of cold wrapped itself around me and I could feel bile rising in my throat. "Don't you think you've done enough to this family already?"

I couldn't help myself: Instinct took over and I ran. I ran as far, and as fast, as I could, glancing over my shoulder to see if he was following. He wasn't.

I slowed to a gasping walk as I neared downtown, where the sidewalks were filled with people. For once I took comfort in their blindness, in my invisibility.

Why could he see me?

I began to calm down only when the doors of the library closed behind me and night began to fall.


Karen

It was just after five when the doorbell rang. Jamie, Ruth, and Stephen had gone home.

Mary was standing on the stoop.

"Hi, Karen." She shifted. "I'm sorry to come by like this. I'm just . . . Is Simon here? I've been trying his cell."

I shook my head. "He's not here. I haven't talked to him since this morning after his meeting."

She looked confused and glanced around herself. "After his meeting?"

I nodded and stepped to one side. "Why don't you come in?"

She hesitated for a moment, then brushed past me, in a wash of clean scent. I closed the door behind her, taking care to turn the dead bolt.

Of everything that had happened since the morning of the accident, Simon being terminated by the firm was probably the least surprising, especially after the newspaper story, and what had happened to Jamie and Stephen.

His voice on the phone as he described his meeting with the senior partners had been fractured, devastated.

"I'm coming home," he said. "I'm on—"

"Simon." I stopped him. "Don't. Don't come home, not like this. Try to work it through or walk it off."

"But I should be there. With Sherry and everything that's—"

"It's fine, Simon. It's going fine."

"Are you sure?"

"You were going to be gone all day, Simon. It's fine."

I couldn't tell if he had been relieved or upset.

"I haven't seen him since this morning," Mary said. "They changed the locks to his office and reassigned me. I thought he would be here." Her words seemed to bubble out of her in a single breath.

"He's not. He said he'd be staying at a hotel downtown. I'm not sure which one. There are some things he needs to work out."

"That's good."

I was stunned. "Do you really mean that?" I asked.

"This . . . When we were up in Tofino, and he saw the newspaper story." She shook her head. "It was pretty clear that this is still his home. This is where he needed to be." Her eyes were bright. "I didn't . . . I know what you must think of me, but I never wanted to be the kind of person who—If Simon was going to be with me, I wanted him to want to be with me, not—"

"And not just running from something else."

Our eyes met, and she nodded.

She leaned back into the couch, spent.

I wished I could hate her.

The doorbell rang.

## Simon

The lobby of the Balmoral Hotel was almost too warm, thick with voices and cigarette smoke from the adjoining pub.

I paid cash in advance for a week, and climbed the stairs to the third floor.

I was surprised to find my room mostly clean, smelling of stale cigarette smoke and fresh cleanser. On the wall above the head of the bed was an atrocious painting of a ship on a dark sea. In the bathroom there was a single glass on the shelf, wrapped in white paper. When I unwrapped it to get a drink of water, it was so badly scratched, it was textured.

I went back to the door, shot the bolt, and hooked the chain lock.

Then I sat at the end of the bed, facing the television, my hands on my knees. My reflection was stretched and distorted, a rumpled caricature of someone I could barely recognize.

Karen

There was a stranger at the door, squinting under the porch light.

I stepped back, bumping into Mary.

"Good evening," he said. He fumbled in his pocket for his identification. "I'm Sergeant Richards, with the Victoria Police." He was a large man, solid but starting to go soft. The sort of man who would always seem rumpled, whose suits never fit quite right.

"You're Karen Barrett?" he asked, folding his wallet back into his pocket.

"Yes."

"I'd like to have a word, if you've got a minute."

"Come in. It's easier to talk inside."

"I waited until the reporters left," he said as I led him toward the family room. "I didn't think there was any need for anyone to read about this in the morning paper."

"Read about what?" Mary asked.

"And you are?"

Mary glanced at me, then back at the policeman. "Mary Edwards," she said, extending her hand.

He shook it firmly. "You're an attorney, right? You work with Mr. Barrett."

She nodded, then corrected both herself and him. "Until this morning."

He seemed surprised. "This morning?"

"Simon was terminated by the firm this morning," I explained.

"I'm sorry to hear that, Mrs. Barrett. I know your husband."

"Really?"

"He did some work for me a couple of years ago. Before your time," he added to Mary. "Really helped me out. Did his dismissal have anything to do with the story in the paper?"

"What do you think?"

Richards nodded. "Yeah. Well, unfortunately, that's why I'm here, too." He took a small notebook and pen from inside his jacket and opened to a fresh page.

"Mrs. Barrett," he started. "We've received some reports that are somewhat alarming, so we wanted to talk—"

"Sergeant, is there a police investigation concerning Mr. and Mrs. Barrett?" Mary interrupted, her voice calm.

He shook his head. "No, there isn't an active investigation. We've received some reports, and we wanted to look into them."

Mary nodded. "That's fine, then. But if it turns out there is a criminal investigation, I think you'll find this interview of little evidentiary value."

"And why is that?"

"Because Mrs. Barrett doesn't have an attorney present."

"You mean you don't represent Mrs. Barrett?" It was hard to tell, but it seemed like the sergeant might be making a joke.

"Sergeant Richards, I don't represent Mrs. Barrett in any way whatsoever."

"Well, I can assure you, Miss Edwards, that there is no active criminal investigation. I've just got a few questions, starting with Donna and Jeffrey Kelly. Can you give me a little background, Mrs. Barrett?"

I took a moment to think through my answer. "Jeffrey Kelly and his mother were two of the people who camped out in our front yard on Thursday night, just after the story broke in the paper."

"The story about your daughter's ability to heal the sick?"

"Yes. He—Jeffrey—is six years old. He'd been diagnosed with leukemia. After we read about him in the paper—"

"You invited them to come in."

"Yes. We wanted to talk with his mother."

Richards made a note. "Do you believe that your daughter can heal the sick?"

"I don't know. There have been a few people—Sherry's nurse, her sister—but we've never claimed that Sherry can . . . can do any of those things."

"Did you ever ask Donna Kelly for money, in exchange for using your daughter's powers to heal her son?"

"No."

"Yet Ms. Kelly claims you told her that unless she paid, you wouldn't let Jeffrey see Sherry."

"Did she tell you that herself?"

He looked up from his notebook.

"Because we've tried calling her—"

"That's probably not the best idea."

"—and we haven't been able to get in touch."

"We're responding to published reports."

"So you haven't spoken to her either?"

Richards shook his head. "So no money changed hands."

"No."

"Have you asked for money from any of the other people who have come to see your daughter?"

"No. I wouldn't have taken any even if they had offered."

"And how many people would you say came through here today?"

"I'd have to check. Between thirty and forty, I think. I've got a list of their names, addresses, and everything if you need it."

He wrote the figure down in his notebook. "That would be handy."

I was about to stand up, to look for Jamie's clipboard, when Mary cleared her throat.

"Have you got a fax number where we can send the list, Sergeant? I'm sure Karen would like to keep her files complete."

"Sure." Reaching into his pocket, he passed me a business card. "All my numbers are on there."

He closed his notebook and tucked it back into his pocket. "I think that's everything," he said. "I can't . . ." He shook his head. "You might be hearing from someone else in the department in the next few days. Depending on if there are complaints or reports." He seemed uncomfortable, shifting slightly from foot to foot. "Mrs. Barrett, I don't mean to pry. I know there have been . . . Will you be talking to Simon?"

I nodded.

"Could you get him to give me a call the next time you're talking to him? Nothing major. I just want to touch base with him."

"Sure. I'll tell him."

"Thanks. And thanks for taking the time."

After I saw him out, I came back to the family room, where Mary was still sitting on the couch.

"That was strange," I said.

She nodded. "Yes, it was."

For some reason, I found Mary's uncertainty disturbing.


Mary

"This all looks good," I said.

I couldn't tell if Karen had meant for me to accept her invitation to stay for dinner, or if she had just asked to be polite.

Karen smiled a little at the compliment, but I could feel a bit of the chill returning. "Do you cook much yourself?"

"No, not too much. I've usually got so much going on, with work, and . . ." I realized suddenly how all of this might be taken by Karen, forced to stay at home with Sherry. I trailed off.

"Do you enjoy it?"

"Enjoy what?" I took a sip of my wine.

"Being a lawyer. I know that Simon loves it, but I've never really understood why." She seemed to be trying to minimize any offense I might take.

I nodded. "I love it," I said. "It's all I ever wanted to do."

"Really? It wasn't something your parents pushed you into?"

"God, no," I said. "I was born in a VW Microbus in North Africa somewhere. My parents have never even been sure what country they were in when it happened. They were in one of those mobile communes, going wherever the wind took them." I shrugged. "We lived in Ireland for a few years when I was little, then came back to Canada. They opened up an organic foods store up-island. They freaked out when I told them I wanted to be a lawyer. God, I might as well have told them that I wanted to be an air force pilot dropping napalm on some village somewhere."

"So I guess you could say they discouraged you?"

"You could say that. They thought that I should be an artist—maybe write poetry, edit a little magazine, do raku. But I liked the stability of the law, the order." I chuckled, taking another sip of my wine, risked a joke. "I was rebellious. Started shaving my legs and everything."

Karen smiled and shook her head. "Did they ever forgive you?"

I nodded. "Oh yeah. Christmas is hard, though. It's like, 'This is Bob, my cross-dressing son, and this is Sparkle, she paints rocks, and this is Mary—'" I dropped my voice to a dramatic whisper. "'—*she's a lawyer.*"

We both laughed.

"I'm just kidding," I finally said. "I don't really have any brothers or sisters." This just started us off laughing again. The sense that there might be anything strange in the two of us sitting there over dinner had mostly disappeared.

"I always wanted to write," Karen said, the smile vanishing from her face.

"I thought you wrote for the *Sentinel,* before Sherry was born?" I took a small bite of my salad.

"I did." She shook her head. "I got the job at the paper to make ends meet while Simon was in law school." She toyed with her fork. "No, I always wanted to be a *Writer.* You know, capital *W.* Short stories, fiction, maybe a novel." She shrugged, as if that part of her no longer existed.

"Why don't you? Write, I mean."

"I did, for a while. Well, all through school I did. I took courses in creative writing. I spent as much time writing stories as I did writing papers."

"Did you get anything published?"

"A few things here and there. I never really sent stuff out."

"Why not?"

"I'm not sure. I guess it seems pretty stupid now that I didn't."

"That's okay," I said.

She shook her head, staring at me. "No. No, it's not. I see you—I look at you and I realize how, how . . . jealous I am. Beginning your career. So many options."

I braced myself.

"I look at you and I realize that somewhere I got off track, I guess."

After a long silence, I said, "So get back on."

She gave a single, sharp laugh. "Right. In my spare time."

My turn to shrug and take another bite.

"You're really something, you know that?"

I looked up, and she was smiling. I didn't speak, uncertain what she meant, what to say.

"I can see why Simon loves you," she said.

"Karen, I—"

She shook her head. "No, don't. Please don't. I know. I know it goes deeper than my husband having an affair with someone at his office. I know that there's more to it than sex, than staying late after work, lying to me on the telephone." She smiled a little at my expression. "I think I knew, even before the accident, that something was going on."

"I'm sorry," I said.

"What's he like when he's with you?" She shifted in her chair.

Stalling, I set my knife and fork on the edge of the plate, dabbed the corners of my mouth with the napkin, and picked up my wineglass. I really didn't want to talk about Simon with his wife, but I couldn't see any way to avoid it. "He's, I mean, he's, well, he's just Simon, I guess. . . ."

Karen leaned across the table and took my hand, squeezing it.

I took a deep breath. "It's hard to describe. I mean, I don't know what he's like with you. How that compares. With me, he's gentle, I guess. I mean, he never raises his voice. Never seems to get upset. I've seen him in court: I know how he can get. You know, how cold. How precise. How vicious. I've never seen that, except in court."

She looked at me like I was describing a stranger. I tried again. "He listens. And he talks to me. I feel like we've got . . . like we had . . . a real connection." I shook my head. "I'm sorry."

"You got him playing his guitar again."

"Guitar?"

"Yeah. The other day he went up to the attic and got his old guitar down. I hadn't heard him play since university."

"I didn't even know he played," I said.

"He's a man with a lot of secrets," she said, almost without bitterness.

"I never used to think so. I always thought that we were really open. With one another, I mean. The problem, I think, is that Simon doesn't really know himself."

She nodded, and then shook her head.

"That's what I told him this morning. I told him . . ." I braced myself. "I told him that I loved him, but that I didn't really think that he knew what he wanted, and that I didn't want to . . ."

I couldn't finish the sentence. Instead, I reached for the bottle of wine in the center of the table and filled my glass, carefully looking away from Karen.

## Leo

I sat in the van in the parking lot of the 7-Eleven where Father Peter had told me to wait, trying to remember everything he had said. I tried to think everything through. Everything he told me made so much sense when he was talking. All that stuff about people attacking our faith, about the forces of darkness being loosed upon the earth. You only had to watch the news at dinnertime to know that he was telling the truth.

But that little girl . . .

I kept the picture of Sherilyn Barrett from the newspaper under the invoices and work orders on my clipboard, right where I could look at it, look at her beautiful sweet face. How could she could be evil?

But no. Father Peter said she wasn't a little girl anymore, not since the accident. That was when the Beast took her, deceiving people with these false healings, luring them away from the truth and finding a home in the darkness within them.

Father Peter says evil can wear many different faces.

Somebody tapped on the window and I jumped. I thought for a moment that it might be the Beast, called to me by my thoughts of him. But it was Father Peter. He waved me out of the van.

I locked the door, and had to hustle to catch up with him. He led me into an alley in the next block. Piles of garbage and Dumpsters leaned against the walls of an old church. The windows were all boarded up.

When I caught up to him, he was unlocking a door with a heavy-looking ring of keys.

"A donation," he said, as he pulled the door open. "From a true believer."

He led me through the messy basement and up the stairs to the empty church. There were no pews, no altar, nothing. Just a big empty room. Our footsteps were loud, and when Father Peter started to talk, his voice echoed.

"One of the oldest buildings in the city, a house of God, now . . . empty. Abandoned. There's no history here." He shook his head. "Brave men died to protect places like this, and now we leave them to rot away."

I didn't understand what he meant, and I think he could tell.

"Someone told me that there used to be a fitness club in this building. They did aerobics here. Right here, where people used to come to worship. Looking for salvation by way of a perfect body. And now this."

He had a candle in his hand that he lit with a lighter from his pocket. He held it high above his head.

"But that's all right," he said, as if he were talking to himself. "We'll claim it back, won't we, Leo?"

"I . . . I guess so." I had no idea what he was talking about.

He turned toward me, holding the candle between us. In the flickering light, his face looked even more like a skull.

"You do know what I'm talking about, don't you, Leo?" he asked, his teeth sharp and shiny in the dim light. "You're a part of this now."

I nodded. I knew it. I was part of it. He trusted me. Had confidence in me.

"That's good, that's good." He seemed to look into me, without blinking. "Because there is going to come a time when I call on you, Leo. When I will have need of you. And I need to know that when that time comes, I'll be able to rely on you to do what needs to be done. I can rely on you, can't I, Leo?"

I thought of the photo of the little girl from the newspaper, of the evil that was hidden inside her, waiting to get hold of anyone who touched her, anyone fooled by her innocence. The mask of the Beast.

I bowed my head. "You can count on me, Father Peter."

## Karen

Closing the door behind her, locking it, I watched as Mary edged her way through the small crowd of protesters on the sidewalk. I waited until she reached her car safely before I turned off the front light.

After feeding Sherry and changing her, checking her stats, I kissed her on the forehead, saying "Good night, sweetheart," and then I climbed up the stairs to my bedroom.

The house was completely, absurdly still. I was aware of the silence in a way I hadn't been since just after Simon left. I went downstairs to check Sherry again. Back in bed, I couldn't find a comfortable position, twisting from side to side, flipping my pillow, throwing off the comforter to cool off, pulling it back up when I got too cold.

Finally, I gave up. Sleep wasn't coming, and I didn't want to read in bed. I pulled on my robe and went down to the kitchen.

The ceiling light turned the darkened patio door into a mirror. I kept catching glimpses of my reflection as I looked in the drawer under the phone for some paper and a pen.

Back in Sherry's room, I took the largest of her books from the basket beside the bed and set it on my lap. Centering the paper on the book, I took the cap off the pen and began to write.

"There was once a princess in a kingdom by the sea. Beset by . . ."

# Part 6

*December 10–23*

*VICTORIA NEW SENTINEL*, TUESDAY, DECEMBER 10
## Can She Heal the Sick?
**Controversy Surrounds "Miracle Child"**

The parents of 4-year-old Sherilyn Barrett, comatose since a car accident last April, opened their Fernwood home to a steady line of injured and ill pilgrims yesterday. Following reports that Barrett had seemingly cured several people . . .

### Simon

I stopped short as I turned the corner onto Shakespeare at about 7:30. There was a crowd in front of the house, and judging from the garbage and the lawn chairs, they had been there all night.

They had leaned their signs against the fence, and most of them were hunched over steaming take-out cups. They were dressed for the weather, but they still seemed cold, stomping their feet and rubbing their arms.

I was in front of Cecil's place next door when they noticed me.

"It's the father!"

The crowd surged toward me, the protesters coming into focus.

A woman in a floral dress with a heavy brown coat shouted, "How can you do this to your child?"

"Why?" A man with a close-cropped beard and glasses, wearing thick socks in his sandals.

"Liar!" A pretty blond girl in her midteens.

I kept walking. I never thought they'd touch me. So when hands shoved my chest, grabbed my arms, I stumbled and lost my balance, almost fell.

"Sinner!"

I righted myself, then lowered my shoulder and pushed through them to the gate.

The protesters shouted behind me, waving their fists and signs, but no one followed me into the yard.

"Are you all right?" The question came from a young woman in a wheelchair, first in the line of six pilgrims at the base of the ramp. The words were thick and hesitant. She looked like she might have MS—it was clearly difficult for her to speak.

It took me a moment to answer. "Yes. I am," I said. "Did they do that to you, too? Block your way into the yard?"

She nodded.

I let myself into the house with a key I hadn't used in months.

"Karen?" I called as I slipped off my shoes.

"I'm with Sherry."

She was smoothing a new nightgown over Sherry's legs.

"How long have those people been out there?"

"The protesters?" She drew the covers up. "Most of the night," she said. "A few of them, at least. More have been arriving since it got light."

I shook my head. "They blocked the gate. I had a hard time getting through. Apparently they've been doing it to the pilgrims as well."

"Are you all right? Is anyone hurt?"

"They pushed me around a bit. I'm going to call the police."

"They were already here."

"What?"

"It was a busy day."

She started by telling me about the previous day with the pilgrims, about Dr. McKinley losing his job. I stopped her when she told me about her confrontation with Father Peter.

"Why didn't you call me?" I asked. "My cell was on."

"It wasn't exactly the best day for you either."

"I would have come."

"I know."

I didn't say anything when she told me about Mary staying for dinner, and she didn't volunteer any details. I was surprised to hear that John Richards had come to the house.

"So he just wanted to ask some questions?"

She nodded. "He said there wasn't an investigation, but that someone else might be in touch. He said you should call him."

By 9:30, the lineup of pilgrims reached to the gate.

Shortly before ten, the television trucks and Father Peter arrived, so close together, it was as if they had coordinated it. No sooner had the crews readied their cameras than the protesters began singing. Up came the signs: WORSHIP NOT FALSE IDOLS. PROPHET, NOT PROFIT. There must have been two dozen of them, marching along the sidewalk, across the width of the front lawn, shouting and chanting and singing.

Father Peter stood away from the group, watching them from the rear of a plumber's van, out of range of the cameras.

"We're ready," Karen said. I let the blind fall back against the front window and turned to face her.

The shouting and chanting were gaining in force and volume as the protesters tried to drive the pilgrims away from the house. The pilgrims ignored them as best they could, and the protesters increased the pressure, leering into the yard, singing hymns. The television cameras devoured it all.

Then Karen opened the front door, and the day's parade of the sick and the dying began.

I spent the morning taking down information as the pilgrims passed through the foyer. I assumed, initially, that it would be better to keep my distance, to maintain my objectivity. That dispassionate distance is one of the first skills you learn as a lawyer: don't fall for a client.

I kept my head down, my eyes focused on my clipboard, only glancing up when someone new came through the door.

"Your name is?"

I was pleased with how smoothly everything was going: by noon, I had more than twenty names on my list.

And then Lorraine Coombs touched my arm.

I was writing her name when I felt her fingers just above my wrist. Her touch was hot, sticky.

I glanced up and met her eyes, liquid blue and bright. She smiled.

Her skin was bright red, damp with sweat. With one hand, she clutched the handle of her walker as if she might collapse without it. With the other, she had reached out.

I couldn't look away.

"Are you all right?" I asked.

"As good as I've been," she said, still smiling.

I set the clipboard down and tucked the pen into my pocket. "Let me help you," I said.

She took my arm, and we walked, halting step by halting step, to see Sherry.

"Thank you," she said in the doorway to Sherry's room, her face lighting up when she saw my daughter.

"You're welcome."

After that, I began to notice how each pilgrim's face lit with hope and desperation when they first saw her. None of them were reluctant, none of them reserved. They hoped—no, they believed. They believed that my daughter could save them, that her touch could help them reclaim their lives.

I envied them their faith, the clarity of their belief.

After the last pilgrim left at three, I followed Karen to the kitchen.

She had been the very embodiment of strength and balance through the day. She seemed to be everywhere at once, and nothing threw her off. She was in the front yard, talking with the pilgrims as they waited in line, learning their names, their stories. She was at the gate, helping them push past the protesters into the yard. She was in Sherry's room, checking on our girl. She was taking over from Ruth, from Stephen, from Jamie, and even me, when we needed a break. I never saw her flag.

We left Ruth and Dr. McKinley working with Sherry. Jamie was sorting through the information that we had collected about the people who had come through the house. Karen had asked her to follow up with the pilgrims a few days after they went through the house.

I was pouring her a cup of coffee when she asked, "It's amazing, isn't it?"

She was sitting at the table, and I set the mug in front of her.

"It is. I wasn't expecting it to be like this."

"Like what?"

I sat down across from her. "So personal, I guess," I said, sipping my coffee. "I've never . . . I've seen a lot of people who were sick or hurt. I've done the best I can for them; that's been my job. But with the case-work, it's so clinical, so detached. I've never felt . . . connected like this."

She smiled a little, and nodded. "It feels important, this. What we're doing."

"Yeah. I . . ." I couldn't put my feelings into words.

Seeing my daughter through the eyes of the pilgrims was a revelation. I had fed Sherry and washed her and dressed her, had sung her to sleep and sung to her when I knew that she would not awaken. She was a beautiful little girl who smelled of shampoo and soap and milky skin, whose laughter had sounded like singing. I had been there at her birth. I had been there at the moment of her death, and when she had come back.

In the eyes of the pilgrims, though, she was something else, something more. At some point in the last few days, she had stopped being my little girl alone and had become a vessel for their hopes and their faith, a glowing symbol where once there had been a child who liked to fill her pockets with stones.

I struggled to reconcile the two visions of Sherry in my mind—my girl and their grail. I wanted to deny the pilgrims their beliefs, to preserve the image of my daughter as just a little girl, but now I couldn't.

I tried again. "It's . . ."

"Real," Karen said.

Our eyes met across the table.

"Real," I said.


### Karen

"Simon's gone?" Jamie asked as I came back into the kitchen.

I nodded. "Guitar case in hand. A wandering minstrel he . . ."

Jamie smiled.

"It was hard."

"Having him here?"

"Letting him go," I said. "I wanted him to stay."

"That wouldn't—"

I shook my head. "No. That wouldn't have been good."

"You don't want to rush into anything."

I couldn't help but smile. "Yes," I said. "Yes, I do. That's the whole problem."

Simon

I stopped at McDonald's on the walk back downtown and wolfed down a burger and fries without even tasting them. But even with the stop, the six o'clock news was just starting as I turned on the TV in my hotel room.

We were about three stories in—not breaking news, but ahead of the first commercial. The piece was short: the pilgrims from the morning, some file footage of the accident scene, Father Peter's protesters singing their hymns on the sidewalk. He was nowhere to be seen—he had a knack for disappearing when cameras turned to him.

After the story, I turned off the television.

I had no idea what to do with myself.

I stretched out on the bed. I was exhausted, but when I closed my eyes my mind sprang to life—no chance of sleep.

I unpacked the bag I had brought from Karen's, refolding the clothes and tucking them into the battered dresser under the TV. I stacked the books on the bedside table, reading each back cover before I put it down in hopes that something would appeal. Nothing did.

Turning the television back on, I flipped through the channels again. Nothing.

I took my time showering, just standing for a while in the hot water as it washed the day away. I toweled off thoroughly, put on a clean shirt, checked my watch.

6:47.

I was at a complete loss.

Hair still damp, I paced around the room. I replayed the day in my mind, thinking about Karen and Sherry, and about the pilgrims. I could see their faces in my mind, the seeming endless line of them, their hopeful eyes, their faith.

And I thought of Lorraine Coombs, and her touch on my arm.

Everything that had consumed me up to now seemed a thin veneer hiding the true texture of the world. A gaudy surface designed to distract, to keep me from pulling aside the curtain, to keep me from looking for the deeper truths I was sensing now.

I sat down on the bed and opened the guitar case. My fingers started picking out a blues, but I stopped myself. The idea of sitting alone in a hotel room, playing "Sometimes I Feel Like a Motherless Child," was too trite to bear.

Then I remembered that among the books I had brought from the house was a collection of traditional ballads. I riffled through the pages, cracked the spine, and started to play.

*The wind doth blow today, my love*
*And a few small drops of rain;*
*I never had but one true-love;*
*In cold grave she was lain.*

There were secrets in ancient songs like the ones Francis Child collected; secrets that I couldn't explain, that I didn't understand. They were all story songs, and you always knew where you were going, verse to verse. But there was an entire world just under the surface. A world of ghosts and angels and demons pulling the strings, all with their own stories, their own motivations, impossible for the characters—or the listeners—to fully understand.

The chords vibrated through me, and it felt like every one of my cells opened to welcome the music like rain. I sang, and for a moment, I felt a part of something larger, something just beyond my understanding. Every word seemed to bring me closer.

Leo

The only light in the empty church was from the candles, stuck with their own wax to the windowsills. I had lit them for Father Peter, saying a Hail Mary as I waited for each wick to catch. Candles always made me think of Jesus, His brightness in a world of dark. They made me feel so proud I could be helping.

Pride. One of the seven deadly sins.

But it felt so right to be doing God's work. To be standing tall against the forces of evil.

Even with the candles, the room was more dark than light, and filled with people. Everyone was waiting. Everyone jumped when Father Peter stepped out of the shadows.

"I apologize for our surroundings here tonight," he said as he walked to the front. "It's not pleasant, but the need for privacy outweighs comfort." He didn't talk loud, but I could hear him all the way in the back. Nobody else was making a sound. Quiet as a church mouse. Church mice.

"I don't want to keep you in this place any longer than you have to be. I'd like to begin with a prayer."

There was a rustle as everyone bowed their heads. We all knew the words.

We said amen after Father Peter; then the room was quiet again.

"You all know why we're here," he began again. "I'd like to take a moment to thank those of you who were with me today at that house, and to think of those who aren't with us tonight, because they are still there, doing the Lord's work in the dark of night."

A few people said, "Amen."

"If you were at the Barretts' house today, you saw those misguided souls, those who believe that Sherilyn Barrett can perform miracles. Can perform miracles! As if she were gifted at the piano, or could paint."

There was angry muttering in the dark.

"Miracles are the province of God!" He lifted his hands over his head, punching the air and almost shouting. "And yet these people continue to insist that this girl is somehow holy. Unbaptized, but holy. Taking money for these miracles, but she is holy!

"I have been inside that house. I have seen that little girl. I have uncovered and revealed their lies for what they really are: a cruel attempt to make money—to make money!—from the pain and suffering of other people. To take advantage of people who are too weak, too desperate, to take solace in the Lord, to put their faith in God alone. It is our job to protect these people.

"I've been in that house. I've looked at that little girl. There are no miracles there, only lies and deception.

"But they will not stop. The Barretts will not stop their lying. The truth has been revealed in the newspapers—you've all seen it. Everybody knows that they are lying, but still they prey on the weakness of the sick, the crippled, the suffering, the weak in God. They must be stopped. We must stop them!"

Father Peter bowed his head. "Let us pray for strength."

### Simon

John Richards was waiting for me at the bar, a bowl of peanuts and a plastic cup in front of him.

He stood up and extended his hand as I approached.

"How are you, John?" I asked, sitting next to him.

"I been better," he said, settling himself back onto his stool. He looked like a boxer gone to seed, big and shambling. His nose had been broken several times. "Nice place you got here."

The bar John had suggested had a reputation as one of the roughest in Victoria. It stank of spilled beer and cigarette smoke. "All the comforts of home," I said.

He waved the bartender over for me. "I'll have a—" I tried to think of a brand they were likely to have. "—a Bud. A bottle."

The bartender shook his ax-shaped head. "No bottles."

"You don't have Budweiser in bottles?"

"No bottles at all. No glasses." He gestured down the bar, and John lifted his plastic cup to me in a mock toast.

"All right. Just a pint of Budweiser."

He pulled the beer and slid it to me. When I opened my wallet, he glanced at John and shook his head at me, waving away my five-dollar bill.

"Are you a regular?" I asked after the bartender turned away.

John shrugged.

I took a swallow of the weak beer. "So what's up, John? Karen told me you came by the house."

"Yeah. I wanted to . . ." His gravelly voice was low, and I leaned toward him to hear. "I'm sorry I had to do that."

I shrugged. "I figured we'd hear from the police, after the story in the paper."

His voice dropped further. "I owe you a lot, Simon." He stared down at the bar.

"Don't sweat it, John. I just did what anybody would have done."

He glanced up at me sharply, locking eyes. I wondered how long he'd been sitting at the bar. "Don't say that. It's not true. Because of you I've still got a job, I've got a pension, I've got my family."

I nodded, uncomfortable with his vehemence. "Sure. Okay."

"That's why I wanted to be the one to go to your house. I thought maybe I could . . . I dunno. I thought I might be able to help. Take a bit of the heat." He shook his head, his eyes tightening in what looked like sadness.

"What's going on, John?" I asked, steeling myself for his answer.

"Charlie . . . you know Charlie, right?"

Charlie Hopkins was John's partner.

"Charlie's got this girlfriend, works over at Monty's sometimes. Dances on the circuit. He sees her when she's in town. Sends her flowers. Nice girl. Clean. No drugs. She makes Charlie happy. Not the sort of girl you want your wife finding out about, though."

"Ah."

"Yeah. You know."

I did.

"Anyway, so Charlie's got this girl. And yesterday he comes in all twitchy. I ask him what's up, but he doesn't say anything. Not at first. But Charlie, he knows a little something about what you did for me, so he pulls me aside and he tells me about this telephone call."

I could see where this was going. "Shit."

"Yeah. He got this phone call at home Sunday afternoon. His wife is sitting right there and this guy starts talking about Clarice, and how if Charlie didn't want his wife to find out . . . Your name came up. Your little girl."

"Right."

John nodded, drained his glass, and waved for another. "Thing is, I'm walkin' around the station today after Charlie tells me this, and nobody's making eye contact. Everybody's twitchy. And I start to think that maybe there were a lot of phone calls on Sunday afternoon. And then the story in the paper came up at the morning briefing. You've never seen a squad room so quiet."

"What are you telling me, John?"

"I'm telling you to be careful. I don't know who you pissed off, but somebody's got it in for you."

I had a fairly good idea. "Are we in danger?"

"I dunno. I can't get a read on it. All Charlie said was that the person who called him told him to be on the lookout for you and your family. And not in the serve-and-protect kind of way."

I couldn't bring myself to take another drink. It was all I could do to hold down my dinner.

VICTORIA NEW SENTINEL, FRIDAY, DECEMBER 13
## Waiting for a Miracle
**Religious Seekers Disturb Neighborhood**

More than a week after the *New Sentinel* first broke the story of miracles attributed to 4-year-old Sherilyn Barrett—and despite conflicting reports concerning her ability to heal the sick—pilgrims continue to arrive daily at the comatose girl's Fernwood home. The increased traffic is creating problems for the normally quiet neighborhood.

"It's like a circus over there," says Cecil White, who lives next door to the Barretts. "The people waiting to see Sherry are fine," says White, who calls himself a friend of the family. "It's the ones on the sidewalk are the problem."

The house has been besieged by demonstrators since early this week, protesting what they feel is a deception on the part of the Barretts.

"I've called the police on them a couple of times," says White. "They're out there all night, singing and shouting. They call themselves good Christians, but good Christians would let an old man get a good night's sleep."

## Simon

I was guardedly optimistic as I walked toward the house and saw that the crowd of protesters was no longer blocking the gate. They were partway down the sidewalk—I didn't have to fight my way through them. I didn't even notice the graffiti until I was in the front yard.

WHORE CHILD

Scrawled on the front wall in black spray paint, bordered by a pair of crosses, the words screamed at me.

SATAN

A crowd of the pilgrims were gathered at the painted wall, talking in whispers, pointing up to where the vandal had sprayed the words across Sherry's window and wall.

I unlocked the door and burst into the silence of the house.

"Simon, what—?" Karen came out of the kitchen as I slammed the door behind myself and headed for Sherry's bed.

"Are you all right? Simon, what is it?"

Nothing was changed from the day before. The light glowed beside the bed where Sherry lay, covers folded on her chest.

I released a breath I hadn't even realized I was holding. "Sherry's all right."

"Of course she is. I just checked on her," Karen said. "Simon, what's wrong?"

I stepped around the bed and opened the blinds. Karen gasped as the morning light struggled vainly past the words WHORE CHILD and SATAN, the writing backwards through the glass. Trails of paint trickled from the letters.

"Oh my God." One hand rose to her throat as she stepped toward the window. She knocked one of Sherry's stones from the windowsill and bent to pick it up.

"I'm going to call the police," Karen said, turning away from the window. "They can't ignore vandalism, can they?"

"Let me," I offered. "I'll call John." I made the call from the kitchen, sitting at one end of the table. "Sergeant Richards," I told the switchboard.

He picked up after three rings. "Richards."

"It's Simon Barrett."

The phone was silent in my hand.

"Hello, Mr. Barrett."

"Getting in or getting out, John?"

There was another long silence. "I'm just coming in. Is there something I can help you with?" His voice was flat.

"Is something wrong, John?"

"Just busy, Mr. Barrett. Is there something I can help you with?" Mr. Barrett. As if he didn't know me.

"I'm sorry for disturbing you, Sergeant. There's been some vandalism at the house."

"I'll transfer you to the reports desk."

"John—"

"It's Sergeant Richards, Mr. Barrett."

"Oh."

"I'm transferring you now, Mr. Barrett." He paused. I could almost hear him struggling to find the words. "I don't know if I'd get my hopes up, if I were you. They don't usually have much luck catching vandals. There's not much we can do." His voice dropped. "Simon, I told you. They know you and I are friends."

"Who are 'they'?"

He ignored the question. "You and your family aren't . . . I'm putting my neck on the line even talking to you like this. Do you understand what I'm telling you?"

Karen was staring at me, trying to make sense of my side of the conversation. "I think so."

"If a police cruiser stops in front of the house, they're not going to be there because you called them. Do you understand that?"

"Yes," I whispered.

"Do you want me to transfer you, Mr. Barrett?"

"No, thank you."

The phone died in my hand.

"That didn't go well," Karen said.

"No, it didn't." I recounted John's side of the conversation. "It's the same thing with Jamie at the newspaper, with my job, and Stephen at the hospital. It's Father Peter."

Karen was pale.

"This is what he was talking about when I let him into the house that day. The 'repercussions' of our decision." I shook my head; I still couldn't believe I had let him in. "Who else could it be?"

"Right."

I started to rummage through the cupboard under the sink.

"What are you doing?" she asked.

"Looking for a bucket and some gloves." I set a bottle of cleaner on the counter. "We need to get some of the paint off."

*The stranger was silent and still in the center of the crowd. The black let-ters on the white wall, covering the window, almost made him smile.*

*It was crass and crude, but he couldn't always control the details—and it served its purpose. Most times, all he had to do was put the spark to the tinder, fan the flames to life, and let the wind take the fire where it would.*

*Would it be enough? He thought it might be.*

*In the years that he had been doing his work, he had learned what worked: a steady escalation of pressure until spirits broke.*

*In these days of little faith, a vague threat and a promise of money were usually enough, and the pretenders were never heard from again. Sometimes, where traces of belief still lingered, he had to go further. Without livelihood, and with their positions in the community under at-tack, most people found it easier to walk away, to abandon their delu-sions and fade into obscurity.*

*It had been a very long time since he had been forced to call his sol-diers to direct action. This pressure would be enough. This family had no faith, nothing to guide them. They were barely a family. Why should they persevere?*

*He allowed himself to smile as the front door opened and the husband emerged, his face a grim mask.*

Simon

The water in the bucket steamed in the cold air.

Standing on a stepladder, I started with the windows. Using a painter's razor, I scraped at the edges of the spray paint, peeling it away from the glass like strips of a shredded garbage bag. It was slow going.

WHORE CHILD.

SATAN.

I took the rubber gloves off to better control the edge of the razor, and soon my fingers ached with the cold. I stopped every so often to breathe into my hands, to rub them together to bring some life back into them, but it didn't do much good.

I caught a movement out of the corner of my eye, and I turned so quickly, the ladder lurched.

One of the pilgrims, a woman with graying red hair and a heavy coat, was dipping a brush in the steaming bucket.

"Oh, ma'am," I called down to her. "You don't need to do that."

Shaking the water off the brush, she said, "It'll be done that much faster if we all help."

As she spoke, I turned around to see several of the other pilgrims following her across the front lawn. People stopped to pick up the rags and the sponges that I had brought.

When the television vans arrived just before ten, the window was cleaned of the curses and the graffiti on the wall had been scrubbed down to a filthy gray blur. The wall would need a coat of paint, but in order to see the words now, you needed to know what you were looking for.

"Thank you all," I said. "I really appreciate your help."

As the pilgrims moved back to their places in line, my eyes met those of Father Peter, who was standing, swallowed up by his black coat, on the other side of the fence. A huge man in plumber's coveralls stood next to him, bouncing a little on his feet and staring at me, too.

I took my time picking up a rag from the grass, scrubbing at the tiny flecks of paint stuck to my hands. It was important to stand up, to seem strong, even if my heart was pounding inside my chest. It was important to gather everything slowly, to clean up after myself methodically, to show him we weren't cowed.

Just before I went into the house I looked back again, and he smiled. That smile—that cold, guileless smile.

It wasn't until I had shut the door that I realized where I'd seen a smile like that before. It had been in court. A friend from law school was defending a man against murder charges, and I had gone to watch. It was an infamous case, standing room only in the gallery, and during sentencing, the accused had smiled in the same way: innocent, but with a deadness, a calculation in his eyes.

As the judge declared him not criminally responsible due to diminished capacity and sentenced him to an indeterminate stay at a psychological treatment center, he had smiled. The devil, he claimed, had told him to kill his wife and three children in their beds.

*VICTORIA NEW SENTINEL,* THURSDAY, DECEMBER 19

## Miracle Casualty
**Tempers Flare at Miracle Home**

Police and an ambulance were called to the home of 4-year-old Sherry Barrett yesterday afternoon when a 45-year-old man, suffering from multiple sclerosis, was injured by protesters while attempting to see the little girl.

Witnesses reported a struggle occurred when protesters tried to restrict the man's entry to the Barrett property and the man was pushed to the sidewalk, suffering injuries to his head and back. His name was not released to the media, and the Barrett family could not be reached for comment.

## Henry

Even into the night there were people in front of the Barretts' house, marching, holding their signs proudly.

I stayed in the shadows, not knowing anymore who might be able to see me, not wanting to risk meeting Peter again. From the dark of the hedge I could watch both the house and people on the sidewalk.

I caught sight of Mrs. Barrett every now and then, the shadow of her against the blinds in the front room as she cared for Sherry. It felt a little strange, almost like I was a Peeping Tom or something, but it wasn't like that.

After midnight all the lights went out inside the house. The protesters set down their signs and sat in a circle on the concrete with candles in front of them, holding hands. Some of them slept in sleeping bags or under blankets while others kept watch.

I could hear the faint sound of whistling from down the block; then a dark figure walked up the middle of the street and stopped in front of the driveway gate, just outside the pool of light thrown by the streetlamp.

Was he one of the protesters? I couldn't tell. He seemed—

"Aren't you cold, my boy?"

"Tim?" I whispered, hurrying toward him. "What are you doing here?"

It wasn't until I saw that he was bundled up in a winter coat with scarf and gloves that I noticed the cold.

"Freezing my ass off," he answered, rubbing his gloves together. "And you, out here in your shirtsleeves." He shook his head, then burst out laughing. "I was just about to tell you that you should be careful or you'll catch your death."

I didn't find the joke so funny. "What are you doing here?"

"I thought I would see where you were going every night. I thought it might be here."

"I just—"

"Henry," he said, cutting me off. "I've got something important to tell you." The humor had left his eyes. "Here, step into the light." Pulling off a glove, he reached into his jacket pocket and pulled out a crumpled piece of paper. There was a downtown address on it, written in spidery black ink.

"What's this?" I asked.

"It's a church. An old church where your friend Father Peter holds his meetings every night."

I flinched, and glanced over at the protesters. "You want me to go to a meeting with Father Peter? Why would I do that?"

"For the same reason that you spend every night here, watching over this family." He took a deep breath, his face tight with concern. "You know you have a role in this."

"But I don't want to have anything to do with—"

"I know."

"What's he got to do with the Barretts anyway? What aren't you telling me?"

"You can't imagine the terrible things he's done, Henry." He shook his head and laid one hand on my shoulder, squeezing. "His actions can't be traced back to him directly, but when things do happen, he's usually around. He's been spotted in the backgrounds of photographs, or people mention seeing him days or hours before . . . I've seen what he's done. I think you need to go to one of his meetings," he said.

"Why?"

He sighed. "Because it is always better to know one's enemy than to simply hope he'll go away."

"Then why don't you go?"

"This isn't about me, Henry," he answered.

"What's he going to do to the Barretts?"

He gestured toward the note in my hand. "I don't know."

"So I'm . . ." My voice trailed off as the full realization hit me. "I have to stop it, don't I? That's why I'm here. Whatever it is he's planning to do, I have to stop it."

"You don't *have* to do anything, Henry," Tim said. "If you want to, you can just walk away from all this. But if you were going to do that, you wouldn't be out here in the cold every night, would you?

"Here," he said, undoing and pulling off his coat. "You hang on to this." He held the coat out to me.

I realized how cold I had been as I slipped into it, his warmth surrounding me. "Aren't you going to be cold?"

"I'm keeping the gloves." He smiled. "Don't worry about it. I'll just steal another from the lost and found. You need it more than I do."

My cold fingers fumbled with the buttons, but once it was done up, the coat felt like armor.


Mary


When I opened my apartment door, it took me a moment to accept that Simon was really there, standing in the hallway. It had been only ten days, but it felt like a lifetime.

"Hey," I said, holding the doorknob tightly.

He shifted from foot to foot. "I guess this is a bit of a surprise."

"A bit."

Part of me wanted to slam the door. Another part wanted to invite him in—to erase the time and the distance between us.

I was afraid he was going to say that he wanted to come back, that leaving had been a mistake. I was afraid he was going to say that it was over, that he was happy with Karen. I was afraid of how I would respond to whatever he said.

"I tried you at the office, and they said you were no longer with them."

"Yeah."

"Did they fire you? Was it because of us, or Sherry, or—?"

"I left." Stepping back, I allowed the door to swing open. "Why don't you . . ."

He nodded and stepped inside.

It was strange to have him in the apartment again. "I don't want to talk about—"

"You worked so hard," he continued, as if he hadn't heard me.

"I didn't want to be there after what they did to you," I blurted. "I know how stupid that sounds. I tried to give two weeks' notice the day after they fired you, and they told me to leave, immediately. Paid out my two weeks."

I preempted the lecture I knew was coming. "I know it was stupid. I know that I've thrown away, well, maybe my whole career. But I'm happier now."

"Have you lined up another job already?"

I shook my head. "I thought I'd take a little time, try to figure out what I really want to be doing. What's important to me."

"That's a good idea."

"No lecture about not being so naïve?"

"I don't think you're naïve. And I'm starting to think that maybe figuring out what really matters isn't such a bad thing. Even if it takes some time. I'm glad," he said. "I'm glad it's working out for you."

He looked down at the carpet.

"I wanted to say I'm sorry," he said, without meeting my eye. "It wasn't fair, what I did to you. Drawing you into all of this, then just leaving you up in the air."

I touched the back of his hand, and he looked up. "Simon, I went into this with my eyes open. You don't get involved with a married man assuming that it's all going to work out perfectly. I never thought we'd be permanent. I never thought that you'd leave Karen. Or Sherry." I smiled a little, and then simply asked, "Are you back with Karen?"

He shrugged. "I don't know. I've been at the house helping, but I'm staying at the Balmoral. . . . It's all still up in the air."

"But you want to be."

"I'm trying."

I thought I'd feel devastated to hear him say that. Betrayed. Instead, I felt relieved.

For a long time he stared, out the window over my left shoulder as I chased words round my head, trying to figure out how to say everything that I needed to say.

"I should go," he finally said.

I nodded, unable to muster anything else. I was happy for him, and I was happy for me, happy that this, at last, had turned out right. But I still felt on the verge of crying as his hand closed around the doorknob.

"Simon."

He turned to face me, his hand still on the knob.

I wanted to go to him, to feel myself against him this one last time, smell him, taste the salt of him. Instead, I whispered, "I hope you work it out. I hope you'll be happy."

He smiled at me. Then he turned away, closing my apartment door softly behind himself. The click as the bolt slid into place seemed to echo through the sudden stillness.

I stared at the door, realizing, for what seemed like the first time, that part of life was never getting a chance to say all that you should to someone before they are gone.

## Henry

I came in just as Father Peter was stepping onto the small platform at the far end of the room. His bodyguard stood several steps behind him. I moved to one side, hidden in the crowd of people and thankful that the candlelight was too dim for him to see me.

"Great God in Heaven," he said loudly. "Please look down on this Your enterprise and favor us with Your blessing."

The room was packed, everyone with their heads bowed.

"Our Lord Jesus, please forgive us our sins and betrayals, and bless us in this Your work. O Holy Spirit, please bathe us in Your glory, and anoint us for this Your task. Amen."

The crowd echoed "Amen" and lifted their heads.

"They have not learned," he started, picking up from a speech that clearly everyone knew but me. "The people keep coming, lining up to sell their souls to that family. Nothing we do or say seems to stop them."

To look at his followers, I could have been at a PTA meeting or a union gathering. Everyone looked so normal. An overweight woman in her fifties clutched her purse tight against her chest, while the young man next to her looked like student, with short hair and wire-framed glasses. A woman with dark hair held a sleeping baby on her shoulder, and three children—two boys and a girl, all fair-haired and under the age of ten—knelt at the very front, their eyes lifted to him as he spoke.

"I'm not angry at those people they are calling 'pilgrims.' The Lord said, 'Forgive them, Father, they know not what they do.' We must forgive those whose illness brings them low, makes them vulnerable to evil.

"I feel sorry for those people. They think they are putting themselves in the hands of the Lord. They clutch their Bibles"—he lifted his up—"they whisper prayers, they kneel . . . They *kneel* before that little girl. Thou shalt worship no false idols before Me! That's the word of God, and yet these people, these people kneel before a little girl, like the Israelites before the golden calf! It is our job to protect these people, from the Barretts and from themselves!"

The older woman clasped her hands and shut her eyes tight, while the young mother swayed in place.

"We must be strong. We must be devout in our beliefs, and coura-geous in our actions. I have gathered you here because our church, our God, is under attack, and we, as the soldiers of the Lord, must go to battle in its defense."

The student and several other people shouted in agreement, their faces lighting up.

"We have been gentle. We have been kind. We have tried to persuade and to remind, to turn people back to the path of true faith, of righteousness. But so long as that family opens their doors, so long as that child is whored out by her own family, our words mean nothing. How can the soft words of the righteous compete with the promises of the evil?"

The crowd leaned toward him, flexing itself like a single muscle. The children in the front folded their hands in front of their chests and closed their eyes in prayer.

"It is time to act. It is time to take steps against the source of the evil. The time for words is over. Now is the time for action! Who is with me? Who will stand with me?"

I couldn't stand it anymore. I ran for the door as people started calling out to him.

The wind had picked up—it drove cold and merciless right through the bulky winter coat—but it felt good. It drove out the echoes of that empty church. It rid my ears of his voice.

I walked as fast as I could up the dark side alley toward the main street. Under a streetlight, I started to feel a little better. The lampposts were decorated for Christmas with lights and ribbons, and I slowed down a bit, drawing the coat up around my neck. I couldn't work up the nerve to look back, afraid Father Peter had spotted me. I passed a few people on the sidewalk—they didn't look like fanatics, but I had discovered that most fanatics don't. The people in that church basement were as normal-looking as anyone I had ever seen, but they all had the same violence in their eyes that Father Peter did, once they heard him speak.

*"Karen, it's Jamie. It's a little past seven, Friday morning. December whatever. Twentieth, I guess. Uhm, listen, I'm not going to be able to make it to the house today. I've got something on the go. I don't want to get your hopes up, but . . . Listen, I'll tell you later, okay? Talk to you soon."*

## Simon

I didn't think anything of it when Father Peter and his bodyguard joined the protesters the next morning before we opened the house. I heard a motor on the street and looked between the blinds of Sherry's window as the plumbing company van that Father Peter's thug drove pulled to a stop. The doors opened and a small group climbed out, carrying signs.

I had just turned away from the window when the glass exploded behind me.

Without thinking, I threw myself at Sherry, covering her with my body as glass sprayed into the room, a series of dull thuds echoing from the walls.

Rocks. They were throwing rocks at the house.

I could hear Karen running down the hall from the kitchen. Something flew through the window and shattered against the coffee table. Shattered.

Bottles. Not rocks. They were throwing bottles.

"Get down, Karen," I called to her. "No—get out. Get out of the way."

Fumbling with the covers, I lifted Sherry, cradling her head to my chest, and scurried across the room, sheltering her with my body. She was surprisingly heavy. Shards of broken glass tore into my socked feet, and I stumbled. Another bottle flew into the room, crashing against the wall at the head of the bed, spraying Sherry's sheets with jagged diamonds.

In the hallway, Karen stood stock still, her eyes wide with panic.

She reached for Sherry. "Simon, is she—?"

I rushed past her into the seeming security of the family room.

## Karen

I fell to my knees at the side of the couch where he set Sherry down. "Is she all right?"

"I think so. I don't know." He stepped away from her, and I saw the blood spotting her face.

"She's bleeding," he said in the same moment. "I wasn't quick enough." Tracing his fingers over her forehead, streaking blood along her pale skin.

"It's okay," I said. The shards of glass had barely broken the skin. "This doesn't look too bad, and Stephen will be here any minute now."

A little nausea rose in my throat—I could still hear the sound of bottles smashing against the house, but that sound was a world away. All that mattered was that my baby was safe.

"Are you okay, Simon?"

I waited for him to reply; then realized I was alone in the room. "Simon?" His bloody footprints led out of the family room, toward the front door.

I heard the click as the door opened, then Simon's voice. "Hey, what do you think—!"

The door closed. And then nothing.


Ruth


The pilgrims were huddled against the hedge as I drove toward the house, and the protesters were in the middle of the lawn. I didn't even have a moment to wonder why before I realized that the protesters were throwing bottles at the house. Sherry's window was broken.

I stopped my car in the middle of the street. I had no idea what to do. I couldn't get to the house, but I couldn't just leave the pilgrims. They seemed so scared.

I was about to run next door to call the police when the front door opened and Simon came out.

He raised his hand to shield his eyes from the morning light. "Hey," he called. "What do you think—"

As he spoke, the biggest of the protesters, the one who usually stood with Father Peter, threw a bottle, which caught the light as it spun through the air. Simon couldn't see it.

The bottle shattered against his head. He stood for a moment, rocking on his feet as if trying to understand what was happening to him, then crumpled to the stoop.

"Simon!" The protesters scattered as I ran through the yard.

His face was masked with blood, his breath bubbling red between his lips.

Please let the door be open.


## Simon

I awoke on the floor of the foyer with shocking suddenness. One moment I was standing on the front porch, catching the glint of something coming at me; then I was flat on my back, looking up at Karen and Ruth.

"What—?" I struggled to rise, but the weight of hands on my shoulders pressed me back down.

"Just rest a moment," Ruth said, from what seemed like a long distance away. "Almost done."

I felt the softness of a hand on my cheek. Karen's. I let my eyes close. Sharp pain in my right foot. I flinched and pulled away.

"That's got it," Stephen said, swimming into view. "I've bandaged . . . Oh, I see our patient is awake."

"He's been in and out," Ruth said.

"How are you doing?" Stephen asked, leaning over me.

It was hard to talk. My lips felt thick, and my face seemed stretched taut. "Sherry. Where's—?"

"She's okay. The doctor checked her." That was Karen.

"What happened—?"

"You got hit." He lifted my left eyelid with his thumb. "With a bottle." A bright light flashed into my eye, and I tried to look away. My left eyelid closed and there was a gentle pressure on my forehead before my right eye was forced open and the light flashed again. "Ruth pulled you inside." He turned to the nurse. "Can you give me a hand?"

"I can do it," Karen said.

"We're going to move you into the kitchen," Stephen explained. "I want you to try and sit up and Karen and I—"

"I can walk," I protested.

"That's one of the things we're going to check," he said as he shifted me to a sitting position. "But right now your feet are probably a little tender."

I had no idea what he was talking about until I tried to stand up and my knees buckled with the pain. I would have fallen if he and Karen hadn't been there to support me.

After we had hobbled to a chair at the kitchen table, Stephen ran a series of tests—vision and reflexes and memory and cognition—as Karen explained again what had happened. It took me a moment to realize that she was holding my hand. Ruth brought me a glass of water, cautioning me to take small sips. When Stephen took his stitching kit from his medical bag, Karen blanched and offered to get me a new pair of socks.

The tug of the thread through the tight skin of my forehead made me feel like I was going to vomit.

"You're doing fine," Stephen muttered in what had to be reflexive reassurance. I didn't feel fine.

"Just a couple more."

"So do you travel everywhere with a needle and thread, Doctor?" I asked him. I hoped that it sounded like a joke—I meant it as a joke.

"What did you think I was around here for, my good looks?"

I smiled, with some difficulty. "No, I think that's my job description."

He finished up, snipping the thread, and took a long look at me. "You may need to find alternate employment, at least for a while." As he repacked his bag, he said, "It's quick and dirty. You'll need to get it looked at. Maybe a cosmetic surgeon."

"Thanks, Stephen," I said.

"Are you okay with these?" Karen asked. She held up a pair of white cotton socks.

I nodded, and bent over to slide them on.

"Do you want me—?" Karen offered.

I shook my head, then reconsidered. "Please."

She was careful, but I had to close my eyes against a sudden dizziness.

"Are you okay?" Stephen asked.

"Woozy."

"Take it nice and slow."

I nodded. "I'll be fine." I took a deep breath and opened my eyes.

The first thing I saw was the concern on Karen's face. "I'll be fine," I said, to her alone.

She tried to smile.

"Is Sherry . . ."

"She's okay. A few cuts, but just minor. The doctor checked her over."

"That's good."

I looked up at Stephen and Ruth behind Karen.

"You all should get back to work, though," I said. "No need to worry about me."

"No," Karen said. "We can't. Sherry's room is a disaster."

"But what about the pilgrims?"

"Simon, we have to think about ourselves, about Sherry. It's not safe."

"That's what he wants," I said. "That's what he's wanted from the beginning."

"He's still out there," Ruth said. "Watching the house. Most of his people ran when you got hit, but he stayed."

Bracing myself against the table, I stood up.

"What are you doing?" Karen asked.

"I'm going out there," I said, walking slowly out of the kitchen.

"What?"

My feet were throbbing, and the walls seemed to inhale and exhale around me. "I'm going out there," I repeated. "We can't just let him—"

"What if they start up again?"

I stopped in the foyer to force my feet into my shoes. I was shocked to see the smears of blood on the floor, and a small pool of congealing red near the front door. My blood, staining the cold tiles of my home.

Karen was staring at the blood. I couldn't read her expression.

"I have to," I said. "If we just let this go, then . . ." I didn't know how to finish, so I just opened the door.

"Wait," Karen said. She was putting on her shoes and pulling a jacket down from the hook. Her face was hard, determined.

I thought of telling her to stay in the house, that it was too dangerous. But I realized I wanted her to come with me; I wanted us to be together. I needed her strength.

I held the door for her.

## Karen

The air was crystalline and cold, the silence so profound, it felt like the world might shatter with a single word. It was still early; there were no reporters or television vans on the street.

Father Peter looked as if he was expecting us. Alone on the sidewalk, he played with his coin and didn't move as we crossed the lawn past the pilgrims who followed us with their eyes.

"You look terrible," Father Peter said to Simon with mock concern. "This is what happens when you put your family directly in harm's way."

As he spoke, Simon seemed to coil into himself, strengthening and solidifying, staring the priest in the eye.

When he spoke, his voice was calm and cold. "I want to tell you what's going to happen next." Simon took a deep breath. "In a few minutes, Karen and I are going to go back into the house, and while I clean up the blood and the broken glass and fix the window, Karen is going to invite these people—" He gestured at the pilgrims. "—in to see our daughter."

He took a step toward Father Peter. The priest stepped back reflexively.

"And that's what we'll do every day. If you or your friends spray-paint obscenities on our walls, we'll scrub them off, and the people will come. If you break our windows, we'll fix them, and the people will come. If you hurt us, we'll wash off the blood, slap on some bandages, and the people will come." He pulled his hair back with one hand to show the priest the gash with its row of stitches. "Do you see this? That's what we'll do. Every day. Any wound you inflict, we'll stitch up. We're not going to stop, no matter what you do. You've showed us just how important this work is. Too many lives are at stake."

I stepped forward, lending Simon whatever strength I could.

"Including your own, Mr. Barrett," the priest whispered. "Do you think it was an accident that you were struck by a bottle this morning?" His eyes were bright, unblinking. "Do you actually believe that God didn't guide the hand of he that threw it?

"One such as yourself," he hissed, "ignorant of the Lord's work, of the teachings of the faith, can perhaps be forgiven for not understanding. Perhaps someone who has chosen to ignore those teachings"—his eyes flicked to me—"might tell you what happens to those who oppose the Lord's work."

He waited a long moment.

"They burn, Mr. Barrett. They drown. The Lord drowned a whole world when it displeased him. He burned cities full of sinners. Are you willing to burn for something in which you do not even believe, Mr. Barrett? Are you willing to consign your daughter to the flames?"

He folded his hands piously in front of him. "I'll let you go back to your work, as I go back to mine."

He turned and walked away down the sidewalk. He didn't look back.

Simon swayed on his feet. "I think," he said, his face white as chalk. "I think I need to sit down."


Simon

"You should see a doctor."

"What?" I lifted my head from the pillow as Karen sat next to me on the bed.

*Our bed.*

"I did see a doctor." Moving made my head swim, and I lay back down.

"You've been out all day. Stephen actually checked on you a couple of times."

"All day?" I struggled to sit up. The effort set off fireworks behind my eyes. "What time is it?"

"About four thirty. Everyone's gone home," Karen answered.

"Oh, shit, Karen, I'm sorry. I only meant to lie down for a second."

She smiled and put her hand on my leg. "You've been through a lot."

"How did everything go?"

"It went fine. It took us a while to clean up the mess, so we didn't start letting people in until noon."

"How's Sherry?"

She stopped rubbing my leg. "She's fine," she said, then paused. "But something strange has happened. Can you make it down the stairs to see her?"

I followed her with tentative steps, trying to figure out if there was any way I could walk to avoid the cuts on my feet. I couldn't find any, but it wasn't as painful as I had feared.

Sherry was back in her own bed.

"You got the window fixed already?"

She shrugged. "I called, some guys came, the window got fixed. But that's not what I wanted to show you. Here—"

I couldn't see what Karen wanted me to see. Sherry looked like she always did, her lips parted in sleep, her breathing regular, her cheeks smooth.

I glanced sharply at Karen. She nodded.

Not trusting what I was seeing, I traced my daughter's cheeks with the tips of my fingers. Perfectly smooth.

"She was—"

"Yes."

Before I had stepped onto the porch, my daughter's face had been cut in a dozen places. And now . . .

"When did this happen?"

She was about to answer when the doorbell rang. She glanced up sharply, and I knew exactly what she was feeling.

But it was Jamie, standing on the front porch with an older woman and a bearded man with a camera. "Karen, Simon, this is . . . Listen, this is Amy Moore. She's a medical consultant for the *Globe and Mail.* And Don Neale, a photographer who is working with us today."

"Working with us? Jamie, what's this about?"

Jamie reached forward and squeezed Karen's upper arm. "I've been . . . Over the last week or so I've been doing some follow-ups with some of the people who have been coming to see Sherry. I didn't want to say anything until I had it nailed."

Karen said, "You'd better come in."

Jamie kept talking. "I've spent the last two days interviewing doctors to confirm what people were telling me. I'm working on a story for the Monday *Globe,* and I'm wondering if you'd like to comment—" She reached into her folio and extracted several file folders. "—on these reports from five doctors confirming spontaneous remissions and inexplicable recoveries in patients who have been to see Sherry in the last ten days?"

THE GLOBE AND MAIL, MONDAY, DECEMBER 23

## Spontaneous Healing

**Sick, Dying Go into Remission after
Paying Visits to Comatose Girl**

by Jamie Keller, special to *The Globe and Mail*

Doctors in Victoria, B.C., confirmed late last week that five patients with chronic or terminal conditions who visited 4-year-old Sherilyn Barrett, comatose since a car accident last spring, have demonstrated clear and remarkable recoveries.

"Of course I'm not going to use the word 'miracle'," said oncologist James Gibson, who spoke to the *Globe and Mail* with the permission of his patient Tanya Ross. "What is clear is that there has been a remarkable spontaneous remission that I am at a loss to explain."

Other doctors confirmed . . .

## Leo

"It should be over by now," Father Peter said, looking at the newspaper again.

We were in the van in the alley by the church. We weren't driving, but I had the motor running so the heater would work.

"This is all happening too fast," he said. "I thought they would have given up—"

He looked angry. Angrier than I had ever seen him.

"Spontaneous remissions. How can that be? How did it get this far? Where do they draw their strength from?"

"From hell," I said, without even thinking about it. Then I looked at him to see if I was right.

He was smiling at me. "Of course," he said. "Of course. That's it. And we know what the righteous do with devils like this, don't we, Leo?"

"We fight them," I said. I tried to remember what he had said at one of the meetings. "We bring the light of the Lord, the flaming sword—"

My watch beeped. "It's quarter to ten."

"And we can't be late," Father Peter said. "Not today. There will be too many questions. From this." He rattled the newspaper. "Those weak of faith and limited of vision will be doubting—"

"Like Thomas."

"Like Thomas. But not you. You're one of us, aren't you, Leo? One of the righteous. The pure of heart. No doubts, no hesitation."

I nodded and stepped on the gas.

"And what do the righteous do, Leo? They fight and they keep fighting. Even when the battle seems lost. Even when the devils seem to have won. They fight until they drop."

I nodded. I didn't know exactly what he meant, but I knew that I would keep fighting. I would never give up.

"This will be the last day, Leo. The last day at the house, I promise you that. This story says that they're stopping for the holidays, that after today they won't allow anyone in to see Sherilyn until the twenty-seventh.

"That gives us three days, Leo. Three days to ensure that they never reopen that house. Three days to bring the wrath of almighty God down on that house of sinners."

When I looked over at him, he was smiling.

# Part 7

*Christmas*

# Karen

The telephone on the bedside table rang well before seven, but I was already awake. I don't think I had slept at all, just watched the red digital numbers on the clock change.

I already knew who it was. "Hello?"

There was some whispered shushing and laughter, and I smiled. I could picture what was happening on the other end of the line. "We wish you a merry Christmas," came the massed voices of my family, two time zones away. "We wish you a merry Christmas . . ."

I could see them all, tatty sweaters and unbrushed hair, clustered around the telephone in the kitchen, the living room a blizzard of torn paper and candy-crazed children. My family did this every Christmas: called all the relations who couldn't be home. When I was a teenager, my brother Barry and I had started calling it the Cunningham Tubercular Choir. Nobody in my family could carry a tune; Simon's rudimentary folksinging had really stood out.

*Simon.*

". . . And a Happy New Year!" The song dissolved into a round of cheering and shouted Merry Christmases before Mom claimed the receiver for herself. "Merry Christmas, honey. And Merry Christmas to our Sherry, too."

"Merry Christmas, Mom." Tears filled my eyes despite myself. "Is everybody there?"

"Oh, yes," she said. "Everybody and their dog." I could see her sitting at the table. She would have brought out the Christmas dishes for the holidays, and the table would be covered with a red cloth, a little the worse for wear after Christmas Eve dinner. "I wish I was with you in Victoria, though."

"You'll be here next week."

"But it must be so hard for you—"

"I know how important it is for everyone to be home for Christmas, Mom. We're fine."

"I just worry about you, that's all."

"So who all's around?"

She let me change the subject. "Well, Chris finally brought that Heather girl he's been seeing."

"And how's that?"

"She seems very nice. A bit quiet. He's wandering around like he just won the lottery, though."

I could imagine. "Did Stan's kids come?"

"They're with their mom. He'll pick them up at the bus in time for dinner."

"That's good." I snuggled deeper under the blankets.

She waited a moment. "And how are you?"

"Just waking up," I lied.

"You shouldn't lie to your mother."

I smiled.

"You could never sleep on Christmas Eve. I hardly think you'd start this year."

"Yeah."

"And how is our little Sherry?"

I shifted in the bed. "I haven't been down yet," I confessed. "She was fine at midnight."

"Was Santa Claus good to her?"

I had to close my eyes and squeeze my face tight to keep from bursting into tears.

"Yes," I managed to say.

"I lit a candle for her last night."

"Thank you," I said, and I meant it.

"I lit one for you, too." She was silent for a long moment, waiting for me to say something. "I wish I could be there for you."

"Don't worry about us," I said, a little glad that she was worrying.

"I just don't like the idea of you being alone on Christmas. It doesn't seem right."

"We'll be all right. I decorated the tree yesterday, and I rented *It's a Wonderful Life* to watch this afternoon. Simon's coming for dinner." I tried to slip that in so she wouldn't notice.

She didn't say anything for several seconds. Then, "That's interesting."

"Let's leave it alone, Mom."

"He ran out on you and Sherry when you needed him most, and you're inviting him for Christmas dinner?"

"Mom."

"Karen, I know you're lonely but this, this is—"

"Mom."

"I won't say anything. You know me. I know how to keep my peace."

I did know her, and braced myself.

"I just think it's a big mistake. I don't know why you haven't been in contact with a lawyer—"

"Jesus, Mom."

"Language, Karen," she scolded. "Not another word. Not from me." A distant crash claimed her attention. "Listen to that. The kids are wanting some breakfast and have started to take the dogs hostage. I should go. Give me a call a bit later when you're up and about. Give a kiss to Sherry."

"I will."

"I love you, Karen."

"I love you, too, Mom,"

We both hung up without saying good-bye, like always. My relationship with my mother was an ongoing telephone conversation.

Simon

I stopped on the front porch with my key in my hand. I'm not sure why, but it didn't feel right to let myself in today.

I rang the doorbell and stood up straight, shifting the weight of the bag in my hand.

Karen opened the door almost immediately. "Hi," she said, smiling almost shyly. She was wearing a light gray dress that seemed to float around her, touching her curves, falling to her knees. Her cheeks were pink—was she blushing?—and she was wearing lipstick.

"Hi," I said, like an idiot. "You look lovely."

Her cheeks got pinker. "Thank you," she said. "You made it through okay?" She gestured toward the sidewalk.

"It was fine. All they're doing today is reading the Bible to each other."

"Maybe the article in Monday's paper took some of the wind out of their sails." She stepped back from the door. "Come on in," she said. "You must be freezing."

For a long moment I felt like all of this was new, that I had never been in this house, that I was meeting this beautiful woman for the first time.

"You brought presents," she said.

"Ho ho ho." I slipped off my shoes and hung my coat.

"You look," she started awkwardly. "I meant to say before, you look nice, too."

I smiled, not sure of how to respond.

"And how's your head?"

I swept the hair back from my forehead. I knew what she was seeing—I had stared at it long enough in the mirror. Where a few days before there had been a jagged split, roughly stitched, now there was only the faintest white line.

I hadn't even noticed the change until I woke up in my hotel room the morning after the attack and started to peel the dressing from my feet. The bandages were stiff with blood, but underneath my feet were entirely healed: not a trace of the cuts remained.

A quick glance in the scratched mirror confirmed my suspicion. The wound on my forehead had vanished as well, leaving behind only a thin line and, on the pillow, a smear of blood and a length of black thread, still knotted from Stephen's stitches.

Karen surprised me by touching my forehead, running her fingers lightly over the skin.

"Does that hurt?"

Her touch was so sudden, so unexpected, I could barely speak. "No, not at all. It's . . ."

"Healed," she finished for me. "I don't even think it's going to scar."

I shook my head. "No, I don't think so either."

She sighed, and shook her head. "Do you want something to drink?" she asked, changing the subject. "There's mulled wine."

I could smell the spices.

"I'd love some. Do you need a hand?"

She shook her head and touched my arm as if to stop me from following her. "I'll be right back. You go say Merry Christmas to your daughter."

I could still feel her touch after she turned away.

Coming from the family she did, Christmas was a big deal for Karen, so I wasn't surprised to see that she had rearranged the room, sliding the couch over and moving the chairs to clear the corner where we always put the Christmas tree. It was a beautiful tree, almost brushing the ceiling, filling the room with a fresh smell of pine. Garlands were draped around the windows, and there was a poinsettia on the coffee table.

And Sherry, still in the middle of it all.

"Hey, pretty girl." I crouched at the side of her bed, setting my bag on the floor so I could smooth the hair away from her forehead. "How are you doing?" Karen had dressed her in a white flannel nightie with reindeer and snowmen playing along the front. "Merry Christmas, baby. I've got some presents in here for you." I pulled packages out of the bag and set them on the bed next to her. "We'll open them a little later."

I stacked the other gifts I'd bought under the tree. I was still looking at it when Karen came back with the warm wine in Christmas mugs.

Strings of white lights flashed slowly from deep within the dark branches, all hung with familiar ornaments. I fingered one, a Renaissance snowflake that we had bought at gift shop at the Met in New York one year. "This is a very nice tree," I said.

"Thanks." She sat down on the couch and I sat down next to her.

We fell silent, looking at Sherry, looking at the tree, looking down at our mugs. Neither of us knew what to say. Was she feeling as strange, as pleasantly confused, as I was?

"This is very good," I finally ventured after another sip of the wine.

"Are you hungry? We can eat whenever you like. I just need half an hour or forty-five minutes' notice. Are you hungry now?" The words spilled from her.

"A little," I confessed. "What's for dinner?"

"Whatever you like. Young's is delivering until eight."

She let the words hang in the air with a strange expression of vulnerability, waiting to see how I would react.

The first Christmas Karen and I had spent on our own in Victoria, rather than making the frantic flight to visit her family—our annual Guilt Trips, as we had come to call them, separate bedrooms and family sing-alongs—we had ordered Chinese, rounding it off with a couple of bottles of wine and a night of lovemaking under the tree. The dinner had become a Christmas tradition, the way some families go to church.

I smiled. "Do you want me to call?"

Her tension seemed to break. She shook her head, and got up. "No, I'll call." As she left the room, she turned back. "You can pay." She grinned at me.

My heart was beating almost in time with the blinking of the lights.


Leo


Father Peter told me to meet him at the church after Mother went to bed. He told me that he would leave the side door open for me.

I bought two turkey dinners from the grocery store, and Mother heated them up in the oven after church. She said the blessing. I didn't say anything when she asked God to watch over that "precious little girl." I just smiled at her and said "Amen." Loose lips sink ships.

I closed the side door behind me. It took me a second to see him in the dark. "Merry Christmas, Father."

He grunted. "Christmas? There's no time for that. We need to talk about what comes next."

Of course. Who had time to waste talking about something silly like Christmas?

"I need your advice."

I couldn't help smiling. My advice. "Okay."

His teeth were shiny in the candlelight. "I knew I could rely on you, Leo," he said. "I knew that from the first time I saw you. Do you know what tomorrow is?"

I was sure I knew the answer. "Boxing Day?"

He shook his head. "Saint Stephen's Day. Do you know who Saint Stephen was, Leo?"

I knew that it was one of the churches in town, but I didn't want to make any more stupid mistakes, so I didn't answer.

"Saint Stephen was the first Christian martyr. The first of us to be killed for the truth, the first to die in the service of God."

I nodded as if I knew that already.

"We've tried to stop them, haven't we, Leo? We've tried every other means. But now, we need to find someone to take the next step in this battle, Leo. We need to find someone who, if necessary, is willing to follow in Saint Stephen's footsteps."

I listened very carefully.

"Think back to the meetings, Leo. Was there anyone you noticed who looked like they might be brave enough to take on this fight against the darkness?"

I tried to think of all the people who had come to the church, but the only face I could see in my head was the man who tried to hide, who didn't pray.

"We're looking for a lion, Leo. A lion of God, willing to kill or die in the Lord's name."

My heart began to race.

"It has to be someone strong, someone powerful. Someone strong enough and pure of heart, to fight off the devils who will try to stop them."

A lion. Leo.

"My name," I said. "I could, I could be the lion of God."

He shook his head. "No, Leo. I couldn't ask that of you. The dangers are too great, I couldn't—"

"I want to. I'm offering. I'm offering my life to the Lord." I stood up taller. "I want to do this. Please? Can I be your lion? Let me do this."

He nodded. I could see he was so proud of me. "Are you absolutely sure?"

"I'm sure."

"You're willing to be the lion of God?"

"I think God wants me to be. I felt . . . I felt Him take my hand when I was throwing that bottle. I think God wants me to be His lion."

"I think so, too." He stepped toward me and put his hand on my shoulder. "In a few hours, it will be Saint Stephen's Day, and we'll go forth. We'll finish this battle with the Barretts."

### Karen

Simon picked up my plate from the coffee table and stacked it on his own. "Do you want anything else? Coffee?" he asked, standing up.

"Just a fortune cookie."

He smiled. "Okay. I'll be right back."

"And bring the wine," I called after him.

I flushed Sherry's feeding tube while he was gone and tucked her under the covers before looking out the front blinds.

"Should I take them out some leftovers?" Simon asked, coming back into the room.

"There's no one there to eat." My words misted the glass.

"What?"

I turned to face him. "They're all gone."

"Maybe they didn't want to miss their turkey dinners."

He was joking, but there was something unsettling about the sudden absence of the protesters.

"It's kind of strange not having them out there."

"I could get used to it."

I didn't know whether I should hope that this might be the end, that maybe they would leave us alone now. I settled for temporary gratitude.

He set the wine on the coffee table and held his hands out toward me, a fortune cookie hidden in each. "Pick one," he said.

I touched the back of his right hand, and it opened.

I suppressed a laugh as I read. "God they're getting predictable with these. 'Fortune favors the bold,' " I read.

"In bed," Simon added, observing our traditional fortune cookie game.

"So let's see what I've got." He broke the remaining cookie. "What the . . . ? 'The only time people prefer crunchy to smooth is in peanut butter.' "

"There's no sensible way to make that dirty."

"Actually, there's no way to make that sensible."

He tossed the slip of paper onto the table and crouched beside the tree. "Should we do the presents now? There's actually quite a bit under here."

"I saved the stuff from my family so we could open them together. Don't get your hopes up, though. I don't think anyone sent you anything."

"I can imagine." He sorted the presents into piles. "Did anything come here from my mom?"

I shook my head. "She called from Maui to wish us a merry Christmas, and to tell us that the gifts should be coming in the mail in the next few days."

"Good old mom."

"Yeah. I didn't hear from your dad."

"I did."

I was stunned. "What? When?"

"I called him."

I couldn't get over the thought of Simon calling his father, on Christmas no less. "And how was he?"

"The same. Unhappy. Alone." He sorted through the gifts. "It was good to talk to him, though."

His voice had dropped as he mentioned his father. I knew how hard it must have been for him to call.

"Shall we open Sherry's first?"

"Sure." I felt like I'd been opening presents for Sherry for weeks: letters from people too sick to visit Sherry, parcels from people who had read her story, gifts from people who had been to see her. Every day more packages came from people we had never met: stuffed animals and nighties, children's Bibles and baubles. I left the letters in a sack by the bed—I hadn't had time to open them—but I had donated the parcels to a gift drive sponsored by one of the radio stations. I didn't think anyone would mind making a different child happy.

Simon had brought her a CD of children's music by Fred Penner and a collection of picture books. Santa and I had brought her new pajamas and a book by Robert Munsch.

"You've got a lot of reading to do, hon," I said.

Simon rubbed my back.

We kept our packages from each other until the end.

"A harmonica," he said, turning it over in his hands.

"I thought if you were doing the whole folksinger thing, you might as well go all the way."

"Thanks," he said. "This'll irritate the hell out of 314 and 318."

"So should I open these now?" I asked, looking at the pair of packages from Simon.

He shrugged. "It's no big deal."

"Your wrapping's gotten better," I joked. When we were together, wrapping had always been one of my responsibilities.

"I had them wrapped at the store. More wine?"

I nodded, and extended my glass to him. "Is there a special order these should be opened in?"

He shook his head. "Doesn't really matter. But I guess—open the big one first."

I picked up the package. "This feels suspiciously like a book."

"Just open it." He smiled. "No fair guessing."

I peeled the paper off carefully, revealing a beautiful, soft plum leather binding tooled with a Celtic design. "It's gorgeous," I said, cradling it in my hands. It was a slipcover, with a plain sketchbook inside.

"I know how much you love notebooks, but you never use the fancy ones with the good paper."

"They're too nice."

"Exactly. This way you can have a nice notebook that you can actually use."

"Thank you, Simon. I love it."

He shrugged, but I could see how pleased he was. "You've got one more," he pointed out.

I picked up the smaller package and opened it just as carefully, already suspecting its contents. Simon has always had a hard time resisting thematic gifts.

"It's German," Simon explained as I took the fountain pen from the gift box. "It's got a good weight, doesn't it?"

I nodded, making small circles in the air with the nib.

"Try it," Simon urged. "I had them fill it before they wrapped it up."

I looked around for a piece of paper, then sat back as Simon opened the notebook on the table in front of me. "Here," he said. "That's what it's for."

The pen laid down a beautiful wet green line. "That's gorgeous, Simon. The ink . . ."

"I've got the bottle in my jacket pocket."

"I don't know what to say."

"Just use it," he said. "The pen and the notebook. I want you to use them. Really use them."

"Thank you," I said, leaning in and kissing him quickly on the mouth before I realized what I was doing.

"You've given up so much, lost so much. I was so happy when you told me that you had started writing again. I don't want you to lose that." His eyes held mine until I nodded. "Good," he said. "Merry Christmas, Karen."

He stood up.

"What are you doing?"

"I thought I'd clean up this mess," he said, plucking handfuls of paper from the floor. I turned the notebook over in my hands, feeling the leather warm to my touch.

"This *is* beautiful," I repeated as he crumpled the paper into the garbage next to Sherry's bed.

"I'm glad you like it," he said, arranging the teddy bear my brother Steve's family had sent into the crook of Sherry's arm, touching her cheek with the back of his hand.

"I'd like you to stay," I whispered. I wasn't sure if I had spoken loud enough for him to hear.

He straightened slightly.

I had wanted to say it for a while; the wine made the words a little easier to pronounce.

He turned away from Sherry to face me.

"Tonight. I'd like you to stay tonight. With me. We can talk about tomorrow in the morning. But—"

He took two steps toward me.

"—I was alone last night. I don't want to be alone tonight."

For a moment he looked like he was about to launch into a speech. Then our eyes met, and he nodded.

"Fortune favors the bold," he said, picking up his glass.

---

## Leo

I waited inside Mr. Perkins's van around the corner from the Barretts' house. It smelled like gas, but I liked it. It reminded me of what I was here to do.

I kept the picture of Sherry that I had torn out of the newspaper in my lap, and I held on to Mother's rosary. I said the Hail Mary over and over again as I stared at the picture.

*Hail Mary, full of grace.*

I felt sorry for the people they had fooled. Thank God for Father Peter, who saw the truth that the sheep couldn't see. Someone brave enough to do something important. Something to save those too stupid to save themselves.

*Blessed art thou among women.*

I was so lucky I met him when I did. Before I had actually knelt by that child of the devil. I would have knelt.

*And blessed is the fruit of thy womb, Jesus.*

All my life I tried to do what is right. I go to church. I go to confession. I say a blessing before I eat, and pray before I go to sleep. I take care of Mother.

But tonight I will be a lion of God, a warrior, bringing the battle home to those evil enough to try to destroy His children. Tricksters and evil crooks. Tonight I will be a lion for God.

*Pray for the sinners now, and at the hour of death.*

## Simon

In the past few weeks with my family, I had learned to savor the little things, to hold on to the moments of grace as they came. Like walking through the still house with Karen, turning off all the lights except for the Christmas tree in the living room, making sure all the doors and windows were locked.

Like the weight of my daughter in my arms as I carried her up the stairs, as I laid her down in her old bed, close to our room.

Like the warmth of my daughter's skin as I kissed her forehead and whispered, "Good night."

Like following my wife down the hallway, my body tingling.

Like the momentary pause as we both looked around the bedroom as if seeing it for the first time.

"Do you want to . . ." She gestured toward the bathroom.

I shook my head. "You go ahead."

"I won't take long." A moment later I heard the water in the sink, the rattling of the hook on the back of the door as she took down her robe. The sounds of our life together.

I let myself sink into the bedside chair and rubbed the heels of my hands into my eyes. It was late, but I didn't feel tired. In fact, I felt electric.

The toilet flushed and the door opened and Karen stepped out, her housecoat loosely belted. "I opened a new toothbrush for you. It's on the counter."


## Leo

No moon. No stars.

No sound.

The lights were off inside the house except for the Christmas tree. Everyone else had been told to leave. All was still.

O holy night.

The witching hour. That's what Mother called it: the witching hour. No good Christian had any business being out at this time of night.

What did she know? This was the holiest time of the night on the holiest night of the year, a time for all good Christians to stand up and be counted, if they were good enough, and true.

I leaned against the van, feeling the lion of God inside me trying to get out. I had to remember to slow down, to do everything right, just the way Father Peter told me.

I opened the back door of the van as quietly as I could. I could barely breathe with the smell, but I knew what I had to do.

I zipped my coat up high around my mouth.

I picked up the gas can.

I didn't shut the van door. I didn't hide. I walked like a man through the gate, right up to the front door. The gas can was heavy, but not for me. Not for the lion.

The porchlight wasn't on. There was no security light. It was just like Father Peter had said it would be. I felt a little scared as I walked up the ramp, but mostly I felt strong. I felt like I could do anything.

I splashed the door with gas from the can. I tried my best to stay dry, but some of it splashed on my coveralls. But I didn't stop. I splashed the walls with gas, up and down, all the way along the flower beds and around the corner down the side to the back of the house.

When the can was empty I threw it into the hedge.

When I got back to the van I was shaking—it felt so good to be doing God's work! Just one more step.

He had tried to warn them. They knew that they were sinning, and that they would be punished. Father Peter had told them.

One more step.

First a prayer, then the fire.

## Simon

She was already in bed when I came out, the comforter pulled up around her neck, her housecoat draped over the chair. It took me several seconds to realize that she was lying on the wrong side. I had always slept on the side of the bed closest to the bathroom. I walked around to the far side of the bed and lifted the covers, sliding in alongside her.

The sheets were smooth, cool, familiar.

"This is kind of weird," she said, her voice low.

"Yeah." It was as if there were a bubble around us, a delicate, shimmering globe that the wrong word, the wrong action, the wrong thought, could destroy.

"It feels . . ." She trailed off.

"New," I finished, unsure of where the word had come from.

She nodded. "Yeah. New."

"Like those nights in the dorm . . . covers up to our necks, Donna in bed just across the room—"

"Trying to be so quiet," she added.

"Not getting any sleep."

"I always wonder how we survived that year. Falling asleep in class—"

"When we went to class at all."

Her hand found my hip. Her fingertips were hot.

It was strange to cross the distance between us. As I reached out, Karen's eyes closed a little and her breathing sharpened.

We both kept our hands in the same safe space, the nonpresumptive area between hip and abdomen, careful not to trespass where we were not yet certain we belonged. We hovered in a soft trancelike state, neither of us quite prepared to take it further.

Then cautiously, I slid my hand until the base of my palm brushed gently against the cool side of her breast, bare and surprising.

Her eyes met mine.

I raised my eyebrows playfully.

And immediately regretted doing so.

Karen pulled away without physically moving, her jaw tensing.

"What is it?" I asked, lowering my hand again to the safer area near her hip.

"I'm not . . . I . . ." She shook her head against the pillow. "I'm too tired to make any sense. I'm sorry."

I didn't move, just waited for her to continue.

"I, I don't want . . . I don't know what I want. I just . . . I'd like, I just want to feel you against me. Is that okay?"

I lifted my hand to her hair, smoothing it. "Of course it's okay," I said. "Of course it is."

She came into my embrace, the space between us disappearing, my arms around her, hers around me. We fit together perfectly, as we always had: she curving where I was rigid, soft where I was coarse. Our foreheads touched, the remaining space between us bridged by our breath.

"When you touch me like this," she said. I felt her words more than heard them. Smelled them in sweet mint.

"What?" I asked after she had been silent for a long time.

"It's the same way you touch Sherry. Smoothing her hair back . . ."

"I'm sorry," I said, afraid that I had hurt her in some way.

"No, no, no. I like it. I like the way it makes me feel." She pulled herself even closer against me.

"How does it make you feel?" I asked.

"Safe," she said, and on that word, on that single syllable, her voice broke like the edge of a wave. Her back shuddered with sobs. I didn't try to stop her, to comfort her with whispered words. Instead, I stroked her back, the buttons of her spine. I cupped the round base of her skull in my hand, gently stroking her soft hair as she cried against me, her tears hot on my cheeks, salty in my mouth.

As she cried, I could feel growing there, as had once before, a presence between us: the tiny perfect form of Sherry nestled between her parents' bodies. Our bodies were shaped by her absence, by the almost unbearable weight of her loss.

## Leo

Father Peter had filled the glass bottle at the church, and as he pushed in the rag, his lips were moving. I thought he was praying, but I couldn't hear the words.

When he handed me the bottle, he had asked, "Are you sure that you can bear this burden?"

I hefted the bottle in my hand. I remembered how it felt when God had guided my hand when I threw the bottle at Mr. Barrett. I imagined the flames, and the lion inside me roared. "Yes, I'm sure."

"I knew you would be," he said. "This is for you. Use it well."

I felt for the lighter in my pocket as I stepped onto the Barretts' front lawn.

My breath made a fog and my fingers hurt from the cold. It didn't matter. In a minute I would be warmed and cleansed by God's fire.

I struck the lighter and touched it to the rag. It burst into blue flame with a loud pop that scared me a little.

I could feel the heat on my face as I closed my eyes, as I prayed for God to guide my hand.

I drew back my arm. "Hail Mary," I whispered, letting the bottle fly.

The flames were blue in the night sky.

Something moved in the corner of my eye.

The bottle tumbled once in the air, bright in its flight.

The man came running out of the shadows and threw himself in the direction of the bottle, reaching out, like he thought he might catch it. But the glass smacked against his shoulder, spraying burning gas all over him.

His arm and chest burst into flames, and around his feet the grass burned where the gas had spilled. He kicked the bottle away as he screamed and dropped to the ground.

He rolled and rolled, trying to put out the fire, but the flames didn't go out, and he screamed again and again.

I knew why the flames weren't going out. I knew who he was, how much he loved the flames.

I threw myself at the devil, swinging my fists. The heat of his flames tried to drive me away, but I didn't give up. I kept hitting and hitting.

"Stop it," the devil screamed, rolling away from me, pulling at his burning coat. "Stop it!"

Flames were eating at part of his face, but I knew him. His long hair, his beard, his eyes. He was the one from the meeting, the devil who wouldn't bow his head to pray.

"Devil!" I shouted, throwing myself at him again.

### Karen

"Simon? Do you hear that?"

He was already awake, rolling out from under the covers and crossing to the window. There was a hint of light as he drew back the curtain. I pulled the sheet with me to cover myself as I leaned toward the glass.

At first, I didn't know what I was seeing. There was a fire—No, someone was on fire! And someone—was that Father Peter's bodyguard?—was . . . punching him, kicking him, as he tried to roll away, as he writhed in the flames—

The scene vanished as the room filled with light. Simon was by the door, pulling on his pants.

I dropped the sheet and pulled open a drawer for something to wear. "Was that Father Peter's . . ."

"I think so." He tugged a T-shirt over his head, and he started through the door. "It looks like he's trying to kill someone."

"What should we—?"

"Call the police."

I grabbed the cordless phone and followed him, looking into Sherry's room before racing down the stairs.


## Henry

So much pain, all at once. I couldn't—

I kept rolling on the ground, trying to smother the flames. I could smell burning meat, and I knew it was me. My face, my arm. If I could just get Tim's coat off—

Then there was a blow and a cracking in my chest and I couldn't breathe. Another burst of pain. Another kick.

"Stop it!" I cried out. Every word pulled at the burned skin on my face. If I could just—

My right hand didn't work anymore. When I tried to move my fingers, the pain was crippling.

Fumbling with the zipper with my left, I shrugged the coat off that shoulder. I shrugged again, but it was stuck. . . .

The fabric of the coat had melted and clung to my skin like glue. If I pulled it off, it would take the skin right off my arm with it.

I couldn't leave it.

Bracing myself, I started to pull.

"Go back to hell, you devil!" More blows rained down on me. I heard a crunch and saw a bright light and I was suddenly choking on blood. My nose . . .

He was still coming at me, arms flailing.

I stumbled away and pulled off the coat, peeling away the burnt skin from my arm. My scream stopped the big man in his path.

I couldn't breathe, and my eye clouded over with the pain. My entire arm was an open wound, so tender that the movement of air across it felt like fresh flames.

Then he punched me again, and again, wherever he could reach. I reeled and stumbled and fell onto my back.

"Go back to hell!" he shouted, drawing back to kick me again.

The pain was too much to bear—

And then there was a sudden brilliance. He looked behind himself at the house. The porch light! The porch light was on.

He ran toward his van. It took me a moment to get my bearings. Grass. Concrete. I was at the edge of the driveway. And right there—

As the van door opened and closed, I pulled myself across the driveway, and into the shadow of the hedge.

Then I surrendered to the dark.

### Karen

Simon's adrenaline carried him out the front door and partway down the ramp before he stopped, clutching the flashlight like a club. I was only a few steps behind, carrying the phone.

"There's no one here," I said. I hung up before the phone connected.

"Look." Down the street, taillights shone in the dark, and a cloud of steam rose from the exhaust as the van pulled away.

For a moment I thought Simon might run after the moving vehicle. Instead, he walked to the base of the ramp and looked around the yard.

"What the hell—?" he muttered.

I was closer to the house and smelled it first. "Do you smell that?"

He lifted his head. "What?" The air was so heavy with the reek, it burned the nose. "Oh, God," he muttered. Crouching, he touched the door just under the knob.

The lower half of the door was wet. Simon touched a finger to the wetness and brought it to his nose. "It's gas."

"There's gas on our door?"

"Check on Sherry," he said, turning on the flashlight and starting down the ramp again. "Lock the door."

Simon looked flushed and scared when he came in. "There's gasoline all over the house. And I found these on the lawn where they were fighting." He had an empty soda bottle in one hand, and a winter coat, partially burnt, in the other.

"Is that—?"

He nodded, a sheen of sweat breaking out on his face. "They tried to burn down the house. But somebody stopped them. It looks like he's pretty badly hurt," he said, turning the coat over in his hands. Half of it had melted into a gnarled clump of plastic.

"Is he still out there?"

Simon shook his head. "I couldn't find him."

The thought was numbing. Someone had tried to kill us all. This wasn't a warning.

"Should I call the police?" I asked. I still had the phone in my hand.

"I don't—" He bit his lip and shook his head, trying to figure out what to do.

"No," I said, setting the phone down. "Probably not. So what are we going to do?"

"I'm gonna try to hose off some of the gas," he ventured. "I'd feel better if you stayed inside with Sherry."

"Be careful."

It took him the better part of an hour to wash down the walls using the garden hose. I spent the time upstairs in Sherry's room, curled up in the chair beside her bed.

When would we ever feel safe again? How could someone do this? The answers just weren't coming. How could someone who professed their faith, their love for God as loudly as Father Peter even consider something like this?

I thought of the God I remembered from when I was a little girl, and I couldn't force the ideas into anything that resembled sense.

"That'll do for a start," Simon said from the doorway. He had taken off his shoes and coat. He was chilled and damp and out of breath.

"Do you think anything we do will be enough?"

Leo

I don't know how Father Peter knew, but he took one look at me and said, "You failed."

I nodded, and then I bowed my head.

"What happened?" he asked quietly.

"I . . . I did everything just right. Everything just like you told me, but there was . . . I saw him at the meeting. He was there. He stopped the bottle, and I knew . . . He was a devil, Father. He was a devil and I fought him and I would have, I would have killed him, but the lights went on and—"

"The lights went on? Did they see you?"

Did they . . . Didn't he care about the devil? "I . . . I don't think so."

He shook his head and turned away. "Thank you, Leo," he said. "You did very well."

"I can go back," I said. "I can go back and try again." I knew I could do it.

"It's too late," he said, still looking away. "It's over."

"I can go back," I said, pulling at his coat. "I can do it. . . ."

"It's too late," he said again. "They've seen you. They know what we tried to do. Tim knows. They'll be ready. Someone will be waiting."

I didn't understand. What did the fat man have to do with any of this? Was he a devil, too? And how could Father Peter just say it was over? There was so much left to do. "What about the sinners? What about saving the people from that girl, from that demon? What about the devil?"

"It's over, Leo."

"It's not over!" I shouted. "The righteous fight, and they fight until they drop. That's what you said. I can do it. I know I can do it."

He looked at me for a long time. He shook his head. "It's time to go home, Leo."

Then he turned and walked away down the alley.

"It's not over," I called after him. "I'll do it. I'll show you."

He didn't look back.

I could do it. I'd show him. I was the lion. I could do anything.

## Simon

I kissed Karen on the forehead, and watched as she climbed the stairs.

Double-checking that I had a key in my pocket and the flashlight, I locked the front door behind myself.

It was frigid outside, and I was grateful for the old ski jacket Karen had found for me. I could see my breath, and I pushed my hands deeply into my jacket pockets.

It was only one night, a few hours, really. In the morning we would call a security company, hire someone to watch the house. We should have done it weeks ago.

I took a slow walk around the house. I paid careful attention to the basement windows, playing the light over the glass and along the frames to ensure they hadn't been opened. The smell of gas was still strong, but not overwhelming. We could all be dead now, the house in flames. I couldn't bear to think about it.

On the porch, I sat with my back to the door, keeping a keen eye on the yard and the sidewalk and street beyond. It was perfectly still, a perfectly silent.

I sat there till dawn, protecting my family. I thought about Sherry, snugged tight in her own bed. I thought about my wife. I watched my breath rise into the cloudless sky. Every fifteen minutes or so I walked around the house, checking.

I've never been so happy to see the sun rise. I lingered on the front porch in the warm glow, watching as the light crept across the yard.

And then I heard footsteps on the sidewalk, the determined click of hard heels.

The sun was bright over the horizon, and I was looking right into it, not seeing anything. I heard the rattle of the gate, and the footsteps coming closer.

All I could see was a shadow against the light, the dark of a long coat. I stepped forward, tightening my grip around the flashlight.

"Mr. Barrett?" The voice startled me. "It's Father Peter. . . ."

# Part 8

*Saint Stephen's Day*

# Henry

I must have passed out in the bushes. When I came to, it was morning, and the curtains were open inside the Barrett house.

When I sat up, every part of me screamed with pain and the ground seemed to swim around me. My arm was raw and oozing, and I couldn't see out of one eye. That side of my face was numb. I could taste my own blood and I wanted to find somewhere warm, somewhere to rest.

I pulled myself to my feet. I needed to get back to the library. I needed Tim to look at my wounds.

I stumbled toward downtown, stopping every so often to rest. It hurt to lift my head, and I watched the sidewalk as I lurched from side to side.

I wasn't paying attention, and somehow I lost my way. I found myself surrounded by noise and crowds, people rushing along the sidewalks with shopping bags held tight to them. I couldn't bear the press and push, the noise, the smell.

I collapsed in a bus shelter on Douglas.

At first, he was just another face in the crowd, another child being dragged along by an adult. From the scowl I could tell he was being propelled against his will. He had a shock of blond hair, clothes a little too big, as if inherited from an older brother, a turned-up nose, green eyes.

Green eyes.

Something about those eyes drew me back to him. Something I should have been able to remember, but couldn't.

As he passed the bus shelter, it came to me.

He had his mother's eyes.

"Connor!" I called out, stepping into the sidewalk. The tide of the crowd pulled him away, pulled the three of them away. "Connor!"

Three of them. A mother, two children.

"Dylan!" I stumbled down the sidewalk after them.

I caught glimpses: Connor's hair, the side of Arlene's face, Dylan pulling on the door as they went into the Eaton Centre. But I couldn't catch up. By the time I got inside the mall, they had disappeared. I ran to the railing, but I couldn't see them either below me or above.

"Connor!" I called out. "Dylan!"

No one turned. No one heard.

A flood of memories tore me apart. A life so like a dream returned to me with the vividness of a blow.

Arlene.

Dylan.

Connor.

All here. Now.

I rode the escalators up and down. I hobbled from one end of the mall to the other, looking into stores. I checked the bathrooms upstairs and down. I ran onto Government Street, looking for Arlene's familiar ponytail in the sea of shoppers.

They were gone. But I knew where I could find them.

Home.

I remembered.

I remembered everything.

How could I have forgotten?

## Karen

"Are you sure?" I asked, still groggy from the sudden waking.

Simon nodded. There were dark half moons under his eyes. "He introduced himself."

"He just came up to the door?"

He was pacing at the end of the bed and he nodded again. "Scared the hell out of me."

"You were outside? Still?"

"Yes."

"What did he say?"

He shook his head. "He just said he needed to talk to us."

"Where is he now?" I asked.

"He's still on the front porch. I told him I was coming to get you."

I threw the blankets off, a little stunned by the news, and went to the closet.

"What should we do?" Simon asked, not looking away as I dressed.

I pulled on a sweater. "I think we should hear what he has to say."

"Are we going to invite him in, or . . ."

"We've let everyone else in," I said as we went downstairs.

When I opened the front door, I felt immediate relief. This man was as far from the threatening specter who had tried to kill my daughter as you could imagine. His face was ruddy on top of his white collar, his hand firm in mine, and he smiled as he spoke. "Mrs. Barrett? I'm Father Peter. Father Peter Shaughnessy. I was contacted by the diocese." He smelled a bit of aftershave, and his voice had a hint of an accent, and the warmth of someone who spent his life talking to people.

"Are you all right?" he asked as we shook hands, meeting my eyes.

I glanced at Simon. "I guess we were expecting someone else."

He smiled reassuringly. "No, it's just me," he said. "I'm sorry I couldn't come sooner."

## Henry

When I got to the library, I found Tim sitting cross-legged on the counter of the ladies' room, his head bowed over the large book open on his lap.

"Tim," I said quietly, not wanting to startle him. The door closed behind me with a soft thud. I recognized the book as a Bible. His finger was tracing along the inner column as he read.

"Henry," he said, looking up at me. "Good Christ, you look awful." He slid off the counter. "Let me look at you," he said, leaning toward my face. "What happened?"

I stepped away from him. "That doesn't matter," I said. "I need to talk to you."

"Clearly," he said, stepping toward me again, staring at the burns on my face. "What happened to you?"

"Last night, at the Barretts'."

"Father Peter did this? But how?" He seemed uncertain for the first time since we had met.

"No, not him. His bodyguard. He tried to burn down the house."

"And you got burned?" He was acting as if he didn't believe what he was seeing.

"Yes, but that's not—I need to ask you about my family."

"You don't have a family," he said. "None of us do."

"No, I do," I protested. "I just saw them. My sons. Arlene. I just saw them."

He backed up a little, and looked even more confused. "You're remembering?"

"I remember it all. Arlene, the boys, the job. My parents. Everything."

"But that's—Did they see you?" he asked.

Hesitating just a moment, I shook my head. "No," I said.

He seemed comforted by the word. "No. Of course they didn't."

"But it was crowded and . . ."

He shook his head. "I'm sorry, Henry," he said. "I know it's hard. It's probably the hardest thing to get used to. I wish I could tell you how to make it better."

"Why do I remember them? Why now?"

He shook his head. "I don't know." He looked intently at my burned face. "But you should try to forget them. Again. Forget that whole life."

"But I don't want to forget them. I want to see them."

He shook his head. "You can't. There's no going back."

"Why not? What if . . . What if this is what I was supposed to do? You're always talking about amends—maybe I was supposed to help save Sherry and her family, and that's why I can remember my life. I saved them. Last night. Maybe I've been given my life back. As a reward—"

"Then why couldn't they see you?"

"I . . . I don't . . ."

"Even if they could see you, what would you say? Where do you say

you've been? How do you explain what's happened to you? All of this."
He gestured at my face, my arm. "And even if you can make your wife
hear you, what happens then? You're not really alive anymore. You
don't eat. You don't sleep. You don't die."

He went on. "Are you ready to watch your wife grow old before
your eyes? To watch your children crippled by time? What will you say
when your grandchildren die, and you haven't aged?"

"But maybe they . . . I don't know. It doesn't matter. She'll understand."

"Henry, it's not a good idea."

"They're my family. They're my life."

"They *were* your life," he corrected me. "Not anymore." His eyes
fixed on me a moment; then he slowly raised his hands, palms upward
and open, gently shaking his head. "I don't understand everything,
Henry. I don't know what's happening to you. But this isn't your path."

"I'll make it work. I'll get my old life back. You'll see."

He shook his head. "I'm sorry, Henry," he said as I turned away.


## Karen

I'm sure I flinched when the real Father Peter first touched Sherry, tracing his fingers over her forehead, down the softness of her cheeks. It
was a reflex, really, nothing to do with the man himself. The air of calm
that surrounded him had quickly put my fears to rest.

"Is she always so warm?"

Simon, Ruth, and I were watching him closely. He had wanted us to
tell him our story before he saw Sherry, and Ruth had arrived while we
were having coffee in the kitchen. She said she knew we hadn't planned
on opening the house on Boxing Day, but had come just to check on
things. When she saw the priest, her hand rose, seemingly, of its own
volition, to touch the small, gold cross she had started wearing on a
chain around her neck.

"She feels warm to the touch, but it's not fever," Ruth said, reaching
for her chart. "Her temperature is normal, consistently."

Father Peter glanced at her. "Don't you find that unusual? Wouldn't you expect her metabolic rate to be slower? Anything I've read about comatose states—"

Ruth nodded. "We thought the same. And yet her pulse rate, blood pressure, temperature, blood glucose—they're all normal. We've never had any problem with bedsores or secondary infection."

Father Peter turned back to Sherry. "She's a very pretty little girl." He leaned in close enough to kiss Sherry's forehead, but turned his head instead to smell her skin, a long sniff. "What sort of soap do you use?"

"Just water. We didn't want to use anything too strong."

I trailed off when I saw him nodding, his head still inclined over Sherry. "Of course not, of course not. You wouldn't want anything very strong at all. Tell me," he asked, straightening up. "Have you noticed any strange smells around her?"

"Smells?" I repeated. "I don't think so. Why do you—?"

"Lilies," Ruth said.

I turned to look at her.

"Yes, yes," the priest said. "I had thought lavender, but I think you're right. Lilies. Have you noticed it often?"

"All the time. I just thought it was the way she smelled."

"Of course," the priest said. "And after a while you'd get used to it. Not notice it. Did you know, though, that in the folklore"—he used the word as if it were the best of several bad choices—"saints are often recognized by how they smell?" He was watching me intently. "Sandalwood. Jasmine. Various flowers. And this was when people didn't consider bathing, or did it only occasionally."

It was as if a shadow had passed over the room, discouraging speech.

"Lilies are for purity," Ruth said softly behind me. "For peace."

## Leo

I went right to the library as soon as Mother was up and had her breakfast. I couldn't go in. The doors were locked, and a sign said that it was closed for the holiday. I was glad that I wore my winter coat. It was going to be cold waiting for the devil to arrive.

This was where Father Peter said the fat man, Tim, was staying. I didn't know if he was a devil, or if the devil was working with him, but I thought that the fat man would know where to find him. He would tell me, or I would destroy him. I would destroy all of them.

First the devils.

And then the Barretts.

I practiced flicking the lighter a few times, and I thought of the whole building full of paper. How it would burn. I would destroy him. I would send him straight back to hell.

I'd wait however long it took.

## Karen

Father Peter straightened up and turned toward us, brushing his palms along his jacket. "You're not used to hearing your daughter referred to as a saint, are you? Surely someone has suggested—"

Simon interrupted him. "We don't use that word," he said. "I think the first time that word was used in this house was by someone with the same name as you, just before he tried to ruin all of our lives."

"Was he a tall man?" Father Peter asked in a voice both excited and startled. "Very thin? Almost cadaver-like? Pale and—"

"You know him?"

"I know *of* him. Our paths have crossed. We may have met once, I'm not sure."

"He implied to us that he was close to the diocese. That he represented them in some capacity," Simon said.

Father Peter shook his head. "No. No, that's not true at all. This man, if he's the one I believe him to be, is in no way affiliated with the Church."

"Then who is he?" I asked.

"The short answer is 'I don't know.'" The disappointment must have registered in my face, because he hurried to continue. "I *do* know that there have been reports, over the years, of a man matching this Father Peter's description interfering with a . . . a possible saint."

"Interfering how?" I asked.

"Usually he tries to discredit the subject in the community and in the Church first. He keeps his distance, never acts directly.

"I was involved in a case several years ago . . . in a small town in Oregon. A young woman seemed to have the gift of healing, through the laying on of hands." He looked down at Sherry's still body, then shook his head as he turned back to me. "By the time I got there, she was dead."

"Father Peter killed her?" Simon asked.

He shook his head. "No, it wasn't that simple. She killed herself. There were rumors, and the local newspaper had begun running stories. She was nineteen. She had had a number of lovers, several of whom spoke to the press. Her parents hadn't been aware." He shrugged his shoulders. "I was too late. I arrived just before the funeral. I didn't really have any need to contact the family at that point, but their priest introduced us after the funeral. It was the girl's sister who mentioned that I was the second Father Peter they had met."

"So his name really is Father Peter," Simon concluded.

He shook his head. "No, I don't think so. I think he just used 'Father Peter' because he knew that I would be coming, and he wanted to create confusion. Like he did here."

"How would he know that?" I asked.

"Because I'm the one who gets sent, in North America, at least. When we get reports of occurrences like this, I'm asked to look into it. My counterpart in Europe is named Joseph. I don't think it's any coincidence that when reports come back from Europe about the Stranger, he's usually calling himself Joseph."

"But who is he?" Simon asked.

Father Peter frowned. "We don't know," he confessed. "There are some who believe—" He stopped cold on the word as he rethought what he had been about to say. "It seems that there are reports of contacts with this man, or another who bears quite a striking resemblance to him, going back several hundred years."

## Leo

It was cold work waiting on the devil.

I never thought Father Peter would be the one to come.

He came out of the dark looking just like a shadow, wrapped up in his long black coat. He walked across the square so fast, it looked like he wasn't even going to stop at the door.

I hid behind the big plant pot, holding tightly to the lighter, and watched him as he pushed on the doors.

What was he doing here? Was he going to fight the devil and his friends himself?

Why wouldn't he have wanted me here with him?

The locked doors opened without a sound. No alarms went off. No watchmen came running.

I wanted to run after him, to tell him that I was there to help him in his fight against the devils.

I followed him into the library. Quiet as a church mouse.


Henry

Limping home was like going back in time. I fell into the old patterns without even thinking about it: the shortcuts across side streets and schoolyards, walking up the narrow roads between Blanshard and Quadra to avoid the worst of the hills. I had to stop several times each block to let the dizziness pass.

Our apartment was in the second building from the corner on the first floor. The white curtains were closed, backlit from within.

I couldn't help smiling, even as my open eye filled with tears.

It was fate. I had been put in that bus shelter this morning to see them, to be reminded, to be given my life back again. To have whatever spell had been cast over me broken.

It was the only explanation I could think of: I had been rewarded for helping the Barretts. I had made my amends, suffered my punishment, and the family in the brightly lit apartment—my family—was my reward.

The bare trees shifted and rasped in the cold wind as I stumbled to the front door. I punched the intercom button for 108 with my left hand, keeping my injured hand buried in the front pocket of the hoodie that I had borrowed from the lost and found.

A moment later the speaker crackled to life. "Who's there?" came a young boy's voice.

I pushed the TALK button. "It's me, Dylan. It's your daddy. Let me in." My voice sounded strange, thick and lispy.

"Hello? Hello? Who's there, please?"

"Dylan, it's me, hon. It's your dad. Press the button." I could feel a cold trickle of fear tracing its way down my spine.

"Who's there, baby?" Arlene's disembodied voice sounded tinny and distant.

"It rang, Mommy. It rang, but nobody said anything," he explained, his voice growing fainter as she lifted the receiver away. "Nobody said—"

There was a harsh click as the receiver was set back into the base on the wall.

I stared blankly at the panel, the cold trickle threatening to become a flood.

I started punching the black buttons on the intercom panel at random, just punching them, ignoring the inquisitive voices from the speaker, waiting, waiting—

There! As the buzzer sounded, pushed by someone too lazy or trusting to bother checking, I grabbed the door handle and let myself in.

"What will you say?" Tim had asked. "How will you explain?"

I had thought about that the entire walk. I would tell Arlene the truth. I would tell her about the accident, about running away afterwards. I would tell her about the state of shock I had been in, the confusion, the amnesia.

I would tell her about the library, and the men who lived there who had taken me in, who had kept me safe. I would tell her about Tim, about the books I had been reading, about finally seeing her and the boys downtown and how they had brought me home at last.

I could hear the sound of the television, the boys playing behind our door. I knocked.

Dylan called out, "Mom, there's someone at the door!"

"She knows, stupid," Connor said, and I could picture him giving his little brother a shove.

"Don't call your brother that." Arlene's footsteps came toward the door. "And stop pushing him."

The chain rattled and the door cracked open. Arlene's green eye looked out into the corridor.

I forced a smile, feeling the tight pull of the burned skin, trying to ignore the racing of my heart. "Hi," I said quietly. "It's me." I steeled myself for her response.

The door opened a little more. Arlene looked directly at me, but there was no shock, or surprise, or recognition. There was no trace of anything at all.

Despite the sick feeling in my belly, I tried again. "It's me. I'm home."

She stepped out into the corridor, almost brushing against me. She was beautiful, her dark hair pulled back into a high ponytail, her skin clear, eyes puzzled. She was wearing a blue T-shirt and gray jogging pants, what she always wore around the house. She had lost weight— she looked like a runner again, like she did in high school. She looked like someone you wanted to spend your whole life with.

I could smell her soap and feel the warmth emanating from her body. "Arlene," I called, even though she was right there. Her brows knit in confusion. "It's me," I said, my voice cracking. "Arlene!"

I waved my left arm in front of her face, lurched directly into her field of vision. She stepped back, as if she could sense my presence, then, shaking her head, turned back into the apartment.

"Who was it, Mommy?" I heard Dylan ask. I could see him inside the door, huddled against the wall. Connor was standing next to him, craning his neck to see but obeying the rule to stay inside the apartment until Mommy or Daddy said it was okay. Where Connor looked like his mother, Dylan looked like me—the brown eyes, the small nose, the brown hair you had to fight to get to lay flat. "Dylan," I cried, stumbling forward.

"No one, hon," Arlene answered him, closing her hand around the doorknob. "Someone playing a prank."

"Dylan," I called again. The door closed in my face.

I sagged against it, pressing my burnt face against the cool of the paint. "Dylan," I whispered. "Arlene." Tears streamed hot down my face, and I couldn't control my trembling. I was cold. So cold.

I wanted to pound on the door. I wanted to be heard. I wanted to will myself to be seen. I wanted to explain to Arlene what had happened.

But when I raised my hand to knock, I couldn't. I couldn't bring myself to see her again, knowing that I would never be able to make her see me. I couldn't bear the idea of seeing her again without being able to touch her, of seeing the boys without being able to hold them.

What was I going to do? Was I just going to wander aimlessly, waiting for some mysterious salvation, for something to break my curse? Was that my fate? To live in limbo for generations, some modern-day Wandering Jew, haunted by that little girl?

And then I knew what Tim didn't know. He had been trying to teach me, all these months, about my future. About *his* past and what he thought was *my* destiny.

For him, whose past had been spent waiting, the future would hold more of the same.

But not for me. The truth had been right in front of me the whole time, but I hadn't seen it. Until now.

I wasn't doomed to live forever, wandering the earth, waiting to make my amends. That was Tim's destiny.

I had made my amends.

I didn't have to wait an eternity to beg forgiveness. My forgiveness was right here.


## Karen

After midnight. The house was silent, save for the coughing and knocking of the heat pipes as they slowly cooled, and the choking noises Simon and I made as we tried to stifle our laughter.

"This is a first," he whispered. "With a priest in the room next door."

"It's what every little Catholic girl dreams of," I answered, burying my laughter in the pillow.

It felt good to laugh with him. To be naked and smiling and sweating and happy. To be together.

"Shh."

"He's asleep," he whispered.

"How can you be so sure?"

"He would have pounded on the wall if he wasn't."

That set us both off again, and I had to bury my face in the pillow. Simon rubbed my back and tangled his fingers in my hair.

"I love you," he whispered.

I turned onto my side to face him. "I love you, too." I brushed my fingertips along his face.

"Do you ever . . . ," he started, then stopped himself cold.

"What?"

"I don't . . . this isn't really the time."

"You might as well say it now—it's out there."

"I was just . . . Do you ever think about having another baby?"

His words knocked the wind out of me. I struggled to catch my breath.

"I wasn't even going to bring it up. I've just been thinking about it. I know, it's insane. After everything we went through the first time, and everything that's happening with Sherry." He shook his head as if he didn't agree with what he was saying. "I just . . ."

"I used to think about it," I confessed. "I haven't recently. Not with everything that's happened. That's still happening."

"I know."

"I wouldn't want to try to replace Sherry."

"I don't think that's what it would be," he said. "I wouldn't want to do that either. But this . . . I want to have a baby. I know that it sounds crazy, and I know that we've got so much to work out between us, but it just feels right to me. I say the words out loud and they sound right."

"Don't you remember the last time, though?" I asked. "All the tests, all the trying. I don't know if I could go through that again. Not with everything else." I thought of Sherry, sleeping downstairs for the first night since the attack on the house.

He shook his head, his eyes soft. "I know. I'm not saying that I'm even really considering it. I'd just, I'd like us to . . . I just feel open to it, to the possibility."

The possibility.


## Leo

Father Peter floated like a shadow into the library, but the fat man, Tim, blocked his path. He stopped, and the two of them just stared at each other.

I hid behind a set of shelves, where I could see both of them. I wanted to be close. I wanted to be there if Father Peter needed me.

I tightened my grip on the lighter.

I wanted to be close enough to see what he would do to these devils. The thought made me smile, made me feel warm after the cold wait.

The two men were still looking at each other.

I waited for Father Peter to strike out, to bring the devil down.

Instead, the fat man smiled, and Father Peter bowed his head.

"Gloating?" Father Peter asked him.

The fat man shook his head. "Just waiting."

"I'd be gloating."

"You usually do. But I'm not you. And there have been far too many innocent people hurt for me to take any delight in how things have turned out."

"It's been a long time since you've won. I suppose you were due."

Tim shook his head. "I don't consider this a game. Besides, it had very little to do with me. Henry's a very bright boy. Thought for himself. And the family was strong. Stronger than I expected."

"Much stronger. And it's done now. *He's* arrived, bringing the bright light and protective arms of the Church. He's at the house right now. If I had had one more night—"

"I've long wondered," Tim said, gesturing at the coin flashing in Father Peter's hand. "Is that one of them?"

Father Peter nodded, looking at the coin. "I spent a lifetime trying to find this," he explained. "Do you have any idea how hard that was? Searching an empire for a single piece of silver?"

"How do you know you found the right one?"

"Well, there were a number of them." Father Peter smiled, showing his teeth. "But I could tell, right away. It burns. From the first moment I picked it up, it has burned me. But I can't put it down."

Tim looked in my direction, then away. Had he seen me? I crouched lower behind the bookshelves, but it was like he knew I was there, listening.

After a moment, Father Peter said, "You can't keep up this fight forever."

"And you can?" Tim smiled. "How many times have we two met? How many alleys? Hillsides? Libraries? Sewers? A wise man once said that the best definition of insanity was performing the same action over and over again, expecting different results."

Father Peter's smile disappeared. "The same could be said of you. What makes you so sure you're right? And so sure I'm wrong?"

"The difference is that I made a mistake once, out of ignorance," Tim said. "Everything I've done since then has been to try to make amends."

"To earn forgiveness."

"To protect the innocents." Tim smiled. "And yes, to earn forgiveness."

"Some of us have a higher calling," Father Peter said. I had heard him say those words dozens of times. "There are things more important than oneself."

"But that's your failing," Tim said. "You made a mistake a long time ago, and you think you've spent that time trying to make amends, but you just keep making the same mistake again and again."

"It's not a mistake. It's you who doesn't see. Who doesn't understand. I made a mistake, yes. I failed Him. But I have been given the chance to make amends."

"By killing children?"

"By keeping the way clear for His return. By dealing with those pretenders and false prophets who draw people away from the true savior. I stand by my judgment."

"You always have," Tim agreed. "But has it ever occurred to you that one of those false prophets you destroy could be Him? That you're killing Him all over again?"

"Don't be ridiculous. I would know Him."

"You didn't before."

He scowled. "There were . . . other factors."

"How many times can you hang for that handful of silver?"

Handful of silver?

"Is that really what you think?" he asked. "That I did it for the money? I thought you were too smart to believe the slander, especially considering everything that's been said about you over the years. Do you honestly believe that I hanged myself out of guilt? Surely you know me better than that."

*And throwing down the pieces of silver, he went and hanged himself. . . .*

290     Robert J. Wiersema

"Then why did you?"

Father Peter shook his head. "I hanged myself to try to find Him. I thought . . . He was always talking about the life everlasting. I thought that if I died, I might find Him there. I thought I would be able to ask for His forgiveness. Instead . . ." He shook his head. "I had to find another way to atone."

Tim looked my way again. "And how do you think you will be judged, on the day that He returns? You who have caused so much pain, so many deaths . . ."

"I have been true to Him. I have stood up for His name when all around me—"

"For His name," Tim said. "But what of what He taught? What of the innocents you have killed in His name?"

"I've known only one miraculous innocent," Father Peter said.

"And you've spent your lifetimes trying to atone for your betrayal, to protect His memory. A memory that doesn't need your protection."

"You're not going to change my mind."

"I know," Tim said. His voice was sad. "And my work here is done."

Father Peter nodded. "So what now, Ahasuerus?" he asked.

"Now we move on."

He nodded gravely. "I thought so. When?"

"Tonight. Right now. We're all ready. I was just waiting to tie up a couple of loose ends. Waiting for you, for one."

"As usual."

"As usual."

"Are you going to wait for Henry Denton?"

Tim shook his head. "He's gone. He's got a rough road ahead of him, but I think he'll find his way. And he'll be able to find us if he still needs us."

They stared at each other for a long silent moment.

"I'd like this to be over," Father Peter said quietly. It didn't sound like his voice.

He started to walk away, then turned back toward Tim again. "Do you think we'll ever be able to sit down together, you and I? Have a drink? Eat? Breathe?"

Tim's eyes looked sad. "Next year in Jerusalem?"

He shook his head and turned away with his hand still raised.

"Good night, Ahasuerus," he said, but he didn't look back. The dark of his coat looked like wings as he walked away.

"Good night, Judas," Tim whispered, standing there alone in the darkness, watching him go.

Judas.

The name seemed to tear something inside me. My knees felt like rubber, and I had to grab the shelf to keep from falling over.

Tim turned to look right at me. I took a step back, trying to hide in the dark.

"Mr. Tanner, I presume?" he said. "Please come out from the shadows. Time is growing short, and we have much to talk about."

### Simon

"I'm not sure about this," Karen whispered as we crept down the stairs.

I don't know who thought of it first, but we had sat up in bed and turned on one of the lamps and talked for hours, talked in circles. We had talked ourselves out.

"I'm not either," I said, holding her hand.

In the end, we had gotten up and pulled on our robes.

At the doorway to the living room, I was stopped by the immensity of what we were considering. In the silvery light through the blinds I saw the shape of her body barely lifting the sheets.

From the window came a light pattering, almost but not quite like rain. Without thinking, I drew the curtain aside. Karen joined me and we peered out, our breath misting against the glass.

Outside, the world was transformed. Wet snow was falling, not yet covering the ground, but spiraling and refracting under the streetlight, shimmering like a galaxy, like a benediction in our front yard. With what we were about to do, it felt almost sacred.

"That's so beautiful," Karen whispered.

I let the curtain fall back into place, brushing the three stones that Karen kept on the sill, and turned to face our daughter, my eyes still dazzled by the snow-bright midnight.

Turning on the lamp, I noticed, for the first time, that Sherry had grown since the accident, that her body was longer in the bed, that her hair was longer, too. I wondered how long she would keep growing, if twenty years from now we would be standing alongside the beautiful young woman we had always imagined her becoming, knowing that she would always be the three-year-old she was the day of the accident. I shook my head against the tears I could feel forming. I couldn't cry. If I started to cry, we would never get through this.

Blowing into my hands to warm them, I gently stroked her hair. "Hi, baby," I whispered.

I wanted to explain to her, to reasssure her that everything was all right, but how could I do that? Instead, I started to sing, quietly, my voice tremulous and near to breaking. "Hush little baby, don't say a word, Daddy's gonna buy you a mockingbird . . ."

Karen was fighting back tears.

"I'm sorry, Sherry," I said to her as I gently drew back her covers. "I know it's cold. It'll only be for a minute." As I spoke, I was praying that she understood. At the same time I was hoping that she was completely unaware.

"Simon, I . . ." Karen's fingers dug into my arm.

"We don't have to do this," I said.

She looked down at Sherry, and shook her head. "No, I think we do."

I met her eye, and nodded. "Do you want—?"

She shook her head. "No, you. You first."

I knelt beside the bed, leaning my head against the cool sheets for a long moment, trying to build my courage. Finally, I straightened up.

"And if that mockingbird don't sing," I shifted her hand gently to my forehead, closing my eyes. "Daddy's gonna buy you a diamond ring." I couldn't stop my tears. Unlike the daddy in the song, I could do nothing to help her.

I kept her hand against my forehead for a full minute, holding in my mind the image of Karen's face at the very moment of Sherry's birth, the pure joy as the sticky, curded bundle of blood and breath was pressed into her arms, that moment when our eyes made contact over the slick head of our daughter.

Our daughter.

I don't know what I was expecting. I didn't feel anything except cold. But as I took her hand away, laying it gently on her covers, I felt strangely comforted.

As we traded places, Karen kissed me, quickly, full on the mouth.

For a moment she stood uncertainly at the bedside; then she untied the loose knot of the belt of her robe and allowed it to fall open.

"Hi, baby," she said quietly. She lifted Sherry's hand with the tender care I remembered her using when she bathed Sherry as a baby, cradled her wrist as she turned her palm and laid it gently on the soft skin of her belly. She closed her eyes and held Sherry's hand there for the space of several breaths, tears running in rivulets down her cheeks.

After she laid Sherry's arm back down and tucked her under her blankets, she threw herself into my arms, and we cried there in the pool of golden light surrounding our daughter.

Before turning off the light, we each kissed Sherry on the forehead. So fragile. It was as if she were only sleeping, as if she might open her eyes at any moment.

"Good night, sweetie," I whispered, taking in the floral scent of her. "Sweet dreams."

I walked Karen to the foot of the stairs. "I'll be right up," I said. "I just want to check the doors and windows."

"Are you okay?"

"Not really," I said. No secrets between us. Not anymore. "But I will be."

"Do you want me to wait for you?"

I shook my head. "I'll be right up."

She laid her hand over mine. "I love you."

"I love you, too."

She walked back upstairs in the darkness as I methodically checked the front and back doors, as I double-checked that the windows were locked. The snow was coming down heavier, a thin crust now covering the ground.

I was about to let the curtain fall back into place when I saw the figure under the streetlight, silhouetted in the falling snow. He was pudgy, in a too-large coat that nearly dragged on the ground. The smoke from his cigar pooled upward with the snow. Another man, taller, broad across the shoulders in a blue ski jacket, followed him. Then another, similarly ill-kempt, then another, and another all walking past the house, little more than shadows in the snow. The last man, huge and gangly, stared into the yard as he passed. He looked almost like Father Peter's assistant, but I couldn't quite see him in the dim light, and he disappeared into the dark before I could be sure. In the end, over a dozen men passed. Street people, I thought. Rousted from somewhere they had been sleeping, searching for another resting place out of the cold.

It occurred to me to call after them, to invite them in, to give them shelter for the duration of the storm, but by the time the thought had fully formed, they had gone, slipping from the pool of the streetlight back into the shadows.

I climbed silently up the stairs, past the closed door of Sherry's old room, through which I could hear the snoring priest, and into the bedroom. After gently draping my robe over the chair, I slid into bed and pressed myself against Karen.

She sighed a little as my cool body came into contact with her warmth. "Everything okay?" she asked slowly, in a drawl that was more asleep than awake.

"Yes. Hey, listen. . . . It's snowing harder now."

"Sherry'll like that," she replied drowsily. "Maybe we'll go for a walk in the morning, make angels. . . ."

I thought that I had cried myself out downstairs, but hot tears coursed down my cheeks, spilling into her hair. I wished for sleep. I wished that I could meet Karen wherever she was, in that world where our daughter was whole, where in the morning they would be making snow angels in the yard.

# Part 9

---

*The Price of Miracles*
*December 27*

## Father Peter Shaughnessy

I was awakened by a soft tapping at the door. "Father Peter?" asked a male voice.

At first I didn't recognize the tiny bed, the animal-print wallpaper, the mobile slowly spinning above my head. Then it all returned to me. "Yes, Simon," I answered. "I'm awake."

"Do you prefer coffee or tea?"

I had fallen asleep with the window open a crack, and the air was cold on my face, but I was feeling very comfortable under the weight of Sherilyn's quilt. "Coffee, please, Simon," I answered. "I'll be right down."

His footfalls faded as I swung my legs out of the bed. Something was different from the day before, something subtle. The air seemed brighter, cleaner.

Snow had fallen overnight, blanketing the yard in several inches of thick, heavy white. Snow was still falling, large wet flakes the size of coins, plummeting, rather than drifting, toward the ground. The street was unplowed, bisected by a single set of tire ruts.

I dressed quickly, checking my watch as I put it on. It was just before nine. I was not accustomed to sleeping in.

Simon was sitting at the kitchen table, reading the local paper. He looked up as I came into the room. "Well, I don't think we're off to a very auspicious start for you," he said.

"I'm sorry?"

Karen waved me to the chair across from Simon, setting a cup of coffee on the place mat in front of it. "Simon's worried that with the snow we won't have many people out today." She gestured toward the chair again. "Go ahead, sit. Did you look outside? Ruth and Stephen already called to say they wouldn't be able to make it in."

I nodded from the chair. "It's still really coming down. I don't think you have to worry, though. I think people will come through . . . well, snow or high water."

Karen smiled.

By the time I had eaten some fruit and cereal for breakfast, there was a line of about ten people waiting in the front yard, pressed against the house under the eaves.

"Should we just send them home?" Karen asked. "It's too wet and cold for sick people to be standing around outside."

Simon shook his head. "No," he said. "We can't do that. We can't just send them home after they've come through the snow."

"We can't just leave them outside, either."

"No." He stretched the word out as he shook his head. "We can have them wait in the family room."

So Karen and I stood in the living room doorway as Simon showed the pilgrims into the house. They left their wet coats and shoes in the foyer. A few of them craned their heads, trying to look past us to see Sherry, but most of them just followed Simon, their eyes on the floor in front of them. They all seemed to be both optimistic and embarrassed, as if they were ashamed at being forced to seek out such help, but unable or unwilling not to take the risk. I had seen it before.

Karen had already cared for Sherry, and now she carefully pulled back the covers, folding them near Sherry's waist as I sat down in the chair nearest the window, opening my notebook onto my lap and taking my pen from my pocket.

"So this is what you do?" Karen asked as I was organizing myself. Leaning behind the chair, she plugged in the lights, and the dark Christmas tree in the corner burst into life.

"I'm sorry?"

"Your job. It's to go around, collect evidence, disprove reports of miracles." Her tone was maybe a little critical, but mostly curious.

"Or to prove them."

"Does that happen often?" she asked, turning the rod for the blinds, the bright, clear winter light spilling through the sheers into the room.

"That I get a chance to prove that a miracle has actually happened?"

She nodded.

"Very rarely."

"I didn't think so," she said.

I shook my head. "Most families, most people put into a situation like you're in with Sherry, don't handle it nearly so well. There's an impulse to pull away, to run from what a lot of people consider such a huge responsibility, such an overwhelming obligation. Very few people open their lives to the needy. We wish more did.

"And of course," I continued, "the other Father Peter does everything in his power to encourage people to turn away. Or to run. I've often had reports of miracles—of healings or visitations—and by the time I arrive at the scene, the family has moved, leaving no forwarding address."

"I don't think we could do that," she said. "Just turn our backs."

"But you can see the temptation?"

She hesitated for a moment, then nodded.

"I still don't like the word *miracle,* though. It just smells too much like church to me. Too much incense and candle wax."

I was smiling at her, about to respond, when I noticed the figure in the doorway behind her. "Hello," I said. I didn't recognize him from the group of pilgrims we had escorted to the family room.

"Did Simon send you in already?" Karen asked.

The man stayed silent. He was in his twenties, not overly tall, wearing faded, dirty jeans, battered sneakers, and a burgundy sweatshirt. His face was mostly hidden in the shadow of the hood. His right hand was tucked into the front pocket of the sweatshirt, and he stood hunched over, as if in pain.

"You can see me," he finally said.

Karen took a step toward him and I rose to my feet, setting my notebook and pen on the chair. "Did Simon get your information?" she asked.

"No," he said, his voice gruff, his tone like that of someone surprised at being spoken to. "I came to see Sherry."

"Well, you have to sign in . . . ," Karen started.

"I knocked at the door," the man explained. "No one answered."

"I guess we didn't hear," Karen answered.

He turned toward Sherry.

Karen put herself between the man and her daughter.

"Can I see her?" he asked. His voice had dropped to a whisper.

With his left hand, he fumbled with his hood and pulled it off. He had the disheveled look of someone who had been living on the street for a while—tangled shoulder-length hair, uncombed for what looked like weeks; a long, tangled beard—but the right side of his face was a raw burn, fresh and oozing. His right eye was swollen shut from the wound, which extended down his neck.

He was completely focused on Sherry, and he didn't even seem to notice our attention. He looked at her with a deep anguish that radiated from him in waves.

"You're burned," Karen said, her voice dropping. She stepped toward him, raising her hand.

"Your arm, too," she said, not releasing his gaze. "And here." She gestured over the right side of her body, mirroring him. Her eyes were wide, and her face opened, as if something suddenly made sense to her.

He nodded, slowly.

"You were here," she whispered. "That night. You stopped the man with the bomb. You got burned." She reached out, almost touching his face. "You saved us."

He turned back to Sherry on the bed.

"Simon," she called, not quite shouting, but loud enough to be heard.

"I just want to see her," he said quietly, stopping inches from Karen, craning his neck. "I *need* to see her."

"Simon," she called again.

I stepped forward. "Listen, if we can—"

"What's wrong?" All three of us turned to face Simon, outlined in the doorway.

Karen's face was tight with uncertainty, and she didn't move from her position between the man and her daughter. "This is . . . This is the man from the other night—"

Simon was looking at the man. "It's you," he said, stepping toward him. His jaw was set, his face hard. The man seemed confused.

"He wants—"

"You don't recognize him?"

"What?"

"I'm not," he sputtered as Simon took hold of his left arm and turned him toward Karen. "I just came to see—"

Karen looked at him, trying to see past the beard, the burns.

"I'm sorry," he said quietly. "I didn't see your daughter."

He glanced between the two of them; then his gaze stopped on Karen. "I didn't see Sherry," he repeated. "I came, I came to say I'm—"

"It is you, isn't it?" Karen asked.

Their eyes locked. "Yes," he whispered.

Before she could speak, he stepped forward again. "I've been . . . I wanted to come. I wanted to see Sherry. I came to say I was sorry."

Simon shook his head. "You can't just—"

"I'm glad you came, Henry," came a voice from behind us.

The tiny, high voice seemed to echo through the room, and we all turned to face the small bed where Sherilyn Barrett had spoken.

She was sitting up, staring at us. Her eyes seemed curiously dark against her pale skin.

"Oh, God, Sherry," Karen gasped, stumbling toward the bed.

Everything seemed to slow down in the moment that Karen pulled her daughter into her arms, squeezing her and rocking gently in place. Sherry's arms were around her neck, and after a moment her fingers began to toy with her mother's hair.

"Oh, Sherry." Karen couldn't stop her tears, but the sob, when it bubbled up, sounded like laughter. "Sherry."

"Don't cry, Mommy," Sherry whispered into her neck. "It's all right."

Karen pulled away from her a little so she could make eye contact when she told her, "No, honey, it's just . . . Mommy's so happy." She cradled one of her daughter's cheeks, letting her fingers linger.

"I know," Sherry said, touching her mother's cheek in return. Her fingers came away wet with tears.

Simon stared, his eyes wide, mouth gaping before his hand covered the lower half of his face, hiding a sob. He fell toward the bed, taking his family into his arms.

His eyes met Karen's as he buried his face in Sherry's hair, breathing her in. Both of their smiles seemed caught somewhere between ecstacy and despair.

"I love you, baby," he whispered into his daughter's ear.

She squirmed at the tickle of his breath. "I love you, too, Daddy," she said. "Can you sing me a song?"

"Anything," he said, meeting Karen's eyes again. Her hand found his on Sherry's lap, and they clutched at one another. "Anything you want."

"I like the one about the mockingbird."

As the Barretts huddled together, Henry Denton took several halting steps to the edge of the bed and crouched there, clutching the covers in his hands.

Sherry looked down at him, and her parents exchanged a glance over her head.

The girl, pale and small, lifted her gaze from the broken man before her and turned back to her parents. "Please call her Lily," she said. "I'd like it if you called her Lily."

Karen made a sound that was somewhere between a sharp laugh and a sob, and tightened her hand around Simon's.

"Henry," Sherry said, as though he and she were the only people in the room. She leaned toward him.

He lifted his head. "I'm sorry," he said to Sherry, not flinching from her wide, dark gaze. "I came to ask your . . ." His face was streaked and stained with tears, his open eye filled with confusion and fear that seemed to melt away as she raised her hand to him.

"I knew you'd come," she said softly. "I was waiting for you." With a look of deep understanding, he lowered his eyes and bowed his head to her, almost touching his forehead to the white sheet.

She took a long look around the room, her gaze lingering on her parents. It was impossible to read her expression: I want to call it beatific, but there was a hint of resolve there, as well as a touch of sadness.

She knew.

Sherry lowered her hand gently to the crown of Henry Denton's head, slowly enough that we could watch his tangled hair give under its weight.

I think that we all realized what was happening at the same moment. Karen gasped, "Sherry?" as Simon raised his hand as if he wanted to try to stop her, but all of us were unable to interfere, none of us knowing, or even able to guess at, the consequences of what we were witnessing.

Sherry knew.

"It's all right, Henry." As her fingers touched his head, her eyelids slowly lowered.

It was like an electrical current passed through them both, as if when she touched him, when she told him it was all right, a circuit was completed.

A single spasm passed first through Henry Denton, who crumpled to the carpet.

Then the girl's back arched, and a force seemed to push her parents away from her. At that moment, I felt a pulse thrum through me, like a sound too low to hear. The light dimmed as the breath rushed out of me and the force brought me to my knees. I struggled for a moment, but the next breath I drew was as sweet as the air after a summer storm.

The light grew bright again, and Sherry sagged, motionless, onto her bed.

For a moment, the silence seemed deeper than that of an empty church. I felt connected to the world. I could feel Simon and Karen on the bed, and I knew that the pilgrims down the hall were on their knees with me. I could hear the falling of the snowflakes in the cold white light outside the window. It sounded like the dryness of wings, the gentle pressure of a final breath. The air filled with the smell of lilies.

"Sherry?" Karen choked, her voice raw and desperate, struggling toward her daughter.

Before I even touched the cool skin of Sherry's throat, I knew it was too late. Her chest wasn't rising; there was no pulse under my fingers.

"Sherry?" Karen whispered, her voice breaking into sobs as she pulled her daughter into her arms. She slumped onto the bed holding the girl close, pressing her face into her hair, cradling her head as she wept. Simon took them both into his arms, and they held one another in the white glow of the room, their daughter still between them.

Neither of them seemed to notice the expression of peace and serenity—of release and comfort—the little girl wore. Nor did they notice, then, that the body of Henry Daniel Denton had disappeared from the room, leaving no trace. It was as if he had never even crossed the threshold.

File # 5485.2
*Barrett, Sherilyn Amber*
—Final Report (excerpt)—
Father Peter Shaughnessy

April 24, 1997
... It is appropriate that I am completing and submitting this report today, a year to the day since the accident that injured three-year-old Sherilyn Amber Barrett and initiated the strange series of events in Victoria, British Columbia, that culminated with her death on the morning of December 27, 1996.

I have spent the four months since her death both working on this investigation and assisting the Barrett family, and their friends, in dealing with Sherilyn's death.

You will find, attached, testimony from over 150 people who witnessed Sherilyn Barrett's healing powers, including petitioners and their medical practitioners, who testify to the complete recovery and remission of those who came in contact with Sherilyn. I will solicit further testimony from these witnesses at the first and fifth anniversaries of their contact, as is the norm in these cases.

Of the twelve people waiting in the Barrett home that morning, we have received reports of seven full recoveries; I am awaiting replies from the remaining petitioners. By mid-January, the Barretts were receiving letters and reports of recoveries from as far away as Toronto, Halifax, and the American South. These people had all written to Sherilyn; their letters of petition were found at her bedside, still sealed.

Pilgrims continue to wait at the Barrett home even now, months later, their numbers having increased after Sherilyn's death. Some of them also report spontaneous recoveries, although such incidents are less common.

I do not know how to make sense of the things I have seen, nor what meaning to ascribe to those events in which I was a participant, however minor.

I have delayed completing this report, hoping that time would provide me with the clarity and distance to help me to understand the events I witnessed and to recount them objectively. Time has not, however, accorded me understanding or distance.

I would like to attach to this report a more personal concern. I have discussed this with my confessor, and have decided that, although personal of nature, this note should form part of the official record.

In August of 1996, I was diagnosed with prostate cancer, which had metastasized. The doctors informed me that it would likely be terminal within a year, and I determined that I would resign my position on December 31, 1996. The inquiry into the miracles attributed to Sherilyn Barrett was to be my last.

Following the events of December 27, however, the cancer disappeared. As of last week, I have been in complete remission for four months. My doctors are "cautiously optimistic," and will monitor my situation. I, however, am certain: I was cured by Sherilyn Barrett on the morning of December 27.

# Coda

---

*April 24, 1997*

I go with them to visit the grave. They can't see me. They have no idea I'm here. But I want to be with them. It's been one year since the accident, and I want to be with them, today of all days.

I follow behind them through the parking lot, through the gate, and along the winding pathways.

They're holding hands, and they walk slowly, not saying anything.

They stop at the side of the grave, and he hugs her to his shoulder. They still don't speak. They just look at the grave with its small white stone, and the pile of flowers and letters and stuffed animals that people have left.

Sherilyn Amber Barrett
Beloved daughter, beloved friend
August 1, 1992–December 27, 1996

I can't look at it for too long. It makes me too sad. Too sad for them.

It's a beautiful spring day. In this place of death, the world is full of life. You can almost hear it singing, all around. The daffodils are waking up after their long winter naps, and their yellow and white heads dance between the rows of gravestones. The grass is green and bright and damp. Mr. Squirrel will be taking off his winter coat.

It rained last night, but this morning it's warm and the sky is clear and blue and beautiful.

I'm wearing my sky blue dress, because it matches the sky.

Without letting go of Mommy's hand, Daddy crouches beside the flowers and teddy bears. "Baby," he chokes, tears running down his cheeks. His hand shakes as he reaches into his jacket pocket and carefully puts a stone atop the grave marker.

After Daddy stands back up, Mommy crouches carefully. She uses Daddy for balance as she puts a stone of her own on my grave, gently brushing the white marker with her fingertips the same way she used to tickle my cheeks. As she stands up, her hand goes to the small swelling of her belly, and she turns herself into Daddy's arms.

There were three stones I gave to Mommy before the accident. There were three stones in Mommy's pocket when the truck hit me, three stones on the windowsill of the winter room where the people came to see me, the room where I died. The last stone, I know, is in her pocket again, near her heart, near the heart of their unborn child, the girl they will call Lily.

My sister.

Lily.

For peace.

# Acknowledgments

No novel is born in a vacuum, and while *Before I Wake* is the result of a lot of predawn mornings in a cold study, it also owes much to many people, some over the course of a lifetime. If there is credit to be had, I share it with the following. Blame, though, I'm hoarding for myself.

First, to my family, by birth, divorce, remarriage, and my own marriage. If we are the sum of our earliest experiences, and of those closest to us, I owe much of what I am to you.

For Mrs. Winstanley, Mrs. Hepnar, and Miss Guthrie, as promised all those years ago. And for Ellen Scarff—I wish you were here to see it.

For Peter and Greg, my oldest friends, who were there at the very beginning of what turned into a dream, and then a life—the cigars are waiting. The good ones.

Special thanks to the early readers of this book: Your interest and support saw me through some rough times, while your advice helped this book in immeasurable ways. I made friends through this book (including people I have yet to meet in person). Thanks, then, to Ruth, Matthias, Nathalie, Peter, Mary, Lee, Mel, Samantha, Nikki, and everyone else who had an eye out and a hand in.

Thanks to Kevin Patterson for his advice and his medical expertise, and to James Grainger for his critical acumen, informed support, and his thorough knowledge of small Toronto bars.

I am blessed to know (and work for, and with) Mel Bolen and Samantha Holmes. A writer could not ask for better employers, fiercer advocates, and stronger supporters. Thank you so much for the kindness you have shown to me, to my work, and to my family. I live in the best of both worlds thanks to you.

To my fellow travelers in the book trade (a finer bunch of people you'll never meet): I am honored to have spent my adult life in your number. And to my coworkers at Bolen Books (and to those in my previous life) I owe a hearty thanks for keeping me down to earth and for suffering my occasional insufferableness.

On the professional side, blessings and thanks to Anne McDermid, the best agent a writer could ask for, and her ever resourceful and supportive cohorts, past and present.

When a book reaches a certain point, it becomes less a force of inspiration and more an act of collaboration. I raise a glass, therefore, to my Canadian editor, Kendall Anderson, who probably didn't realize what she had signed up for, and to my American editor, Nichole Argyres, who knew what she was getting into and took the plunge anyway.

More than anyone else, though, this book—and my life as a writer—owes everything to my wife, Cori Dusmann. Supportive first reader, fiercest first critic, it is she to and for whom I write. Without her, I hate to even imagine where I would be.

And for Xander, who wasn't born when this novel was and who is seven years old as it is published, I promise: The next one has sword fights, some magic, and people jumping heroically off cliffs. No hamsters, though.